W9-BYZ-497

IT TAKES A

Hero

...to sweep you off your feet

ENJOY THESE CLASSIC LOVE STORIES BY THREE MUCH LOVED AUTHORS!

About Caroline Anderson:
'Your emotions will seesaw with Caroline
Anderson's latest as she touches your heart with a
gripping premise and poignant scenes.'
—*Romantic Times*

About Carol Marinelli:
'Carol Marinelli is very sensual and dramatic, with
interesting characters that hold your attention.'
—*Romantic Times*

About Sarah Morgan:
'Sarah Morgan's latest is a steamy, passionate,
explosive love story.'
—*Romantic Times*

Caroline Anderson has the mind of a butterfly. She's been a nurse, a secretary, a teacher, run her own soft-furnishing business and now she's settled on writing. She says, 'I was looking for that elusive something. I finally realised it was variety, and now I have it in abundance. Every book brings new horizons and new friends, and in between books I have learned to be a juggler. My teacher husband John and I have two beautiful and talented daughters, Sarah and Hannah, umpteen pets and several acres of Suffolk that nature tries to reclaim every time we turn our backs!' Caroline writes for the Mills & Boon® Medical Romance™ and Tender Romance™.

Carol Marinelli is a nurse who loves writing. Or is she a writer who loves nursing? The truth is Carol's having trouble deciding at the moment, but writing definitely seems to be taking precedence! She's also happily married to an eternally patient husband (an essential accessory when panic hits around chapter six) and is a mother to three fabulously boisterous children. Add a would-be tennis player, an eternal romantic and a devout daydreamer to that list and that pretty much sums Carol up. Oh, she's also terrible at housework! Carol writes for Mills & Boon® Modern Romance™ and Medical Romance.

Sarah Morgan trained as a nurse and has since worked in a variety of health-related jobs. Married to a gorgeous businessman, who still makes her knees knock, she spends most of her time trying to keep up with their two little boys but manages to sneak off occasionally to indulge her passion for writing romance. Sarah loves outdoor life and is an enthusiastic skier and walker. Whatever she is doing, her head is always full of new characters and she is addicted to happy endings. Sarah writes for Mills & Boon Modern Romance and Medical Romance.

IT TAKES A

Hero

...to sweep you off your feet

CAROLINE ANDERSON

CAROL MARINELLI

SARAH MORGAN

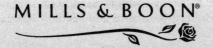

MILLS & BOON®

DID YOU PURCHASE THIS BOOK WITHOUT A COVER?
If you did, you should be aware it is **stolen property** as it was
reported *unsold and destroyed* by a retailer. Neither the author nor
the publisher has received any payment for this book.

*All the characters in this book have no existence outside the imagination
of the author, and have no relation whatsoever to anyone bearing the
same name or names. They are not even distantly inspired by any
individual known or unknown to the author, and all the incidents are
pure invention.*

*All Rights Reserved including the right of reproduction in whole or in part
in any form. This edition is published by arrangement with Harlequin
Enterprises II B.V. The text of this publication or any part thereof may not
be reproduced or transmitted in any form or by any means, electronic or
mechanical, including photocopying, recording, storage in an
information retrieval system, or otherwise, without the written
permission of the publisher.*

*This book is sold subject to the condition that it shall not, by way of trade
or otherwise, be lent, resold, hired out or otherwise circulated without the
prior consent of the publisher in any form of binding or cover other than
that in which it is published and without a similar condition including this
condition being imposed on the subsequent purchaser.*

*MILLS & BOON and MILLS & BOON with the Rose Device
are registered trademarks of the publisher.*

*First published in Great Britain 2005
Harlequin Mills & Boon Limited,
Eton House, 18-24 Paradise Road, Richmond, Surrey, TW9 1SR*

IT TAKES A HERO © Harlequin Enterprises II B.V., 2005

*Captive Heart, The Outback Nurse and The Doctor's Runaway Bride
were first published in Great Britain by*
Harlequin Mills & Boon Limited in separate, single volumes.

Captive Heart © Caroline Anderson 1998
The Outback Nurse © Carol Marinelli 2001
The Doctor's Runaway Bride © Sarah Morgan 2002

ISBN 0 263 84579 6

109-0805

*Printed and bound in Spain
by Litografía Rosés S.A., Barcelona*

CONTENTS

Captive Heart

CAROLINE ANDERSON

Dear Reader,

'How about somewhere exotic?' my editor said. Exotic? My brain isn't very good with exotic. The word always makes me think of crowded beaches, millionaires and weird-coloured drinks. 'How about an Indonesian island?' I offered sneakily and promptly invented Pulau Panjang. Well, it sounded exotic. It turned out to be far from it, but it fitted with 'Changing Places', certainly a change from England where we take modcons for granted, and where culture means going to the opera, not sitting three parts naked round an open fire smeared with wood ash and eating fruit bats!

I grew up in Malaysia, and despite the mosquitoes, bats, snakes and jellyfish it was a most glorious and enviable childhood. I had absolute freedom because children are sacred to the Malays, and I will never forgot the kindness of the people I met there, most particularly my nanny, Rom, whom I ran ragged! She was wonderful. In fact just as soon as I can manage it, I'm going back with my husband and children to see if I can find my island!

Caroline Anderson

CHAPTER ONE

HE LOOKED like something out of an old B-movie.

Faded khaki shirt and shorts, feet propped up on the veranda, hat tipped over his face, chair tilted onto its back legs—and he was in the shade, which was another reason to dislike him on sight.

Gabby could feel the heat of the sun scorching down on her unprotected shoulders—the skin would probably be burned already. No doubt her nose was covered in a smattering of little freckles, with the rest of her programmed to follow in short order, but that was what you got for being a green-eyed redhead—sunburn and a lousy disposition!

She studied the man on the veranda again as she drew closer. As there was no one else around and no other dwellings in the vicinity, it must be him she was looking for, and he was every bit as clichéd close up as he'd been from a distance. She stifled a little laugh. She'd come all the way across the world and she'd stepped into the set of a Trevor Howard film, with the neighbourhood MO cast in the leading part!

He was quite well put together, however, despite the air of old-Colonial dissipation that hung over him. No doubt some Hollywood director would be thrilled to have him, she thought, examining him with clinical detachment. 'In fact, forget Trevor Howard,' she mumbled to herself, losing her clinical detachment, 'think Harrison Ford as Indiana Jones…'

His shirtsleeves were rolled up to expose deeply tanned and hair-strewn forearms, rippling with lean muscle, and long, rangy legs, strewn with more of the same gold-tinged wiry hair, stuck out of the bottoms of crumpled shorts. His feet were bare and bony, with strong high arches and little tufts of hair on the toes. They were at her eye level as she approached the steps to the veranda, and a little imp inside her wondered if they were ticklish.

She couldn't see his face because of the battered Panama hat tipped over his eyes, but his fingers were curled loosely around a long, tall glass of something that looked suspiciously like gin and tonic. The outside of the glass was beaded with tiny droplets of water, and in the unrelenting tropical heat it drew her eyes like a magnet. She swallowed drily and wondered if he'd mind if she pinched it.

Mind? Of course he wouldn't mind—he wouldn't know! He was fast asleep, a soft snore drifting out from under the hat at intervals—he looked so relaxed that Gabby had an insane urge to kick out the two legs of the chair on which he was balancing and knock him onto his indolent behind.

Only two things stopped her. One was her natural good manners. The other was the fact that he was a darned sight bigger than she was and would almost certainly get just a tad cross about it.

So she plopped down onto the edge of the wooden veranda, propped her back against the nearest post and cleared her throat.

Nothing. Not a flicker of reaction.

Damn. She was going to have to kick the legs—

'I'm asleep.'

She blinked at the deep growl that emerged from under the hat. She thought she saw the gleam of an eye, but she wasn't sure. He hadn't moved so much as a single well-honed muscle.

She swallowed. 'I know. I'm sorry. I hate to disturb you—'

'So why do it? I don't entertain bored tourists,' he drawled. 'It's not in my job description.'

'Well, excuse me,' she muttered under her breath. She stood up, banging the dust off her bottom and stomping down the steps, pausing on the rough track to turn and glare up at him. All she got for her pains was a view up the leg of his shorts which her grandmother wouldn't have approved of and which did nothing for her blood pressure.

'For the record,' she said tersely—petulantly? Probably. Oh, heck. She dragged her eyes away from his shorts. 'For the record,' she began again, 'I'm not a tourist, I'm Gabrielle Andrews—Jonathan's cousin. Penny sent me up here to tell you lunch will be ready—'

The chair legs crashed to the floor, making her jump, and he tipped back the hat with one finger and studied her out of startling blue eyes.

'In a minute,' she finished.

'Well, why didn't you say so?'

She scowled at him. 'I just did,' she said crossly.

His grin was lazy and did further damage to her blood pressure. So did his eyes, tracking equally lazily over her body and back to her face. That did it. She wondered if she looked as angry as she felt, standing there in the muddy road with her head tipped back at a crazy angle and her hair—the red hair that was a dead give-away for her temper—clinging to her forehead in sweaty tangles.

She brushed it impatiently back out of her eyes and glared at him. 'Well?'

'Well, what?'

'Are you coming?'

'To lunch?' He leant forward and propped his elbows on the railings, the cool, inviting glass dangling from those lean and very masculine fingers, and grinned that lazy grin again. 'Tell Penny I wouldn't miss it for the world. And by the way…'

'Yes?'

'You shouldn't stand about in that sun with your fair skin—you'll burn in seconds.'

Gabby had noticed. She stifled the little scream of frustration and smiled viciously at him. She thought she probably looked more closely related to a barracuda than to her mild-mannered cousin at the moment, but she was too hot and too cross to be nice—not to mention exhausted. 'Thank you. I had realised,' she retorted and, spinning on her heel, she walked back down the rough track to the bungalow where her cousin lived.

What a pain! Idle, indolent, laconic, self-serving pig! Doctor? 'Huh! Not in this lifetime,' Gabby muttered crossly.

Penny greeted her with a glass of something cold, tropical and absolutely delicious that improved her humour immediately. 'Mmm, yum,' she murmured, pressing it against her hot cheeks. She'd only been in the country since early that morning, and it would take her a while, she imagined, to get used to the heat. In the meantime, the icy glass felt wonderful—

'Did you find Jed all right?'

She stifled the urge to tell her cousin's wife what she thought of the cliché she'd found sprawled on the veranda. 'Yes—he said he'd come. I would have thought he'd be here now—he wasn't exactly busy.'

'I expect he'll be taking a *mandi*—a bath.'

Gabby blinked. 'In this heat? Surely he'd shower.'

Penny laughed. 'He hasn't got a shower—the bungalow's not that sophisticated, I'm afraid. He's using the *mandi* at the back of the bungalow—it's a bamboo enclosure with a big tank of water in it. You stand in it and bail water all over yourself out of the tank with a big scoop. Actually, it's wonderful.'

It sounded wonderful—more refreshing than the shower she'd taken just before she'd wandered up the road to call Jed for lunch, and which had already lost its impact in the tropical humidity.

Penny settled down beside her in the rattan lounger, took a long swallow of her drink and turned to face Gabby. 'So, how was the journey? You don't look too bad, considering how tired you must be. Are you sure you don't want to lie down?'

Gabby shook her head. 'I'm still too wound up. Perhaps later.' She thought of the flight from London to Kuala Lumpur, the two-hour stopover for fuelling, the short flight to Jakarta, and then stepping out onto the runway at the airport at two in the morning. It had been like walking into a sauna, and the five-hour wait with little Katie had been hot, smelly and at the wrong end of an exhausting journey.

They had had to transfer to the other airport for the local island service, and even in the middle of the night Jakarta had been seething. The airports had been crowded with travellers and they had spent the last couple of hours perched on their cases, dozing against each other.

That had been the easy bit. Their arrival shortly after dawn in the unbelievable crate in which they had made the last short leg of the journey had been nothing short of a miracle. Her heart had been in her mouth most of the way as she'd listened to the engine cough and splutter—

'So, how was the journey?' Penny asked again, breaking into her thoughts.

How was it? 'OK,' she replied, always the master of understatement. 'Although I would have had more faith in the last plane if I hadn't seen the pilot tinkering around under the engine cowling with a spanner just before we took off.'

Penny laughed. 'They're quite safe—well, mostly. Some of them are a bit rough, but it's not exactly a hot tourist route—well, not yet.'

Gabby looked around her. Below them, stretched out into the muddy estuary on stilts, was a bustling little wooden town, the shacks roofed with corrugated iron or palm leaves, the fishing boats tied up at the makeshift piers rocking gently in the swell.

A seedy hotel, a handful of shops, a bank and not much else comprised the westernised part of the town, legacy of the Dutch influence which had also been responsible for the few bungalows at the top of the hill, in one of which they were sitting. That was it, however. Behind them, just yards away, the jungle began and civilisation, such as it was, ended.

'Not exactly on the beaten track,' she agreed drily.

Penny laughed, and for a moment Gabby thought she sounded a little strained. 'Hence the resort. It's going to be very expensive and very exclusive, so we're told, and with minimal impact. That's why they want the hydro-electric power plant instead of generators—so they don't have the noise in the resort village.'

'Where will it be?'

Penny waved an arm at the little headland beyond the town. 'Over there, in the next bay. It's a fabulous spot, I can see the attraction for the tourists once it's done.'

'But not now,' Gabby said softly, instinctively reading Penny's unspoken words.

She shrugged. 'Perhaps not while it's quite so primitive. Jonathan loves it here, and the little ones are very happy. I just hope Katie settles down like the others have—I can't thank you enough for bringing her back to us.'

Gabby chuckled. 'She was no trouble at all—and, anyway, I got a free tropical holiday in the middle of winter out of it! What more could a girl want?'

'A swimming pool?'

'What, with a bar in the middle and some fancy waiter in a grass skirt, serving bizarre blue cocktails with parasols floating in them?' She shuddered theatrically, and Penny relaxed and smiled.

'Yes, they can be pretty tacky, some of those pools— and they aren't necessary really. The sea's wonderful if you don't mind the odd jellyfish. Still, sometimes I wonder if this doesn't go too far the other way. It will get busier, of course, once Jonathan's built the power station and we have real electricity—then the resort will get under way and prosperity will happen and, whatever they say, it'll get just like Bali in the end, which will be a shame in a way because it is beautiful like this, so unspoilt.'

'Will it be spoilt? I thought the developer wanted to keep it very low impact.'

She shrugged. 'He does. He's quite emphatic about that, but it might just open the floodgates for other firms to come in the slipstream, so to speak. He's supposed to have an arrangement with the government, but things change with time. Still, a little more civilisation wouldn't go amiss. It would be nice to be able to buy butter that wasn't rancid, for instance, but they haven't got a cold storage facility here yet, and they won't until they have a proper and reliable source of power.'

Gabby laughed. 'Something to look forward to.'

Penny shrugged. 'By the time they have I expect we will have moved on to another primitive site in Brazil or Africa.'

Was that a wistful longing Gabby could see in her eyes? 'Don't you ever wish Jonathan had a proper job—you know, nine to five, Monday to Friday, in Basingstoke or wherever?'

Penny smiled, and again for a second the strain showed. 'Of course, but he wouldn't be happy doing that so here we all are. If we didn't have Jed I'd probably refuse to live here, but having a doctor on the spot makes it much safer and there are wonderful hospitals in Jakarta and Singapore.'

Gabby thought of their 'doctor on the spot', and hoped no one was about to be ill. He looked much too laid-back to cope with anything faster than ingrowing toenails.

She remembered her last job, a three-month stint in A and E, and almost laughed aloud at the thought of Pulau Panjang's resident MO caught up the hurly-burly of real medicine. Still, what did she expect? No doctor worth his salt would give up a decent job to live out here quite literally at the edge of civilisation, if not somewhat beyond it—but, anyway, he was quite decorative in a rather rough-hewn sort of way so she could probably forgive him so long as she remained healthy!

The object of her musings ambled into view, dressed in equally faded but freshly pressed shorts and shirt, his dark blond hair still wet from his bath, and bounded up the veranda steps with a grin that, to Gabby's utter disgust, did stupid things to her insides.

He looked even more like Indiana Jones, and she regretted the weakness she had for the type. She thought of all the old-fashioned and appropriate words, like 'cad' and 'bounder' and 'rascal'—all oddly flattering. Damn.

He grinned at her, waggled his fingers and turned to their hostess.

'Hiya, Pen. How are you doing?' he said cheerfully

and, bending over, dropped a casual kiss on Penny's cheek.

She caught his hand and patted it. 'Hi, yourself. Can I get you a glass of juice?'

'I'll get it.' He wandered into the house and emerged a few moments later with a tall clinking glass and a jug. 'Top-up?' he asked the two women.

Gabby held her glass out and wondered if she hadn't judged him a little too harshly, but then he blew it all away by dropping into a chair, hooking his feet over the veranda and closing his eyes.

'Bliss,' he said with a muffled groan, and within seconds he was asleep. Gabby was astonished at the rudeness of the man. Didn't he have more respect for his hostess than to come for lunch and go to sleep?

'He's been up all night,' Penny said under her breath, as if reading Gabby's mind. 'Jon'll be here in a minute—I'll wake him up then.' She settled back in her chair, sipped her drink and levelled a searching look at Gabby. 'So, tell me about your job,' she demanded. 'Got anything lined up yet?'

Gabby shrugged. 'Not yet. I don't want to go back to London, and there's nothing in my line anywhere else at the moment.'

Well, there was, but she would have had to cancel her holiday to attend the interview and wouldn't have been able to escort little Katie home. After the bout of appendicitis which had struck Katie while they had been on leave Gabby's temporary lack of employment had seemed like a godsend. It had meant that Katie hadn't had to travel alone once she was fit—for which service, Gabby reminded herself, she had been well paid despite all her protests that it wasn't necessary.

And there was no way she would have passed up the opportunity to see this wonderful tropical island, a tiny jewel in the Indonesian archipelago. Called Pulau Panjang, or Long Island, in Bahasa, the universal language of Indonesia, it was easy to see why from a map—and indeed from the air. Several times longer than it was wide, her first view had been of a huge, vivid green crescent in the turquoise sea.

As the ancient little plane had circled overhead she had had the most spectacular view of the thick unbroken green of the jungle with its winding rivers, slicing through the hillside on their way down the mountain, the deserted sandy coves and the isolated little settlements scattered here and there.

It was like something out of *Robinson Crusoe*, she'd thought, only bigger, and then at one end, clustered round an estuary, she'd spotted a larger settlement with an airstrip no bigger than a pencil line.

Around the town there was a terraced area of *padi* fields where she was told the locals grew rice and soya beans in rotation, but apart from that there was little sign of cultivation on the island. Because of the shape it was also known as Pulau Pisang, or Banana Island. Apparently, so Penny told her, Indonesian places often had more than one name, which just added to the delightful confusion.

The airstrip lay to the south of the town, on a spit of land sticking out into the sea, and although it was a little bigger than it had appeared from the air it was still barely adequate. What would happen if the plane failed to stop didn't bear thinking about, but it was hardly a jet. The little twin-engined monstrosity would probably just bellyflop into the sea and be towed back to land by a group of cheerful Indonesian children, yelling, 'Hello, Mister!'

It was the sum total of their English, apart from 'Give me money, give me sweets', which was the tail end of the refrain she had heard ever since her arrival in Jakarta that morning. Katie had been wide-eyed. For Gabby, it summed up the influence of the west on the innocent children of the east, and she felt faintly ashamed.

This island, though, had been unlike that, the children simply friendly and curious and the adults likewise. They had been courteous, voluble and charming—which was more than could be said for the company doctor.

A soft snore rippled the air, and she glowered at him and willed him to wake up and not just lie there.

She got her way. As she watched, his fingers relaxed their grip on the almost full glass of juice and ice and it tipped up on his chest. He gave a startled yelp and sat up, blinking and swatting at his shirt, but the damage was done.

That'll teach you, Gabby thought, stifling a laugh, but she was the one who suffered in the end because he stripped off his shirt, mopped the hair-tangled expanse of his deep, muscular chest with the soggy bundle and dropped back into the chair with a sigh.

'I suppose you want another one,' Penny said with a grin.

He flashed her a smile full of wry self-disgust, and to her horror Gabby found herself warming towards the rogue.

'Shirt or drink?' he asked ruefully. 'It was my last clean shirt. Last night was a bit heavy on them.'

Penny stood up. 'I'll get you one of Jon's. Can't have you frightening the natives—or Gabby. Help yourself to the drink.'

She left them, and Gabby felt his eyes graze her skin, sending a shiver over it. 'I don't think I frighten you, do I, Gabrielle?' he murmured, his voice a little husky. 'Rather the opposite, I feel.'

She blushed and glared at him, and he chuckled, a

deep, warm sound that was nearly as attractive as the expanse of bronzed skin that filled Gabby's line of sight. She shifted slightly and turned her eyes to the little town below them, the houses clustered along the curve of the bay and stretching up towards the brilliant green of the terraced *padi* fields.

She hoped he would leave her in peace, but no chance. That deep, slightly husky voice teased at her senses again like a caress. 'Pretty, isn't it? Especially if you don't have to live here.'

She turned back to him and tried to avoid ogling his body. 'Don't you like it?'

He shrugged. 'It's where the work is. You do what you have to do.'

Like sleep on verandas. Gabby was less than sympathetic, and it probably showed, but she really didn't care. As far as she was concerned, what he seemed to be doing couldn't possibly be construed as work. She thought of the sick people of the world, and of him passing the prime of his life with his feet on the railing of some tropical veranda, and despaired of the waste of talent.

If he was, indeed, talented. Perhaps he'd been struck off?

'How long are you here for?' he asked after a pregnant pause that she refused to fill.

'Three weeks—and, don't worry, I won't expect you to entertain me.'

He said something under his breath—not an apology, she was sure. She turned and met his eyes, her own glittering with challenge, and that sapphire gaze locked with hers. The same sparkling blue as the tropical sea beneath them, they issued their own challenge.

'That's just as well,' he said mildly. 'I'm much too busy to play nursemaid to a tourist—even if she is related to the boss.'

'Busy?' Gabby couldn't keep the scepticism out of her voice, but he either chose to ignore it or it went over his head, which she doubted. Most likely he had a skin like a rhinoceros.

Penny re-emerged, clean shirt in hand, sparing them the necessity of any further conversation. He stood up and pulled it on, and Gabby noticed with interest that it was a little on the tight side, compared to his other one. Not surprising, really. He was somewhat larger than her cousin, better muscled—heavens, she must stop looking at his body!

She was just wondering how she was going to get through lunch, without disgracing herself by being rude or ogling him, when a Jeep appeared on the horizon, horn blaring, bearing down on them in a hurry.

With a muffled exclamation Jed was on his feet and running over the lawn to meet the Jeep before it came to a halt. Penny and Gabby followed a little more slowly, and arrived at the Jeep to see Jonathan in earnest conversation with Jed.

'Just serviced two days ago,' Jonathan was saying worriedly. 'I can't understand it.'

'Where are the men?'

'Up at the compound. I didn't think it was safe to move them without you. Derek's giving them first aid.'

'Right. I'll get some gear. What injuries are we talking about?'

He was getting into the Jeep, and Gabby put a hand on Jonathan's arm. 'Can I help?' she asked.

'I hardly think this is going to be a spectator sport,' Jed growled, but Jonathan ignored him.

'Thanks. Get a hat and put on something with sleeves—we'll pick you up shortly. Oh, and wear sensible shoes.'

She ran back to the bungalow with Penny, opened her

case and pulled out thin cotton trousers, a long-sleeved cotton shirt and trainers. She was back in the road in seconds, Penny following her to plonk a hat on her head, and as the Jeep came careering past she jumped in before the vehicle had even come to rest.

'Pity about lunch,' Jed said. 'You should have stayed and kept Penny company.'

Jonathan, she noticed, was missing. Ignoring Jed's barbed remark, she asked where her cousin had gone.

'Phoning for an air ambulance to take the men out—sounds like it might be necessary. God knows why you wanted to come—I expect it'll be somewhat gory. Just keep out of the way and don't faint on me, all right? I don't need any more casualties and if you're anything like your cousin you'll go green at the first drop of blood.'

'I think I can cope,' she told him drily. 'After three months in A and E as staff nurse, I'm sure one more accident won't turn my stomach.'

His head snapped round and he stared at her in amazement. 'You're a nurse? God, woman, why didn't you say so?'

'You didn't ask—and don't call me "woman".'

A brow climbed into his hairline, and those full, firm, well-shaped lips quirked at the corners. 'Yessir,' he said with a grin. 'Right, hang on tight, it gets a bit rough here.'

For the next twenty minutes she was heartily relieved that she didn't have a roof over her head because she would have smacked into it countless times. She was also glad that she hadn't had her lunch. 'A bit rough' turned out to be the understatement of the century.

'The road's the next thing on the list, once we've established where the plant's going to be,' he yelled over the scrabbling of the tyres and the grinding roar of the engine. 'Obviously we can't do anything in the way of construction with the road like this, but until the feasibility study's been completed there's no point.'

Gabby just hung on and wondered if anyone had done a feasibility study about staying in bouncing Jeeps at fifty miles an hour on jungle tracks.

And it really was jungle, she realised when the mud forced Jed to slow down enough for her to focus on her surroundings. All around them the trees soared skywards to the canopy, their trunks straight and tall and leafless, and at the edges of the road the undergrowth was rioting in the light and air let in by the narrow channel the road had cut through the canopy.

She didn't recognise a single plant—not that she was much of a botanist but, even so, she was surprised that things were so strange and different.

'What's happened to the men?' she asked belatedly.

'Nobody's quite sure. They were driving back from town this morning and crashed.'

She wasn't surprised. It didn't take a genius to work out that the road was dangerous. They passed the tangled remains of a Jeep in the undergrowth on a bend, and then suddenly she could see light and they were in a clearing. Wooden prefabricated huts clustered round a central square, and Jed slid to a halt outside a hut labelled somewhat grandly INFIRMARY just as the rapidly blackening sky opened.

Gabby gave a little shriek as the first fat, heavy drops hit her, and then Jed was jumping out of the Jeep and telling her to hurry. 'Bring the rest, could you?' he yelled, and then, grabbing bags and boxes of equipment, he ran up the steps and inside, leaving Gabby to follow. She straightened her hat, scooped up the last remaining supplies and went after him at a run.

It was like an oven inside, and the sound of rain on

the tin roof was deafening. She looked out of the window and saw it fall in a solid sheet, flattening the exposed plants at the edge of the clearing and turning the area to a sea of mud in seconds. She felt sweat break out on her skin and run in rivers down her spine, and she longed for a cool shower or the *mandi* Penny had spoken about. No time for that, though, there was work to be done.

The hut was dimly lit, with four beds arranged around the single room. Men lay on three of them with others clustered around, trying to help. Two seemed reasonably comfortable, if a little bloody. The third, the one Jed had gone straight to, looked awful. A young Indonesian, he was pale and sweating, his lips were blue, his eyes were rolling and he was obviously very seriously injured.

'Thank God you're here,' an Englishman yelled over the noise of the rain. Derek presumably, Gabby thought. About thirty years old, lean and bespectacled, he was covered in blood and dirt, and he looked harrassed and weary. 'Right out of my league,' he continued. 'I'll go and tell Ismail to bring boiled water. Anything else you need?'

Jed shook his head and bent over the man, examining him quickly. 'Chest,' he said economically, and proceeded to sound it, his face impassive. 'Tension pneumothorax—we'll have to put a drain in before we can move him. I've got some stuff in there somewhere that we can use.'

'I'll set up—you check the other two,' Gabby said quickly. 'Is there somewhere I can wash?'

He rattled off instructions in Bahasa, and one of the men left the room and reappeared moments later with a bowl, fresh water and a towel that looked reasonably clean. She used one end and left the other for Jed, and went back to prepare their patient.

She knew where he would want to enter the chest wall, and she swabbed and wiped it, washed it with io-dine solution and left it to dry while she fished around in the bag he'd shown her. All she could find of any use was a urinary catheter, some tape, a couple of pairs of rubber gloves, a scalpel, a pair of scissors and some local anaesthetic and suturing equipment.

She drew up the lignocaine into one of the syringes, recapped the needle and turned to him. 'Ready when you are.'

He nodded, came over and checked the things she'd set out on a sterile paper towel and then injected the local into the area around the fourth rib space, before washing his hands. Gloved up, he swabbed the area again, sliced neatly with the scalpel and then inserted the point of the scissors, twisted and opened.

There was a hissing sigh of air out of the chest cavity, and behind them a dull thunk over the noise of the rain. 'Hello, one of the boys has bitten the dust,' Jed said softly. 'Can we find a bottle of water to put the end of the catheter in? Boiled water, tell them.'

'I can't,' she reminded him, handing over the catheter. 'I don't speak a word of Indonesian.'

There followed another stream of instructions, thrown over his shoulder as he deftly pushed the catheter in, taped it to the chest wall and stood up. 'Right, let's get this air out.' He pushed gently on the chest, listening to the sighing exhalation of air from the tube, and as he released the pressure he folded the end of the tube over to prevent air re-entering the chest cavity.

Immediately their patient started to look better. His colour improved, and he groaned and his eyes fluttered open. '*Obat*,' he whispered.

'What's that?'

'Medicine—he wants some painkiller, I expect.' She

drew up a shot of pethidine while he spoke quietly to the man in his own language, running his hands lightly over the bruised and battered limbs and gently palpating the abdomen.

'Seems to be fairly all right, apart from the chest and a broken arm. I'll just check the others again—give him the pethidine and watch him, would you?'

He turned to the man who'd fainted on the floor behind them and was now coming round, leaving her to her own devices. Gabby found herself lost without a language in which to communicate so she spoke in English, murmuring gentle reassurance. It seemed to work. The man relaxed his death grip on her hand, but when she soothed his head and touched his forehead his eyes widened.

'Careful—the head is sacred. You never touch it unless you've asked permission, and never with your left hand—it's an insult. Never take or give anything with your left hand, either. Always use the right.'

Jed's quiet advice made her aware of how little she knew. How could she really be of help amongst these people about whom she knew nothing? She could offend so easily without any idea of what she had said or done. Perhaps she should just go outside, sit down and wait for him before she did something truly awful—

He was beside her again. 'Don't get bent out of shape—it doesn't matter. I'll explain.' He broke into the native tongue again, and the man relaxed and almost smiled.

A few moments later Jed beckoned to her and they went out onto the veranda. The rain had stopped, and the air was cooler and fresher. It felt wonderful. She turned to Jed. 'Sorry about that—I didn't realise about the head. What did you say to him?'

His grin was wicked and did silly things to her insides. 'I told him you were a healer. Healers can do anything.'

She gave a hollow laugh. 'I wish. It would come in awfully handy sometimes.'

'Tell me about it,' he muttered. 'Right, we need to get these limbs splinted up for the journey down to the airstrip. Both these others have got fractures—one arm, one leg.'

They worked side by side without comment, strapping limbs to makeshift splints made of bits of wood wrapped in clean towels. They padded them and supported them as well as they could, but even so Gabby knew it was going to hurt, bouncing down that hillside to the town.

They laid two of them in the back of the Jeep, but the third, the man who had the chest drain, Jed propped up on the front seat between them so Gabby could keep an eye on him and the bottle of water as they travelled slowly and carefully down the hill.

It took nearly an hour, almost three times as long as it had taken to drive up, and when they arrived they could see the little plane just taxiing to the end of the runway. Jed drove along the edge of the strip to the plane, and then they loaded their patients, handed them over to the medical crew and sent them off to Jakarta for treatment.

As they watched the little plane climb into the sky and bank away towards Jakarta, Jed turned to her. 'Thank you for your help—it was invaluable,' he said quietly. 'Most things I can manage on my own, but there are times like this when a skilled assistant makes all the difference.'

She felt heat brush her already warm skin, and looked away, confused by the sudden rush of pleasure his words had given her. 'It was nothing—I only did what I'm trained to do,' she replied diffidently.

'Nevertheless, you did it well. Thanks.'

A silly grin crept onto her lips and she turned away, walking back to the Jeep so that he wouldn't see her response. Why would those few words of praise mean so much?

Because he was competent and skilled himself, of course. She'd seen that in the quick, precise movements of his hands, the assessing eyes, the searching fingers—he was a natural physician, and his praise did matter.

She grinned again, and swung up into the Jeep. 'Get a move on, I'm hungry,' she told him as he ambled up.

'Typical woman—always complaining.'

'Typical man—always providing something to complain about,' she returned.

It was almost four o'clock when they got back to Jonathan's and Penny's house, and as Gabby went to have a shower and change into clean clothes she heard Jonathan and Jed in conversation.

They were talking in low tones about the accident, too quietly for her to grasp more than the general drift, but one word jumped out of the urgent exchange.

Sabotage...

CHAPTER TWO

LUNCH turned into an early supper.

They sat on the veranda and ate their delayed meal of cold chicken in spicy sauce, rice and avocado salad and wonderfully exotic fruit. It was delicious, but Gabby couldn't concentrate on it. She was too tired to enjoy the food, and all she could think about was the three injured men who had been airlifted to hospital, and the possibility that their injuries had been caused deliberately.

It was the sole topic of conversation, in any case.

'It seems that the brakes failed,' Jonathan told them. 'The driver told Derek that they were working one minute, and the next there was nothing there at all. He was completely helpless. You know that stretch of road—all hills and bends. It's lethal enough with brakes. Without them it's suicide.'

Jed frowned. 'Has anybody checked out the vehicle?'

Jonathan shook his head. 'No, not yet. Derek's going to do it now.'

'But surely it could just have been a simple failure. Why would anybody want to tamper with the brakes?' Gabby asked, puzzled.

'To frighten us off?' Jonathan suggested.

'But why?'

'That's what we don't know,' he replied. 'It's the third or fourth incident in the past couple of weeks. The first was nothing much—a generator was smashed. It was irritating vandalism, we thought. Perhaps some of the boys from the town out looking for mischief. Then the cookhouse was burned down. It could have been an accident—a spark lodged in the roof or something. Then one of the Indonesian engineers left suddenly without explanation. We still don't know why, but he seemed very frightened and it spooked the others.'

'And now this,' Gabby said thoughtfully.

'And Mohamed last night.'

They looked at Jed. 'Mo?' Jonathan said. 'I thought he slipped and fell?'

'But why? He won't talk about it. By the time he went out on the plane this morning he was still refusing to discuss it, and he seemed scared. I think he either saw or heard something, or someone pushed him. Whatever, I don't think he just fell down that cliff.'

Penny licked her lips nervously. 'But why? Why are they being targeted? Do they want us to use workmen and engineers from the island?'

'Or do they just want us to go away?' Jed said quietly.

'But why?' Penny asked again. 'What are we doing that's upsetting them?'

Jonathan shoved his hands through his hair and sighed. 'Lord knows, darling, but I don't think you need to worry. It seems to be restricted to the Indonesians at the moment—I think it must be some local thing. There's a lot of rivalry between the different areas, but I'm sure we're all quite safe.'

Gabby shot Jed a look and saw him shake his head slightly, as if in mute disagreement. Did he think they were in danger?

She didn't have a chance to find out because at that moment the children finished their nap and came and joined them, and the topic was dropped instantly. Later, though, a messenger came from the compound and Jonathan excused himself and left, his face troubled.

Jed went too, and Gabby, exhausted from her trip,

suddenly ran out of steam. 'Penny, I need to go to bed,' she told her hostess.

'Oh, heavens, how dreadful of me, you must be exhausted!' Penny exclaimed. 'Oh, Gabby, I'm so sorry. I'll take you up there now.'

'Up?' she asked, puzzled. There was no 'up' in the bungalow.

'To the guest house. I'm afraid you'll have to share it with Jed,' she said apologetically, 'but it's got two quite separate bedrooms and a large living area and veranda in between. I don't think you'll be too much on top of each other. It's just that both our bedrooms in this house are already overstretched, but it's a very nice bungalow—I'm sure you'll be quite comfortable.'

Share. With Jed.

Great.

She dredged up a smile, heaved her case off the veranda steps, swung her flight bag over her shoulder and followed Penny up the uneven road to the bungalow where she had found Jed that morning.

'Rom has made your bed up ready—if you want anything just ring and one of the servants will come and see to you. We all eat at our house—it's got the only decent kitchen. Make sure you put plenty of insect repellent on—and have you started a course of anti-malarials?'

Gabby nodded. 'Of course. So's Katie.'

'Oh, yes. Right. Well, here you are…'

She threw open the door of a plain but spotlessly clean room. The windows were open but had mesh screens over them, as did all the doors and windows, and there was a fan on the ceiling that creaked slowly into life when Penny pushed a switch.

The bed was made up with crisp white sheets, and dangling over it was a thick, net rope suspended from the ceiling.

'That's a mosquito net—you spread it out and tuck it into the edge of the mattress when you go to bed. It cuts the air circulation down a bit, but it's better than being eaten alive and, although the screens help, the odd bug gets in through the doors. When the power station's built we'll get air conditioning, of course, but the generator can't manage it.'

Gabby didn't care about air conditioning. She just wanted to get her head down and get some sleep. First, though, she was going to explore the *mandi*.

She opened her case, found a cool cotton nightshirt and some fresh underwear, grabbed the thick white towel off the end of the bed and padded out to look for the bathroom.

There was a loo and basin off a corridor at the back of the bungalow, but the *mandi* was located, as Penny had said, outside the back door. There was a wooden walkway and a bamboo structure like a little shed, and she opened the door and peered in.

A cold stone floor and a big tank of deliciously cool water convinced her she wanted to try it. She shed her clothes and looked about for somewhere to put them, but there didn't seem to be anywhere. 'Oh, well,' she shrugged, put them on the floor in the corner, piled the fresh ones on top and tipped a scoop of water over her head.

A little shriek escaped before she could control it, but she was expecting the next scoopful. It was cold against her hot skin, but wonderfully refreshing. There was a bar of soap that smelt like Jed, and she rubbed it over her body and wondered if he'd done the same.

What a curiously intoxicating thought, she thought, humming cheerfully. Strangely intimate.

She rinsed, grabbed the towel from over the door and

rubbed her hair, threw it back out of her eyes and then looked at her clothes.

Soaked. Not just damp, but sodden. She must have been flinging the water around with even more abandon than she'd realised!

Oh, well, there was no one about. She wound the towel around her body and tucked it in over her breasts like a sarong, scooped up her soggy clothes and went back inside.

It was getting dark rapidly now at the end of the day. The light was fading fast, night literally falling, plummeting her into a velvet blackness.

She paused for a moment, listening to the sounds of the night from the jungle behind her, and a shiver went down her spine.

Primeval forest, full of strange plants and even stranger creatures. She felt as if someone was watching her, and a shiver ran through her again. Clutching the towel tighter round her, she hurried inside.

The bungalow was gloomy without lights, the rooms almost completely dark now, so the sudden movement of a white-clad figure startled her. With a little scream she stepped back, thumped her heel against a low table and sat down on it with a bump.

'Feeling a little jumpy?' Jed said mildly.

She swore somewhat colourfully under her breath, and rubbed her heel. 'Where did you come from?' she snapped. 'I didn't hear you drive up.'

She could hear the laughter in his voice, though. 'I'm not surprised, with all the splashing and singing,' he teased. 'I gather you enjoyed it.'

She hoped it really was dark and that it wasn't just her eyes because she could feel the heat scorching her cheeks. Had she really been singing? Oh, Lord.

'It was wonderful, but my clothes got wet.'

'You're supposed to take them off—'

'On the floor,' she said drily.

'Before you go in.'

'Oh.' She had a sudden vision of Jed going to the *mandi* stark naked, and the colour in her cheeks grew yet brighter—just as he flicked the lights on.

'You've caught the sun,' he said softly, bending to brush her burning skin with his knuckles. The light touch against her cheeks sent a tiny shock wave through her, and she stood up, dodging past him, and went to her room.

'I'm going to bed,' she told him. 'I'll see you in the morning.'

'Running away?' he asked with gentle mockery.

She turned back to him, hanging onto her temper with difficulty. 'I'm tired. I've had an incredibly long and trying forty-eight hours, and I'm wiped. Anyway, I thought you didn't want to entertain me.'

'I don't,' he said bluntly. 'It appears, however, that I don't have a choice.' His face was stony and he was clearly unimpressed, but there was nothing she could do about it.

She tried again. 'Look, I don't like the idea of having to share your accommodation either, but we're just going to have to be civilised about it. I'm sure if we try hard we can manage to act like grown-ups,' she said sweetly, and, going into her room, she shut the door with a definite little click, looked for a bolt and was disappointed.

Well, she'd just have to rely on his good manners— if he had any. So far she hadn't seen much evidence of them, but she'd give him the benefit of the doubt for now. She was too tired to do anything else.

She dragged a comb through her hair, spread a dry towel over her pillow and lay down on the bed, arranging the mosquito net over herself as Penny had said.

It was the last conscious thing she did for eleven hours.

'Tea, mem.'

Gabby's eyes struggled open and she sat up, fighting the layers of mosquito net that were tangled round her.

'Come in,' she called, and the door swung open to admit a young Indonesian girl with a smiling face and a very welcome pot of tea on a tray.

'Where's Jed?' she asked, wondering if it was safe to use the *mandi*.

'*Jalan-jalan*,' the girl replied, and then with a little bob and a smile she was gone, leaving Gabby with her tea.

She wondered where Jalan Jalan was. The compound? The town? She looked at her watch, and discovered it was six o'clock. Plenty early enough not to worry, she thought, and sipped her tea with gratitude. It was flavoured with the powdered milk she was beginning to get used to, and which she dimly remembered from a short spell in Sarawak in her early childhood.

She looked out of the window and saw that it was light again. Wonderful. She felt better—positively energetic. She disentangled herself from the mosquito net, stripped and wrapped herself in a towel and went out to the *mandi* for another delicious slosh around.

This time she managed to get back to her room without being caught, and she dressed quickly and went down the road to Penny's and Jonathan's bungalow. There the same girl who had brought her tea informed her that *Tuan* had gone out and *Mem* and the children were still in bed.

'*Doktor* come back,' she was told and, looking over her shoulder, she saw Jed strolling up the road from the town, a string bag dangling from his fingers.

'Morning,' he called, and she went down off the veranda towards him.

'Morning. I gather you've been to Jalan Jalan—is that the town?'

He laughed, showing even white teeth that gleamed against his tan. '*Jalan-jalan* means to go for a walk but, you're right, I have been to town. I wandered down to the market in Telok Panjang for some fruit. Join me for breakfast?'

Join Jed? She was astonished at the invitation after last night's cool rebuttal, but she was starving and it sounded wonderful. 'Sure you've got enough?'

He grinned, showing those teeth again. 'If I ate all this lot I'd be really ill,' he said with a chuckle.

Gabby fell into step beside him, thinking that if she wasn't so busy being critical of him professionally she could probably enjoy the man's company—and why was she thinking that? He'd already made it clear how unwelcome her presence was, from the comment about entertaining tourists through to his lack of enthusiasm the night before over having her as a house guest.

She was probably the last person he'd seek out as a companion—and, anyway, she wouldn't want him to because she couldn't separate Jed the doctor from Jed the Hollywood cliché. She'd seen him at work the day before, after all, and knew he was capable of working efficiently and well—so why wasn't he?

Unless, of course, they were going to continue to have accidents like that one, in which case his expertise would be well and truly put to the test.

'Did you find out what happened about the brakes?' she asked as they climbed the veranda steps.

His face clouded. 'No. The Jeep was burned out.'

She frowned. 'No, it wasn't. We saw it.'

'They must have done it after we came down again

with the casualties. When Derek went to look at it, it was a heap of smouldering ash. They were lucky there wasn't a forest fire, but I suppose the rain would have made it safer by damping everything down.'

'Damping?' She laughed, thinking of the slashing torrents of water that had fallen. 'Does it always rain like that?' she asked, amazed yet again that the sky could hold such vast quantities of water.

Jed grinned. 'Every afternoon. That's the beauty of it—you can get about in the sun in the morning, even in the monsoon season. It just makes the mud a bit deeper and the roads even worse.'

That was hard to imagine. The thought of the track up to the compound getting any worse was mindboggling. She just hoped she wouldn't have to travel it again if it did.

She followed him into the kitchen area at the back, and he washed the fruit, piled it into a bowl, picked up two plates and some knives and spoons and headed back to the veranda, leaving her to bring from the fridge the glasses of juice he had poured.

They settled themselves down on the veranda out of the direct heat of the sun, already scorching at only eight in the morning. The fruit looked wonderful, and Gabby realised she was ravenous. She had hardly eaten anything the day before, and it seemed for ever since she'd had a decent meal.

'What's this?' she asked, picking up a fuzzy little pinkish red fruit.

'Rambutan—it means hairy. Just peel it and eat it, but be careful. There's a stone inside.'

She pulled off the skin, bit into the translucent white flesh and sighed with delight. 'Oh, wow.'

He chuckled. 'Lovely, aren't they? I managed to get a couple of mangosteens, too,' he said, proffering a dark purple ball the size of a small orange. 'It's a bit early in the season for them, but one of the traders owed me a favour. Crush it in your hands to split the skin, then it's easy to peel.'

Gabby found herself wondering what sort of favour he'd been owed as she peeled one of the precious mangosteens, then promptly forgot to worry about it as she tried the fruit. Segmented like an orange and with firm white flesh like the rambutan, it, too, tasted wonderful. Silently thanking Jed's favour-owing friend at the market, she moved on to sample a wedge of mango, a slice of papaya and a pomelo, before admitting defeat.

'I'll be ill if I have too much before I'm used to it,' she said and, sipping her drink, she lay back in the chair and opened her mouth to quiz him about local customs.

She didn't get a chance, though, because he smacked down his glass and stood up with lazy grace.

'Right, I must get on. See you later—and don't forget to cover up if you go out, remember to take your anti-malarials and drown yourself in insect repellent—and don't go near the jungle. There are snakes.'

'Yes, Mum,' she replied, trying not to look at those well-made legs only inches away from her face.

'Just doing my job as camp MO,' he said mildly, then left her to it, bounding down the veranda steps and heading off towards a battered old Jeep. It started with a cough and a rattle, and set off up the road with a little spurt of dust. The clutch was obviously less than subtle—or else it was Jed's driving.

She leant back, closed her eyes and dozed for a while, then Penny came and found her. 'Hi. How are you feeling?'

'Tired—it hit me last night and my system's all confused. All I want to do is sleep!'

'So sleep. We aren't doing anything today—Jon wants

to sort out this business of the crash yesterday, put out a few feelers. I'm sorry you had to go and work when you're supposed to be on holiday. It was very kind of you.'

She dismissed the remark with a wave. 'It was nothing. I couldn't sit here and twiddle my thumbs and let people bleed to death, could I?'

Penny laughed. 'No, I suppose not. Why don't you come down and spend the day with me? I don't want to leave the children, and Katie's still catching up on her sleep. Perhaps later we can go and explore the town.'

They did, at four in the afternoon when the worst of the heat had worn off. They walked down because the Jeeps were now one short, and the children skipped and scuffed up stones and seemed full of energy.

Gabby was too hot to skip, but she felt a bubbling excitement just the same. The noises and smells and sights were all strange and yet familiar from her very early childhood, and they saw things she'd forgotten.

On one street corner a man was grating ice over a huge plane, then packing the chips into a ball and covering it in hideously pink raspberry juice. He put it inside a folded cone of newspaper, then prepared another with condensed milk, grated coconut and chopped banana over the top.

'Gross,' Penny said with a shudder, but to Gabby, who was steaming gently in the tropical heat, it looked unbelievably inviting.

'The ice isn't safe, I suppose,' she said wistfully.

'Absolutely not. The water's probably straight out of the river. Come on, I want to go to the draper's and get some white cotton. I've run out.'

They went into a tiny shop, run by a wizened little Chinese woman with quick fingers and more wrinkles than Gabby had ever seen, and then they came back along the main street.

Penny indicated a sort of café, with people eating at tables on the pavement. 'This is a *rumah makan*—literally a food house. It's our only restaurant, and the food's brilliant. Indonesian and Chinese, and the kitchen's so clean you can see your face in the counters, so we're told. It's the only place to eat so it's just as well! We'll take you one night. It's a real treat, and ridiculously cheap.'

As they walked on Gabby was sure she could hear the unmistakable roar of a football crowd. 'It's the satellite TV over the restaurant,' Penny explained. 'They rent out space to watch it—the Indonesians are all football-crazy, and they love the Australian and American soaps. After the restaurant it's the town's most popular venue!'

'Do they have *Children's BBC*?' Katie asked hopefully.

'Sorry, darling, no,' Penny told her oldest daughter. 'When we get electricity we can have a TV with a satellite dish, and you can watch cartoons—OK?'

'But we've got electricity,' Katie reasoned.

'But only a tiny generator and it's not big enough to run a television. Sorry, darling.'

But it didn't pacify her. Katie trailed up the hill behind them, scuffing her toes and looking mournful.

'Oh, dear. It's one of the adjustments she's going to have to make,' Penny said. 'There's so much that's different. Still, the others managed to get used to it quite quickly. I expect she will.'

They made their way slowly back to the bungalow and were greeted by Rom with a brimming jug of freshly made lemonade for the children and steaming tea for the adults.

Gabby eyed the lemonade longingly but, as Penny assured her she would, she found the tea actually very refreshing.

Not so refreshing that she didn't very soon excuse herself and go back to bed until supper, and then escape again to return to her bed as early as she could decently do so.

It was worth it, though. She emerged the following morning after her *mandi* and early morning tea feeling refreshed and ready to start enjoying her holiday at last.

Jed was stretched out on the veranda, sipping fruit juice, with a little heap of papaya skins beside him on the table. She greeted him cheerfully, and he turned his head and looked up at her, without moving.

'Morning,' he said, and his voice sounded husky and interesting.

All that gin, Gabby thought. It probably wrecks the throat. She didn't dare look into those astonishingly blue eyes.

She helped herself to some fruit and sat down, nibbling as she looked out over the bay. It looked sparkling clear and inviting, and she longed to be out on it.

'We're going out in the launch today, I think,' he told her, as if he'd read her mind. 'There's nothing more we can do about the Jeep, and Derek's making some discreet enquiries about the other incidents. Until we find out what's wrong Jon thinks we should just carry on and not pay too much attention to it.'

'Do you agree?' she asked him, sensing that he was reluctant to criticise her cousin in front of her.

'I think he might be underestimating the situation,' he said carefully. 'I don't know what's wrong, but something's making them jumpy and someone's going to get badly hurt before long if this goes on.'

She remembered something her cousin had said the

night before last. 'Do you think it's just the Indonesians being targeted?' she asked.

There was a second's pause and then he shook his head. 'No. Anybody could have been driving that Jeep. Derek's wife could have been in the cookhouse—she's living up there with the others. She's an engineer too, and part of the team. They got married two months ago.'

'A female engineer? Doesn't that cause problems?'

He raised an eyebrow. 'Sexist?' he said softly.

She blushed. 'Not at all. I just thought, with all those men in the primitive conditions up there—well, bathrooms and that sort of thing—it's a bit difficult, I should think.'

'It's better now they've tied the knot. Indonesians can be a bit funny about women on their own. Married women, on the other hand, are quite safe. That was why I was a bit wary about you sharing the bungalow with me—I didn't want your reputation to suffer so that you lost respect.'

'My reputation matters to you?' she asked, feeling guilty for judging him so harshly last night but not at all convinced that he was genuinely concerned for her virtue and it wasn't just an excuse to get out of entertaining her.

'Well, perhaps not directly,' he said with a lazy grin. 'It might enhance mine, of course, which could be good news, but Jon's reputation could be affected and he needs to remain in a strong position to lead the team.' He stretched out his legs and propped them up on the veranda rail right in front of her eyes.

'As for the safety thing, I think we should all be vigilant. Jon's checking over the launch now, and making sure it hasn't been tampered with. The last thing we want is for it to break down and leave us adrift in the sea in the middle of the day in this heat.'

He eyed her bare arms critically. 'You'll need to cover up and smother yourself in sunblock,' he warned. 'And don't forget to take your anti-malarials.'

'Yes, Mummy,' she teased. 'Am I going to get this lecture every morning?'

He gave a wry grin. 'You can't be too careful. What pills are you taking?'

'Mefloquine—now you're going to tell me that's wrong.'

He laughed. 'I'm not—it's fine. It's the recommended drug. Just watch out for side-effects, but even they're better than dying of falciparum malaria.'

'What do you take?' she asked, somehow knowing it would be different.

He grinned. 'I'm trying a combination of other remedies.'

'What—marinading yourself in sweat and gin?' she said before she could stop herself.

To her relief he gave a short bark of laughter. 'Don't forget the tonic. The quinine in tonic was an early attempt to kill the malaria parasite spread by the *Anopheles* mosquito—you do know it's the female of the species that causes all the problems, typically?'

'Sexist?' she said softly, returning his little barb, and he grinned.

'Only mildly, and it is true. The female is the carrier of the parasite. Quinine was first used as an anti-malarial by the Indonesian folk doctors or *dukun*. Unfortunately this means it's been around for ages and so there's a lot of immunity to it now.'

'Hence the introduction of mefloquine.'

'Exactly. Chloroquine combined with proguanil, or alternatively doxycycline, causes fewer problems than mefloquine, but since none of them are especially desirable long term I'm trying to find out if anything else works any better—'

'Hence the gin and tonic.'

'Amongst other things.' He grinned. 'Hey, a man has to have some recreational activities, and what else do you see around here? Anyway, it's a good idea to take in plenty of fluids to replace the huge amount lost in sweat, and the juniper oil in gin acts as a natural insect repellent. Of course, rubbing yourself with a solution of tobacco juice is also effective—'

She wrinkled her nose. 'Nice,' she said with a grin. 'I could go off the tropics.'

He laughed again. 'There are hazards. The best thing to do is stay in the shade, cover up, use insect repellent and stay inside a screened area at dusk and during the night to avoid being bitten. The fluids are the easy bit. Want another drink?'

He was on his feet, heading for the kitchen, when Penny hailed them from down the road. 'We're off soon—are you ready?'

'Be with you in two shakes,' he called back. He looked at Gabby's arms and frowned. 'Cover up—have you got any long-sleeved shirts?'

'Only one clean one, and it's tight fitting and quite thick—and black.'

He rolled his eyes. 'Borrow one of my shirts. You can roll the sleeves up and tie the bottom, but it'll give you more protection. The sun shining off the sea will burn you in no time flat—and don't forget to put sunscreen on under your eyebrows and chin. Everybody gets sunburned there because they forget about reflections up from the water.'

'Mothering me again?' she said drily, heading for the kitchen with their plates.

He followed her. 'Just a little friendly medical advice.

I don't want to end up having to nurse you through malaria or heatstroke—and don't forget the hat.'

She rolled her eyes and he threw up his hands in mock surrender and backed out of the kitchen. 'OK, just don't say you weren't warned.'

She did cover up—in one of his shirts, freshly laundered and pressed to perfection, tied at the waist over loose cotton trousers and cotton tennis shoes.

'All right?' she asked, appearing outside her bedroom as he emerged from his.

He scanned her quickly, then those gloriously blue eyes locked with hers. 'Fine,' he said, and she wondered if it was her imagination or if he had sounded a bit curt.

He crammed the Panama hat down over his eyes so she couldn't really see them any more, and looked down at the bag in her hand. 'Got your swimming togs?'

'Of course—they're on, and I have spares. Now you're going to tell me I have to swim in a wetsuit because of jellyfish, and I'm probably going to hit you.'

'Oh, I love a bit of violence in a woman,' he teased, and pushed her gently out of the door. 'Come on, they'll be waiting.'

She was glad he couldn't see her face because the touch of his hand against her back had brought soft colour flooding to it. She had to fight the urge to lean back against him—and as much to escape from herself as from him—she hurried down the hill to where the others were now waiting.

'Where are we going?' she asked Penny as they drove down the road to the town. They were all squeezed into the Jeep, the children chattering excitedly beside them.

'A little island called Pulau Tengkorak—Monkey-Skull Island—so called because of the shape. It's fabulous—unpopulated except for a few monkeys and lizards, and of course the jellyfish, but they're mostly further out. Just keep your eyes open.'

She did, looking over the side of the launch into the sparkling clear water as they sliced through it on their way out to the island. She could see jellyfish, and flying fish jumping just yards from the launch, and she thought of the freezing fog and grey drizzle of England in November and forgave Indonesia its malaria mosquitoes. 'I can hardly wait to get in the water,' she told Penny. 'It looks so inviting.'

Penny nodded. 'It is. Warm and refreshing and wonderful, and of course there's plenty of shade from the palm trees. There are coconuts on the island—if any have fallen we can eat them with our lunch. The fresh ones are delicious, nothing like the dried-up remains that get into English supermarkets.' She pointed ahead of them. 'There it is.'

Gabby saw a little green dot growing on the horizon, and then within minutes they were there, pulling up near the beach and anchoring the launch to a buoy that floated in the surf.

'We have to wade the last few yards,' Penny told her. 'Keep your shoes on—in fact, keep them on the whole time, even for swimming. You never know what you might tread on.'

She climbed over the side into the knee-deep water, and found herself in Jed's warm and firm grip. 'OK?' he asked gruffly, before releasing her, and she could hardly function enough to nod in reply.

What was it about the man that every time he touched her she turned into an inferno? She shook her head slightly, scooped Katie up into her arms and carried her up the gently shelving slope to the shore. 'OK?' she asked her little travelling companion.

Katie nodded and grinned, quite happy to be carried

to the beach by the woman who had become her friend over the past few weeks. 'Yes, thanks,' she grinned. 'Are you going to swim with me?'

'I expect so. Shall we ask Mummy where we should put all our things?'

'They're up there,' she said, nodding up the beach to the edge of the treeline.

They walked up the sandy slope to the others, and Gabby wondered if she'd get away with spending all day with the children so she didn't have to spend any of it with Jed because she honestly thought she'd make a fool of herself if left to her own devices.

She wasn't to be that lucky. He appeared at her elbow with a bottle of factor 25 sunscreen, and ordered her to undress to her swimsuit.

'Even if you put your clothes back on it's a good idea,' he told her, and then stood waiting until she'd stripped off his shirt and her trousers and was standing in just a skimpy costume. Had she known he was going to do this she'd have worn the more modest one, but it was too late now. He turned her round, spread a dollop of cream over her neck and shoulders and smoothed it down her arms and back, then turned her round again, did her face and throat and down her chest until she pushed his hands away.

'I can manage now,' she told him firmly, and finished off the low neckline herself. Not for all the tea in China was he getting his fingertips down the neck of her costume!

He handed her the bottle. 'Return the favour?' he asked, and, as if it hadn't been bad enough to have him touching her, she now had to run her hands over acres of bronzed Hollywood potential. 'I'll do your back,' she muttered, and went round behind him.

She was a little on the rough side in self-defence, but

it was either that or linger longingly on the supple, satiny skin that her fingers itched to explore. She finished off with a last defiant swipe, squirted enough into her hand to do her legs and handed the bottle back to him.

'Thanks,' he said, and she could have sworn his voice was a little gruff.

Him too, eh? That could make life interesting. Too interesting. She wasn't into holiday romances, and she had no doubts about Jed. He was a love 'em and leave 'em man if ever she'd met one, and there was no way he was loving and leaving *her*.

She slapped on the last of the sun cream, helped Penny spread some on the children and then went to explore the sea.

She was just about to dive into the gently rippling surf when a hand clamped on her shoulder, making her jump. 'Mind—there's a jellyfish beside you.'

She looked down to where Jed pointed, and saw a soft, pale parachute, undulating gently in the water. Almost invisible, it was beautiful to watch.

'Are they dangerous?' she asked, fascinated by the slow movement.

'Not those. They sting a bit—and they sting where they're washed up on the beach, too, so be careful where you walk. You should also keep an eye out for rocks under the sand and avoid them. This beach is fine, but others have stonefish and sea urchins, and they're deadly, quite literally. Remember to keep your shoes on and your eyes open.'

He drew her to the side. 'Here, I've checked this bit. Just wallow. It's wonderful.'

She sank down under the water, revelling in its gentle caress, and sighed with delight. 'Oh, it's glorious.'

'Glad you came?' he asked softly.

'Oh, yes.'

'Despite the malaria and the flukes and the leeches and the hepatitis and the rabies and the filariasis and—'

'Yes!' she said with a laugh. 'Even so! Are you trying to put me off?'

He grinned, his head floating above the water just inches from hers. 'Would I?'

'Probably,' she said drily.

'Oh, I don't know. I'm beginning to think having you over here for a holiday may not be all bad after all. If all else fails, you can always help me with the sick list.'

'What sick list?' she scoffed. 'You don't have a sick list. You ship them all off to Jakarta!'

He grinned. 'Rumbled. Ah, well. You can help me with my malaria research—'

She chucked a handful of water in his face and swam away from him, laughing. She thought she'd got away with it until she felt long, strong fingers close around her ankle and jerk her backwards. She shot through the water and cannoned into him, and the sudden contrast of coarse hair against her back and legs did nothing for her composure.

He stood up, drawing her to her feet, and turned her into his arms. 'Forfeit,' he said softly, and then before she could move his lips were on hers and her mouth was opening to him. Heat flooded her, and with a little moan she leant into him and felt the solid pressure of his response.

That nearly finished her. With a little cry she pushed him away, and turned and swam back to the others, wondering if they'd seen and if so what they'd make of it.

They were all engrossed in a game of water polo, and she went and joined in. Jed, she noticed out of the corner of her eye, went up the beach to their bags, took out a towel and lay down in the shade with his hat over his eyes.

Good. She didn't need any more challenges to her nervous system like that one. She was beginning to think that in terms of mortal danger malaria was the least of her worries!

CHAPTER THREE

THEY stayed all day on the tiny island, playing in the water until it was too hot, then lurking in the shade at the fringe of the palm trees and eating the picnic that Rom had prepared for them.

There were little sticks of spicy chicken satay with a tasty peanut sauce, cold roasted chicken legs, avocados and, of course, lots of fresh fruit and plenty to drink. Jed wandered off and came back with a couple of fresh, young coconuts, and with a vicious-looking knife called a *parang* he laid about the green husks, poked out the three eyes in the top of each nut and poured the sweet, translucent coconut milk into a jug.

Then he hacked the coconuts into chunks and handed them out, and they used their teeth to scrape off the tender white flesh from the hard shell. Gabby couldn't believe the flavour.

'Good?' Penny asked with a smile.

'Amazing—it's nothing like the ones you can buy in supermarkets in England!'

'Told you. You'll be spoilt now—you'll have to keep coming back.'

Gabby stretched out on her towel and sighed. 'It could certainly be addictive,' she agreed. 'Just think, back home it's cold and rainy—foul!' She wriggled a little on the towel, rearranging the soft sand under her back to conform better to her contours, and shut her eyes.

The conversation droned quietly around her, and she lay completely relaxed and tried to follow the words, but

47

it was too much like hard work. Perhaps she'd just lie there…

The next thing she knew was a tickling sensation around her ribs. Her eyes flew open and she lifted her head to find Jed, sitting next to her dribbling fine sand over her midriff. There were little piles of it all over her costume, tiny slithering pyramids that ran together when she moved.

His smile had a slightly alarming quality, rather like the smile of a tiger. There was no sign of the others, she noted with a little shiver of panic as she looked around.

'They've gone for a wander round the island,' he told her, as if he'd read her mind, and made another pyramid on her stomach. 'I volunteered to babysit.' His teasing grin did silly things to her, and her memory would keep re-running the kiss, which did her no good at all.

'Why do I need to be sat on?' she asked a little breathlessly, watching the sand. 'I'm hardly going to get into mischief.'

'Snakes,' he said calmly. 'They come down out of the jungle and curl up on you when you're sleeping—I had to guard you.'

She gave him a sceptical look. 'You, guard me?' She snorted softly. 'You're joking, of course.'

He grinned that devastating grin of his. 'Of course—there aren't any snakes that dangerous on the island, but it was worth a try just to get you looking adoringly at me as your saviour.'

'I didn't,' she said dampeningly.

The grin widened. 'No—great shame. Still, I'll keep trying. Want a drink?'

She sat up, spilling sand all over her legs. 'Yes, please. What is there?'

'Beer, lemonade, coconut milk, fruit juice.'

She opted for lemonade as the safest choice. She'd

had a great deal of fruit already, and until her system adjusted she didn't want to push her luck.

It was freshly made, cold and sharp and gorgeous. He was pretty gorgeous, too, she had to admit. He was wearing his shirt open over his swimming trunks, and the little glimpses she had of his chest were almost more enticing than the lemonade.

'Fancy a stroll?' he suggested, and she dragged her mind back under control.

'Around the island? Is it far?'

He didn't answer because Jon came running back just at that moment, carrying little Tom who was screaming and thrashing in his arms.

'Uh-oh. Looks like he's been stung by something,' Jed said, getting to his feet. 'Problems?' he called, sprinting towards them.

'Jellyfish—he stood right in the middle of one on the beach. I told him not to, but he didn't realise it would squelch over the top of his shoes.'

They came back to Gabby, Jed examining Tom's foot as they hurried over the sand. 'Any idea what sort?' Jed asked, rummaging in a bag.

'Not really—big pink job.'

He nodded and, taking off the shoe, held Tom's foot firmly in a bowl and sloshed something dark brown over it.

'What's that?' Gabby asked, peering over his shoulder and sniffing.

'Vinegar—it's the cheapest and most effective remedy. That and meat tenderiser paste—don't ask me why, I haven't got a clue, but it really takes the sting out. It's brilliant for Portuguese man-of-war stings, too.'

'Whatever happened to good old-fashioned antihistamine cream?' Gabby said wryly.

'It's a bit low-key for some of these things. I do use

conventional antihistamines and adrenaline in case of emergency and anaphylactic shock, and I always carry it with me wherever I go just to be on the safe side, but for this sort of thing cooking ingredients seem to have it licked. Right, Tom, my old son, how does that feel now?'

'Better,' the boy said with a sorrowful sniff. 'It hurt vewwy badly.'

Jed ruffled the boy's hair and stood up. 'Where are the girls?' he asked, searching the beach.

'Probably looking for us. I didn't have time to let them know what was happening, I just picked him up and ran. I don't suppose you'd like to go and find them? They were just near that rocky outcrop when we saw them last.'

Jed screwed the lid on the vinegar and turned to Gabby. 'Fancy that stroll now?' he asked.

Alone? With him?

'I dare you,' he said softly, so softly that Jon and Tom didn't hear over the little boy's sniffling.

Their eyes locked. 'Really daring,' she murmured somewhat scathingly, and pretended that her heart wasn't thumping at the thought of being alone with him. Nevertheless, she got to her feet, brushed the sand off her legs and put her shoes back on.

Murphy's law being what it was, she lost her balance and swayed against him, and felt the hard thrust of his thigh against her hip. By the time she'd straightened up she'd coloured beautifully and, being the gentleman he was, he grinned knowingly at her and made the situation worse.

She stepped well away from him, looked back over her shoulder and tipped her chin up a touch. 'Well? Are you coming?'

He bent over Tom. 'All right now, little man?'

Tom nodded, and Jed straightened, picking up a bottle of the lemonade and dangling it from his fingers. 'Let's go, then.'

She put his shirt on again to protect herself from the sun, then fell into step, although not quite beside him. She maintained a careful distance between them, but if she thought she'd got away with it, without him noticing, she was wrong.

'I don't bite,' he said mildly, strolling some ten feet away from her. 'You'll be walking in the water to get away from me soon, and you shouldn't be in the sun anyway. Come back here in the shade and stop behaving like a Victorian virgin. I promise you, I'm quite harmless.'

She snorted. Jed, harmless? And she was a monkey's uncle!

He did behave, though, after she came back in the shade, and then she had to deal with an emotion that felt suspiciously like disappointment.

It didn't last long. Gabby was too busy enjoying the strange vegetation and the sparkling clear blue sea and the cloudless sky—except that it wasn't cloudless. Rainclouds were building fast over Pulau Panjang and heading towards them, and she got the distinct feeling it was about to rain very, very heavily—

'We're going to get caught in that,' Jed said as she thought it, and, taking her hand, he led her at a run along the beach to the place Jon had mentioned where the rocks stuck out into the sea. There was a big outcrop with an overhang, and clustered underneath it they saw Penny and the girls.

'Hi,' she called. 'Have you seen Jon and Tom?'

'Back at base camp—Tom's trodden in a jellyfish,' Jed told her. 'It didn't seem too bad—I've dealt with it.

They sent us to tell you where they are and make sure you were all right.'

'We're fine. We've been puddling about in rock pools, haven't we, girls?'

The girls nodded excitedly and began to tell them about all the funny things they'd seen.

'You didn't put your hands or feet into the water, did you?' Jed warned.

Penny shook her head. 'No. We know about nasties that live in rock pools. Anyway, we looked up and saw the sky, and came in here to shelter from the rain when it comes.'

'Which is now,' Jed said with a laugh, and pulled Gabby down and under the shelter of the rock just as the rain swept up the beach from the sea and flung itself against the little island. Once again she was amazed at the torrential streams that fell, blocking out their view of the sea and turning the beach to a river.

They played games and told stories to keep the children's minds off the storm, but it was short-lived. It stopped after about half an hour, and they crawled out from under their rocky umbrella into glorious sunshine.

'Look, a rainbow!' Daisy said excitedly, and pointed at the horizon.

'Oh, Mummy, wow!' Katie breathed.

Gabby could have echoed her. There was a perfect arch spanning the sky, the colours more radiant and glorious than she had ever seen. She stared at it, spellbound, for endless seconds, before sighing and turning to Penny. 'Why is it that the colours here are brighter and more— more *coloured* than they are at home?'

Penny laughed. 'I suppose they are—I don't know why. It must be something to do with the light.'

'Perhaps you're just more relaxed?' Jed suggested.

Relaxed? With him two feet away?

'I think it must be something to do with the angle of the sun,' Gabby said, ignoring his suggestion.

'Possibly. Come on, girls, let's go back to Daddy and let Jed and Gabby get on with their walk,' Penny said to the children, and herded them gently back in the direction of the boat, ignoring Katie's protests.

Jed turned to Gabby. 'Want to carry on round? It'll take about half an hour.'

'What about Tom's foot?'

Jed shrugged. 'It was a simple sting. He'll be fine. Anyway, I want to talk to you. I've got a proposition to put to you.'

Gabby's eyes widened and she backed up slightly, making his lips quirk.

'Don't jump to conclusions,' he teased. 'Come on, let's walk and talk.'

They walked, but for a long time they didn't talk—or at least not about what Jed wanted to discuss. Gabby was so busy being fascinated that she wasn't really paying attention, and he didn't seem to be in a tearing hurry to broach whatever subject he had in mind.

Perhaps, she thought with mild curiosity, he was biding his time—or perhaps it had just been an excuse to get her alone on the other side of the island, away from the others.

And do what? she scoffed at herself. Seduce her?

She was being ridiculous. Whatever else he was, he was easygoing and good-natured. If seduction was in his mind and she said no, he'd accept it, she was sure. She was less sure that she'd say no, and that worried her just a touch. Maybe he knew that, too? Even more worrying!

She managed to convince herself that he didn't want to talk to her at all but just wanted to get her alone, and so she continued to plague him with questions about the trees and undergrowth and the composition of the sand, which was smooth and tracked with rivulets after the downpour—anything rather than silence.

Not that there was much of that, either. Lizards scuttled about, birds flashed overhead and she saw and heard monkeys screeching in the trees and swinging from branch to branch with casual ease. Every now and then one would stop for a moment and watch them with bright, intelligent eyes.

'I wonder what they think of us?' she murmured, returning the level stare of a young male.

'Not a lot, if they've got any sense. We either ruin their habitat or eat them, depending on how civilised our culture is. Either way, I don't suppose they're exactly grateful.'

Gabby laughed softly. 'If you put it like that, I suppose you're probably right. I wonder if they can philosophise?'

He rolled his eyes and carried on walking, and she fell into step beside him again and wondered when he was going to make his move.

She didn't have to wait long. Apparently the time was right because he turned to her and tipped his head towards the trunk of a fallen tree. 'Come and sit down,' he suggested, and made himself comfortable on the trunk. He uncapped the bottle of lemonade and handed it to her.

Warily, she sat a discreet distance away from him and took a swig, then handed it back and waited.

He drank deeply, recapped the bottle and put it down. 'Do you like it out here?' he asked after a second or two.

'On this island?' she asked, surprised. This was not what she'd expected.

'Pulau Panjang.'

She shrugged. 'It's only been three days. I suppose

it's all right. The scenery's gorgeous, the town's colourful and noisy and smelly, and the people seem friendly enough if you discount the trouble up at the power station compound—why?'

He shrugged and grinned at her. 'I was just wondering. I heard you talking to Penny about not having a job so there's no need for you to rush back, I imagine, unless there's some significant other you haven't told me about?'

'No significant other.' Or insignificant, come to that, she thought with an internal sigh. Nobody that cared or mattered at all, depressing though it was. 'Why?'

He shrugged again. 'I could do with a research assistant,' he told her with a lazy smile.

'Research assistant?' she exclaimed, staring at him in amazement. 'What on earth for?'

'My anti-malarial research project, of course,' he said as if it was obvious. He was totally deadpan, and she thought again what a loss he was to the film industry—or poker.

Research project indeed, she thought, and laughed. 'You must be joking! You seriously imagine you can persuade me to stay out here and join you on that veranda, sousing myself in gin and tonic and watching the world go by while I wait to get malaria? Get real, Jed! Life's too short to spend playing Hollywood bit-parts to the natives.'

'There is rather more to it than that,' he said mildly, but she didn't let him finish because the light had dawned and she suddenly realised exactly what he was suggesting. Yes, his aim had been seduction, only not now but later, longer term and pre-arranged. Rather more to it, indeed! She hung onto her temper with difficulty.

'No, thank you,' she said firmly.

'Sure I can't persuade you? The terms and conditions are very flexible,' he said with a grin.

'I'll bet.' She gave a huffy sigh. 'Look, Jed, I'm not in the market for an affair. I want a real job, thank you, not some thinly disguised excuse to get me into bed. Find a nice little native girl to cuddle up to if you're lonely at night, but leave me out of it. I'm sorry, I'm not buying. You don't interest me.'

He stared at her in stunned amazement. 'My God, you're arrogant,' he murmured.

She exploded. 'Me, arrogant? Just where the hell do you get off calling *me* arrogant? You have the infernal nerve to suggest setting up some cosy little love nest in the name of your bogus research—research, for heaven's sake! What research? You're such a fraud, Jed Daniels— and, for the record, you leave me cold.'

She stalked off but he followed her, grasped her arm and turned her back, pulling her hard up against his chest.

'Liar,' he said softly. His eyes glittered dangerously, and she wondered what she'd done, angering him when they were so far from the others. After all, what did she really know of him?

'I am not,' she protested, pushing feebly against his rock-hard chest. It didn't budge an inch. 'Idle lounge-lizards are not at all my type,' she added, just to ram the point home.

'Is that why you kissed me back this morning?' he murmured just inches from her mouth.

'I didn't,' she protested, but he cut off her argument by the simple expedient of sealing his lips over hers and stifling the words. His mouth was firm and yet soft, and after a few moments it softened further, coaxing, sipping and teasing, and she felt her resistance ebbing away.

She was powerless to resist the probe of his tongue,

and her mouth opened to him, giving him what he so gently demanded. She felt the silken stroke of his tongue over hers, hot and salty with a faint trace of lemon from the drink they'd shared, and then her body exploded into molten heat and she sagged against him with a little cry.

He might have been a gentleman, but he wasn't a saint. He took only what she offered, and when his large, hot palm closed over her breast she gasped and leant on him even harder. His other hand cupped her bottom and lifted her hard against him, and the tattered remains of her mind seemed to flutter to the sand at their feet.

'Yes,' he sighed against her throat as she trailed her tongue over his jaw. Her fingertips threaded through the hair on his chest, seeking the hot, damp skin beneath. Everything was hot, she thought vaguely. Hot and humid and torrid and a little like a dream, not quite connected to reality. What on earth was she doing?

His fingers were kneading her breast and her head felt too heavy. It fell back, and she felt the heat of his mouth on the vulnerable slope of her throat. There was a gentle suck, and a nip, then the soothing sweep of his tongue over the tender skin.

It nearly drove her wild. She felt herself clawing at his clothes, pushing the open shirt off his shoulders, whimpering slightly as the fabric resisted, and then suddenly he was releasing her and stepping back.

She nearly fell at his feet.

'Now tell me you're not interested,' he said dangerously softly, and, turning on his heel, he walked ahead, leaving her standing there rooted to the spot.

'Damn you, Jed,' she muttered under her breath. 'Damn you to hell and back—*I am not interested*!' she yelled after him.

She trudged after him through the soft, thick sand that sucked at her feet and made her calves ache. She didn't dare take her eyes off the ground she was walking on unless she trod on a snake or lizard. Beside her the monkeys screeched and ripped through the trees with ridiculous ease, and she wished she could do that. At least she wouldn't have to walk through the sand!

It probably only took about ten minutes to get back to the others, but it seemed more like hours. She was hot, she was tired and she was ready to kill. She was also embarrassed at herself.

Penny shot her a searching look but she avoided the other woman's eyes and wouldn't be drawn. 'How's Tom's foot?' she asked, exhibiting a professional interest.

'Oh, Jed's dealt with it—it's fine. It's so reassuring having him around.'

She heard a soft snort from the man in question, but she didn't look at him either. They were packing up to go home, and she helped with the loading of the bags onto the boat and the ferrying of the children.

Once on the launch she found herself a nice secluded spot in front of the wheelhouse, well away from Jed and Penny and the children, and sat under her hat, enjoying the cool breeze as they chugged across the stretch of water to Telok Panjang.

The water was magical. As they were approaching the town the sun was low in the sky, and the phosphorescence in the water was wonderful. She imagined at night it would be stunning, the sparkling green trails left by the flying fish and the wake of the boat quite spectacular.

It would be wonderfully romantic to share it with a lover, she thought in a moment of weakness, and then remembered Jed and his proposition. Maybe she ought to stop being such a prude and take him up on it?

Although she was by no means the Victorian virgin he'd accused her of being, she was very far from liberal in her morals. Perhaps it was time to make a change, she thought, and then remembered that she'd rather burned her boats in that department.

And they had to go back to the bungalow and live together for the next three weeks! She groaned inwardly, wondering how she could have put him down without being quite so forceful so that they were both left with a shred of dignity instead of the awkward and uneasy silence that had existed between them ever since their 'talk'.

Penny came and sat beside her and smiled a little warily. 'OK?' she asked.

'Fine. It's beautiful up here, I'm enjoying the view.'

'Good. Um—look, Gabby, is everything all right with you and Jed?'

She stared at the island, feigning interest. 'Of course. Why wouldn't it be?'

'I just wondered,' the other woman said softly. 'Only Jed seems a bit crusty and irritable, which isn't like him at all. He's normally so easygoing. I just wondered if anything happened on your walk—but it's none of my business. Ignore me.'

'Good heavens,' Gabby said with a false little laugh. 'Whatever could have happened on our walk? Penny, relax, everything's fine.'

And the moon was made of cheese.

Oh, hell.

As they drew near the jetty they could see a cluster of people, waving and shouting, and Jed came round beside the wheelhouse and held his hand above his eyes, peering at the crowd. His mouth was tight, and Gabby looked away. Was he still mad with her? Or was he worried?

She looked at the jetty and saw people were gesticulating at them to hurry.

'Something's wrong,' Jed murmured, squinting at the crowd. 'What the hell's happened now?'

Penny came up beside her and joined the inspection. 'Oh, no. Whatever can it be?'

They scrambled to their feet and headed back to the well of the boat, ready to disembark as soon as possible, and as they drew up alongside the jetty she saw Rom, the pretty young Indonesian servant who worked for Jon and Penny, weeping and calling out to Penny.

There was also a crowd of men in uniforms, and as they tied up and climbed out of the boat, one of the men with more gold braid than the others stepped forward, his eyes flicking from Jed to Jon.

'Tuan Andrews?'

'That's me,' Jonathan said. 'What's the matter?'

The man looked unhappy. 'We have a situation,' he said in stilted English. 'Some of your engineers—they seem to have been captured by men from the hill tribe.'

Gabby felt the blood drain from her face.

'Captured?' Jon said in a shocked voice. 'Who?'

'Tuan and Ibu Beckers, Ismail Barrung, Jumani Tandak and Luther Tarupadang.'

'Derek and Sue,' Penny said with a wail. 'But Sue's pregnant!'

'Sorry, mem,' the chief of police said to her. 'It's a bad business. Very bad.'

'Mummy, what's happened?' Katie was asking. 'What's wrong?'

'Nothing, darling,' she assured her, and gathered the children close. 'Nothing at all.'

But her eyes were wide with fear, and Gabby knew this was what she'd been dreading for two days. It was no longer just the Indonesians. They could no longer pretend.

All of them were in danger.

CHAPTER FOUR

'I WANT you to leave the island.'

Jonathan's voice was rough with worry, but Penny was implacable.

'I'm not leaving you,' she said firmly. 'I think we should all go. It clearly isn't safe—'

'I can't leave,' Jonathan said just as firmly. 'I have to stay here and get to the bottom of this. The engineers' lives could depend on it.'

'Your life could depend on you getting away,' Penny replied, and they could tell the strain was getting to her by the shake in her voice. Jed shook his head and looked across at Gabby, sitting with him on the veranda just outside the bedroom where Jon and Penny were having their argument.

'Do you think we should all leave?' Gabby asked softly.

Jed shrugged. 'Who knows? Until the chief of police comes and we find out more about what happened, I don't think we can tell, but I have to say I'm not concerned about the children. Indonesians dote on children, they wouldn't hurt them. Children are sacred, whatever their parents may have done.'

'You seem very sure.'

His smile flashed white in the darkness. 'I am sure. They're quite safe. Jonathan is probably most at risk of the five of them.'

'What about you?'

'Me?' He sounded surprised. 'I'm not at risk—I'm just the doctor, I'm not really anything to do with the

project.' He tipped back his chair, propped his feet on
the rail and stared out over the dark sea. A boat carved
a gleaming, greenish wake in the phosphorescence, and
here and there lights twinkled.

Behind them she could hear Penny weeping quietly,
and her cousin's gentle reassurance.

Gabby's mind stayed locked on their problem. 'Will
the developer come out to see what's going on?' she
asked.

'Bill Freeman?' Jed shrugged again. 'Maybe. He's
been quite involved up to now. It depends what the problem is, but I don't think Jon's told him about the sabotage attempts yet.'

The lights of a vehicle appeared on the track up from
the town, and the battered old police car spluttered to a
halt near the veranda.

Jed unfolded himself from his chair and ambled down
the steps to greet the police chief, while Gabby went in
to tell Jonathan of his arrival.

'Stay with Penny, she's upset,' her cousin pleaded,
and so she went in to the other woman and comforted
her. Outside on the veranda they could hear the murmured conversation of the three men, and then the sound
of a vehicle clattering to life signalled the end of the
police visit.

Jonathan came in again and sat heavily on the end of
the bed. 'No news. They still don't know why it's happened, but they're sending an officer up to the next village to find out what he can. They expect him back by
tomorrow night, and in the meantime they've left an
armed guard to protect us, just as a precaution.'

Penny's eyes widened. 'Armed?' she whispered.

'Just to be on the safe side—he's not convinced it's
necessary. I had to talk him into leaving the man at all.'

Gabby eyed her cousin thoughtfully. He was lying,

she could tell. Was the situation worse than they'd been told at first?

'Excuse me, I think I'll go back to the bungalow now,' she said to them, and slipped out. Jed was on the veranda, as she'd expected, and she beckoned him.

He stood and followed her up the track. Out of the corner of her eye she could see the guard, lolling against a tree, and she could smell the sweet, heavy scent of the clove tobacco he was smoking. He didn't look much of a deterrent to determined and desperate men, Gabby thought with a little shiver of nerves.

'What did he say?' she asked once they were out of earshot.

'They came at two in the afternoon when the men were resting. They always lie down for a while after lunch and start work again after the rain when it's a bit cooler. They came while they were asleep, and took them.'

'How?' Gabby asked. 'Surely the road doesn't go very far.'

'They were on foot, so had the alarm been raised quickly it might have been possible to catch up with them, but by the time the cook-boy got back from town at five they were long gone and the trail had been destroyed by the rain.'

'So how do they know when they were taken?'

'A note from Derek, apparently dictated by the captors and translated by one of the engineers.' He stopped, obviously reluctant to say any more, but Gabby pressed him.

'What did it say apart from that?'

Jed sighed quietly. 'Just a threat to kill them if the project proceeds.'

'Oh, my God.'

'Quite. These boys aren't messing around, they mean business.'

He looked at his watch. 'Fancy dinner?'

'But Rom isn't up to cooking—wasn't her husband one of the engineers who was captured? I thought Penny had given her the night off so she could go home to her family?'

'I meant in town, at the *rumah makan*.'

She stared at him in amazement. 'They could be killed and you want to go out for dinner?' she exclaimed, her voice rising. 'Anyway, I thought you didn't entertain tourists.'

He gave her a level look. 'I don't, but I still have to eat. Anyway, before you get carried away about why I want your company, I want to go down to town and sound out a few people I know, but I don't want to leave you here on your own and I think Jon and Penny could do with a little privacy right now.'

'I'd be all right on my own—'

'No, and, anyway, you have to eat as well. We'll go to the *rumah makan* and have a meal, and then wander through the town as if I'm giving you a guided tour. We'll be quite safe, but I can casually make a few enquiries while we're down there.'

'More people who owe you favours?' she asked with a thread of sarcasm. The last thing she felt like doing was going out for a meal to celebrate. 'What did you do, save their children's lives?'

'Actually, yes.'

Colour scorched her cheeks and she was suddenly ashamed of her suspicious mind. 'Sorry. That was un-called-for. Yes, of course I'll come.'

They set off in the Jeep, after telling the others where they were going, and Gabby discovered to her surprise that she was actually starving. While they were waiting for the food to be put in front of them they sat at a table on the street outside amongst the other customers and the smoking mosquito coils, and while her stomach grumbled quietly to itself Gabby marvelled at the way Jed networked the locals.

'Nobody wants to talk,' he confided under his breath at one point. 'They all know more than they're saying, but they're keeping out of it.'

The food arrived then, great heaps of *nasi goreng* or fried rice, with *satay* and dried salt fish and curry and sweet and sour chicken and innumerable other side dishes, all spicy and tasty and quite delicious.

'Save some room,' Jed warned as she piled in, eating—as he did—with her fingers, balling the rice into neat pellets with her right hand and popping them into her mouth. It was, in fact, an easy way to eat once she'd mastered the art of making the grains of rice stick together, but again there was the question of the right and left hand—the right for eating and greeting, the left for toilet purposes.

So much to remember, she thought as she ate yet another strip of the salty dried fish.

'Why do I need to save room?' she mumbled around the tasty fragments.

'Because we're going visiting, and the Indonesians are such hospitable people they just have to feed visitors.'

Gabby groaned, thinking of the vast amount she'd just put away. 'You might have warned me sooner!'

'You'll cope.' He caught the waiter's eye, haggled for a moment over the bill and then paid up once honour was satisfied on both sides. They took the Jeep and drove down to the harbour, then parked it and wandered along the seafront.

The town was slightly L-shaped, wrapped around the mouth of the river on one side. On the other side was a small *kampung*, or village, a much poorer community altogether. It was to there they were headed, she discovered.

Jed hailed a water-taxi, a rickety little boat with a hissing kerosene lantern, hanging from a bamboo pole, and an outboard that had seen better days. It spluttered to life once they were seated, and the boat chugged across the estuary to the little settlement on the other side. Jed asked the boatman to wait, and then handed Gabby ashore and ushered her along the jetty, a makeshift raft linked to the wooden walkways that stretched out over the water like fingers.

Between them were simple houses, lit with the yellow glow of kerosene, all family life taking place behind the open doorways. 'They don't go much on privacy, do they?' Gabby murmured.

'Only for certain things. Men and women never touch each other in public except in a very asexual way, and they never hold hands or kiss like we do in the west, but they have much more contact between people of the same sex. Indonesians are great touchers and huggers.'

He turned left and right and left, and then finally stopped outside a sorry little shack with a thin, tired-looking woman sitting on the step nursing a baby.

Jed crouched down and greeted her, and she scrambled to her feet and ran inside, calling to the others and beckoning the visitors in.

'Take off your shoes—and don't touch the children's heads,' Jed muttered, and then they were inside the little room and being greeted by all the family.

There was the now familiar smell of mosquito coils smouldering quietly near the doorway to deter the worst of the villains, and also the sweet, cloying scent of the clove cigarettes that were so popular. Drinks were brought out—the incredibly strong and sickly sweet coffee she'd learnt to avoid—and tiny cakes, nuts and other delicacies were spread out in front of them on the floor. Although she couldn't understand a word, the women kept giving her sidelong glances and giggling behind their hands.

'Do they think we're an item?' she asked Jed in a lull, and he laughed.

'Probably. You might be kind and play along with it—I've been religiously celibate and they think there's something wrong with me.'

She chuckled. Jed, celibate? Surely there was no need. The young women were looking at him as if they could eat him, and at least two of them were nursing babies!

Finally, after all the social niceties had been satisfied and Gabby had eaten more sickly little cakes than she thought she could keep down, Jed and Jamal, the head of the house, seemed to turn their talk to other things. They went into a huddle in the corner, and Gabby suddenly found herself the centre of attention.

The young women touched her clothes and smiled shyly, and one fingered her hair, marvelling at the colour and texture, so unlike their own. A baby crept onto her lap and tugged at a curl, and she laughed and hugged it, just stopping herself from kissing its head.

It used her as a climbing frame, pulling itself up and bouncing on her lap just like her nieces and nephews did, and she held onto the chubby little brown arms and let it bounce, laughing when it sat down with a plonk.

She looked up then to find the other children clustered round her, all reaching out to touch her hair. They didn't seem to have the same inhibitions as the adults about touching heads, and as she had none at all she sat there and let them maul her gently.

A hand on her shoulder made her turn her head, and

she looked round to find Jed standing behind her, an enigmatic look on his face.

'Time to go?' she asked wistfully.

'If you can tear yourself away.'

She stood up, and one of the young women went out the back and returned with a length of batik cloth, beautifully dyed in the most wonderful jewel colours, and pressed it into Gabby's hands.

She turned to Jed. 'It's lovely—why's she showing it to me? Did she make it?'

'It's a gift,' Jed told her. 'A sarong.'

'A gift? Oh, but I couldn't possibly accept!' she protested, stunned by the girl's generosity.

'You have to. They'd be desperately insulted if you refused it.'

'Really? Could I offer to pay for it?'

He shook his head. 'Absolutely not. Just take it, Gabby.'

She turned back to the girl, unbearably touched, and hugged her. 'Thank you,' she said simply, blinking away the tears that filled her eyes, and all the women hugged her and patted her and sent her on her way with a warm glow she hadn't felt in years.

She clutched the cloth against her chest all the way home, amazed that she should have been made such a gift.

She stroked the fabric, and found it was fine and soft and felt quite wonderful against her skin. 'Why did they give it to me?' she asked Jed as they climbed the road out of the town.

'The man with the pneumothorax is her intended— you helped to save his life. They've heard you're a healer, and your unusual colouring backs that up.' He shrugged and grinned. 'Seems like they just wanted to say thank you.'

'I wonder where they got the idea from that I'm a healer?' she murmured drily, still stroking the cloth.

He laughed and pulled the Jeep to a halt outside her cousin's bungalow. Lights were burning brightly in the sitting room, spilling out across the veranda. 'They're still up—let's go and tell them what we've found out,' Jed suggested.

The security guard was asleep under a tree and jumped as they approached. Jed spoke to him in rapid Indonesian and he struggled to his feet and straightened his uniform, grinning sheepishly.

'Useless,' Jed growled. 'They just aren't taking this seriously, but they'd better.'

Gabby shot him a keen look in the dim light from the windows. 'Why? You still haven't told me what you found out. Why do we need to take this so seriously?'

'Because they mean business. Come on.'

He pushed open the screen door and went in, to find Jonathan and Penny sitting together on the sofa. Penny had been crying, and Jon looked distracted and tired. They both jumped up as Jed and Gabby went in.

'You're back—thank God,' Penny said, looking relieved. 'I was worried about you.'

'There's no need,' Jed assured her. He folded himself into a chair, crossed one leg over the other and sighed, dropping his head back against the cushions.

'Well? Did you find anything out?' Jon asked urgently, clearly irritated by his casual attitude and impatient to hear the news.

'Oh, yes. Jamal wouldn't tell me why they want us to stop, but these hill people apparently are quite fierce and have powerful magic.'

'Magic? I thought this lot were Christians?' Jon said, looking confused.

'They are—after a fashion. Indonesian beliefs are all

a little tangled. Anyway, everyone's a little afraid of this lot, although they very rarely venture down to the town. They're hunter-gatherers in the main, rather like the Dyaks, and their religion is largely animist with the odd fragment of Christianity.'

'Are the two compatible?'

Jed laughed softly. 'In Indonesia almost all religions are compatible, and if they aren't they alter them until they fit. Whatever, these people could be dangerous, and they mean to stop us building the dam. What we don't know is why, but you can bet your life it's tied up in *adat*.'

'*Adat*?' Gabby repeated. 'What's that?'

'Custom, tradition, social order and behaviour patterns, ways that things are done or not done. There's a tremendous amount of ceremonial attached to all their religious practices, whatever the religion. What we need to do is find out whose toes we're treading on and why, and then we might stand a chance of negotiating a settlement.'

'Did Jamal think—? Are they—? Oh, Lord, Jed, they will be all right, won't they? I can't bear to think of Sue pregnant and going through all this.'

'I'm more worried about Derek and his diabetes. If he didn't take insulin with him he could be in trouble already,' Jed told them.

'Bill phoned—he's arriving tomorrow afternoon. He's bringing his plane so you can overfly the site and get a closer look, see if that sheds any light.'

'We might also see if we can spot any woodsmoke or signs of habitation further up—give us an idea of where to start looking.' Jed jackknifed out of the chair and looked at Gabby. 'Time for bed, I think. Tomorrow could be a very long day.'

She nodded and stood up, following him out past the dozing security guard.

'That man's a waste of space,' Jed muttered as they went into the bungalow. 'I think it might be a good idea to sleep together tonight.'

Gabby shot him a look. 'Excuse me?'

'Relax, I have no designs on your virtue. Actually, I think it's probably me taking the risk, but I'll tough it out if you promise to be gentle with me.'

She had to laugh. It was that or scream. 'Do as you wish. I shall be in my room, in my bed, alone. Where you choose to sleep is up to you.'

She went into her room, undressed and wrapped herself in a towel and went out to the *mandi*. When she came back it was to find Jed sprawled on another bed apparently dragged in from his room, wearing nothing but a sarong fastened round his waist.

She raised an eyebrow witheringly—she hoped. It didn't wither him. He smirked, vaulted off the bed and snagged his towel on the way out of the door. 'Yell if you need me,' he said with a grin.

'In your dreams,' she muttered under her breath, and he laughed and shut the door. She pulled on her nightshirt, slid under the covers and arranged her mosquito net over her mattress, then lay down to wait. Five minutes later he was back, his body beaded with moisture from the *mandi*, the sarong clinging to his damp body and leaving little to the imagination.

She dragged her eyes away and hauled in a breath, and turned firmly on her side away from him. 'I think you're being ridiculous. We've got a security guard—'

'Who's asleep again. I just checked. He's about as much use as a eunuch in a brothel.'

'That's disgusting.'

'Oh, Gabby, give over. We need some rest. Your virtue's safe. Just go to sleep.'

She couldn't, though, not for ages. She lay and listened to every creak, every scream and wail from the jungle just yards away, and then there were the soft snores that drifted out from under Jed's makeshift mosquito net.

Dawn seemed to take ages to break, and when it did she fell into a deep and dreamless sleep. Jed woke her at nine with a cup of tea and the news that he and Jon were going up to the compound to look around, and he was then going back to town to continue his sleuthing.

'More people who owe you favours?' she asked without any real rancour, and he grinned.

'Comes in handy at times. I'll see you later.'

The day dragged without him around. She spent most of it with Penny, trying to amuse the children and distract them and Penny from their worries. Despite her protests of the previous day, Penny was packing to leave the island, taking just a few things and going to Jakarta with the children for a while until things settled down. She persuaded Gabby to pack and come with her and, as she could see little point in staying without Penny, she agreed.

They were to leave late next morning on the little local plane. Jon was relieved that they had both seen sense, and Jed, too, nodded his agreement when he came back at ten that night. They talked with Bill, the developer, for some time, and then Jed rose to his feet and stretched.

'Bedtime,' he said to the assembled company. 'Tomorrow could be quite eventful.'

Gabby was happy to agree. The sleepless night before had taken its toll, and she slept like a log, comforted this time by Jed's presence.

He'd said nothing about what he'd discovered the previous day, but he'd had a thoughtful look on his face, and she wasn't surprised when she woke at dawn and found he was gone. She slid her feet over the edge of the bed, ducked under the mosquito net and padded softly out into the sitting-room area in the centre of the bungalow. She could hear him moving around in his bedroom, and she looked through the open door to see him packing medicines into a flight bag.

'What are you doing?' she asked.

His head whipped round and he searched her eyes, as if he wasn't sure how much to tell her.

Eventually he spoke, measuring every word. 'Derek needs insulin. The others need anti-malarials, probably antibiotics and anti-inflamatories, and there could be all sorts of other emergencies—dysentery, fungal infections, burns and wounds that won't heal—the jungle's a nasty place.'

'And how do you intend to get this little Red Cross parcel to them?' Gabby asked, plopping down on the edge of a chest and waiting.

He hesitated again, and she felt a sinking feeling inside. 'You're going to try and go to them, aren't you?' she said, following her unerring nurse's instinct.

'There's a scout gone up there—he may be able to get a message to them.'

'And pigs fly. You're going to walk up there, aren't you, if you can get an idea of where it is?'

He sighed and sat back on his heels. 'Yes. I think I stand a better chance of negotiating than your cousin or Bill and, anyway, I'm a bachelor. It's reasonable I should be the one to go.'

'And how will you know the way?'

He shifted, and she fixed him with a steely glare. 'How, Jed?'

'Jamal knows a man from there—he's an outcast, but he knows the way. He'll be able to show me how to get there. We'll set off later this morning.'

'So why didn't you tell Jon last night?'

He laughed softly. 'Because he would have had a fit, and so would Penny. I went up with Bill yesterday to fly over the site and see what we could see but, as I suspected, it was nothing. Before they get up I want to go and look at the site from the ground—the compound, the area where they've been drilling and blasting for the feasibility study—all of it. See if I can work out what the problem is.'

'Can I come?'

He quirked a brow. 'Can't keep away from me?'

She blushed. 'Not at all. I just thought two pairs of eyes might be better than one, and our plane doesn't go for ages.'

'Do you know what to look for?'

'Do you?'

He shrugged in submission and grinned. 'No, not really. It might just be a holy place—there might be nothing *to* see. I just want to look, that's all—and, yes, you can come if you're ready now.'

She glanced down at her nightshirt. 'Give me ten seconds.'

She was back in about ninety, just as he put the last of his pills and potions into the flight bag and zipped it up. 'I'll take this with me—there are one or two things up at the compound I need to pick up as well.'

The Jeep, bursting into life, woke the security guard with a start, and he grinned and waved and rubbed his eyes.

'What a waste of a good skin,' Jed muttered, and gunned the engine.

Gabby said nothing. She was too busy hanging on like

grim death because Jed clearly didn't intend to waste any time on this trip. They hurtled up to the compound, disturbing another security guard who slept peacefully in the shade of a veranda, and then, after collecting a few more drugs and supplies from the infirmary and making a cursory check around the immediate area, they set off again for the proposed site of the power station.

It wasn't far, a third of a mile at the most, but the road was every bit as bad as the other one, and as they grew nearer so it became worse, more winding and twisting as they negotiated rocky outcrops and the huge trunks of fallen trees.

Finally Jed pulled the Jeep up in a little clearing and turned off the ignition. The silence was deafening. Gradually, sounds began to return—birds screeching, monkeys whooping and yelling, the chirring of the cicadas, and underlying it all the dull roar of water. The sounds all seemed distant, though, as if there was an uneasy silence over the area.

'Come on,' he said briskly, and slid out from behind the wheel. She followed him, almost running to keep up with his long stride, and then finally they emerged on the edge of a rocky cliff.

Below them, falling almost vertically for fifty feet or more, the river crashed downwards towards Telok Panjang and the sea, a foaming torrent of water that threw up a veil of mist. Gabby could quite see how harnessing its power would provide electricity for the town and the new resort.

'The plan is to divert some of the water over here, and build a turbine house to take the generators,' Jed yelled over the roar of the waterfall. 'That will mean damming it and putting weirs in the side of the lake— it might be that there's something here that's sacred. Let's take a look.'

They retreated from the edge of the cliff, to Gabby's relief, and studied the area Jed indicated. A little lake lay sparkling in the sunlight, a natural weir-pool and the perfect pick-up point for the water they would need to power the turbines.

It was beautiful, peaceful and cool and restful, and there didn't seem to be anything—any artefacts or man-made structures—that could be shrines or tombs or any such thing that might be of significance. The only strange thing was the wonderful peace she felt steal over her as she stood there in the dim light of the jungle.

Gabby tipped her head and looked up through the soaring trunks of the jungle giants that fringed the edges of the lake. They were amazing, great gnarled trees with massive boles and leaves so far removed from the roots she wondered how they could possibly pump the water such a long way.

Some of them had a strange chequered effect on the bark—an almost square pattern of astonishing symmetry that clothed the lower part of the trunks.

She nudged Jed. 'Look at those trees—the bark's really weird.'

He looked, and his eyes narrowed for a second. 'My God—I think that might be the answer.'

'What might?'

He looked at her, his eyes strangely bright in the artificial twilight. 'Grave trees,' he said.

'What?'

'They have them in Tanatoraja, in Sulawesi. They're animists, too, and it's possible the two tribes could be related. One might be an offshoot of the other. Whatever. They believe that if infants die without touching the earth their souls go directly to heaven, and so for the first few months of their lives they're carried everywhere and never put down. If a baby dies they cut a hole in the bark of a grave tree, chisel out a cavity and put the baby's body inside, then replace the bark and put a little door over the hole. That way the baby never has to touch the ground.'

Gabby swallowed. 'So those trees contain dead babies?'

He peered closely at them. 'Could be.'

She laid a hand over her chest, conscious of a great feeling of sadness. A cold chill ran over her. 'Oh, Jed. No wonder they want to protect them.'

'They're right in the line of the turbine house and the weirs. They'd have to be felled without a doubt if the plant was to be sited here.'

'But it can't!' Gabby protested. 'They can't be allowed to cut them down!'

'They could be hundreds of years old. Those marks aren't new by any stretch of the imagination, Gabby. It might be a red herring.'

She knew it wasn't, though, just as she knew that the strange feeling of peace came from the souls of those children.

Tears welled in her eyes. 'Jed, they can't cut them down, no matter how old they are. They must be left in peace.'

He turned to her, saw her tears and cupped her face gently in his big hands, smoothing the tears away with his thumbs. 'I think I'll let you negotiate with Bill. He's a sucker for pretty women.'

She smacked his hands away and turned, wrapping her arms around her chest. 'I mean it. They can't be allowed to desecrate this area, Jed. Can't you feel it?'

His hands closed over her shoulders. 'Oh, yes, I can feel it. I agree with you. I'm just wondering how Bill will feel about all the money he's spent on this project so far, and how much it would cost to relocate it.'

'Tough,' Gabby said uncompromisingly.

Jed squeezed her shoulders and she heard a soft laugh. 'I think we'll definitely let you tell him.'

Her shoulders drooped, and he eased her back against his chest and rubbed the tense muscles of her neck with his thumbs. 'We'll talk to him. With the lives of the others on line I'm sure he'll see reason—if we're right and that is the problem.'

She looked up at the trees again, and sighed. 'Why didn't anybody notice before?'

'Because nobody was looking. The area's uninhabited now—Jamal told me the hill tribe moved north years ago when the Dutch arrived. What seemed like a natural clearing where we parked the Jeep is probably the site of the old village. This graveyard is all of a hundred years old, if not more.'

'That doesn't stop it being sacred.'

'No, but nevertheless I don't suppose anyone was looking for grave trees when they did the feasibility studies. Like I said, they're exclusively Torajan, or I thought they were. Obviously these people have never been studied.'

'Perhaps because of their powerful magic?'

'Maybe.'

'Or perhaps just because they're very fierce.'

His hands fell to his sides. 'Perhaps. Come on, let's get back and tell Jon.'

They turned, and then stopped dead. Five men stood around the Jeep, naked except for bark loincloths and tattoos. Their skins were smeared with what looked like ash, and they held long things in their hands, not spears but something else. Blowpipes?

'Hell,' Jed said quietly.

'I'll go for that,' Gabby mumbled from beside him.

One of the men stepped forwards. '*Docktor*?'

Jed nodded and pointed to his chest. '*Docktor*,' he repeated.

The man jabbed his blowpipe upriver, at a barely discernible path in the jungle. '*Jalan-jalan*,' he growled.

'I don't think he's negotiating,' Gabby said softly.

'No. I'll take the medicine and go with them, you get in the Jeep and go like hell for the town. Tell them what we've found out, and start the negotiations rolling. OK? And get them to follow us.'

She nodded, and he winked. 'Attagirl.'

He stepped forward, picked up the bag from the Jeep and turned to the waiting men. As he moved, Gabby got into the Jeep and reached for the ignition, but there was a yell and one of them pulled her out. There was an urgent exchange, and she felt the press of cold steel at her back.

'I think they want me to come too,' she said as steadily as she could manage. Her heart was pounding, her mouth was dry and she thought her legs were about to give way, but she was damned if any of them would know that.

She lifted her chin a notch and noted the approval in Jed's eyes. A lot of good that would do her.

'No problem. I'll try and talk to them.'

He spoke in Bahasa, then in the native dialect of Pulau Panjang, but he was met with a blank wall of silence. Incomprehension, or just a stubborn refusal to listen?

The ringleader jabbed his blowpipe at Gabby. '*Jalan-jalan*,' he repeated, sounding angry now, and the man holding her thrust her forward so that she staggered against Jed.

They were looking at the flight bag, and Jed unzipped it. '*Obat*,' he told them. Medicine. They nodded, and they turned towards the jungle. Three of them went first, melting into the jungle along an almost invisible path. Jed turned to her. 'Stay close,' he ordered.

The others fell in behind, and within seconds the undergrowth closed in behind them and the last trace of civilisation vanished...

CHAPTER FIVE

IT TOOK Gabby about two seconds to work out that if they went any further into the jungle she wouldn't be able to find her way back to the Jeep.

It took about another two seconds to tell herself it was a crazy idea, but so what? So she was crazy. So they had blowpipes. One quick poison dart was probably preferable to walking all day in the jungle in nothing but a pair of thin trousers, trainers and a long-sleeved shirt.

She was too hot, and she'd already discovered that the trousers gave little protection against the whipping stems of some of the more vicious jungle plants she'd already encountered—and they'd hardly started their journey, she was sure of that! And, anyway, she might be the last chance the hostages had. She had to get back to Jon and explain about the grave trees and do something positive before the situation escalated out of control.

She scuffed her shoe heel down, loosened it, then casually walked out of it and stopped dead. As she bent over to refasten it Jed and three of their captors had moved ahead, and there were only the two men following her.

They looked reasonably harmless, she thought, if one ignored the blowpipes and nose-bones. She smiled and made a great production of putting her shoe on again, then, as the others disappeared from view ahead of them, she turned and threw herself against one, catching him by surprise and knocking him over. Using her old netball skills, she ducked past the other and ran back down the path towards the Jeep.

At least, she'd meant to, but in her haste the jungle blurred into a mat of foliage and the path vanished. She pushed the stems aside, hurling herself forwards against the vegetation to cleave a path through it, and ran straight into a mass of thorny stems.

The vicious spikes ripped her clothes and skin, and with a scream of frustration and pain she fought to free herself.

Hands stopped her, trapping her arms and pulling her backwards out of the savage clutches of the monster plant and back against a hard, muscled chest. The arms were like steel bands, and once she was free of the plant they half dragged, half carried her back towards the others.

'Let me go!' she protested, but the arms didn't move and she was propelled relentlessly back through the undergrowth, kicking and screaming.

Not that it did any good. Her captor's arms simply tightened and, apart from a grunt of pain when her heel connected with his shin, she slowed him down so little she might as well have been a gnat.

She could hear yelling in the distance, and as they neared the rest of the group she was released and thrust forward so that she fell at the feet of the ringleader.

'That was a bit bloody stupid,' Jed said angrily, and, ignoring the men, he pulled her roughly to her feet, hauled her up against him and hit her hard across the face.

She screamed, blood trickling down her lip, and raised her fists to pound on his chest. He caught them with one large hand, trapped them and then glared at her—but not angrily. 'Don't say a word,' he growled. 'Just play along. You're my wife, you do as I tell you, I'm responsible for you. It's the only way you'll be safe.'

'The Indonesian didn't hit me,' she grated back at him.

'No, he's just ready to rape you, and if you get away from the others again he probably will. He's looking at you as if he'd like to eat you. Now cast your eyes down, look ashamed and I'll try and explain that you're a difficult wife but I'm taming you gradually.'

He pulled her round to his side none too gently, looked at the boss-man and gave a man-to-man shrug, then he grasped a vine and indicated to one of the men that he would like it chopped. With a quick twisting motion he wound it around her right wrist and shackled her to his left.

'What the hell are you doing?' she muttered furiously.

'Ensuring your safety and proving that you're my chattel. Now shut up!' He held up their wrists, rolled his eyes expressively and winked.

To her relief and fury, they laughed and the party set off again. There was no further chance of escape, of course, but it seemed there was none anyway so she probably hadn't lost anything except her dignity and several inches of skin.

Bitter disappointment settled like a lead weight in her chest, and gradually as the sweat trickled down her body into the cuts and scratches the pain became almost unbearable. Her mouth hurt where he'd hit her, the vine was chafing on her wrist and she was sick of trailing just behind Jed with one arm outstretched to accommodate her shackle. It wasn't necessary anyway, she thought crossly, but at least, being so close behind him, his big body took most of the sting from the undergrowth.

Then she stumbled over a root and fell, only Jed's arm tied to hers preventing her from falling right down.

A little sob broke from her lips, and he turned and helped her up again, then tipped her chin and winked at her.

'Keep going,' he murmured comfortingly. 'You're doing well.'

'Liar,' she grumbled.

'I'm sorry about your face. I had to make it look real.'

'That real?' she said bitterly.

His thumb brushed the bruise on her swollen lip. 'I'll make it up to you. Just hang on in there, it can't last for ever—the island's not that big.'

But it was, of course. She'd seen it from the air, and she knew just how big it was. Anyway, distances couldn't be measured in normal ways because progress was so slow.

She tried a smile, and he dropped a hard, quick kiss on her lips and turned away again. As he did she caught the eyes of the man who'd chased her, and realised with a chill that Jed had been right. His eyes were glittering with a strange fever, and she just knew that given the slightest chance he'd try and get her alone.

Which was a problem because just then she wanted to be alone, just for a moment or two. She tugged at Jed.

'I need the loo,' she hissed.

'Fine. Can you hang on? They have to stop soon.'

'I hope you're right.'

They trudged on, however. The heat was relentless, steamy and intolerable. Her mouth was dry, and she thought she'd have given her eye teeth for a long glass of ice-cold beer.

She began to fantasise about it, to such an extent that when their captors called a halt she didn't even notice and cannoned into Jed's hot, sweaty back.

It was probably no hotter and sweatier than her front

so she leant against it, exhausted, and waited for some instructions.

As she listened she heard the sound of rushing water, and realised they were still near the river. The cold, wet, clean, thirst-quenching river—

'I think he's saying we can drink and bathe, and I think they've got some food,' Jed said softly over his shoulder.

She straightened and looked around, and found they were in a little clearing beside the river. The air was cooler, and the water looked wonderful. Just then the men disappeared one at a time and came back, adjusting their loinclothes.

'Jed, I need to go!' she muttered. 'Take this thing off—'

'No. We'll go together.'

Jed waved his arms about in some ghastly sign language, and the ringleader nodded. Unfortunately he also accompanied them out of the clearing, standing over them with his arms folded.

'Jed, I can't—'

'I think you're going to have to. I'll stand between you and him.'

'What makes you think you're any better than he is? Jed, I want a private pee! Is that so much to ask?'

He grinned. 'If it's any consolation so do I, and I'm not going to get one. I'll turn round and face him, and you can turn your back to me—'

'Can't you just untie me?' she pleaded for the nth time, but he was emphatic about it.

She was too hot and tired to flounce so she turned round and then discovered the impossibility of undoing her clothes with her left hand and squatting down over prickly undergrowth full of unmentionable creepy-crawlies—

With a yelp she catapulted to her feet, forgetting the shackle and almost dragging Jed over on top of her.

'What the hell?' He turned towards her to steady her, and then looked down. 'You've forgotten something.'

She yanked up her knickers and trousers and to her embarrassment had to enlist Jed's help in refastening them.

'Want to tell me what that was all about?' he asked calmly when she was reassembled.

'I felt something tickling me,' she muttered, furiously embarrassed.

'Is that all?' he asked with a chuckle. 'I thought at the very least you'd been bitten on the bottom by a cobra.'

Her eyes widened. 'A what?'

'Forget it. I needed cheering up.'

'At my expense?'

There was a wicked twinkle in his eye and if she hadn't been so damn tired she would have hit him. As it was she leant her head on his chest for a second, then straightened again, tilted her chin and nodded.

'Any chance of a wash?' she said wistfully.

Again Jed went through the pantomime, and they were led through the trees to the river. It tumbled over rocks, looking clear and cool and absolutely the best thing in the world to Gabby, and she almost fell into it in her haste.

'Steady,' Jed murmured, and then he was beside her on the rocks, sloshing water over his head and face with one hand while the other went up and down to hers, shackled to her arm.

One particular scratch was stinging furiously, and she turned back her cuff to look at it.

'When did you do that?'

'When I tried to play the hero,' she said drily. 'There was a great spiky vine thing—'

'Rattan. It's wicked. Let me look.'

He rolled up her sleeves, tutting and mumbling, and washed all the scratches thoroughly—too thoroughly in some cases. Then he rolled up her trouser legs and did the same thing with those, and by the time he'd finished and smeared antiseptic over them from his box of tricks the hill men were looking bored and irritated.

They were each handed a little bunch of bright yellow fig-shaped fruits, and then nudged on the way.

'Can't we sit and rest?' Gabby pleaded, but apparently they couldn't.

She fell in behind Jed, examining the fruits with suspicion. 'What do you suppose they are?'

'Figs. They'll probably give you the runs, but they taste good.'

The runs? While she was shackled to him and in front of an audience? Not in this lifetime!

She lobbed them into the forest and trudged on, ignoring the rumbling of her stomach. She'd rather starve than go through that.

Four hours later she was regretting her impulse. They'd had another quick pitstop, but there was nothing else to eat and she thought if she didn't wrap herself around something substantial soon she was going to fade right away.

Melt, in fact. She remembered the old saying, 'Ladies glow, men perspire, pigs sweat.' Clearly she was a pig.

A tired pig. She put one foot in front of the other without any real awareness of where she was going, except that she was following Jed. She couldn't see for the sweat and dirt that was running down her face, although that was probably marginally preferable to the rain that had fallen. The air was still soaked, a fine misting drizzle falling from the canopy, and every third or fourth step some kind-hearted leaf generously poured a couple of pints of water down the back of her neck as she went underneath, but at least the unrelenting downpour had stopped.

The path was slippery now, and there was something on her wrist which she had an idea was a leech.

'They're medicinal,' she told herself, and ignored it. Some while later it had dropped off, and there was a little red spot where it had been, with a thin trail of blood leaking from it.

'I'm going to bleed to death and Jed won't know until he looks round and finds my corpse, dangling behind his wrist,' she mumbled.

He stopped dead and she crashed into his back. 'What?'

'Nothing. I'm bleeding to death.'

He turned abruptly. 'What? Where?'

She showed him her wrist, and he gave a huff of laughter that sounded suspiciously relieved and ruffled her hair. 'Chin up. You're doing fine. Look, we must be nearly at the village, the path's much clearer now.'

She looked and, lo and behold, she could actually see where they were heading for the first time since they'd set off on their tortuous journey.

Not that she'd been exactly looking hard.

'Yippee,' she said expressionlessly, and he gave her a quick hug and turned back, setting off again. Their captors, who had stood patiently waiting during this exchange, picked up the pace and within minutes they were surrounded by a group of chattering children, darting back and forth and giggling.

'This must be it,' Jed murmured, and moments later they were in a clearing in the forest. A few large huts clustered around the fringes under the shade of the canopy, simple huts roofed with leaves of some sort, capable of sleeping several families.

The families themselves were standing round, studying them, their bodies all smeared with ash like their captors', and then into the throng came a white woman Gabby had never met.

'Jed—oh, thank God!' she wept, and threw herself at him.

He hugged her, a little awkwardly because of the shackle that still tied him to Gabby, and then eased her away. 'How are you, Sue?'

'Sick as a pig but that's just because of the baby. Derek's awful—I don't suppose by a miracle you've got any insulin?'

He nodded, and Sue's eyes closed with relief. 'Thank God—he's almost in a coma, Jed. Come on…'

She started to drag him forward, and together they were herded into one of the huts. They had to climb a ladder to reach the entrance. Once inside it was gloomy and Gabby had to blink and screw up her eyes to see.

What she saw did nothing for her. Derek was pale and sweating, his eyes sunken in his grey and slightly stubbled face, and his breath was an instant give-away.

'Pear drops—his blood sugar must be sky high,' Gabby mumbled, and Jed nodded. Kneeling down beside the sick man, Jed untied the vine from his wrist to free Gabby, told her to stay close and quickly examined him.

'Has he been vomiting?'

'Yes.'

'Drowsy?'

'Yes—and slurred speech. He sounds drunk—well, he did. He hasn't spoken for an hour or so, but I don't think he's in a coma. I can rouse him still, just about,' Sue told them.

Jed passed Gabby the bag of goodies and asked her

to pull up a very high dose of insulin, about twice or three times the normal amount. This was to deal with the high level of blood sugar that was causing Derek's symptoms and would push him before long, if Gabby wasn't mistaken, into a coma.

She'd seen diabetic comas, both hypo- and hyperglycaemic, and knew exactly what to do. It was a good job she did because she was definitely on autopilot.

She drew up the insulin and looked at what Jed was doing. Her eyes widened when she saw the dark green-blue of the testing stick on which he had put a drop of Derek's blood.

'That's dark.'

'Almost black. It's well off the scale, which goes up to 44. Normal should be about 8. That's what I'm aiming for in the next twenty-four hours. Got that insulin ready?'

She handed him the syringe and watched as he injected it. 'There—he should be feeling better in an hour or so, and within twenty-four hours he should be fine.'

He looked up. 'What about the rest of you?'

The three Indonesian engineers were sitting around on the other side of Derek, watching Jed anxiously. At his question one proffered a foot with a nasty cut on the ankle, but that was the only problem. Jed cleaned it and squirted it with antibiotic spray, gave him an injection of antibiotics and dished out anti-malarials to everyone. Then finally, when everyone had been seen to, he turned to Sue.

'We need to wash and have some food—how strictly are you guarded?'

She gave a hollow laugh. 'Guarded? Where would we go?' She scrambled to her feet. 'Come with me, I'll show you where you can wash—have you got any clean clothes?'

He shook his head. 'No. Nothing except the drugs, by a miracle. I was just getting them ready in case I got a chance to get them up to you somehow, and we'd just collected the last few things from the compound. They took us from the power-station site—and I've got something to tell you about that, as well, after we've washed. I don't suppose you could rustle up some food?'

'Sure. It might be a little strange but none of us have been sick yet. They seem to be taking good care of us. They've almost been hospitable, crazy though it seems. I don't think they want to harm us.'

'No. I don't think they do—I think that's why they came for me. They must have been waiting at the compound and followed us on foot.'

'They knew Derek was sick right from the start. He grabbed what insulin he could, but of course there wasn't enough up at the compound and it ran out yesterday morning. They seemed to understand he was ill, and we saw the men who brought you leaving the village by the path we'd come on. They might have had time to get down there before dark.'

Jed nodded. 'Makes sense. Without us they would have made better time, and downhill as well would have been easier.'

Gabby wasn't sure about that. She almost fell down the ladder she was so tired, but the sight of a clear pool in the rocks at the foot of a long sloping waterfall was enough to wake her up. 'Let me in,' she mumbled, and, pulling off her shoes, she walked straight into the water without stopping.

It was freezing on her hot skin, but the pain of her scratches and bites faded instantly and she lay back in the water with a sigh of relief and shut her eyes.

'Wow,' Jed murmured from beside her, and disappeared under the water for endless seconds. He came up just when she was starting to panic, shooting up through the surface and shaking his head like a dog, sending water droplets flying.

Then he grinned, and he looked as fresh as a daisy.

She wanted to kill him.

She also wanted another bathroom stop, but she thought she might wait and ask Sue about that. She sluiced her hair again, squeezed the water out of it and then wondered what to do about her dripping clothes.

'Take them off and wring them out, then put them back on. They'll soon dry and they'll keep you cool.'

She gave him a sideways glance and saw he was following his own advice, standing on the rocks at the edge of the pool in a pair of skimpy briefs, looking more delicious than he had any right to look after the day they'd just gone through.

She pulled herself out of the water, peeled off the sodden clothes and squeezed them out and then, after her skin had stopped streaming, she went to put them on again.

'Hang on.'

Jed's hands touched her gently, turning her this way and that in the soft green light, and he shook his head. 'You're a mess—why didn't you say how bad the scratches were?'

She shrugged, standing there in her soggy undies, all but naked. 'What would you have done—admitted me to hospital? It wouldn't have made any difference.'

He looked at her and through her bleary haze she thought she saw respect in his eyes. 'Come on,' he said gently, and helped her into her clothes. He had scratches and bites too, she noticed as she returned the favour. He hadn't said anything either. She promised herself she'd put some cream on them once they were back at the hut.

Sue was waiting for them. She showed them what

passed for a bathroom, then on their return greeted them with some food—vegetables baked in leaves, boiled rice and some sauce, which Gabby avoided because it smelt so strongly of chilli she thought it would finish her off.

The meal was strange but palatable, and as they ate it darkness fell. The temperature fell with it, dropping sharply up here in the hills as it didn't nearer the coast. She remembered climbing Ben Nevis once and being astonished at the temperature difference. Somehow in the tropics she just hadn't expected it.

Someone lit a candle, a makeshift affair that smelt vile but probably kept the mosquitoes out. By its meagre light Jed told the others about the grave trees they had found. The Indonesians particularly were very excited at this.

'I think it must be the reason they want us to stop,' Luther said. 'They have been chanting and the priest has been wearing ceremonial robes and dancing and they sacrificed a pig today. I think they are using their strongest magic.'

'All we need to do is tell the others,' Sue said. 'Got any bright ideas?'

Jed grinned and, like a conjurer pulling a rabbit out of a hat, he produced a thing like a mobile phone from the bottom of the flight bag.

'The Magellan GCS! Jed, you're wonderful!' Sue cried.

'What?' Gabby asked, confused. 'Surely a mobile phone won't work.'

'No, it won't—but this will. It's a global communications system, and I can send an e-mail to anywhere in the world, telling them where we are and what's going on. All I have to do is remember the e-mail number—and that's the problem. I can't. The only one I can remember is my own, and I don't know if anyone will check my e-mail at work, or how often. My secretary might, but perhaps not for a day or two. Still, it's the best chance we've got.'

He keyed in a few brief words about the grave trees, their reunion with the other hostages and their state of health, and sent the message winging on its way, before shutting the machine down. 'I must keep the batteries going as long as possible—we have no idea how long we'll be here,' he told them all. 'If I remember a more relevant number I'll try sending our whereabouts to that.'

'Our whereabouts?' Gabby said with a laugh. 'A jungle hut in the middle of God knows where? How precise.'

'It is. It's a satellite GPS—a global positioning system. It tells them where we are to within fifteen metres.'

Gabby's jaw dropped. 'It's that precise, and you've just done it? Just like that?'

He nodded.

'So they might come and rescue us?'

He looked thoughtful.

'Well? Will they?' she pressed.

'Yes—when the message is picked up. And that's the problem. I don't know when the message will be picked up, or even if it will. I'm sorry.'

'Doesn't it have a memory for addresses?' Sue asked.

'Yes—but I haven't got round to programming them in yet. I've only had it a few days.'

Sue's face fell. 'It isn't Derek's?'

Jed shook his head, and she dropped her face into her hands for a moment. When she straightened she looked calm but tired. 'I suppose we'll just have to wait, then,' she said pragmatically. 'It can't take for ever. How much insulin did you bring?'

'Enough for two weeks.'

Sue perked up immediately. 'Well, it won't be that long, will it?' she said more brightly, and then turned to Derek. 'How are you?' she asked him.

'Horrible—I need Jed.'

'Jed's here—he's brought his Magellan. We're going to be all right, Derek. They'll find us soon. It's OK, love, we're going to be all right.'

Gabby, hearing the optimism in the other woman's voice, felt a cold shiver of fear run over her. Perhaps it was her still-damp clothes, or perhaps the fact that two weeks wasn't really all that long in the great scheme of things. If the e-mail didn't get picked up—

'OK?'

Jed's voice was soft and right beside her, and she looked up at him and tried to smile.

'I'll be better once I've got some cream on these scratches and I can go to sleep,' she told him.

'Easily done. I gather we're all sleeping here together in this hut. The men are together in one part, then Sue and Derek, and we get the last bit. We'll stick to the myth that we're married—you'll be safer that way.'

'Definitely,' Sue assured them. 'They might not want to do us any harm, but there are plenty of healthy young men here who would be fascinated to sleep with a white woman. I think telling them you're married is an excellent idea.'

Gabby yawned and Jed unfolded himself and stood up, then pulled her to her feet. 'We'll go and settle down now. See you in the morning. Call me if you're worried about Derek—I've given him another shot of insulin and his blood sugar level's falling steadily. I think he'll be all right soon.'

They padded along the little corridor to the room at the end, a small area screened off by a beaten bark curtain over the doorway, and in the middle of the floor was a heap of bedding—rush mats, sarongs and a couple of woven rugs.

They sorted out the beds and Gabby took off her outer clothes, pulled on the sarong she'd been left and fastened it. Then Jed, as much by touch as by sight, spread cream over her lacerated arms and legs, and around her wrist where the vine had cut in during the day.

'You're a mess,' he said huskily, and she remembered the sun cream. It seemed weeks ago—months. In fact, it had been only forty-eight hours earlier. She was exhausted, she had aches where she hadn't known she had muscles, and yet at his touch her body seemed to find another life.

She felt the pain ebbing, the aches soothing, and a mellow warmth seeped through her. She lay bonelessly, letting him move her arms and legs around, rolling onto her front when he prodded her, and all she could think about was the feel of his hand on her skin.

All too soon he stopped, and she rolled over and looked up at him in the darkness. A candle was burning in the little passage outside, and in its dim light she could make out his shadowed features. She reached up a hand and cupped his cheek.

'Thanks,' she murmured languorously.

He capped the tube and turned away. 'You're welcome.'

'How about you?'

He made a choked sound and looked back at her over his shoulder. 'How about me?'

'Want me to do your scratches?'

He looked at her for endless moments, before turning away. 'I'll do them. You rest.'

She lay and watched him, then took the tube and did his shoulders and back, anyway, where the occasional particularly determined vine had coiled round him. His skin was hot, like damp silk, and she had to struggle to resist the urge to lay her lips against it—

'That'll do,' he muttered, and his voice sounded slightly strangled.

She lay back and watched as he got ready for bed, then lay down beside her. The noises of the jungle seemed incredibly loud and close, and they could hear the shufflings and soft snores of the others on the other side of the wall.

He turned his head towards her. 'You did well today, Gabby,' he said quietly. 'Well done.'

'What about you? You must have been exhausted when we arrived, but you dealt with Derek straight away.'

He laughed softly. 'I didn't think Derek had time to wait while we freshened up—and, anyway, you helped.'

'Only a bit. I don't think I could have walked any further, though,' she told him.

'No, nor me. Good job we didn't have to.' His hand reached out and squeezed her shoulder. ''Night,' he said softly.

'Goodnight.' She turned on her side to face him, but she didn't sleep. Tired as she was, too much had happened for her to relax. She lay for ages, then she thought she heard him sigh.

'Jed?' she whispered.

'Mmm?'

'I can't sleep.'

'I can't sleep either,' he murmured. 'Too much to think about.'

The candle had gone out, and in the darkness the noises all seemed louder. Knowing the others were close by was strangely comforting, but she still felt very alone. She wriggled a little closer to Jed. It was chilly now, and she wished she'd got something a little thicker than the mat and a sarong and little woven rug to cover her.

'Penny will be worried sick,' she said.

'If she knows. She might have thought you'd changed your mind, and gone without you. Jon and Bill will be worrying, though, and I expect the chief of police will put another dozy security guard on the case, for all the good it'll do.'

Gabby thought back to their capture and the appearance of the men in the clearing by the Jeep. 'I wonder how they knew who you were and where to find you?'

'They have their contacts, I expect—Jamal's exile friend for one. Anyway, it's a good job they did. Without medical help for Derek, he would have been dead in twenty-four hours. I expect they realised how sick he was and couldn't afford to risk him dying. Anyway, as Sue said, they don't seem to mean us any harm.'

Gabby gave a hollow laugh. 'I wish I had your confidence. My legs and arms certainly feel harmed, and my feet are killing me.'

He laughed gently at her, then reached out a hand. 'Are you warm enough?'

'Not really.'

'Nor am I. Come over here and warm up.'

She hesitated for a nanosecond—certainly not long enough for decency—and then shuffled across the mats to his side. He pulled her light covering across them both, tucked her bottom into his lap and draped an arm round her waist. 'Better?' he murmured.

'Mmm.' She snuggled closer, comforted by the solid warmth of his body at her back, and fell instantly asleep.

CHAPTER SIX

GABBY woke to find her head cradled on Jed's shoulder, her hair spread across his chest and cramp in her foot.

'Ow,' she moaned, and he pitched her off him and sat bolt upright.

'Wha—?'

She flapped a hand at him to shush him. 'Nothing exciting,' she whispered. 'I've got cramp.' She folded over and grabbed the offending foot, and Jed took it from her and stretched the toes up towards her knee, straightening her leg and pulling the muscles tight in her arch. Then he dug his thumb into the offending muscle and she wailed softly.

Pig that he was, he laughed at her, a kindly laugh but a laugh for all that. She decided he needed punishing so she put her foot in the middle of his chest and pushed.

Unfortunately he still had hold of her foot so he didn't fall. Instead a dangerous glint appeared in his eyes and he dodged her foot and sprawled across her, pinning her to the floor, his stubbled face hovering just inches from hers.

'Want to play games, do you?' he asked softly, and there was a curious rasp to his voice that did crazy things to her nerves.

She couldn't move, couldn't speak, couldn't do anything. She was trapped, pinned down as much by the look in his eyes as by his arms. Against her leg she felt his body stir, coming to life in response to her closeness, and with a tiny moan she closed her eyes and accepted his kiss. His beard scraped her face softly, sensitising her skin further, making her forget common sense.

Her sarong had ridden up around her hips and he shifted, one hard-muscled thigh nudging between her legs and settling against the ache that was growing with every touch of his lips on hers. She was conscious of the coarse, wiry hair against the tender skin of her thighs, the contrast of his hard, masculine frame aligned with her softer, more yielding body.

He shifted so he could gain access to her breasts, tugging the sarong down and closing one large, hard hand over her softness. She had never felt so much a woman, or been touched by so much a man. She arched against him, against that thigh that chafed with such devastating accuracy against her, and as she did so the cramp that had woken her returned with interest.

She wrenched her mouth from his with a yelp and reached for her foot, and he rolled away and took it from her, stretching and kneading it again in a strained silence broken only by their ragged breathing.

Finally, when the knot had dissolved and her foot was relaxed again, he set it down with great care and looked at her.

His eyes were smouldering, and she was suddenly aware of the sarong rucked up around her waist, the top unfastened to expose the soft swell of her breasts...

She covered herself hastily and sat up, pushing the hair out of her eyes, and saw him withdraw into himself.

'Saved by the bell, eh?' he murmured softly.

He stood up and turned away from her, but not before she'd seen that he was still aroused. His briefs hid nothing, and the ache returned, slamming into her so hard that she had to bite back the moan that rose in her throat.

He pulled on his clothes, slid his feet into his shoes

and went out, leaving her sitting there in the midst of their bedding, frustration her only companion.

She could hear the others moving about, and next door through the thin bamboo wall she could hear Jed murmuring to Derek and Sue.

Had they heard everything? Oh, Lord. She buried her face in her hands and sighed. Why had she tried to push him over? When would she learn not to bait the tiger?

She scrambled to her feet, pulled on her clothes and dragged her fingers through her hair. Then, on the principle of getting unpleasant things over and out of the way, she went along the hut to the end where Sue and Derek were sitting, staring out of the doorway.

'How's the patient?' she asked brightly, avoiding Jed's eyes.

'Which one?' Sue said weakly. 'Derek's better but any second now I'm going to throw up.'

'No, you're not,' Jed said reassuringly. 'Come on, have some fruit. That'll stay down.'

Gabby saw they had fruit and cold rice and bamboo tubes filled with coconut milk set out on the floor in front of them. As they settled down to eat, Sue eyed the food with horror and then covered her mouth.

She leapt to her feet and ran, threw herself down the ladder and fell to her knees in the dirt, retching helplessly.

'Ginger,' Jed said, standing with Gabby in the doorway of the hut and regarding the poor woman dispassionately, a banana skin dangling from his fingers.

'Ginger?' Gabby repeated.

'Mmm. Good anti-emetic. It's used a lot now for travel sickness. I wonder if we can get any—would you like to ask the women? They might know.'

She stared at his retreating back. Ask the women. Just like that. No language barrier, of course!

She went down the ladder to Sue, put a comforting arm round her shoulders and helped her back to her bed, then went out into the village again. A pregnant woman was sitting with her back propped against the stilts of her house, pounding something in a coconut shell.

She was beautiful, her black hair long and lustrous, her flawless skin a deep golden brown. She was wearing only a loosely woven skirt, slung around her hips under the prominent swelling of her baby, and Gabby approached her with a cautious smile.

The woman put down her makeshift pestle and mortar and smiled back at Gabby, then pointed to the place where Sue had been sick and said something unintelligible.

Gabby made a cradle with her arms to show it was pregnancy sickness, wondering as she did so if these very healthy-looking people actually had such a thing.

Evidently they did. The woman smiled and nodded, then beckoned to Gabby and led her into the hut. She gestured to her to wait in the first room, went off and came back a few minutes later with a gnarled piece of root.

She indicated that Sue should chew it, and handed it to Gabby. She remembered to take it with her right hand, thanked her with a bow and smile and went back to Jed. 'A pregnant woman gave me this when I explained the problem. Do you suppose it's ginger? It looks a bit like it.'

He frowned at it, turned it this way and that and tried to break it, but it was too tough and fibrous. One of the Indonesian engineers pulled out a penknife and Jed cut into the root and sniffed, then chewed the little piece he'd removed.

'Hmm. It tastes a little different, but it's very similar.

It might be a wild form. Did she understand? I mean, it's not an abortifacient, I hope?'

Gabby shook her head. 'No, I'm sure it's not. Hang on.'

She took the root back and returned to the woman, who was pounding again. She held it out and pointed back to the hut, then pointed to her stomach and mimed retching. The woman nodded happily. Then Gabby pointed to her stomach, cradled her arms again and made a flushing away gesture with her hands to indicate losing the baby. The woman shook her head vigorously and started to talk nineteen to the dozen, miming chewing and pointing to her own distended abdomen.

Gabby nodded, sure she was now understood, and went back to the others. 'She got very agitated when I mimed losing the baby, and indicated that she'd taken it. I'm sure it's just to stop the sickness.'

'I think we could risk it, then,' Jed said slowly, and Sue waved a hand at him.

'In which case, for God's sake let's do it. I can't cope with this,' Sue muttered, and Jed cut her off a small piece and handed it to her.

After a few minutes she sighed with relief and lay down again. 'Thank God,' she said fervently.

'Better?' Jed asked.

'Much.'

'So much for drug trials,' Gabby said with a laugh. 'I'll go and thank our friend.'

The woman had finished her pounding and was sitting with a wicked-looking *parang* and chopping up strange oval fruit of some kind, prickly and olive-green. She beckoned to Gabby and patted the ground beside her.

It was cool and shady, the house behind casting a shadow just wide enough to sit in. Gabby smiled and sat down cross-legged next to her new friend and inspected the food she was preparing.

The green things looked like aubergines inside, and Gabby thought they might be jackfruit. Whatever they were, they were all cut up and put in a huge iron pot. The woman moved on to slice some lengths of what looked like young bamboo, and then some other things, the identity of which Gabby couldn't even begin to guess at. She imagined it was all edible, provided too many of those bright little chillies didn't end up in the dish!

Garlic she recognised, going into the pot with the other ingredients, and then the pot was set on some hot embers and given a stir, and the paste that had been pounded earlier was scraped into the pot. Water from a jug was poured over the top, and Gabby reckoned she'd seen her first native Indonesian vegetable stew created.

The girl then sat back on her heels, grinned at Gabby and said, '*Makan*.'

At last! An Indonesian word she had heard before! She smiled and nodded, then pointed to herself. 'Gabby,' she said. Jed was wandering across the open area and she beckoned him over. 'Jed,' she said, pointing to him, then to herself, 'Gabby.'

The girl smiled and pointed to herself. 'Gabby,' she repeated.

Gabby shook her head. 'No.' She pointed to her breasts, then to the girl's, and said, 'Woman.' Then she pointed to Jed in the region of his shorts, and said, 'Man.'

The girl giggled deliciously and covered her face with her hands. Then Gabby did the Gabby and Jed routine again, and the penny dropped.

She pointed to Gabby and repeated her name, then to Jed and repeated his, then to herself. 'Hari,' she said.

Gabby felt a grin almost split her face. 'Hari,' she

repeated, pointing at the girl, and laughed with delight. Such a simple accomplishment, to learn someone's name, but what an achievement.

She almost forgot that the girl's tribe was responsible for her capture. She pointed to the bubbling cook-pot, repeated, '*Makan*,' and turned to Jed. 'I'm learning,' she said with a grin.

His smile was indulgent. He took her arm and drew her gently to her feet, then bowed at Hari and led Gabby away from the village to the bathing pool.

'Do I smell or something?' she asked with a grin, still ridiculously pleased with herself.

He returned her grin. 'No worse than me. I wanted to talk to you out of range of the others.' He stripped off to his briefs, slid into the chilly water and beckoned to her. 'Come on, then.'

She did, only because the water looked so inviting and not because he said so. She pulled off her shoes, shirt and trousers and went into the water in her underwear. To hell with modesty—she was steaming.

'What did you want to talk to me about?' she said, once she'd got her breath back from the shock of the water.

'I want to get Derek stable, then I think we need to get him out of here. I have no idea when my e-mail will get picked up or even if it will. I'm relying on my secretary to use her initiative. She usually does, but I don't want to take her for granted. I've been sending her research results by e-mail so she may be on the lookout, but I have a horrible sinking feeling she has a week's holiday some time now.'

Gabby rolled her eyes. 'Great. Isn't there anyone else?'

He gave a shrug. 'Not offhand. I don't suppose you know anyone's e-mail number?'

'By heart?' She shook her head. 'No. I've tried, but I can't think of anyone. I'm not really a computery sort of person.'

He tutted at her and she poked her tongue out at him and lay back in the water. 'Just imagine, these people live here without any of these so-called necessities, eking out their simple existence by gathering food from the forest—'

'Nature's bountiful harvest?' Jed said with a little snort. 'They're riddled with parasites, plagued by malaria and filariasis, dysentery and malnutrition. They have no health service, no surgery, no antenatal care, dentists don't exist—'

'But if they don't eat refined sugars they probably don't need dentists,' Gabby reasoned. 'And, anyway, it's probably better than dying of stress-related illnesses like we do in the West. I'm sure they have all sorts of herbal remedies that are very effective—probably some of them even more effective than the ones we've come to rely on. You can bet your life no Indonesian village in the mountains is plagued by the MRSA bug!'

He laughed. 'You're just an optimist. You wait till you get sick and see what you want, western medicine or Indonesian *jamu*.'

She sobered, thinking of Derek for whom the Indonesians would have no treatment. 'How's Derek's blood sugar?' she asked.

'Coming down. It's still a little high, but I want to get the last bit down gradually. He's all right now, just a little queasy, but that's natural. I've given him some of Hari's ginger, too. It seemed to help a little.' He climbed out of the pool and sat on the rocks by the side, dripping all over the stone and giving Gabby altogether too much to look at.

'I want to have a meeting with the priest,' he was

saying. 'He seems to be the doctor as well, and I might be able to impress on him the need to have us released. I also want to tell them about the grave trees and ask if they're the reason, but without language it's a little tricky. I don't suppose you can draw?'

'Me?' She shrugged. 'A little—but do we have any paper?'

'Derek brought some, and a pen. We could try drawing the lake and the trees, and see if we get a reaction—'

Something flew low over his head and he ducked, flinging his arms up instinctively and losing his balance so he fell back into the water. When he came up Gabby was laughing. 'Well, that certainly got a reaction,' she choked.

He was at her side in two lazy strokes, and pushed her under the water. She came up spluttering and fighting, her fists connecting with his chest and her legs tangling with his, so that she could feel—

'Oh,' she said softly, her eyes widening with surprise.

He stared into her eyes for an age, then his head lowered and his mouth brushed hers. 'Gabby, I want you,' he said softly, 'but it isn't going to happen. There's too much else going on—we need to keep our heads clear.'

She pushed away from him, treading water while their eyes locked, and then with a sigh she turned and swam to the edge and climbed out. 'Fine,' she said in a choked voice. 'Just stop getting me alone and winding me up and it'll be easy.'

She pulled on her clothes and left him there in the water, cooling off. Do him good. Who did he think he was talking to? So he wanted her, did he?

And she wanted him. She bit back a little moan of frustration and stomped back towards the clearing. She saw a shadow above her, and ducked from another of the swooping whatevers, glanced over her shoulder and then suppressed a shriek.

A bat nearly two feet across?

She headed back to the hut almost at a run, and went up the ladder and into the relative sanctuary of the dimly lit interior like a rat out of a trap.

'Hi, folks!' she said brightly, and plopped down on a heap of folded bedding near Derek. He was lounging against a post, looking better than he had at breakfast and infinitely more human than he had the night before, and she considered again the miracle of modern medicine while her heart settled down again.

'How are you feeling?' she asked him, sure of what the answer would be.

He smiled wanly. 'Almost back to normal, thanks to you two. I'm sorry you got dragged into this mess.'

Gabby grinned. 'Actually, daft though it might seem, I'm almost enjoying myself. It's an opportunity to see an untouched culture and get to know a genuinely friendly people—'

'Very friendly,' Jed said drily, entering the hut behind her. 'So friendly they insist on you coming to stay with them.'

She swivelled round and fixed him with a look. 'We want to desecrate the graves of their children,' she said very slowly and clearly. 'I think they have a right to be a little bit antsy about it!'

'There are ways of communicating—'

'By e-mail?' she said sweetly. 'Anyway, talking of communication, I thought you were going to have a chat to the doctor-priest fellow.'

'I am. I want you to come too. Let's scrounge up some paper and go to it.'

She got reluctantly to her feet and did as he suggested, then they went out and stood at the bottom of the ladder and looked around. 'OK, so which one is he?' Gabby asked.

Jed shrugged. 'Let's ask your friend, Hari.'

She was busy parcelling up little pieces of some indeterminate meat in leaves and burying them in the ashes around the pot as they approached her. She sat back on her heels and gave them her lovely smile.

'Gabby,' she said.

Gabby smiled. 'Hello, Hari.' She squatted down beside the woman and waved a questioning hand at the village. 'Doctor?' she said hopefully.

Hari looked puzzled so Jed crouched down too and pointed at himself. 'Jed, doctor,' he told her. '*Obat—jamu—dukun.*'

'*Dukun!*' Hari exclaimed, and broke into a torrent of her unintelligible native tongue.

'What's a *dukun*?' Gabby asked Jed.

'An Indonesian folk-doctor—like a sort of witch-doctor with an amazing battery of natural remedies. Some of them are quacks, but some are fantastic. Your friend seems to be getting very excited so we might be in luck.'

'Hari, is there a *dukun*?' Gabby asked, pointing round the village.

She scrambled to her feet, wiped her hands on her skirt and led them over to a hut. Gesturing to them to wait, she approached a gnarled old man sitting in the shade under the ladder, fanning himself with a huge leaf.

She spoke to him rapidly, waving at Gabby and Jed, and then the old man stood up and drew himself to his full height.

He reached almost to Gabby's chin, and he was dressed like all the other men in a hammered bark loincloth and tattoos. He had a gleaming white bone through his nose and ash over his dark, withered skin, and he looked ancient. His eyes, however, were like polished conkers, bright and lively and incongruous in so lined and venerable a face.

He looked only at Jed, giving Gabby a cursory once-over and dismissing her. Taking Jed's arm, he led him under the hut into the shade and they sat down cross-legged. Gabby, standing in the full sun, began to wonder about the natural order of things that dictated that women toiled in the sun while men sat in the shade, smoked their evil clove cigarettes and drank out of tubes of bamboo.

Perhaps there were things about this wonderful and untouched culture that weren't quite perfect!

Jed caught her eye and winked, and she smiled sweetly and stood there until he beckoned her.

'Draw the lake and the trees for him. I've tried and I can't do it well enough. I don't think they're exposed enough to 2-D images to understand.'

She tried not to smile at his efforts. Art was obviously not his forte, but one couldn't be good at everything and he was a hell of a kisser...

She dragged her mind back to the subject at hand and thought for a moment, then tried to recreate the scene from memory. As she drew the trees and put the squares on the trunks the old man seemed to become very agitated, and when she drew a baby and pointed from the baby to the tree he nodded vigorously.

Then she drew the trees cut down and lying on their sides and a building in their place, and he got very angry and started to mutter and chant.

Gabby touched his arm gently, took the page and screwed it up then put it into Hari's fire. When she returned he was looking puzzled. She drew the scene again, extended the river and drew the power station at a different site. She didn't know where she'd drawn it, and just hoped it wasn't on the site of some other burial ground or sacred spot.

Obviously it wasn't. He stared at the paper for a long while, turned it this way and that and then took the paper, folded it and tucked it into his loincloth. He turned away, and Hari touched them on the arm and beckoned them away, indicating that their audience was over.

'I suppose that means he's going to think about it,' Jed said drily as they walked back to their hut.

'He'll probably do what an Anglican priest would do and pray over it, only I expect he'll sacrifice something and wait for the gods to tell him the way forward. Not so very different.'

'At least he seemed to understand the drawing.'

'By a miracle. I thought he was going to have us killed when I cut the trees down and put the power station there.'

Jed laughed softly. 'You and me both. That might have been a little rash.'

'It told us what we needed to know, though. It *is* the trees that are the problem. I should add an addendum to your e-mail.'

'For all the good it'll do us.' He sighed and sat down in the shade near the hut. 'I wonder what's for lunch? It seems a long time since we had that fruit for breakfast.'

'I wonder what the meat was in those parcels?' she said speculatively.

'Don't ask,' Jed advised sagely. 'Probably bat or monkey.'

She shuddered. 'Just as long as it isn't snake or frogs, I don't care.'

He laughed. 'I remember listening to a radio programme about some scientists who were taken hostage on Irian Jaya. They said that rat was tough, pig was fatty but the frogs were delicious.'

Gabby gave him a sceptical look, firmly unconvinced. 'How many of them died?' she asked drily.

'None from food poisoning. I think if the natives eat it we can assume it's safe for us to, but we need to boil water for teeth and drinking unless we stick to coconut milk and *tuak*. Rather nice stuff, that. The *dukun* gave me some.'

'I saw you drinking away with him,' she sniped, remembering being left out in the sun. 'Was it nice and cool?'

'What's the matter—didn't you like standing in the background, being servile?'

She threw a bit of twig at him and laughed. 'Tell me about this *tuak*. What is it?'

'Palm wine. They tap the sap from a palm tree and pour it into lengths of bamboo and seal it for a day or so. It ferments naturally and gives a lovely warm glow.' He grinned. 'A sort of naturally occurring gin and tonic without the quinine.'

'No doubt you'll have to research it heavily,' she said innocently.

'Oh, of course. Perhaps you can persuade your friend, Hari, to show you how to make it for me as befits your station. After all, you are supposed to be my wife.'

She snorted. 'Don't hold your breath. My acting skills aren't that brilliant.' She doodled in the sand. 'So, anyway, now they know we know about the trees, do you think they'll let us go?'

He shrugged. 'Depends on what the gods tell our friend, I guess. Maybe, maybe not. We'll have to play it by ear. I wouldn't hold your breath, though, we could still be here for weeks. What we need, of course,' he continued after a pause, 'is an interpreter—some way of communicating with them. We could also do with having a chance to talk to Bill about the possibility of re-siting the power station.'

'I wouldn't have thought he could refuse—not with seven lives at stake,' Gabby pointed out, but Jed shrugged again.

'The Indonesian government gave him consent and passed all the plans. He's got permission for his holiday resort because he was going to provide free electricity to Telok Panjang. At the moment it struggles on kerosene and the odd generator, and the government obviously thought it were getting a good deal. They may decide to throw their weight behind Bill and send troops in to deal with this little insurrection.'

'And we'll all get caught in the crossfire. Great.' Gabby stood up. 'I want to go for a walk around the village.'

'To see if you can find a way out?' Jed said wryly.

'Oh, yeah. Absolutely.'

He stood up and brushed the dirt off his trousers. 'I'll come. Your friend still seems to be watching you so I'd be careful about being alone anywhere too isolated.'

They wandered down to the mountain pool where they had swum that morning and turned left, following the river downhill for a while. There was a path which was quite well used, and it crossed others, a veritable network of tracks and trails that criss-crossed the area around the village.

They wove through them, keeping an ear out all the time for the sounds of children playing and making sure they didn't go too far.

Not that it would have mattered. They were followed at a discreet distance by a gang of little children, tittering and squeaking like a litter of baby mice. They pretended to ignore them, and looked around at the forest.

One tree caught Gabby's attention because of its strange structure. It had a network of stems stretching up in a circle around a hollow core, as if the tree had grown up like a fungus from a ring of roots, and the children were playing hide and seek inside it.

'It's a strangler fig,' Jed told her. 'They germinate halfway up one of the forest trees, send down aerial roots to the soil and then continue to grow upwards. Eventually they link up with each other in a band and strangle the host tree, which dies and rots down to provide nourishment for the growing fig trees. It's probably several trees, not just one. Look, there are figs on it.'

There were, but she shunned them, mindful of the effect they might have. They continued on their way, circling the village until they were almost back, then suddenly the children vanished and an eerie silence descended.

A chill ran over Gabby, and she moved instinctively closer to Jed. 'Everything's gone quiet,' she whispered. 'Even the monkeys are quiet.'

He pointed ahead of them at a tree, and there in the trunk she saw a number of neat, square patches on the bark. Most had started to heal but there was one, though, that was unhealed, indicating a grave tree in current use and, judging by the look of it, used very recently.

She closed her eyes and a tear slipped out. 'Oh, Jed,' she said and, turning, she buried her head in his chest and sobbed.

'Hey, softy, it's a fact of life,' he told her gently.

'I know,' she mumbled, wiping her eyes on his soggy shirtfront. 'I'm just being silly. It's because they're babies, and there seem to be so many little holes for so few people. They must lose their babies all the time.'

'Perhaps that's why the children that are still alive are

strong and healthy—perhaps nature sorts them out early so that only the really tough ones make it.'

She sniffed and straightened up. 'Don't be logical,' she told him, and with a last lingering look at the quiet glade with its sad little secrets she turned away and carried on with her walk.

Jed fell into step beside her. 'If you get so emotional and weepy about a few babies you've never met, how on earth do you cope with losing a child you've nursed?'

She gave a humourless grunt of laughter. 'Badly,' she told him with characteristic honesty. 'Usually I fall apart afterwards, but I have been known to cry at the time more often than I care to remember.'

'How did I know that?' he murmured and, slinging his arm around her shoulders, he gave her a quick squeeze. 'Come on, my stomach tells me it must be lunchtime. Let's go and find out what that meat was that Hari was putting in the fire.'

'If it's fruit bat I'm not eating it,' she warned, and he laughed.

'You could get awfully thin in the next few days.'

'So be it,' she said firmly. 'But I'm not eating bats for anybody!'

They walked back into the clearing arm in arm and laughing, to find two men on their knees in the middle of the open ground. A cluster of what looked like village elders stood around them with spears pointing menacingly at them, and at their head was the *dukun* in full ceremonial dress, chanting tunelessly.

'Damn,' Jed said softly.

'What?'

'It's Jamal and his friend Johannis, the man who's an outcast from this village.'

'Isn't that good?'

Jed looked from the group to her and back to the

group. 'I somehow don't think so,' he said softly. 'I think, if they aren't about to kill them, we've just got ourselves two more fellow-hostages.'

And with that he strode into the middle of the group of men, stood in front of the *dukun* and began, so Gabby imagined, to intercede.

CHAPTER SEVEN

'HE's off his trolley,' Sue said quietly, appearing at Gabby's elbow. 'Come into the hut out of the way—it could get nasty.'

Gabby needed no second bidding. She'd always thought Jed was a bit of an Indiana Jones, but surely he didn't have to take it quite so seriously? She followed Sue up the ladder and sat, watching anxiously from just inside the doorway through a crack in the bark-covered wall.

Jamal and his friend stayed where they were, but she noticed that Jed was speaking to the other man, who was in turn speaking to the *dukun* and relaying messages back.

The conversation was inaudible, but after a moment the *dukun* waved away the men with their spears and told Jamal and Johannis to get up. They were then led to a hut and thrown in, and a guard was posted outside the door.

Then the *dukun* waved his spear at Hari, who was standing on the fringe, and went back to his shady spot under his hut. The elders with their spears stood, looking disgruntled, for a moment, then turned away and shuffled back to their business, and Jed was left standing there in the middle alone.

After a second they saw him shrug and make his way towards them. Hari was serving food to the *dukun*, and nobody seemed to make any attempt to stop Jed. Within seconds he was up the ladder and they all pounced on him.

117

'Well?' Sue said impatiently. 'Are there others behind them? Are we going to be rescued?'

Jed sighed and shook his head. 'No. The elders were going to kill them, but I managed to persuade the *dukun* to spare them so we can use them as interpreters to negotiate between us and the tribe and the Indonesian government and Bill. I said it would be a terrible tragedy if they were unable to communicate their concerns and the trees were destroyed, without proper respect being shown for the burial site.'

'Crafty thing,' Derek said with a chuckle. 'I thought you'd had your chips, Jed. I thought for sure you were going to bite the dust back there.'

Jed gave a quirky little grin. '*You* thought that? How do you think *I* felt!'

Hari appeared in the doorway with a huge wooden platter laden with food, and passed it in to them. She gave Gabby a shy smile, bobbed her head at Jed as if he were some kind of spirit and backed away again.

'Great,' he said, reaching for one of the charred little leaf parcels they had seen being put on the fire. 'Let's see if it's rat or bat.'

Sue groaned, turned away and reached for another little piece of the ginger root. 'Jed, you are foul,' she muttered and, turning her back on them all, she chewed her way back to equilibrium.

If Gabby had thought the arrival of Jamal and Johannis signalled a change in their circumstances she was wrong. The days seemed to drag by with more of the same nothingness, and after a week everyone was getting crabby and difficult.

Every night Jed checked the Magellan instrument to see if he'd had a reply and every night he sighed, switched it off and put it away as their hopes crumbled in the dust.

He tried to talk the *dukun* into letting Jamal go back to Telok Panjang but he wouldn't hear of it, presumably because it would give away their whereabouts. The men were guarded night and day, although Jed seemed to be allowed to go and talk to them, and he discovered that everyone was convinced they had all been murdered.

Penny had been sent back to Jakarta as planned, he told them all, and Jon, a government official and Bill Freeman, the developer, were in endless meetings. At least they had been. By now they might have decided to track the tribe down but, since Johannis was the only man to know the way, it seemed unlikely they would be discovered.

Gabby found the waiting very difficult, and passed the time as well as possible by making friends. She spent time with Hari, getting to know her in a strangely silent way, and by observing her carefully through the days she realised Hari was very tired and uncomfortable, although she never complained.

She spoke to Jed about it one night, carefully separated by a foot of floor and maintaining a strict rule of no physical contact through the night. It was less frustrating that way, they'd discovered, and by an unspoken agreement had settled into the companionable but slightly distant routine.

Tonight, though, she didn't want to be distant. She rolled on her side to face him, pillowing her head on her arm, and tapped his shoulder to get his attention.

'Mmm?' he murmured drowsily.

'It's about Hari,' she said softly. 'She's huge and she doesn't seem to be showing any signs of going into labour, but she's very uncomfortable. Today she was really bad.'

His eyes flickered open in the half-dark. 'Yes, I'd noticed. I wonder if she's got a breech? It might not be triggering her uterus to contract if so, or just feebly.'

'So what will happen?'

'Nothing until it's too late, then weak contractions that get nowhere. She might have an antepartum haemorrhage and die, or the baby might turn and everything will be all right, or she might go into very strong labour and rupture her uterus and die that way. Or she might just work like stink and get away with it if there are enough people to help her who know what they're doing.'

'Like us?' Gabby suggested.

'Forget it,' he told her. 'Even if we could get near her, what could we do?'

Gabby rolled onto her front and propped herself up on her elbows, her head close to his so they could hear each other without disturbing the others. 'We have to do something, Jed. We can't just ignore her, can we? Surely we can do something?'

He snorted. 'How? We haven't got access to any diagnostic tools, we can't scan her or X-ray her or even examine her. I don't suppose for a moment I'd be allowed to perform an internal on a young pregnant woman, do you? Think about it. I bet the only birth attendants will be the older women—and the *dukun* if things get really bad. No way will they let me in there.'

'How about me?' she suggested.

'More likely, but still not very probable. It depends how desperate they get. Of course Jamal thinks you're a healer so that could work in our favour. I'll talk to him in the morning.'

He didn't get a chance, though, because they were woken later that night by a woman's screams.

Gabby leapt up instantly. 'Hari,' she said with conviction. 'Jed, I want to go to her.'

'Try getting dressed first, then,' he suggested, stopping her in her tracks.

Bemused, she turned back and pulled on her clothes in place of the sarong, freezing as the air was ripped again by another cry. A shiver ran down her spine. 'Jed, please come too. If they let me in I can perhaps talk to you through the wall, but something's dreadfully wrong. Women don't scream like that normally.'

'God, I haven't done obstetrics since I was twenty-seven—I doubt if I can remember what's what,' he muttered.

'Let's just hope you're better with obstetrics than you are with e-mail numbers, then, or I might be better off without you.'

'Ha-ha,' he growled, dragging on his trousers and following her out of the hut.

The action was all taking place in and around Hari's hut, they discovered. Her husband, a strong and healthy-looking young man, was sitting at the fire with another man, whom they recognised as the chief, smoking clove cigarettes and talking in muttered undertones.

'You know Hari is the chief's daughter, do you?' Jed murmured as they approached.

'Yes, I'd gathered. That must be why he's here. I wonder where the *dukun* is.'

'Inside, I expect, chanting and giving her ghastly potions. I should think he's given her something to speed up the contractions, hence the screams.'

'Don't,' Gabby said with a shudder. 'How am I going to get inside?'

'Just go in. You're a woman. If you're humble enough they might let you help. I'll see if I can talk them into letting Johannis out to interpret.'

She climbed the ladder and slipped into the hut un-noticed, and found everyone clustered round Hari who was lying on the floor, writhing. Everyone in the room was a woman, with the exception of the *dukun*, who was squatting beside her chanting as Jed had predicted.

He looked up at her and stopped, then pointed at the door and said something that was obviously telling her to leave. She shook her head and knelt down on the other side of Hari, facing him, and pointed to herself. 'Gabby, *dukun*,' she said, hoping he would believe her and enlist her aid, or at least allow her to help.

Would he feel threatened, as if his magic was no good?

He sat back on his heels, folded his arms and stared at her defiantly—challengingly. Gabby swallowed and bent over Hari, stroking her hair back from her face and murmuring soothingly to her.

A woman pressed a damp cloth into her hand and she used that, wiping away the beads of sweat on Hari's clammy skin. 'Hari? Hari, it's Gabby,' she told her, and the girl's eyes flickered open.

They were glazed with pain and fear, and she clutched Gabby's hand and began to weep silently. Gabby used the other hand and laid it on the hugely distended ab-domen, palpating it thoughtfully. It was years since she'd done much obstetrics, but she knew that what she was feeling now wasn't run of the mill.

For a start, she realised with a shock as she palpated the edges of the woman's abdomen, Hari was having twins, and—if she wasn't very much mistaken—it was a double transverse lie, one baby in the lap of the other, both crosswise.

'Gabby?'

She lifted her head at Jed's voice. 'She's having

twins—a double transverse presentation. Jed, she doesn't stand a chance without a section.'

He swore, softly but succinctly, and called to her to come out. 'Johannis is here, he can interpret. We've been talking to the husband. Apparently she's been in labour for a day off and on, without complaining, but she's starting to have much stronger contractions.'

'I can tell,' she called, her hand still resting where it was. There was suddenly a tremendous tension under her palm, and Hari cried out and rolled up into a ball, tensing all her muscles.

Gabby stroked her back soothingly, talking reassuringly to her, and when the contraction was over she slipped out of the hut and went to see Jed. 'Her contractions are horrendously strong, and she's never going to make any progress. Jed, she's going to die unless we can operate.'

Jed stabbed his hands through his hair and looked up at the sky for inspiration. 'I can't, Gabby. There's no anaesthetic, no light, no after-care—she'd die anyway, and if we've interfered we'll probably die too.'

'So you're just going to leave her to it?' she said furiously. 'Jed, you can't. We can do it—surely you've got some painkillers in that box of tricks.'

He snorted. 'Nothing that strong. I've got a couple of phials of pethidine, that's all, and no antibiotics strong enough to dare risk it, not in these unsterile conditions.'

She twisted her hands together worriedly. 'There must be something we can do.'

'Only if the *dukun* has a narcotic available in his arsenal of natural remedies, and he might well have—and if he's prepared to help us, which he might not be.'

'Ask—get Johannis to tell the chief his daughter's going to die unless we help her. Get him to tell the man that we're healers too. Get him to order the *dukun* to help.'

'Just like that?' He shook his head in despair and turned to Johannis, and explained the situation to him through Jamal.

'Wah,' the man said, rolling his eyes in fear and starting to babble.

'I think what he means is he can't tell the chief that because he'll cut his head off,' Jed translated.

'I'll cut his head off—Johannis, please, tell the chief his daughter's dying,' she pleaded.

Just then another scream cut through the night, and the chief looked anxiously at the hut. Gabby, not one to hang about in the face of such an emergency, pushed Johannis over to the fireside. 'Tell him,' she snarled.

So the poor man, shaking and trembling, translated their message. The chief's eyes widened in fear, then glazed and filled and he started to sob. The husband fell on him and they wept together.

'Oh, this is hopeless,' Gabby said impatiently, and pulled the two men apart. 'Jed, *dukun*,' she told them firmly. 'Hari…' She pulled her finger over her throat. 'Jed help.'

They looked at her as if she were mad. 'Johannis,' she wailed, and he spoke again. She turned to Jed. 'Make sure he tells them about the operation.'

There was a muttered exchange between Jed, Jamal and Johannis, and then their intrepid translator tried again. This time the chief got to his feet and went to the door of the hut and called out.

The *dukun* appeared in the doorway and they had a brief, fierce exchange. Jed got Johannis to translate, and then relayed it to Gabby.

'The *dukun* doesn't want to help us. He's now admitted he can't do anything and, yes, she will die.'

At this the chief produced a knife and threatened the man.

'Things are hotting up—he might be on our side,' Jed muttered to Gabby, rubbing thoughtfully at the beard on his chin. He turned to Johannis and said something which the man then translated, and the *dukun* nodded, his face surly.

'I don't think he wants to help, but on the other hand I think he's quite happy being alive. The chief's just told him that if Hari dies he dies too.'

'So I guess the same will apply to us.'

Jed grinned at her. 'I love a challenge. We need to scrub, kiddo. I think we're about to do surgery al fresco style, and the anaesthetist has got a serious case of the sulks.'

Adrenaline, Gabby thought some half an hour later, was a wonderful thing. Talk about sharpening up your wits!

Hari had been washed and sedated with the *dukun*'s herbal remedy, and was now sleeping peacefully in her hut. The women had been herded out, only the woman's mother, the *dukun*, Jed and Gabby remaining, with Johannis outside the door to translate if necessary.

They had scrubbed as well as they could and sprayed their hands with antibiotic spray, and Jed used more of it to sterilise the incision site. 'I'll do a longitudinal section because I don't want to cut the babies, and this light's awful. Anyway, it's quicker and she's less likely to have problems later with another delivery.'

He picked up the knife he'd been given by their reluctant assistant and which he'd sterilised as well as possible by boiling it in water for ten minutes. 'Let's hope this sedation works,' he said to Gabby, and without further ado he ran the knife down the skin.

A thin beading of blood appeared along the line, and

Hari moaned and moved a little. Her mother soothed her with trembling hands, tears streaming silently down her wrinkled face, and Jed stroked again and again until he was through the muscle layer and the uterus was revealed.

'It's very thinned at the base—I think it would have ruptured within another hour or so. I wish I could do an ultrasound scan to find out where the placentas are,' he muttered. 'Let's just pray I don't hit one of them.'

He stroked the knife over the uterus, pierced it and then, by sliding his fingers under the knife the wrong way up, he opened the uterus far enough to reveal the babies.

'So far so good. Right, let's see what we've got here.'

'Wah!' the mother keened softly as Jed reached in and lifted the first tiny infant out. It squalled healthily, and he grinned and handed it to Gabby. She laid it on Hari's chest and waited for the second child. It wasn't long coming, and also squalled vigorously.

Jed turned to Johannis and asked something, which was relayed to the astonished *dukun*. He reached in his bag of potions and produced a root, which he slivered with a knife and handed to Hari's mother with an instruction.

She placed it under Hari's tongue, and a few minutes later the uterus contracted steadily and the placentas came naturally away.

'Well, I never. Oxytocin, as I live and breathe.'

Jed smiled grimly. 'So far so good. Right, let's separate these babies from their placentas, take them out and get her closed up before too many moths fall inside.'

He closed quickly, more quickly than Gabby had ever seen it done and probably nearly as neatly, using the antibiotic spray liberally as he went along. Then he cleaned up his hands, washed the site down and sprayed

it again, before covering it with a non-adherent sterile
dressing.

Then he sat back on his heels and looked at Gabby.

'Well? What have we got?'

'Two boys, both well and fit and hungry. I don't suppose he's got a natural antidote to that sedative so she
can feed them?'

Jed laughed. 'I think we'd better let her sleep it off,'
he said. 'The longer she's out of it the better. I'm sure
another woman can be persuaded into service as a wet
nurse.'

He spoke to Johannis, then turned to the *dukun* and
held out his hand with a grin.

After a few seconds' hesitation he took it and smiled,
and said something to Johannis who translated.

Jed relayed it back to Gabby. 'He says together we
have powerful magic,' he said with a grin. 'I reckon we
were just damned lucky.'

'So far,' Gabby agreed, looking at the sleeping woman
who had been all but unaware of the procedure. 'Never
mind the magic—thank goodness he had a powerful
enough painkiller. Let's just pray she doesn't get an infection.'

'I'm sure our friend here has something as impressive
in the way of a natural antibiotic. I'd make up a garlic
paste dressing and lay it on if all else failed, but he's
probably got a whole battery of goodies up his sleeve.'

He stood up, moved to Hari's head and squatted down
by her mother, who was cradling the babies in her arms.
They were both squalling furiously, and were quite obviously well and healthy. They were very certainly alive,
at least.

Jed smiled at the woman who smiled back tearfully
and hugged the babies even tighter, then she struggled
to her feet and went over to the doorway, holding the

babies up. There was a cheer from outside and she turned back to the *dukun*, obviously thanking him for his part.

He bowed graciously, then began chanting over Hari and the babies, sprinkling them with something from his bag. 'Doubtless thanking some powerful god for the safe deliverance not only of the babies and their mother but also himself,' Jed murmured to Gabby.

She laughed softly. 'And us. I think I might join in.'

Jed hugged her, dropping a quick kiss in her hair, and together they left the hut to the greetings of the women who were still waiting for a proper look at the babies.

They were led to the fire by the happy, laughing throng and asked to sit with the chief and Hari's husband, and they were brought strong, sickly coffee and even sicklier cakes made of palm syrup in order to celebrate.

The *dukun* came out about half an hour later, smiling and bearing the babies in his arms, and they were handed to the women, who immediately took charge.

'They'll be fed and washed and looked after now,' Jed said confidently. 'The Indonesians are wonderful with children. If parents die the children are always instantly absorbed into another part of the family, and they often seem almost to share their children. I'm quite sure those babies will be fine now.'

'And Hari?'

Jed turned and spoke to Johannis who was squatting on the fringe of the group, waiting to be asked to translate again, and after a brief discussion with the *dukun* he relayed that Hari was fine and sleeping peacefully.

'Should I stay with her?' Gabby asked.

'Perhaps we all should. I don't think he would, but the *dukun* has the power, I'm quite sure, to kill her and have the blame fixed on us. I think this guy is OK, but a lot of these healers are quacks and totally unscrupulous, and they'd stop at nothing to protect their own reputations.'

'Even murder?' Gabby murmured.

'Possibly. I think, just to be on the safe side, he should have an audience at all times and, anyway, I'd rather be near Hari just until she comes round.'

In the end they stayed up by the fire until the sky began to lighten, popping in and out of the hut every few minutes to see the sleeping woman and her relieved mother. Both were fine, and after a while Hari stirred and moaned a little. The *dukun* gave her a potion which quietened her, without sedating her, and Gabby and Jed were both happy with her condition as far as they could tell.

The babies, too, were cuddled and admired once they had been fed, and they were passed around the group at the fireside with pride.

Gabby held one and Jed the other, and Gabby felt a huge lump in her throat.

'I'm so glad they didn't end up in a tree,' she said and, without thinking, she held the baby tight against her and closed her eyes.

When she opened them and looked up at Jed, his eyes seemed very bright in the firelight. He took the baby from her and passed it on, then took Gabby by the hand and led her back to their hut.

'I think she'll be all right now,' he told her and, leading her along to their bedroom, he turned her into his arms and held her tight. 'Thank you for making me do that,' he mumbled into her hair. 'I really didn't want to but, you're right, she would have died. I just thought we were bound to kill her.'

'And we didn't. I just couldn't bear to see her die, she's such a lovely person.'

'So are you,' he murmured, and his lips closed over hers. Her tiredness was forgotten, the drama of the night behind her, and only she and Jed existed.

They lay down without a sound on the scattered bedding, and Jed undressed her with trembling fingers. Everywhere he touched her skin it turned to fire, and by the time she was naked she was shaking all over.

Her fingers didn't work, and he dragged his shirt over his head, ripped off his trousers and briefs and settled beside her with a tiny sigh.

'I love you, Gabrielle Andrews,' he murmured. 'You're my little angel, do you know that? I've wanted to hold you like this for so long...'

His mouth found hers, teasing and tormenting until she thought she'd go crazy for him. His hands moved over her, cupping and cradling and stroking, making her weak with longing. She searched his body, her own hands restlessly fluttering over his back, over the skin that was like hot, damp silk in the tropic dawn. So hot, lit with the fire that was consuming them both. Amazing that he could feel so hot—

He shifted slightly and her hand found its way around and down, cupping the heavy fullness of his masculinity, dragging a groan from deep inside him.

His own hand responded, stroking the damp nest of curls that hid such a wild need she thought she'd die of it.

'Jed, please,' she whispered, and then he shifted across her and buried himself deep inside her.

She couldn't hold back the cry, couldn't help the little sob of relief at being part of him at last. He dropped his head against her shoulder with a shudder, and was still for an endless moment.

Then he lifted his head and met her eyes in the pale

light of dawn. 'Oh, Gabby,' he breathed raggedly. 'It feels so right—it's like coming home.'

Tears filled her eyes and she blinked them away, anxious to see his face—to remember every moment of this precious union. 'Jed, I love you,' she whispered.

'Oh, angel, I love you, too, so very much.'

His lips touched her face like the wing of a bird, soft, open-mouthed kisses that left a trail of fire over her eyes, her nose, her jaw, and finally her lips.

Their mouths went wild then, hungry and demanding, clinging fiercely and searching as their bodies rose to meet each other and the relentless passion broke in a devastating climax that left them both weak and shaken.

Jed collapsed against her, his breath scorching against her neck.

'God, my head aches,' he murmured a few moments later, and then his body slumped bonelessly onto hers.

'Jed—Jed, get off, I can't breathe,' she whispered.

There was silence, broken only by the harsh rasp of his breathing, and it dawned on Gabby that something was horribly wrong...

CHAPTER EIGHT

'JED?'

He was heavy on her, so heavy she could hardly roll him off. She pushed him, hissed at him, shook him, all to no avail. He seemed oblivious to her, and now that the wild heat of passion had cooled in her Gabby could feel that the heat coming off him in waves was far from normal.

In fact, it was worryingly abnormal, coupled with his lack of reaction and the headache he'd spoken of. Now he seemed to be unconscious, his body shaking violently.

She gave a mighty heave and rolled his shuddering body off her, then knelt beside him. 'Jed? Talk to me, damn it!'

He mumbled something unintelligible and curled into a ball, hugging his arms around himself as if he was cold, and Gabby covered him with one of the loosely woven rugs, pulled on her clothes and went out to see the others. There was a deep chill of fear settling round her heart, and she needed Jed's advice.

Unfortunately he wasn't in a position to give it to her.

She found the others grouped round in the living area by the door, eating their breakfast. Conversation stopped dead as she walked in, and she realised that in the flimsy hut their love-making had probably been quite clearly audible.

Tough. She had other things to worry about.

'Have any of you ever seen cerebral malaria?' she asked them.

'I have,' Ismail said.

'I don't suppose you'd recognise it?'

'Jed?' Sue asked her, the curiosity on her face replaced by concern.

'I think so. He complained of a headache, and he's burning up and shivering and I can't seem to get through to him. He might just be very tired, but I don't think so.'

Sue was on her feet in an instant, following Gabby back to their bedroom, with Ismail behind her and the others trailing at a distance.

Jed was pale and sweaty, his sunken eyes shadowed in his bearded face. 'He looks awful,' Sue said bluntly, and knelt down beside him. 'Jed? Come on, wake up!'

He mumbled something and stirred, but his eyes didn't open and he didn't really respond.

'He's out of it—how long has he been like this?'

Gabby shrugged. How long was it? 'Twenty minutes? Half an hour? Not that long.'

'Looks bad, mem,' Ismail said, squatting down beside him and touching his hot skin with a tentative hand. 'My cousin died—'

'Thank you, Ismail, we can manage now,' Sue said quickly, but Gabby felt a chill run right through her.

'You don't suppose it could just be flu, do you?' she asked, knowing as she did so that she was clutching at straws.

'No. I think it's almost certainly malaria. There's a leaflet about treating all the different types in the medicines he brought with him, and I'm sure he would have brought the right things to treat it. We just have to get the drugs into him.'

And that, Gabby knew, would be almost impossible without his co-operation or an intravenous drip. She

found the flight bag, dug about in it for the leaflet and
then read it quickly.

'''Severe headache, fever, drowsiness, delirium or
confusion may indicate impending cerebral malaria'','
she read aloud. 'Blah blah—''chloroquine-resistant
strains—quinine, pyrimethamine and a sulphonamide
orally, or chloroquine dihydrochloride IV if unconscious''.'

She looked up at Sue. 'I would say he's unconscious.
I think I ought to try injecting him very slowly intravenously, just to get something into him, and then try
orally as soon as he comes round a bit or we can get
him to co-operate. Will you help me?'

'Of course. What do you want me to do?'

And that was the problem, of course. There was nothing she could do except provide moral support, and
Gabby said so. 'Just stay with me. I'm so scared he'll
die…'

She dropped her face into her hands and choked down
a sob, then lifted her head, took a deep breath and
dredged up a smile. She had to think—

'OK. The first hurdle is saline solution. There isn't
any.'

'You'll have to use boiled water.'

Gabby rolled her eyes. 'I could be giving him God
knows what. OK, I'll use boiled water. Could you organise some?'

While Sue went in search of boiled water in something reasonably sterile, Gabby read and reread the leaflet until she was sure she'd understood the treatment,
then she looked through the medicines and found everything she needed.

'Thank God he brought it,' she muttered, and looked
up just as Sue came back with not only a bowl of water
but the *dukun* in tow.

She wasn't sure if she was relieved to see him or not, but he might have some magic cure up his sleeve that wouldn't hurt as adjuvant therapy, and just now Gabby would settle for all the help she could get!

He squatted down by Jed's head, laid a hand on his scorching forehead and then pulled up his eyelids. Jed moaned a little, and the old man shook his head slightly and turned to Gabby, pointing to his head and holding it as if in pain.

She nodded, and hugged her arms around herself to show he had been shivery, and then fanned her face to show he was hot.

The old man unfolded himself and disappeared, presumably to fetch something. Gabby watched him go, and turned back to Sue. 'Did you ask him to come?'

'No. He just followed me. I had to talk to Johannis to get him to explain what I wanted, and he must have got wind of it. I wonder what he's gone to get.'

'Hopefully Johannis, amongst other things, so we can have an intelligent conversation. Could you hold his arm for me?'

She pulled up some of the water in the syringe, prayed that it was all right and drew up the chloroquine. Then she tied Jed's belt around his arm to raise the vein, slid the needle in and checked she'd entered the vein, then released the belt. Then gradually, millilitre by millilitre, she squeezed the contents of the syringe into his arm.

She was about halfway through when the *dukun* came back, and he watched her impassively as she delivered the drug. When she had finished, withdrawn the needle and bent Jed's arm up over a pressure pad against the vein, he produced a small cup of liquid, lifted Jed's head and tipped it into his mouth.

He swallowed convulsively, the reflex triggered by the liquid in his throat, and Gabby was relieved to see he was not as deeply unconscious as she had feared. She thought it might be safer, that being the case, to give him medicines orally instead of intravenously in view of the absence of sterile saline solution as a carrier.

The *dukun* was now fishing about in his bag and pulling out a variety of things—brilliantly coloured feathers, a shrivelled frog, some claws off a nameless animal, a piece of fur—there seemed no end to the bizarre collection of items he came up with. He laid them in a ring around Jed's head and began to chant, and Gabby settled back to watch.

Clearly, this was the theatre of his work, the drink having been the real treatment. This spectacle was now for psychosomatic relief, the psychology of medicine that was so effective in witchcraft and African juju.

She knew it wouldn't hurt him, and there was nothing she could do. Who could tell—perhaps the ritual would invoke the help of some god she had never heard of? At this point, she wasn't prepared to turn away any aid at all—cerebral malaria could and did kill in six hours.

She closed her eyes and hugged her arms tight around her body. Please, no, don't let him die, she said silently. Don't take him away from me now when I've only just found him. Don't let me lose him like this.

There was a soft touch on her shoulder, like a butterfly, and she opened her eyes to find the *dukun* regarding her compassionately. He patted her hand and then, beckoning, he went out of the hut.

She followed him down the ladder and across to Hari's hut. Hari! Heavens, in the confusion she'd forgotten all about the young woman!

She was lying propped up on brightly coloured rugs, a baby in each arm, and she looked wide awake and well. When she saw Gabby she smiled broadly and beckoned her over. Gabby knelt down beside her and hugged her, then sat back and looked at the babies.

She wanted to say, 'How are you? The babies are beautiful, you're a lucky girl. I hope you aren't in too much pain.' But it was impossible. Perhaps her face said it for her. Whatever, she couldn't keep the smile off it.

She patted Hari's abdomen and raised her eyebrows in enquiry, and Hari pulled a little face. So she was in pain, but not so bad that she couldn't hold her babies and feed them, with help. Her mother was there, of course, beaming broadly and pressing Gabby's hand to her head in a gesture of gratitude.

Gabby checked the incision and found the dressing had been replaced by a poultice of leaves bruised in hot water, by the look of it, and the incision line under the leaves looked clean and healthy and without any sign of infection.

Yet. She hoped it would continue.

She smiled her satisfaction to Hari, who was obviously nearly as proud of her stitches as she was of her babies. They offered her coffee and more of the little palm cakes, and she was going to refuse before she saw the look in Hari's eyes. The new mother wanted company, and to show off her babies to her new friend who had helped to save their lives, and Gabby didn't have the heart to refuse.

So she sat and drank a quick cup of the thick coffee and ate two of the little cakes. Then, bowing to the *dukun* who was busy mixing something in the corner, she left them and went back to Jed.

'How is he?' she asked Sue anxiously. 'I had to go and see Hari and there didn't seem to be a polite way to get out of it.'

'He's the same. He doesn't seem any worse, anyway,

and he's a bit less fidgety. He's talking, though—something about angels?'

Gabby gave a shaky little laugh, wondering what on earth he'd said. 'Angels?'

His lids fluttered and he looked straight at her, his eyes sparkling a vivid blue. 'My favourite angel,' he slurred. 'The angel Gabrielle herself. I love you. C'm'ere, you sexy thing.'

They fluttered shut again, to Gabby's relief, and he went quiet.

Sue laughed. 'Oh, well, at least we know he's not dreaming about dying. He spooked me for a minute. Want any more help?'

Gabby looked around. The room was hot and stuffy, and she wondered if there was any way to ventilate it better.

'It's getting so hot,' she murmured to herself. 'I wonder if we can cool him down?'

'You might find it cooler under the hut in the shade—shall I get the men to carry him out for you? You probably ought to sponge him down too, he's still very hot.'

'I think so—yes, please, Sue, could you do that?'

She waited until Sue had left the room and then tugged Jed's briefs on more or less properly. He was heavy and uncooperative, though, and it wasn't easy. Sue came back with Ismail and Luther, and they took an end each and carried him, slung between them, out of the hut and down the ladder to the shady spot underneath.

Gabby carried the mats and rugs and made up a bed on the ground, and they laid him down in the cooler air and then sat beside her. Sue fetched cool water and a cloth, and Gabby sponged him down, keeping an eye on the time.

He would need oral therapy, if she could get it into

him, as soon as possible, but for now she wanted to keep sponging and see if she could lower his temperature. It seemed to be climbing even higher, and every now and then he had a rigor, a shuddering fit almost like a convulsion.

People came and went, sitting quietly with her for company and helping her with the endless little tasks. Hari's mother sat for a while, and her sister, and Sue was never far away.

Derek spent some time talking to Jamal about the situation back at base, but he was still quite weak and spent a lot of the day resting. Gabby, though, didn't rest. There wasn't time.

The *dukun* came and gave Jed more of the vile green decoction, and she managed to crush up the malaria pills and dissolve them in honey and coax him to swallow the mixture. That in itself took nearly an hour.

During the afternoon Sue came and sat down with her back against one of the posts and regarded Gabby thoughtfully. 'You look awful. Why don't you let me take over and go and have a sleep? You were up all night with Hari, and you'll have days of this ahead of you. You ought to pace yourself.'

It made sense, but she didn't dare leave him. She went down to the pool, though, and washed herself and her clothes by the simple expedient of walking into the water fully clothed. She washed out Jed's clothes as well, and then went back and changed into the sarong.

Her shoulders were bare, but in view of the near-nakedness of the other women she didn't think it would matter. She smothered herself in insect repellent, hung the clothes over a beam and went back out to Jed.

'Go and lie down for a while,' Sue ordered her.

'I can't. I won't sleep. I need to be with him.'

Sue sat back on her heels and regarded Gabby

thoughtfully. 'You love him very much, don't you?' she said shrewdly.

There was no point in lying. 'Yes,' she replied. 'I do. I can't let him die, I know that.'

She plucked at his skin. It was still plump and taut, but she needed to keep getting fluids into him if she could or he might become dehydrated. 'Help me give him a drink,' she said to Sue, and together they propped him up and dribbled cool boiled water into his mouth.

He swallowed barely any, most of it dribbling out of the corner of his mouth and running down his chest. Sometimes, though, he did swallow, and for those few times it was worth it.

She stayed with him all that day and all the following night, and as dawn broke on the second day the *dukun* came back and squatted down beside her in the hut. He said something she couldn't understand, and then some men came and lifted Jed up like a rag doll and carried him outside under the hut again.

She made as if to follow, but the old man pointed to her bed and ordered her to stay.

'But I need to look after him,' she argued.

However, he was having none of it. There was no need for language. He simply pointed to her, pointed to the bed and walked out, dropping the bark-cloth door curtain into place as he left. He might just as well have locked it, the meaning was so clear.

Exhausted, beyond thought, she lay down obediently and slept for two hours. Then she woke up in a panic and got up and went to Jed, to find a strange woman bathing him with cool water.

The woman smiled at her and patted the ground beside her, and she sat down and looked at him.

He was still alive, despite her desertion. Gabby's shoulders drooped with relief, and she opened the flight bag and took out the next dose of quinine, pyrimethamine and sulphonamide. She crushed the tablets into the honey and smeared the paste on his tongue, then stroked the underneath of his jaw to stimulate the swallowing reflex.

As she did so she noticed that his skin was beginning to show signs of dehydration, and he was still almost unconscious. She propped him up and gave him a drink, and was rewarded by him dribbling over her trousers.

'Really, Jed, I've just done the washing!' she grumbled, and to her surprise he turned towards her voice and mumbled something.

'Jed?'

'Head aches,' he said almost inaudibly. She bent and pressed her lips to his forehead, and he moaned softly and turned his face into the softness of her breasts.

'Gorgeous,' he mumbled. 'Sexy, sexy lady. I want to make love to you.'

She looked up to see Derek there, grinning, and went beetroot red.

'Don't be silly, you're sick,' she reminded him a little breathlessly.

'Not silly—love you. Marry me, angel.'

She smiled. 'Of course I will—just as soon as you're better. Now go to sleep.'

'Sick, Gabby,' he mumbled. 'Head hurts.'

'I know,' she murmured soothingly, and smoothed his hair back from his face, forgetting Derek. Jed was hot and she tried to move away a little but he hung on, and so she held him like that for ages while the tears ran down her face and dripped onto his hair. Eventually she felt the light touch of the *dunku* on her shoulder.

She lifted her head with a sigh, and he tutted at her and moved her out of the way. More of the vile green liquid was coaxed into Jed, and more incantations were said, and Gabby joined in with prayers of her own.

Then he gathered up his trappings and beckoned Gabby to follow him to his hut. There he gave her food and drink, and if there was anything in it she didn't care. She was sure now he was a good man, and any fears Jed might have had about him being a quack had been long dispelled. If he wanted to give her medicine for anything let him, she thought.

Anyway, she was starving.

She ate the rice and vegetables and some of the sauce, drank the coconut milk and stood up. 'I have to go back to Jed,' she told him, not expecting him to understand, but he nodded.

'Jed,' he said, and let her go.

He was hovering on the fringes constantly for the next few days, quietly coming and going, taking care of her and Jed and Hari, and she was immensely grateful for his loyal support.

Derek continued to recover and was much stronger, and the others seemed to be remaining well, to her relief. She had her hands more than full as it was.

Jed, meanwhile, continued to be oblivious of the rest of the world. He kept talking rubbish, some of it utter gibberish, some unfortunately quite easily understandable to the inevitable audience, keeping her company in the shade under the hut.

At one point he opened his eyes and looked at Gabby with a glazed expression. 'You are one hell of a sexy woman,' he told her gruffly. Derek and Luther, sitting nearby, laughed softly, and Gabby felt herself colouring.

'Jed, shut up, you don't know what you're talking about,' she told him.

'Yesido,' he slurred. 'Sexy legs, sexy eyes, sexy everything.'

'You sound drunk.'

'Because I fancy you? C'mere. I wanna hold you—'

'Jed,' she said warningly, and he giggled.

'Never learnt to take a compliment,' he told her, and lunged towards her.

She dodged out of the way and he collapsed on the mats and started to snore. She sighed and glared at him.

'I think I like you better unconscious,' she muttered at his comatose form. 'At least you're less embarrassing.'

He mumbled off and on for the next couple of days, coming and going like a tide as the drugs fought the parasite for supremacy. Then on the morning of the third day he opened his eyes and looked at her.

'I have got one hell of a headache,' he said gruffly. 'Have I been ill?'

To her humiliation she burst into tears, dropping her face into her hands and weeping silently with relief.

'Gabby?' he murmured. 'Gabby, what's the matter?'

She sniffed hard and pulled herself together with an effort. 'You've had malaria.'

'Again?' he said heavily. 'Damn. What sort?'

'Cerebral—falciparum malaria, we think.'

His eyes widened. 'Really? No wonder my head hurts.'

She nodded. 'I've been following the instructions and treating you, and the *dukun* has been giving you something green and gruesome and chanting over you—whatever, it seems to have worked...'

She swallowed the tears again and gave him a rather watery smile. 'It's nice to have you talking sense. You've been a bit—well, away with the fairies.'

He groaned and rolled his eyes. 'Sorry.' He moved his head and groaned again. 'Could I have a drink?' he asked.

'Sure.' She poured some cool, boiled water out of a big container into a coconut shell and held it to his lips, and he sipped it and lay back.

'Thanks,' he sighed, and then his eyes drifted shut and he slept again. He continued like that off and on for the rest of the day, and although there were no more episodes of delirium he was still a bit confused and obviously sick.

That night, though, for the first time he seemed to be sleeping normally and, when she checked it, his skin seemed to be a normal temperature.

Relieved that he seemed to have turned the corner, she relaxed and slept heavily for the first time in almost a week, and when she woke he was gone.

'Jed?' she called, scrambling out of bed and pulling on her clothes.

Sue stuck her head round the doorway. 'Derek's taken him down to the pool for a wash—he felt hot and sticky. He wants to know what drugs he's had so I told him he'd have to ask you. He seems fine.'

Gabby sighed with relief and sagged against the wall. 'I didn't know where he was. I thought he might have wandered in his sleep.'

Sue laughed. 'No, just gone to freshen up. I can hear them coming back now.'

Sue's head disappeared and Gabby gathered up the bedclothes and took them down under the hut in the shade. Jed was sitting against a post, looking exhausted after his exertions, but at least he looked a little fresher.

'Feel better?' she asked him, arranging the bedclothes.

'Much. Thanks—I think I'll have a rest. I feel so weak.'

'I'm not surprised, you've been at death's door,' Derek told him bluntly.

Jed rolled over onto his hands and knees and crawled

onto the bedding, then collapsed. 'Tell me about it,' he muttered.

The others left them so Gabby could settle him to sleep, but after a moment he opened his eyes again. 'I don't suppose there are any headache pills in that flight bag?' he asked her.

'Paracetamol,' she told him.

'I'll have two—and what treatment have you been giving me?'

She helped him take the pills, then sat down beside him with the drug chart she'd improvised on the back of the leaflet and told him what he'd had and when.

'How long have I been out of it?' he asked in puzzlement when she started to list the third day.

'Four days altogether,' she told him.

He looked thoughtful. 'Oh. Right. I can remember odd bits and pieces but I didn't realise it was that long.' He took her hand, but didn't meet her eyes. 'Look, Gabby, I don't know what I said and did—I gather some of it was pretty embarrassing. It's just the way I am with malaria. It makes me a bit unihibited—just ignore it, and if I offended you I'm sorry. I've been known to do all sorts of things in the past but it doesn't mean anything.'

She grinned. 'Forget it, Jed, you didn't do anything.'

'I didn't? Good. Only I wouldn't want to have embarrassed you.' He gave a wry laugh. 'I gather I asked you to marry me once—crazy. I hope you had the good sense to ignore it. It doesn't mean anything.'

Her heart jerked painfully. 'Yes, of course I did,' she said with a little laugh. Was it as hollow as it sounded to her?

He closed his eyes and sank back against the bedclothes. 'I don't suppose there's anything interesting to drink, is there?'

'Drink?' she said numbly. 'Yes, of course. I'll get you something.'

Just ignore it? she thought. It doesn't mean anything? Nothing? None of it? Not the love-making before, either?

Of course, she realised with a shock, he'd had malaria then. Probably Hari's operation was the last thing he'd done when in full control of his faculties. So when he'd told her he loved her was that just the malaria speaking?

Hot colour scorched her cheeks when she thought of the uninhibited way she'd responded. Well, if she was lucky he wouldn't remember any of it, and so she could pretend it hadn't happened and spare them both some embarrassment.

She got some fresh coconut milk in a cup and took it in to him, and he drank it eagerly—too eagerly.

'Steady, not too much at once,' she cautioned, taking it away, and he lay down again and gave her a wry grin.

'So, what's happened while I've been out of it?' he asked after a moment.

'Not much to anyone else. Hari's much better.'

'Hari?' He blinked. 'Did I dream it, or did we—? No, we couldn't have done.'

Do what? she wondered. Make love?

'Tell me we didn't do a Caesarean section by candle-light with only herbal anaesthesia.'

So he didn't remember—yet. 'We did. She's fine, incidentally, so are the babies.'

'Babies?' Jed repeated, half sitting up then falling back with a groan and clutching his head. 'Oh, God, I want to die.'

He rolled to his side and shut his eyes, and seemed to sleep for a while. She left him to sleep until it was time for his drugs again, then she washed his face and hands and changed the rug over him for a cooler, drier one.

'I gather you looked after me almost on your own.' he said quietly as she finished.

She avoided his eyes. 'Yes, most of the time. The *dukun* helped, and so did some of the women—they sponged you down and helped me give you drinks and medicines.'

'I don't remember it. I remember hearing people talking to me and making me drink something ghastly, but nothing else. I just know it seemed endless.' He looked up at her. 'You look bloody awful,' he told her bluntly. 'Have you had any sleep?'

Sexy legs, sexy eyes, sexy everything? Only in his delirium, evidently. 'A bit last night. You kept me rather busy before that,' she told him, perhaps rather sharply because he seemed to withdraw.

'I'm sorry. I'm very grateful. I would have died without your help.'

She choked back the sob of protest. 'You didn't, though. That's all that matters. Get some rest now.'

She scrambled to her feet and all but ran down to the pool, then, heedless of any eyes on her, she stripped and dived into the chilly water. Her heart was breaking. She couldn't pretend or hide it any longer, and the noise of the waterfall that filled the pool would at least muffle her grief.

He didn't remember.

She did, though. She thought of the tenderness of his hands, the light in his eyes, the care he had taken with her. She thought of him telling her it was like coming home, and a sob rose in her throat.

Meaningless, all of it. Just empty words.

'Marry me, angel.'

She cried for what seemed like ages, then the chill of

the water drove her out and she wiped the water off her arms and legs and dressed again. When she looked up the *dukun* was standing watching her with gentle, understanding eyes, and another sob tore its way out of her chest.

'I'm just so tired,' she said. She closed her eyes, and the next thing she felt was his arms around her, cradling her very gently as she wept. Then he wiped her eyes with his gnarled old thumbs, patted her shoulder and led her back to the village.

He sent her in to Hari, who took one look at her and made her lie down on a mat in the corner. She was asleep in seconds, and she must have slept for hours.

When she woke, it was to Sue shaking her shoulder and saying something excitedly.

She opened her eyes and struggled into a sitting position, fighting the pins and needles in her arm. 'What?' she mumbled. 'Is it Jed?'

'He's got an e-mail,' Sue told her. 'It's OK, Gabby— help's on its way. We're going to be rescued!'

CHAPTER NINE

GABBY went back to their hut and found everyone in a state of great excitement.

They were clustered round Jed in his bed under the hut, and he was grinning wearily. 'My secretary just got a rise,' he announced. 'Bless her heart, she checked the e-mail, contacted Bill Freeman's office and mobilised a search party, then replied to me, telling me what was happening.'

'What *is* happening?' Gabby asked, her feelings very mixed. She'd made friends in the village, despite the language barrier—Hari and the *dukun*, and some of the other women—and she had felt herself grow closer to Jed over the twelve days they had been there.

Now, it seemed, it was all going to come to an end— possibly in the next day or so—and she wasn't sure how she would go back to her ordinary life. She would miss them—especially Jed, and she was sure their relationship would be over. He'd as good as told her that.

Derek was explaining that a group including Jon and Bill were setting off from Telok Panjang and making their way on foot from the compound, following the river and using the Magellan GCS to communicate with base and with them.

'Unfortunately, I think our battery might be about to give up the ghost,' Derek said. 'Still, at least they know where we are and can make their way towards us.'

'I need to speak to Johannis,' Jed said from his pile of bedding. 'We need him primed to deal with their arrival, and he needs to be sure exactly what it is we're able to negotiate on.'

'I agree,' Derek put in. 'I'm sure the power station will have to go ahead. The only variable will be the positioning of it, and they need to understand that.'

'Don't get overtired,' Gabby warned them both. 'You've both been ill—you must be careful. You never know, you might have to walk out of here and just at the moment you, Jed, particularly, aren't in a fit state to do it.'

'I'm fine, don't fuss,' he told her, and turned back to Derek.

'OK,' she said under her breath. 'Suit yourself.'

She walked off, leaving the others to their endless confab. So he was quite happy to let her wait on him when it suited him, but as soon as it came to taking advice, oh, no, he was fine!

'Men!' she muttered. She walked out of the village along one of the paths, her feet instinctively leading her towards the grave trees. She needed the peace and tranquillity that she found there, the almost church-like atmosphere of hushed reverence.

She was still feeling bruised inside, angry with herself for thinking that all those tender words were real and not just the product of his illness. So she'd thought that the delirium had made him more honest and uninhibited? Apparently, it just made him lie and flatter—perhaps that was the man he really was after all, a womanising flirt with a laughing eye and a ready compliment.

Damn him.

She walked under the towering grave trees and turned her face up to them. They had a quiet dignity that she needed just now, and she sat down against the trunk of one and rested her head back against it.

They were about to be rescued, and she had no idea

how she was going to cope without him. Would she ever see him again? She doubted it somehow. All the camaraderie they'd built up in the week before his illness seemed to have gone out of the window, and he was almost like a stranger now.

She stared at the little squares on the trunk of the tree facing her, and wondered about the women who'd buried their babies in there. How had they coped?

How much less significant was her own sorrow.

The crackling of a twig startled her, and she saw the man who'd been so interested in her on the day of their capture standing a few feet away, his eyes fixed on her.

In his hand was a *parang*, a sharp jungle knife, hanging loosely by his side, and the light in his eyes was chilling. He must have been waiting all this time to get her alone.

She swallowed and tried to stare him out, but he didn't move, except to coil his fingers more tightly round the handle and slowly raise the knife above his head.

Fear clawed at her. He was going to throw the knife at her!

He said something, very softly, and held his other hand up as if telling her to sit still.

'You have to be joking,' she muttered, but then out of the corner of her eye she caught a movement, a slow, weaving movement, repetitive—

There was a *swoosh* beside her ear, and she screamed, darting away from the tree as something thrashed against her, and then the man caught her in his arms and stopped her headlong flight, turning her back to face the tree.

The blade of the *parang* was buried in the bark, blood staining it, and on the ground at the base of the trunk, still twitching, lay the body of a snake.

'Oh, Lord,' she whispered. Cold sweat broke out on

the palms of her hands, and she scrubbed them against her legs.

Her 'assailant' grinned, picked up the snake and slung it over his shoulder, then picked up the head off the ground and showed it to her, pulling out the flaps of skin on each side.

A cobra. Great. Marvellous.

She gave him a sickly smile. 'Thank you,' she said fervently, and he laughed cheerfully, obviously pleased that she was impressed.

He hooked the *parang* out of the trunk, wiped the blood off it on the undergrowth and turned away, beckoning her to follow him back to the village.

She needed no second bidding. She was right there with him, almost standing on his heels in her haste to get back to safety.

As she entered the clearing Jed looked up from talking to Johannis and his eyes narrowed. She smiled at the man who'd rescued her, and to her surprise he blushed beneath his dark skin and turned away with an embarrassed giggle.

He's just shy, she thought to herself, not shifty at all, and he's fascinated by me, poor deluded boy.

Suppressing a smile, she crossed over to Jed and he glowered at her.

'If you've quite finished consorting with the natives, we've got things to sort out,' he growled. 'I want to send a reply to this e-mail, and we'll need scouts unobtrusively circulating on the outskirts of the village to leave pointers, just in case they get lost. I want you and Sue to go to the washing pool, and take the track from there downstream towards the town. The rest of you take the other tracks—not all at once. Pace yourselves and take turns.

'Leave pointers if you can, footprints of your shoes in

the track—that sort of thing. Of course if it rains it'll mess things up, but they might come before then and if not we'll have to go out and do it again.'

He looked round at everyone. 'Any questions?'

Luther nodded. 'How long will it be before they come?'

'Any time in the next few hours or days, I would guess. That depends whether or not they can find the track, if they can follow it, how many of them there are and so forth. We'll just have to be patient.'

And that, of course, was the problem. Waiting was going to be hell on nerves already stretched taut. Leaving the others, Sue and Gabby set off for the pool and found children laughing and splashing in the water.

'I'll miss the little ones,' Sue told her. 'They're so sweet and friendly, and there's one in particular who keeps bringing me little stones and things as presents.'

Gabby laughed. 'My nephews and nieces do that on walks, and sometimes I can hardly get home for the weight in my pockets!' She lost her smile then, looking round at the women and children. 'I'll miss them, too, especially Hari. She's been really sweet to me, and her babies are so lovely. I hate leaving her before she's properly healed, just in case anything goes wrong, but I suppose we'll have to.'

'I think the *dukun* will look after her,' Sue said confidently. 'He's a wonderful man, they're very lucky to have him. I think Jed wants to get to know him and learn some of his secrets. I shouldn't be at all surprised if he doesn't come back, once we're all released, just to find out more.'

Gabby leant against a tree and toed the earth idly. 'What about you and Derek? Will you stay and finish off the power station if they can agree a new site?'

Sue shrugged. 'I don't know. I didn't intend to get

pregnant, but these things happen and neither of us are getting any younger. We're both thirty-four now so I suppose it's the right time for us. I don't want Derek out here on his own, but on the other hand I don't know how I'd feel about having a baby out here.'

'I wonder if Jon and Penny will stay?' Gabby mused.

'Who knows? If Penny's here it will be easier, of course, and more fun.' Sue shrugged away from her tree and headed off casually down the path. 'Come on, we've got to make tracks, so to speak.'

They were careful to leave pronounced tracks back towards the village, deliberately treading in muddy bits to leave lasting footprints, but, of course, there was no guarantee that they would survive the rain or even be noticed.

'Do try and keep Derek quiet,' Gabby advised as they returned to the village. 'I know he thinks he's better, but he really ought to be careful. He might be less stable now, and the insulin should have been refrigerated, of course, so it might not be as good as it ought to be.'

Sue sighed. 'I'll try, but he's every bit as stubborn as Jed in his way. I'll do my best, though. What are you going to do about Jed?'

Gabby gave a short laugh. 'I think I've been told my services are no longer required,' she said a little bitterly.

'Oh, dear. I wonder if that's Derek's doing? I think he told him this morning about what he'd been saying when he was delirious, and he was apparently very embarrassed and worried he'd humiliated you.'

Gabby laughed awkwardly. 'I think I'm made of sterner stuff than that.' Anyway, it wasn't humiliation that was her problem, it was losing him.

They rejoined the others, but Jed was deep in conversation with Derek, drawing plans and discussing alternative sites and so on, and so she went to see Hari.

She was up and about now, just doing a little bit here and there, but Gabby was very much afraid she'd do too much too soon and burst her stitches. She tried to explain that to Hari in mime, and ended up having to get Johannis, with Jed's help, so she could explain the importance of being careful for the first few weeks.

The wound was healing nicely, she saw when she examined Hari, and her uterus was going down well. The babies were positively blooming, and it seemed almost impossible that five days before they'd been on the point of death.

Gabby stayed with her for lunch, holding one of the babies while Hari ate, and after they'd finished their meal she went back to the others.

'How is she?' Jed asked without preamble.

'All right, I think. Healing well, babes both fine. You did a good job.'

Was it her imagination or did his skin colour? 'Just don't ask me to do anything like that again,' he said gruffly.

Raised voices behind them made him turn his head, then sigh. 'I think the tension's getting to everyone. Waiting now is going to be the hardest part.'

'Waiting is always the hardest part of anything. Waiting for you to come back to us was pretty hellish.'

He looked down at his hands, fiddling with a twig for a moment. 'Thanks for sticking by me,' he muttered. 'I'm sorry I said all those things.'

'Actually, some of them were quite complimentary,' she said with forced brightness.

He shot her a searching look. 'I doubt if any of them did you justice. I gather I was a bit crude at times.'

She blushed and trailed her fingers through the sand, sifting it. 'Look, just forget it, Jed, OK? I have.'

He looked as if he was about to say something else,

but then he shut his mouth and turned back to the twig, tearing it into tiny little pieces. 'Luther's got a low-grade fever and bloody diarrhoea. I think he's got dysentery. Have we got anything to give him?'

'Nothing much. The rest has all been used up. I'll ask the *dukun*.'

'He'll start charging,' Jed said with a smile, the first one he'd given her all day, and she nearly cried.

'I'll bat my lashes.'

She went over to his hut and greeted him, and he put down the stick he was whittling and unfolded his frail form, following her back to the hut. She showed Luther to him, and after laying his hands on him for a moment he disappeared and came back with a few black seeds.

'Papaya seeds,' Luther said weakly. 'It's an old remedy. It works.'

'He's holding up two hands—is that ten a day? An hour?'

'A day,' Luther said. 'You have to chew them.'

'We've got a couple of sachets of electrolyte solution,' Gabby told Jed. 'Shall I make one of them up for him?'

'Yes—give him as much as he can cope with. Hopefully we'll get out of here soon and he can have proper medical attention.'

The papaya seeds seemed to help, and by the end of the afternoon he was feeling a little better although he still had a fever and diarrhoea. The *dukun* brought him something else, a powder that made him sleep and that she suspected might be related to opium. Whatever, he wasn't going to be here long enough to get addicted and sleep was the best thing for him.

It would have been the best thing for Jed, but he was too busy planning to rest. He slept for an hour, but he looked like death warmed up and wouldn't give in.

The rain had come after lunch, of course, drowning out conversation and washing away all their careful tracks, and because it was the start of the rainy season there was a spectacular thunderstorm so even if he'd wanted to sleep it would have been difficult.

Now it was evening, the sky darkening to a velvet blackness in minutes, and they gathered in their hut by the doorway and looked out at the village, settling down for the night.

'I thought we'd be gone,' Derek said, voicing everyone's thoughts and disappointments. 'I thought for sure they would have been here by now.'

'Maybe the rains have held them up,' Gabby suggested. 'Perhaps they've had landslides—some of the tracks round here are showing signs.'

'Maybe they've got lost.'

'With the technology they've got available to them? They could be put down anywhere on earth and know exactly where they were. They aren't lost,' Jed pointed out. 'I expect they've found the village and are waiting for the morning to make their move. I suggest we all get an early night so we're ready for whatever the morning brings.'

'And most particularly you,' Gabby told him firmly, and chivvied him off to bed.

It took some time to settle everyone down, but finally Gabby crawled into her bed next to Jed and lay there, listening to the jungle. After the threat with the snake earlier, it didn't seem quite the friendly place it had seemed before, and she found she was tense with the waiting and unable to sleep.

Jed, too, seemed to be wakeful. She turned her head and found him looking at her in the dim candle light. 'How's Luther?' he asked.

'Still suffering, although less so, and the powder

seemed to help. I'll have to get some more for him in the morning.'

'What about Derek?' he asked in a low undertone.

'I'm concerned about him. I think he's becoming a little hyperglycaemic. Perhaps the insulin's deteriorated with the heat.'

Jed nodded. 'That's what I was afraid of. Please, God, let them come tomorrow.'

She turned on her side, facing him. 'What do you think's holding them up?'

'Not knowing the route? There are lots of ravines and things—if you didn't know the way it could be quite tricky. It wasn't easy even on the right track.'

She chewed her lip for a second. 'What if they can't get to us? What if they never make it?'

'They'll make it,' he promised and, reaching out a hand, he cupped her cheek. His thumb idly stroked her temple, soothing her, and she felt silly tears well in her eyes. She closed them so he wouldn't see, but he must have sensed them because the next minute she was in his arms and he was cradling her against his chest.

'It's all right, Gabby,' he murmured. 'We'll be OK. You'll be out of here soon, you wait and see. It's nearly over, sweetheart.'

She slid an arm around him and moved closer, drawing comfort from his nearness. He was thinner, she realised with a shock. The malaria had drained his resources, and yet here he was, being strong for all of them when they should have been looking after him.

She felt him relax against her, and his breathing become more even. Then, when he was asleep, she let the silent tears slip down her cheeks and soak into his shirt. Was this the last time she'd ever hold him?

'If they don't come today I'm walking out of here.'

'Derek, don't be ridiculous,' Sue told him firmly.

'You'll do no such thing. Without any insulin you wouldn't get anywhere.'

'Well, I can't stay here without it, can I?' he snapped. 'I might as well take my chances in the jungle.'

'You're being absurd. Just rest and conserve your energy, and don't have too much sugary fruit.'

'I'll eat what I bloody well like—'

'Hey, hey, boys and girls, let's not fight. None of us wants to be here under these conditions, and it's almost over. Just bide your time.'

'I'm sure if we got Johannis and Jamal out of their hut we could make it back down—'

'Before they get us with their blowpipes? I don't think so,' Jed said drily. 'They might be friendly and pleasant at the moment because there's nothing at stake, but once they decide if they're going to go and negotiate this change of site we might find we're much more closely guarded. I think at the moment they're keeping us here to make Bill and the government sweat. It suits them to do so, and they know we won't do anything silly without Jamal or Johannis to guide us. That's why they're always so closely guarded.'

'They could have told us the way,' Derek argued. 'We haven't even asked them!'

'You can get lost in the middle of London with an A to Z!' Sue told him bluntly. 'What are they going to say—turn left at the big fern? Get real!'

'Well, we could try—'

'And die in the attempt. Thanks, but no thanks—'

'Hush! What's that?' Gabby said.

They all stopped talking then, cocking their heads and listening.

'Have I gone off my trolley or is that a helicopter?' Jed murmured quietly.

'My God!' Derek said. 'I'll stick my head out of the door and have a squint.'

He left the room, and they waited, listening, until it was obvious that, yes, it was a helicopter and, yes, it was coming in to land, or at least to hover just overhead.

They all ran to the door, to find Derek on the ground, waving frantically at a craft about fifty feet above the ground. The dust was swirling up around the huts, and the villagers were running, screaming, men, women and children scattering in all directions as a hatch opened and a ladder was thrown out.

Bill was the first to descend, followed by Jon, another man in shorts and T-shirt and a government official in a safari suit. As soon as the last one was off the ladder the helicopter lifted up and away, and as the dust settled so the villagers began to creep back out from their hiding places, spears and blowpipes at the ready.

Derek, Sue and the Indonesians ran towards them, but Jed hung back. 'Why couldn't they just walk in?' he muttered, and Gabby turned and looked at him.

'You look like death—you should be lying down.'

'And miss this? No way,' he replied, and then ruined it all by swaying against the ladder and nearly falling over.

'Stubborn fool,' she said firmly and, tucking herself into his armpit, she draped his arm over her shoulder, hung onto his wrist and almost carried him across the clearing to the others.

Then there was lots of hugging and backslapping before Jed called them all to order.

'I think, gentlemen, we should get down to business,' he said. 'Jamal and Johannis are here and ready to trans-late—I think it might be politically correct to introduce you to the key players. You do understand about the grave trees?'

'Oh, yes,' Bill assured him. 'We've examined the site and agree with you. We can't possibly build it there. We just have to negotiate an alternative.'

Gabby felt the tension drain out of her shoulders. She was sure it would now be all right.

With Gabby supporting him, Jed went over to the edge of the group of villagers, where the chief and the *dukun* were standing together in hastily donned ceremonial garb, and smiled and bowed at them.

'Jamal? Johannis?' Jed asked, and the chief waved at a man who brought the men to the edge of the circle.

'Jamal, ask Johannis to tell them these men have come to talk about the grave trees and to apologise for having threatened the sacred place.'

They waited while the translations were carried out, and then the chief and the *dukun* looked at Jon, Bill and the two other men and bowed their heads slightly.

'The chief says the trees must stay,' Jamal informed her.

'We understand that. There are other ways. Please will they talk about them?'

The message came back that, yes, they would talk.

Jed introduced the chief and the *dukun*, and Jon introduced himself, Bill and the other two, one of whom was from the government, the other from the International Red Cross. The men disappeared under the chief's hut, and Gabby, heart in mouth, followed them and sat down at a polite distance in case she was needed. The others joined her, straining their ears to listen to the conversation.

Coffee was served first, and once the ceremony had taken place the negotiating could begin. She saw the *dukun* produce her drawing, and the government inspector nodded and looked at Bill, who produced a sheaf of paper from his pocket.

The papers were handed backwards and forwards, considered and studied, thought about and argued over, and then once again the *dukun* took them and tucked them into his belt and turned away.

'OK, guys, I think your audience is over,' Jed told them softly. 'Come and see the others. The *dukun* will talk to the elders and consider it. It's all down to him now.'

Jon had brought insulin in case Derek had run out, and Jed tested him and found his blood sugar soaring again. Tutting, he gave him a double dose of the new, fresh insulin, and after an hour he began to feel better again.

Luther, though, was still causing concern and Gabby could tell Jed was worried. What they needed—what they all needed—was to get out of there and have a proper medical check-up. She met Jed's eyes and he winked reassuringly, as if to say, 'Don't worry, it's nearly over.'

Nothing in Indonesia moves fast. It took five hours for the elders to agree—five hours in which the tension rose to unbearable levels. They were closely guarded now, herded together into the hut with Jamal and Johannis, and by the time they were summoned tempers were well and truly frayed.

The key players disappeared again with Johannis and Jamal, and after another hour Jon came up the ladder, grinning.

'You're free to go. We're going to renegotiate the site—we're meeting the elders down there in a couple of days, and we're going to get you all airlifted out of here in the next couple of hours. Gabby, tell me, who's first?'

'Derek,' she said emphatically. 'He needs stabilising in hospital. Sue—she's pregnant and needs checking up.

Luther has dysentery, and Jed's been extremely ill with cerebral malaria and needs proper treatment. The rest of us are well.'

He nodded. 'I'll get those four sent out first, then, and next you and the others, and Bill and I can go last with the interpreter.'

He left the hut and went out to the others, and a very short time later they heard the whop-whop-whop of the returning helicopter.

It returned for Gabby after an hour, and she bid a tearful goodbye to Hari and the *dukun*. As they rose up in the air the village seemed to disappear, swallowed by the trees, vanishing like a myth.

'I'm sure it can't be anything serious.'

'You look awful—you're suffering from lassitude, nausea, tiredness, lack of appetite—you're coming in for a whole battery of tests, young lady, and that's all there is to it. You could have picked up anything.'

She looked at Jed, fit and well now, sitting on the edge of his desk in the tropical diseases hospital she gathered he worked in when he wasn't swanning about in the tropics, and sighed. 'All right, if you insist.'

'We'll keep you in overnight,' he told her, and her silly heart did a crazy leap. She'd see him! That was worth any amount of tests.

'What are you looking for?' she asked him.

'Anything unusual. My secretary will arrange your admission. I have to fly, I've got another clinic, but I'll see you later.'

He patted her shoulder on the way past, leaving her with a sense of emptiness when he had gone. Funny how it seemed so much colder without his presence.

'Miss Andrews?'

She stood up. 'Yes. I gather I have to come in.'

She'd met his secretary, the woman who had had the initiative to check his e-mails, and she now discovered she was extremely efficient. She flipped open a diary, ran her finger down the days and turned to her. 'Tuesday to Wednesday—all right?'

'That's tomorrow.'

'Yes. Is that too short notice? I think he wants to get the results quickly.'

She shook her head. 'That'll do. I've got my things with me, I was going to stay with a friend.'

'In which case, could you make it today? He thought you probably couldn't, but I think he'd prefer it if you were able to.'

'Fine. If I could just use the phone to ring my parents and my friend, I can stay now.'

'Good. Here, use Jed's phone. I'll come and get you in a minute—I'll just notify the ward.'

His office was functional but very pleasant. She wondered what kind of research assistant he was, and how he came to have his own secretary. Perhaps his research into malaria was a little more organised and well orchestrated than she'd realised…

The tests were apparently endless, involving copious blood-letting and samples from every conceivable part of her. They were sent off to labs, and her heart and brain waves were all charted and inspected and reported as normal.

On the Tuesday her parents arrived to visit her and wait with her for the results, and although some might not be available for a few more days they were going to take her home.

Jed didn't seem to be around much during all of this, to her disappointment. She'd missed him so badly in the past two weeks she couldn't imagine how she would get through the rest of her life, but she'd thought at least she'd see him while she was in the same hospital.

He'd popped in the evening before and told her that they'd agreed a new site for the power station and it was now going ahead with everyone's blessing. 'Johannis has apparently been forgiven for his indiscretion because of his part in the negotiations, and he's been allowed back into the tribe, so I'm going back there in a few days to try and find out what I can from the *dukun*. Anyway, someone has to take out Hari's stitches.'

'They will have dissolved by now.'

He grinned. 'Maybe. I ought to check, though.'

'You're a sucker for punishment,' she said with a smile. 'I knew you'd go back. Give Hari my love when you see her.'

'I will. You get some rest now, you're looking peaky.'

And he'd left her alone to consider the fact that he was leaving the country shortly for heaven knew how long. It was silly to feel so bereft. He'd never promised her anything, except, of course, in the throes of malaria, and she could hardly hold him to those extravagant words.

She'd slept fitfully in the strange bed, and now she was up and dressed, sitting on the edge of the bed talking to her parents about the tests and waiting. Would she see him today?

The Nigerian doctor who'd been dealing with her came in and smiled at her and her parents. 'Well, we've got all the results back that we need,' he told them cheerfully. 'There's nothing to worry about, you'll be pleased to know—'

The door opened and Jed came in, wearing a white coat and looking for the first time like a real doctor.

'Ah, Professor,' Dr Mgabe said.

Professor?

Jed? A professor?

'I was just telling your patient that we have all the results now and there's nothing wrong with her at all. In fact, she's a very fit and healthy woman. She is simply pregnant.'

'What?' Gabby took a deep, steadying breath and looked at Jed, hope flaring in her heart. 'What?' she said again.

'You're having a baby, my dear—nothing more complicated than that.'

Jed looked stunned. He stared at her as if he'd seen a ghost, and then with what looked like a huge effort he sucked in a breath and let it out again. 'Well—that's good, I suppose. Nothing nasty. Fine. Right. Well, ah— I suppose this is it. Um—take care. I'll send you a postcard.'

And he turned on his heel and walked out.

'Well, that's it, you can go home just as soon as you're ready,' Dr Mgabe told her with a smile, and he followed Jed out.

'Darling?' Mrs Andrews said softly.

Gabby stood up on wooden legs. 'We'd better go, then. Um—I've got a case—'

'I'll pack it,' her father said quietly. 'Meg, I think she needs a hug.'

'No!' She moved away, holding herself rigid with enormous effort. 'No. Don't touch me. I'm all right. Just get me out of here.'

They did. They put her in the car and drove her home to their farm in Gloucestershire, and her mother made her a drink and put her to bed, and then went out, clicking the door softly shut behind her.

Then and only then did she allow herself to cry...

CHAPTER TEN

JED pulled up at the end of the drive and sat for a moment, looking at the house. Big, built of stone, it looked a real family home—the sort of place you could retreat to, where your family would close ranks around you.

He switched off the ignition and picked up his mobile phone, keying in her number. A woman answered, sounding like her and yet not.

Her mother?

'Mrs Andrews?' he hazarded a guess.

'Yes.'

'Could I speak to Gabrielle, please? It's Jed Daniels.'

There was silence for a second, and then her mother said, 'She's not here.'

'Oh.' Disappointment and relief fought inside him, and disappointment won. 'Can you tell me when she'll be back?'

'Well, she is here and she's not. She's in one of the cottages, but she's not on the phone yet. Can I get her to call you? I'll see her later.'

'Um…' He hesitated, then said, 'I'm at the end of the drive. Perhaps I could just call and see her.'

There was another pause. 'Well, I suppose so—come up to the house. I'll give you directions.'

He pulled up outside the front of the house and Mrs Andrews came down the steps to meet him, wiping her hands on an apron. She'd been baking, he imagined from the smudge of flour on her nose. It made her look more approachable.

She stopped at the bottom of the steps and he got out

of the car. They stood there for a moment, weighing each other up.

'The cottage is over there,' she said without preamble, pointing across a field. 'You have to go back down the drive and take the track off it. She's probably in the garden—go round the back.'

'Are you sure she won't mind?' he asked, suddenly doubtful about the wisdom of this.

'No, I'm not sure of anything except I think it's about high time you came to see her. She's had a lot to cope with, and she could have done with some support.'

He ducked his head. 'I'm sorry. I've been away again—back to Pulau Panjang. It's not very easy to pop in from there.'

'Well, you're here now, that's all that matters. Just don't upset her.'

He scuffed the ground, feeling like a teenager. 'Is she OK? The baby?'

'They're fine. She'll tell you.'

He nodded and got back into the car, turned it around and headed down the drive. She was still standing there on the steps, watching him.

He found the grassy track, followed it and pulled up outside a pretty little cottage, with flowers blooming in colourful disarray all around the front. He cut the engine and got out, closing the door softly.

Crazy. His palms were sweating, his legs felt like jelly and his mouth was dry. For two pins he'd have got back in the car and driven away, but that wouldn't help at all. He retrieved the parcel from the back seat and knocked on the front door, but there was no reply. Taking Gabby's mother's advice, he went round the back to the garden.

She was there, standing with her back to him bending over a rose, and he stood there riveted to the spot and just drank in the sight of her. She was wearing the sarong Jamal's daughter had given her, and it looked soft and faded and well loved.

He thought she was probably naked under it, and desire raked through him just as she straightened and turned, and he realised with a shock that she was still pregnant.

Pain stabbed him, taking his breath, and then common sense resurrected itself and he dragged in a lungful of sultry summer air.

'Hello, Gabrielle,' he said softly, and she looked up and froze.

'Jed,' she whispered, the roses she had just picked falling unheeded at her feet.

He bent and picked them up, handing them back to her with trembling fingers. 'How are you?' he asked gruffly, and cleared his throat. God, how could he behave normally when all he wanted to do was drag her into his arms and tell her how much he'd missed her?

'All right. What brings you here? Run out of research material?'

She turned and went back towards the cottage and he followed her into the kitchen. 'I've finished. I've brought some photos to show you—of Hari and the babies, and all the others.'

'How are they?' she asked with a smile.

'Fine. Gorgeous. You're a legend over there, you know—the woman that bullied the *dukun*.'

She laughed. 'Someone had to force the issue. She was dying.'

'Yes.' He put down the bag he'd brought from the car and propped his hips against the worktop, looking at her. She'd filled the kettle and was getting mugs down out of a cupboard.

'Tea?' she asked.

'Anything.' He looked at her swollen body and felt a great surge of protective instinct. 'I thought you would have had the baby by now,' he said, struggling for small talk.

'No—it's not due for another fortnight.'

'Oh.' Funny, he'd thought— Oh, well, never mind. He hadn't been thinking clearly then. 'You—um—you haven't got married?'

'Married?' She dropped two teabags into a pot and looked at him. 'No, I haven't got married. Should I have done?'

'I thought—maybe the father—?'

Something happened in her eyes, something sad that made him want to take her in his arms. Anger flickered inside him at the unknown man.

'The father isn't interested,' she told him bluntly.

'Oh.' How could he not be? How could any man turn away from her and her child? Hell, he couldn't, and it was nothing to do with him!

'Is there—um—you know—any—ah—other man—?'

She eyed him straight. 'No, Jed, there's no other man.' She turned to pour the water on the teabags. 'No one at all.'

Hope dawned in him, but he suppressed it. She wasn't interested. She'd said so, at the top of her voice on Monkey Skull Island.

His next words came unbidden, without permission.

'I've missed you.'

She looked up at him sharply and looked away. 'Have you?'

'Yes. Every day.' He looked down at his fingers. 'Funny, I never knew you were missing from my life until I met you, and since then nothing's felt the same.' He gave a short laugh. 'Crazy, isn't it?'

'Jed, what are you trying to say?'

He looked up at her but he couldn't read her expression. She was good at hiding her feelings—all those years of nursing, he supposed.

'I don't know. Only that I want you in my life, and—well, I know it's different these days and loads of women have babies on their own, but if you didn't want to—well, I'm around—'

'Are you offering to be there for the birth?' she asked somewhat incredulously.

'Well—not exactly. Yes, if you wanted me to, but I had in mind perhaps the next fifty-odd years, really.' He swallowed. Hell, this was difficult. He'd never proposed to anyone in his life and he was floundering like a beached whale. 'I think I'm asking you to marry me.'

She gave him a suspicious look. 'Have you got malaria?'

He laughed, a little nervously. 'No, of course not.'

'I just wondered. So, why would you want to marry me?'

He stared at her. 'Because I love you.' He waved a hand. 'I know you don't necessarily love me, but I promise I'd look after you and the baby, and treat it as if it were my own, and perhaps later we could have others, if you wanted…' He trailed to a halt and stopped.

'Forget it. I can see it doesn't appeal. I'm sorry.'

'Oh, you're wrong,' she said softly. 'It does appeal—it appeals enormously. I just wondered what changed your mind about me.'

His brows pleated together. 'Changed my mind? When?'

'When we came home. Well, before, really, but you were very preoccupied and you'd been ill so I could forgive that, but when that doctor told us all I was pregnant you just said goodbye and went, in seconds. I thought you hated me.'

'Hated you? I loved you. I was going to get you better and finish my research, and when everything had settled down again I was going to ask you out, but then I realised that there must be someone else and I felt a fool. You'd told me, after all, that there wasn't anyone so it came as a bit of a surprise.'

'There wasn't.'

'So when—if the baby's not due yet,' he said, going back to the thing that was nagging in his mind, 'when did you—? Was it after we came back?'

She shook her head.

'So there had been someone.'

'No. It happened in Indonesia. I met someone and fell in love.'

Pain stabbed him again. 'Oh. I see.' He cast his mind back through the time they'd been together, and drew a blank. 'Who?' he asked. 'Not your cousin, surely, or Derek?'

'No.'

'Bill.' He said it flatly, as if it left a bad taste in his mouth.

'No. Not Bill.'

'One of the Indonesians, then? Luther?'

She shook her head. 'You've forgotten someone, Jed.'

He thought of the young man who'd lusted after her. He'd seen them coming out of the jungle, laughing, the day before they'd been released. Had they started a relationship while he'd had malaria?

'Who?' he asked hoarsely.

'You.'

The word didn't register for a moment, and when it did he felt the blood drain from his face. 'Me?' he said soundlessly.

His eyes dropped to the swollen abdomen under the sarong, and a great lump formed in his throat. 'Me?' he said again, and emotion rose up and choked him. He turned his head, fighting the foolish tears that prickled at the back of his eyes.

'But—I'd remember—'

'You had malaria.'

He looked back at her, seeing the truth in her eyes, and the tears spilt over and splashed onto his shirt. 'Why didn't you tell me—'

He scrubbed a hand through his hair and fought for composure. 'Damn it, all this time you've needed me here to look after you and you didn't tell me—Gabby, I missed you so much—'

His voice cracked and he scooped her into his arms, hugging her fiercely to his chest. He could hardly reach her for the baby between them so he hooked out a chair with his foot and sat down, pulling her onto his lap and burying his face in her soft breasts.

Wave after wave of emotion washed him—relief, shock, love, hope for the future—swamping him so that he could hardly think.

'I ought to be able to remember,' he said eventually. 'Imagine doing something so fundamental as making a baby and not remembering it afterwards.'

'You were very ill. It was right at the beginning—straight after we operated on Hari. We stayed up till dawn, then went to bed and—well, it just happened.'

He tipped his head back and looked into her eyes, striving for a memory. 'Was it all right? I didn't hurt you or anything? If I was delirious I might not have been very communicative—'

'You were wonderful,' she said softly and, bending her head, she kissed him, then slipped off his lap and took his hand. 'Come to bed,' she murmured.

'But—the baby—'

'The baby's fine. I'm not. I've missed you so much.'

Her façade crumbled and tears welled in her eyes. 'I thought you didn't love me. I thought you just wanted me out of your life. I thought you thought the baby was just the excuse you needed—'

'Sounds like you thought much too much,' he said gently.

'I've had nothing else to do for eight months.'

'Oh, darling.' He wrapped an arm round her shoulders and squeezed. 'Where's the bedroom?'

'Here.' She pushed open a door and they went into a pretty, airy little room with white bedlinen and soft, floaty curtains.

It made him smile, but only until they reached the bed. Then she freed the top of the sarong and it fell to her feet, and his breath jammed in his throat.

Reaching out trembling hands, he laid them on the warm skin of her abdomen, over his child, and tears welled in his eyes again. 'Oh, angel,' he murmured brokenly. 'I love you so much.'

She undid his shirt buttons and pushed the garment off his shoulders, then freed his belt. His fingers came back to life and he stripped off the rest of his things and lifted her, setting her down gently in the middle of the bed.

'Are you sure this is all right?' he asked.

'It's fine. It might be a little complicated, but it's possible, I'm told.'

He laughed softly, then sobered. 'Just stop me if I hurt you or it's uncomfortable.'

She didn't stop him. She just held him, and cried out, and he lost himself in the magic of her body. She was right, it was complicated, but it was beautiful to hold her, to feel the child kick against his abdomen and know that it was his.

It reduced him to tears again but it didn't matter because Gabby was crying too, and he just shifted so he was lying on his back and she was on her side, one leg draped over him, and he held her tight until their hearts slowed and their tears dried on their cheeks.

'OK?' he asked her, and she nodded, her hair like a halo around her head. He stroked it, loving the feel of it—the feel of her.

'I feel as if I've come home,' he said softly, and she lifted her head and stared at him.

'You said that before.'

'Did I? I've never felt like this with anyone else. It just seems so right to be here with you like this.'

'Good. It needs to because it's where you're going to be for a jolly long time, Professor Daniels.'

He felt his skin colour. 'Don't call me that, I hate it.'

She laughed softly at him. 'I thought they were joking at first. I didn't realise you were a real professor. It was only then that I realised your research might actually be valid and genuine, you know.'

'I kept telling you.'

'I know. I just didn't listen. I'm sorry.'

He hugged her. 'Don't be. It's all right—now.' He shifted his head so he could see her. 'Perhaps you'd want to tell your mother you're OK. She was a bit wary about me.'

'Of course she was. She knows you're the father of her grandchild, and she thinks you dumped me.'

'I had malaria! Anyway, you didn't seem to want to know. I didn't want to push myself in where I wasn't welcome.'

'I'll speak to her. I suppose she'll want to start planning a wedding. It'll have to be September or October now, of course—'

'What?' He sat bolt upright and looked down at her. 'Sorry, darling. I'm an old-fashioned man. This baby's going to be born in wedlock if it kills me—just resign yourself to getting married in about three days. If you want a big palaver with lots of relatives, we can have a church wedding later with all the pomp and circumstance you could dream of, but we're getting married just as soon as the registrar can do the paperwork.'

To his relief she smiled. 'Good. I agree. I just didn't want to hassle you. I don't want a big wedding at all, just a few friends and family.'

Women had a gift for hyperbole, Jed discovered three days later. 'A few friends and family' turned out to be over fifty people, a hastily erected marquee and a catered finger buffet.

'Thank God you didn't want a big wedding,' he said laughingly to her as they stood side by side, preparing to cut the cake.

'What?' She looked round and chuckled. 'This is Mum. I had nothing to do with it. I was busy trying to find a dress that didn't look like another marquee or a set of net curtains in a stiff breeze.'

He hugged her, laughing till the tears ran down his face, and then held her at arm's length. 'You look beautiful,' he assured her proudly. 'I can't wait to get you away from here.'

'Where are we going?' she asked for the hundredth time, but he just smiled and refused to tell her. 'You'll find out,' he promised. 'Now, smile for the birdie, the cameraman wants our attention again.'

'Open your eyes.'

She looked around at the elegant façade of the familiar and very exclusive hotel and smiled. 'It's lovely. It's always been one of my dreams to come here. How on earth did you find a hotel like this so close to home with a vacancy at this time of year?'

He grinned, obviously pleased with himself. 'Easy. Friends run it. They were able to jiggle it, but only for three days.' He slid out from behind the wheel and came round to open her door. 'We've got a little private lodge on the edge of the woods, with its own hot tub and maid service and telephone, and we can either have room service or eat in the main building, depending on what you want.'

'Room service,' she said instantly, making him laugh. She grinned. 'I do. I don't want to get up at all the whole time we're here. I can't think of anything more wonderful than lying about in a hot tub and relaxing. They can send the food over and you can feed me.'

'You'll come out like a prune.'

'I don't care. I just want to be pampered.'

His eyes darkened. 'Good, because I have lots of that in mind for you.'

'I said pampered, not seduced.'

He laughed again and helped her out of the car, then, offering her his arm, he led her inside. It was cool, the interior lofty and quietly elegant. It must be costing a fortune, she thought, and then put it out of her mind. It was once in their lives, and she was going to love every second of it.

'Mr and Mrs Daniels,' he said to the girl behind the reception desk.

'Ah, yes. You've got the honeymoon lodge. I'll get Nick to take you over.'

A young man in livery appeared and showed them down a tree-lined path to the little lodge, nestling in the trees at the edge of the park. 'I'll bring your car round with your luggage, sir,' he said to Jed, and disappeared, leaving them to look round.

Gabby sat on the comfy sofa and bounced. 'Oh, it's lovely—soft but firm. I wonder what the bed's like?'

He opened a door and whistled, and she got up and went and peered round him. 'Oh, my. A four-poster.'

'And French doors out to the private patio with hot tub.'

'Mmm.'

'Just hang on. He'll be back in a minute with the car and you can do what you like.'

Jed's BMW slid to a halt outside, and Nick came in with the keys and the cases. 'There's champagne on ice on the house, and the hot tub's full and ready to go. Will there be anything else, sir?' he asked.

'No, thank you, that's fine.' He handed him a folded note, took the keys and turned to Gabby. 'Right, my darling, about this tub.'

They played in it for ages, sipping champagne, then moved to the bed and made love slowly and languorously. Room service brought a light supper of cold smoked salmon and salad with fresh crusty rolls, and they curled up on the sofa and watched a soppy old film on the television, before going to bed early.

The next day was more of the same, and by the evening she was feeling totally relaxed.

The next day, though, she woke with dull backache. 'I thought the bed was a bit soft,' she said ruefully. 'That's the price you pay for comfort.'

'Turn over,' Jed ordered gently, and rubbed her back, then nibbled her neck.

She laughed and swatted him away. 'I'll have breakfast in the hot tub,' she told him, and slid her feet over the side of the bed and vanished into the bathroom. By the time she came out he'd uncovered the tub, called room service and their coffee and croissants were on the way.

He fed her in the tub, little bites of croissant with rich strawberry conserve, and trailed little nibbly kisses over her neck and throat as she swallowed.

She giggled and swatted him away again. 'Stop it, you're tickling me.'

'Sorry.' He put down the plate, took her into his arms and kissed her thoroughly. 'Is that better?'

Would she never tire of looking into those beautiful blue eyes?

'Much better,' she said with a smile.

His hand ran lightly over her abdomen and left a shivery trail in its wake. 'How can I be so pregnant and you still want me?' she asked, faintly amazed. 'Come to that, how can I still want you?'

His mouth quirked in a smile. 'We always did have something pretty explosive in the way of chemistry,' he reminded her. 'Hopefully, Mrs Daniels, we always will.'

She ran her finger over his jaw, feeling the stubble and remembering Pulau Panjang. 'Mmm, we did. Call me Mrs Daniels again, I like the sound of it.'

'Mrs Daniels. Mrs John Daniels.'

She swivelled her head. 'Why *are* you Jed and not John?'

'Because my father's John, and the alternative was Jack. I didn't fancy being called after a whiskey so I opted for my initials—John Edward Daniels. Simple.'

'It doesn't sound like a professor.'

He grimaced. 'I hate being a professor. It sounds so erudite and formal.'

'Or mad. I shall have to watch you as you grow older. Only five years to go and you're forty. Maybe you'll go off the rails then.'

'I thought, according to you, I already was.'

'Ah, but you had the good taste to marry me.'

He grinned. 'So I did.' He bent his head and blew the

bubbles away from the slope of her breasts, then trailed a finger across the pale skin. 'I don't suppose you want to finish this off in bed?' he asked softly.

She smiled and held out her hand, and he stood up and pulled her to her feet. As he did so she felt a massive tightening in her abdomen, a hugely powerful gathering of forces. Her eyes widened. 'Jed?'

'What is it?'

'I think we're going to have to put off finishing this for a while,' she said, struggling to breathe normally.

'What's wrong?'

The cramp eased and she smiled uncertainly at him. 'I think I'm in labour.'

His jaw dropped, and then he scooped her up and carried her through to the bedroom, setting her down gently on the bed. 'I'll call for a doctor.'

She laughed. 'You are a doctor. Just give me a minute and I'll get dressed and we can go to the hospital. It's only a few minutes away.'

He sat down, and a moment later she had another contraction, this one even more powerful. She tried to relax, but it was just too strong and she had to push—

'Aagh!'

Jed ran for the phone and called Reception, and told them to get a doctor to them quickly. Then he ran back.

'Just stay with me,' she panted. 'You can deliver it— you delivered Hari's by Caesarean section in candlelight with a kitchen knife and they all survived—I'm sure we'll be all right.'

He took her hands and held them tight. 'I love you,' he told her fervently. 'Just remember that when you end up hating me because I got you pregnant.'

She laughed. 'I won't hate you. I love you much too much—oh!'

Ten minutes later, when the door opened to admit the

doctor and the receptionist, Jed was sitting on the side of the bed with his daughter in his arms and a rather thunderstruck smile on his face.

'Good job I hurried,' the doctor said drily.

Gabby just smiled. She was glad the doctor had been too late because nothing on earth could compare with being alone with Jed and seeing his face when he lifted their baby in his hands...

EPILOGUE

HE LOOKED like something out of an old B-movie.

Faded khaki shirt and shorts, feet propped up on the veranda, hat tipped over his face, chair tilted onto its back legs—and he was in the shade. Gabby should have disliked him on sight.

His shirtsleeves were rolled up to expose deeply tanned and hair-strewn forearms, rippling with lean muscle, and long, rangy legs strewn with more of the same gold-tinged wiry hair stuck out of the bottoms of crumpled shorts. His feet were bare and bony, with strong, high arches and little tufts of hair on the toes. They were at her eye level as she approached the steps to the veranda, and a little imp inside her nearly tickled them.

She couldn't see his face because of the battered Panama hat tipped over his eyes, but his fingers were curled loosely around a long, tall glass of something that looked suspiciously like gin and tonic. The side of the glass was beaded with tiny droplets of water, and in the unrelenting tropical heat it drew her eyes like a magnet.

She reached for the glass.

'Don't even think about it.'

She blinked at the deep growl that emerged from under the hat. She thought she saw the gleam of an eye, but she wasn't sure. He hadn't moved so much as a single well-honed muscle.

'I'm thirsty.'

'So get your own. I need this, I've been busy.'

She poked her tongue out and his arm snaked out and grabbed her leg, hooking her closer. His hand slid up the inside of her thigh and curled possessively around it, his palm icy from the glass. 'Go and put on something with long sleeves, and some sensible shoes and trousers. I've got a surprise for you.'

Long sleeves? She'd been about to head for one of the resort's many pools. 'What about Bethany?'

'She's all ready. We're waiting for you.'

'You've got shorts on.'

'I'll change.'

The chair crashed to the floor and he unfolded himself, tipped back his hat and grinned at her, clearly pleased with himself.

'Where are we going?'

He tapped the side of his nose. 'Just go and change.'

She did, wondering what on earth he had in mind. A trip to Monkey Skull Island? Hardly a surprise—they'd done it once. The power-station site? Ditto.

It was too far to the village, the only other place she really wanted to go, and not even Jed was mad enough to have hired a helicopter.

He scooped Bethany out of her playpen and blew raspberries on her tummy while Gabby changed, then fastened her securely into the baby seat of Sue's and Derek's Jeep that mysteriously seemed to appear just around the corner in the shade.

They headed up the hill out of the resort, past Telok Panjang and the bungalows where Jon and Penny and their children and Sue and Derek and their little boy lived, and up towards the power station. The road was vastly improved—but she knew that, just as she knew that the grave trees and their surroundings were now protected by an enclosure, with a sign that explained what they were and asked people to treat the area with respect.

'This,' she said drily, 'is not a surprise. We've been here.'

He just smiled and turned into a clearing in front of the resited power station, and there, sitting on the ground, was a gleaming white helicopter with *Freeman* written on the side in red.

She looked at Jed. 'Where *are* we going?' she asked, excitement catching her for the first time. 'Tell me, dammit. We're going to the village, aren't we?'

He just grinned, lifted the baby out of her seat in the back and straightened her sun hat, then headed towards the helicopter.

'Hi, Bill. All ready?'

The developer grinned down at Gabby from the cockpit. 'Morning, Gabby. Happy anniversary.'

She climbed up beside him. 'Morning. Thank you. Jed, where are we going? Is it the village?'

But Bill fired up the engine and the rotors started to turn, drowning out his reply. The door slammed, they were strapped in and then they were off, swooping low over the canopy and following the line of the river up into the hills.

Suddenly a tiny clearing appeared ahead, not much more than a gap in the trees, and Bill was setting them down on the familiar patch of bare earth in the centre of the village.

He cut the engine and opened the door so that they could climb out, and as they stepped out into the sunshine the wide-eyed children started to seep back out of the fringe of trees.

'Gabby?'

She turned at the voice, and saw a graceful young woman with two gorgeous little children clutching her legs standing in the shade of a hut.

'Hari? It *is* you!' She ran towards her and hugged her,

tears clogging her throat. Then she crouched down and looked at the babies, twin boys with bright, curious eyes and chubby cheeks. 'They're beautiful,' she said softly, and had to swallow hard. They could so easily have died. She stroked their shoulders and they turned their heads away and clung to their mother, clearly overawed.

Gabby straightened with a smile, just as Hari patted her on the shoulder and looked towards Jed. He was coming towards them with the baby, and she took Bethany from him and handed her to Hari. The little one beamed, a great gap-toothed smile with sparkling blue eyes inherited from her father, and Hari laughed when the baby pulled her hair and explored her face with chubby little hands.

'There's somebody else to see you,' Jed said softly, and she turned just as the crowd parted and a wizened old man limped towards her.

'The *dukun*—oh, yes!' And, without any thought for cultural differences and social standing, she ran over to him and hugged him, then stood back and looked at him. 'Oh, I've wanted to see you so much,' she said, choked, and to her surprise Jed translated.

The old man's face lit up in a beaming smile that almost matched Bethany's, and he patted her shoulder and drew her into the shade under his hut. Jed, the chief and Bill followed, and the children were whisked away by the older girls and the women.

Hari brought them coffee and little cakes, and then sat and joined them, and Jed and Bill managed to act as translators. They talked about the resort, and the trees, and little Bethany, and the *dukun* took Gabby's hand in his and looked searchingly at her, then said something to Jed.

He looked puzzled, then something dawned in his

eyes. The *dukun* handed her a piece of wizened root, and she smiled in understanding and put it in her pocket.

Then it was time to go, and they bade their friends an emotional farewell. It was only later, after they were alone again and the baby was asleep, that Jed turned her in his arms.

'Was he right?'

She smiled. 'The old man? Of course.'

'We're having a boy.'

'Are we?'

'So he said. Do you need the ginger root?'

She patted her pocket. 'I'll keep it for insurance—just in case. Sue says it works better than the commercial variety. I wonder what Bethany will make of a little brother?'

Jed laughed. 'Mincemeat, if she's as bossy as you are with me. Poor lad, I feel sorry for him already.' He rested his forehead against hers. 'How about slipping out of those things and putting on something cool and refreshing?'

'Like what?'

'A *mandi*?'

She leant back in his arms and smiled. 'With you?'

He grinned wickedly. 'Of course. That's the best thing about this resort of Bill's—he's taken the best bits of everything and put them together. After we've played around in the water we can come back into the air-conditioned cabin and—well, play some more.'

She laughed softly. 'Again?'

'It is our wedding anniversary.'

'So what's your excuse every other day of the last year?'

He chuckled. 'How can it be my fault if you drive me crazy?'

She smiled and pulled off her clothes. 'Last one in the *mandi*'s a rotten egg,' she laughed over her shoulder, and ran…

The Outback Nurse

CAROL MARINELLI

For Dad, with love always.

CHAPTER ONE

'BUT there must be some other work—anything?' Olivia fought for control, trying to keep the note of panic from her voice.

'Ms Morrell, we have plenty of work on our books, particularly for someone with your casualty experience. However, as you've said you will only consider a live-in position, it makes things very difficult. Even the large teaching hospitals are cutting back on their living accommodation—the agency nurses just don't get a look-in.'

Olivia nodded. She had heard it all before. This was the fifth agency she had tried and the only one that had actually come up with a job—a live-in position nursing a recently disabled gentleman in Melbourne. The work in itself didn't worry her, but in her present emotional state Olivia doubted if she would be much good at bolstering the young man's spirits.

'Well, thank you for your time.' Olivia stood up, smoothing her smart grey skirt. Trying to blink back the ever-threatening tears, she reached for her bag. 'If anything comes in, you will let me know?'

Miss Lever looked up from the files she was half-heartedly flicking through. Suddenly she felt sorry for Olivia for despite the designer clothes, immaculate hair and make-up she obviously wasn't as together as she first appeared.

'Just a moment.' Miss Lever tapped the keyboard of her computer. 'I'm sure this won't remotely interest you, but I did receive an e-mail today from our New South Wales office. It would seem they're having trouble filling a particular vacancy. It is live-in, but I can't imagine....' Her voice trailed off as she printed off the particulars.

'Tell me about it,' Olivia said sitting down sharply. Surely there must be a job for her.

'The position is for a charge nurse with advanced nursing skills to work in general practice.'

'It sounds perfect.' Olivia nodded enthusiastically.

'I think you'd better let me fill you in a bit before you go getting too excited. The practice is in Kirrijong—have you heard of it?'

Olivia nodded. 'Vaguely. It's way out in the bush, isn't it?'

'That's an understatement. It's very pretty apparently, but also very isolated. The practice covers a vast area and the surrounding townships. But when I say ''surrounding'', you could hardly say they're close by. Kirrijong isn't close to anything. They're actually in the process of building a small cottage hospital to service the area, which is due for completion in three to six months. The position is available until then, but if you like it...' Miss Lever gave a cynical smile '...I'm sure they'd be delighted to keep you on.'

She looked over at Olivia, expecting to see a look of horror on the well-made-up face. This was, after all, no modern city surgery. Instead, she was surprised to see Olivia closely reading the e-mail, her face full of interest. Perhaps she would get her commission after all. 'You did your midwifery training in England, I see, as well as your general training.'

'Yes, but I came straight out to Australia afterwards, and I've been in Casualty ever since. Apart from the odd surprise delivery in the department, I haven't practised.'

Miss Lever shrugged. 'They only say midwifery training desirable. You're more than qualified and, anyway, they're desperate.'

'What do you mean?'

'Well…' Miss Lever shuffled uncomfortably in her seat. 'Look, I'm not aware of your circumstances and, of course, it's none of my business, though it does appear you need a live-in job in a hurry.'

Olivia blushed. Was it that obvious how desperate she was?

'I just feel I should emphasise this is not the sort of job you're used to. Apart from your regular hours, you will be expected to help out in emergencies at any given time. It's an extremely busy surgery, with a large, complicated patient list. A lot of procedures that in the city would be done in a hospital are undertaken there.'

'Would I be the only nurse in the practice?'

'Yes, and if there's a seriously ill patient there will be no cardiac arrest team to bleep, no surgeons waiting scrubbed up in Theatre. Just you and the good doctor until the road or air ambulance arrives, and that can take a long time.' She paused a moment, before continuing, 'I ought to tell you that by all accounts Dr Clemson isn't the most pleasant of personalities.'

'In what way?'

Miss Lever leant over her desk and lowered her voice. 'Well, according to the last two girls sent there—who, incidentally, only managed two weeks between them—Dr Clemson is recently widowed and extremely bitter. He's supposedly very moody and demanding.'

Olivia let out a sigh of relief. For a moment she had thought Miss Lever was going to say he had made a pass at the other nurses. The very last thing she needed right now was to be stuck in the middle of nowhere with an elderly doctor and his roving hands.

'That doesn't worry you?'

'I've had more than my share of moody, difficult doctors, I can assure you. I'm not going to collapse in a heap if he barks at me. I can give as good as I get. As long as Dr Clemson can cope with that, I can manage his tantrums.'

Miss Lever looked at Olivia's determined face and the fiery red hair. She had no doubt she could.

'You sound as if you don't want me to take the position,' Olivia added.

'On the contrary...' Miss Lever smiled '...I just want to be sure you know what you're letting yourself in for. I'm not too keen on being on the receiving end of the formidable Dr Clemson's temper if I send someone unsuitable. I actually think you'll do very well—you've got a marvellous résumé. Three years in charge of such a busy casualty department must prepare you for just about any eventuality.'

'Just about,' Olivia agreed.

'Look, why don't I go and rustle up some coffee and leave you on your own for a few minutes to think it over?'

'Thank you, I'd appreciate that.'

Miss Lever walked to the door and, turning to ask how Olivia took her coffee, thought better of it, seeing her brimming eyes as she fished in her bag for a handkerchief. Closing the door quietly behind her, she shook her head. It was most unlike Miss Lever to put someone off a job— usually she was just interested in the commission. But there was something about Ms Morrell, a vulnerability behind that rather brittle exterior that made you not want to add to her troubles. She obviously had enough already.

Olivia leant back in the chair glad to be alone. Under normal circumstances she'd have had hysterics at the thought of a job out in the bush, with only a bitter old doctor as her colleague. But, then, who'd have thought, she reflected, she'd ever be in this situation, practically begging for a job? Sister Olivia Morrell, always so immaculate and in control. How happy she had been—a job she'd loved, Unit Manager in the emergency department at Melbourne

City Hospital, wonderful friends and, to cap it all, engaged to Jeremy Forster, Surgical Registrar, dashing, successful and good-looking.

Closing her eyes for a second, Olivia flashed back to the fateful day when Jessica, a dear friend and trusted colleague, had come into her office and asked for a private talk. How clearly she remembered the disbelief and horror as Jessica had gently told her that Jeremy was having an affair with his intern, Lydia Colletti.

At first Olivia had thought it must have been some sort of sick joke, a ghastly mistake, but, seeing the pain in her friend's eyes, she'd known she'd been hearing the truth. Looking back, it all seemed so obvious. Jeremy's mood swings, the exhaustion, the constant criticism. She had put it all down to the pressure of his work. He was due for a promotion soon to junior consultant and the competition was stiff. If they could just get through this, she had reasoned, surely he would be happier?

To add insult to injury, despite knowing the long hours and close proximity Jeremy shared with Lydia, she had never once felt threatened. She had trusted him. What a fool, what a stupid trusting fool.

Painfully, Olivia recalled their final row. She had confronted him, of course, and he'd sung like a bird, telling her in all too great a detail her faults, but Olivia had refused to take the blame for his infidelity.

'How could you do this Jeremy? How could you make love to her and then me?' she demanded, but Jeremy was unrepentant.

'Oh, come on, Olivia, when did we last make love? Our sex life is practically non-existent.'

'And that's supposed to be my fault?' she shouted, her anger welling to the surface. 'It's you who's always too tired or too busy. And now I know why, don't I? You were too damned exhausted after being with Lydia!'

'Well, at least she enjoys it Olivia. With you it's like making love to a skeleton, and about as lively.' He spat the words at her, his guilt and desire to end the discussion making him brutal.

Until finally, exhausted and reeling, all that was left to do was to throw a few hastily grabbed items into a bag and get out with as much dignity as she could muster, desperate to put some space between them.

It seemed that everyone except her had known about the affair. She couldn't go back to face the sympathetic stares and embarrassed silences. The only solution was to hand in her notice, which unfortunately meant surrendering the city apartment she leased from the hospital. Jessica's spare room provided a welcome haven but they both knew it was only temporary.

'Sorry I've been so long.' Miss Lever placed a cup and saucer on the desk in front of her and Olivia forced a smile, suddenly remembering where she was.

'I took the liberty of ringing Dr Clemson and telling him about you. You are still interested, I hope?'

Olivia nodded.

'Good. He was very keen.'

Olivia took a deep breath. 'How soon would he want me to start?'

'How soon can you get there?'

Hauling her suitcases off the train onto the platform, Olivia noticed she was the only passenger getting off at Kirrijong. In fact, the train only passed through once a day. Not for the first time, it hit her just how isolated she was. Gradually the city and suburbs had faded into endless bush, the lush green grass paling into sunburnt straw, acre after acre of dry cracked land. She had heard how the drought and dry winter had affected the farmers but, seeing for herself the parched bush and emaciated livestock, it made her realise the drought was far more than just a news bulletin or a page in the newspaper. Times were really tough here.

'G'day there, I'll get these. You must be Sister Morrell,' a friendly, sun-battered face greeted her, his eyes squinting in the setting sun. 'Jeez, how many cases have you got?'

Olivia blushed. It did seem a bit excessive, yet most of her clothes were still back at home. Throwing caution to the wind, Olivia had sold the car Jeremy had bought her as an engagement present, freeing up some cash. Jeremy would be furious. Blowing some money on a wardrobe more suited to the bush than her designer Melbourne gear had been a good tonic, at least for an afternoon.

Olivia was slightly taken back by the warmth of the man's welcome, having expected, from Miss Lever's description, a far more aloof greeting. Judging him to be in his mid-fifties, wearing dirty jeans and faded checked shirt, with a battered akubra shielding his face, Dr Clemson certainly didn't look the ogre Miss Lever had predicted. 'It's a pleasure to meet you, Dr Clemson.' She offered her hand, startled when he started to laugh.

'Youse didn't think I was the doctor? I can't wait to tell the missus. I'm Dougie, Dougie Kendall. My wife Ruby is Clem's housekeeper. I do a few odd jobs around the place, help out with the land.' He started to laugh again.

Olivia seethed. Did he really find it so funny? It was an obvious mistake. 'Well, Mr Kendall,' she said evenly, 'it's a pleasure to meet you.' It wouldn't do to get the locals offside quite so early.

Climbing into his dusty ute, Olivia winced as Dougie carelessly threw her expensive suitcases in the back. All the windows were wound down, forcing her to shout responses to Dougie's continual chatter. He pointed out the various residences as he hurtled the ute at breakneck speed along the dry, dusty road.

'That there belongs to the Hunts, a beaut family. Just had

a baby, a little fella, so no doubt youse'll be seeing them soon. And the land from now till the crossroads belongs to the Rosses.'

Olivia looked at the vast acreage and huge brick residence, far more formal than the weatherboard homes they had passed.

'They own a lot of land—mind, not as much as the doctor. Their daughter Charlotte is a model, well, that's what she calls herself anyway, I could think of a few other things.' He looked over at her, awaiting a response, but Olivia didn't rise to the bait. She wasn't interested in gossip. 'Charlotte's forever flitting in and out. One minute London the next Italy. She's supposed to be living in Sydney, but manages to put in an appearance here often enough and grace us with her presence. She's out with the doctor tonight—that's why he couldn't meet you.'

'Really?' Despite her earlier disinterest, Olivia sat up, suddenly intrigued. How rude. Surely he could have taken a night off from romancing someone young enough to be his daughter to welcome a new colleague.

'It's no business of mine, but she's a bit touched.' Dougie tapped his head and laughed. 'Clem wanted to come and meet youse himself but Charlotte rang with yet another ''emergency'' and of course he ends up running off to sort her out. Charlotte's a bit of a drama queen, if you know what I mean.'

Olivia knew what he meant all right. Wasn't that Lydia's game? Playing the helpless female, waiting for Jeremy to dash to her rescue. Olivia swallowed hard. While she had been bending over backwards to make their relationship work he had been rushing around comforting Lydia for every trivial hiccup or imagined problem that came her way.

'We're coming up to the surgery now.'

Night seemed to have fallen in a moment, with no dusk

to ease it in. Through the darkness Olivia could make out a huge rambling federation-style house with an array of plants hanging from the turned veranda posts. Dougie drove slowly past, the ute crunching on the gravel driveway. 'That's the doctor's house. The front of it is the surgery and he lives in the back part—it's pretty big.' He drove on for a couple more minutes and brought the truck to a halt. 'This is you.' He gestured to a pretty weatherboard with a huge veranda. The same array of hanging plants and terracotta pots adorned the entry and a wicker rocking chair sat idle in the front.

'Just for me?'

'Yep, all yours. My wife will be in through the week to take care of the cleaning and laundry. She'll show youse the ropes better than I can.'

'There's really no need. I can manage my own cleaning. I'm quite capable—'

'Sister,' he interrupted, 'youse'll be busy enough without running around doing housework. Anyway, don't be doing me missus out of a job.' He spoke roughly but his eyes were smiling.

'Oh, well, if you put it like that,' Olivia replied.

Dougie brought in her luggage as Olivia inspected 'home', her shoes echoing on the gorgeous jarrah polished floorboards that ran the length of the house. The lounge was inviting with two soft cream sofas littered with scatter cushions and a huge cream rug adding warmth to the cold floor. Someone thoughtful had arranged a bowl of burgundy proteas on the heavy wooden coffee-table. A huge open fireplace caught her eye. Olivia doubted whether she'd need it for, though dark outside, the air still hung heavy and warm.

'There's some red gum chopped. Ruby will set a fire up for you tomorrow. It still being spring, we get the odd chilly evening, though not for much longer. There's a fan heater in the kitchen cupboard, youse'll need that in the morning to take the chill off.'

Olivia smiled. 'It's a lovely house, beautifully decorated.'

'That was Kathy's work.'

'Kathy?' Olivia questioned.

'Yep, Kathy—Clem's wife, or rather late wife. She loved decorating. Spent weeks on this place, painting, stencilling, finding bits of furniture here and there.'

He spoke in the same casual manner but Olivia could hear the emotion in his voice.

'Anyway…' he gestured to the kitchen '…there's plenty in the fridge and cupboards to get you started. Ruby will be over in the morning to take you to the surgery. We don't want you feeling awkward on your first day.'

'Thank you, that's very kind.'

Dougie waved his hand dismissively. 'No worries. I'll leave youse to get settled in but, mind, if you need anything there's our number by the phone in the kitchen.' With a cheery wave he was off.

Olivia noticed he didn't even close the front door, just the flyscreen. This obviously wasn't the city, but old habits died hard. Olivia closed the door and turned the catch. A pang of homesickness hit her but, determined not to feel sorry for herself, she set about unpacking, until finally, with every last thing put away, she put the suitcases into the study wardrobe. This was home for now.

Peering in the fridge, Olivia smiled. There was enough food to last a month—a dozen eggs, bacon as thick as steak, milk, cheese. The pantry was just as well stocked. Tackling the Aga, Olivia put the kettle on. She'd earned a cup of tea and then she'd go straight to bed. The day seemed to have caught up with her all of a sudden.

A sharp knock on the door made her jump. Glancing at the clock, she saw it was edging on ten. Tentatively she opened the heavy door. Leaving the flyscreen closed, she peered at the large figure outlined in the darkness, trying to sound assured. 'Can I help you?'

'Olivia?'

'You are…' she said questioningly.

'Jake Clemson, but everyone calls me Clem.'

Olivia blushed, fumbling with the catch. 'Please, come in.' He was her new boss and she was treating him like some madman from the bush.

'I didn't mean to scare you.' He shook her hand firmly. 'Welcome to Kirrijong.'

Olivia smiled, taken aback not only by the unexpected friendliness but also by his appearance. Why had she assumed he'd be older? The man standing before her must only be in his thirties. She had imagined some austere, elderly doctor in tweeds. Jake Clemson, standing well over six feet, with battered jeans and an equally well-worn denim shirt, certainly didn't fit the image she'd had of him. His dark curly hair needed a good cut—he looked more like an overgrown medical student than a GP.

'I had hoped to meet you myself, but something came up.'

Olivia shrugged. If she had been expecting an apology or even an explanation she obviously wasn't going to get one. 'No problem. Mr Kendall was very helpful.'

'Dougie's a great bloke. I knew he'd take care of you.' He peered over her shoulder into the living room. 'Time for a quick chat?'

Olivia blushed again, suddenly feeling very rude. 'Of course. Come through—this way.' It was his house. As if he wouldn't know where the lounge was she thought feeling silly, but he just smiled.

'If I know Dougie and Ruby, there'll be a few stubbies in the fridge. Do you fancy one?'

Nodding, she followed him into the kitchen as he casually opened the fridge and helped himself to the beer.

Opening two stubbies, he made his way back to the living room. Obviously, if she wanted a glass she'd better get it herself!

'So how do you feel about coming to work here?' he asked in a deep, confident voice with only a hint of an Australian accent.

Olivia busied herself pouring the beer and managing to spill most of it. 'I'm really looking forward to it,' she lied. She could hardly tell him she was having a full-on panic attack and wondering what on earth had possessed her. 'The agency gave me quite an extensive brief. It all sounds very interesting, though I wish I had a bit more midwifery experience.'

He stared at her, taking in her slender frame and long red hair. The cheerful, confident voice belied her body language. Those huge green eyes were looking everywhere but at him, and her long hands were clutching that glass so tightly he half expected it to shatter. 'Ms' Morrell obviously wasn't as confident as she would have him believe.

'There is a lot of obstetrics here, but don't worry about that for now. I'll hold your hand, so to speak, for the first few weeks, and if I'm not around for some reason you can always call on Iris Sawyer. She used to be the practice nurse up until a couple of years ago. Iris is retired now, and happily so, but she doesn't mind missing a game of bowls to help out now and then, and her experience with the locals is invaluable.'

Olivia nodded, reassured by the confidence in his voice.

'Your résumé is rather impressive. I see you worked under Tony Dean in your last job. He gave you a glowing reference. I know him well. We're old friends.'

'You are?' Just the fact that this huge, daunting man was a friend of her beloved Mr Dean, the senior consultant in her former casualty department, made him somehow seem much less intimidating.

'Yes. Tony Dean was a junior consultant in Sydney when I was a mere intern. Later, our paths crossed again when I went back as a paediatric registrar. That would be five or six years ago. He moved on to Melbourne and I came here, but we still keep in touch. He's an amazing man as well as a fine doctor, but you don't need me to tell you that. Many times I've rung him for advice about a patient, or had them flown there by the air ambulance. I've probably spoken to you on the phone at some time.'

He smiled. It was a nice smile, genuine. Olivia managed to sneak a proper look. Judging by his qualifications, he'd have to be at least in his mid-thirties, but he appeared younger. He was undeniably handsome in a rugged sort of way. Unruly dark curls framed a tanned face with just a smattering of freckles over the bridge of his nose. She had been right first time—he really did look like an overgrown medical student.

'How long did you work there? I know it's in your résumé, but I can't remember offhand.'

'Five years, three as Unit Manager. I'd just left all my family behind in England, so I was feeling horribly homesick and foreign.'

'Had you been to Australia before?'

Olivia nodded. 'Yes but just on a working holiday, which is when I met my...' Olivia hesitated. 'My ex-fiancé. He was an intern then. Anyway,' Olivia added hastily, because the last thing she wanted to talk about was Jeremy, 'Mr Dean started within a couple of weeks of me. We were the ''new kids on the block'' together.'

'Why did you leave?' His question was direct and he watched as her shoulders stiffened, her hands yet again tightening convulsively around the glass.

'Personal reasons,' she answered stiffly.

Thankfully, he thought better than to push it—there

would be time for that later. Instead, he explained her new position.

'A contrast to Casualty, but there are a lot of similarities. As well as the usual coughs, colds and blood pressures, we're up against whatever they present themselves with at any hour of the day or night. From heart attacks to major farming accidents, we're the front line. You need to keep your wits about you. They breed them tough out here and they don't like a fuss. It takes a lot of skill to read between the lines. What may appear quite trivial can often be far more serious. Most tend to play down their symptoms.' He noticed her suppress a yawn.

'I'm not boring you, I hope?' he asked sharply.

Olivia sat upright, taken back by the first glimpse of him being anything other than friendly. 'Of course not.'

Clem stood up, and Olivia reluctantly admired his athletic build. 'You must be tired. You've had a long journey and it's almost midnight. I seem to think everyone else keeps my ridiculous hours. I'll let you get some sleep and I'll see you in the morning, Livvy.'

'It's Olivia, not Livvy,' she corrected him, following him to the door. 'And thank you for coming over, Dr Clemson. I'm looking forward to getting started.'

'Good. Hopefully you'll enjoy working here. And it's Clem, remember?'

Olivia suddenly felt embarrassed at how prudish she must have sounded, but she hated her name being shortened.

She watched him depart in long deliberate strides.

'Watch out for Betty and Ruby. Don't believe a word they say about me,' he shouted jokingly over his shoulder as he disappeared into the night.

As Olivia closed the door and firmly locked it, Clem rolled his eyes heavenwards. She wouldn't last five minutes. She was obviously well qualified and extremely intelligent, but she was as jumpy as a cat, and he somehow couldn't imagine her on a search and rescue. Sure, she looked stunning, he thought reluctantly then checked himself. She was probably anorexic—you didn't get a figure like that on three good meals a day.

CHAPTER TWO

OLIVIA awoke an hour before her alarm, determined to get the day off to a good start. Dougie had been right—the house was freezing. Reluctant to light a fire, instead she pulled on a pair of socks and a large jumper over her skimpy silk nightie and turned on the tiny fan heater. Jeremy would have had a heart attack if he could have seen her. Not sure how or where she'd get lunch, Olivia took advantage of the well-stocked fridge and prepared an enormous breakfast of bacon, eggs and wild mushrooms.

Mopping up the creamy yolk with a third slice of toast, she tried to decide what to wear for her first day. The usual white uniform seemed so formal, and according to the forecast it was going to be too hot for trousers. Settling on a pair of navy culottes, teamed with a white blouse and navy jacket, Olivia finally felt happy with her selection—smart but casual. She was nervous. What if the patients hated her?

With shaking hands, somehow she managed to put on her make-up, carefully trying to create a natural look. It had been a standing joke between herself and Jessica, the effort Olivia took over her appearance.

'Honestly, Olivia, you look smarter coming off duty than I do going on,' she'd often joked and Olivia would laugh back.

But her appearance was important to her. It had mattered so much to Jeremy that eventually it had rubbed off. Somehow she felt so much more confident with her 'face' on. After smoothing the wild mass of Titian ringlets into a chic French roll, she was finally satisfied.

'G'day. It's only me, Ruby.'

Olivia walked into the hall and watched as a huge woman burst through the front door. She had a mass of keys in her hand, as well as an array of brushes, a bucket and mop.

'Here let me help you with that,' Olivia offered.

'I'm right.' Ruby deposited her burdens on the hall floor. 'So you're Livvy? Dougie said you were a beaut, he wasn't wrong. I'll fix us a nice cup of tea before I get started. Youse must be feeling a touch nervous but, no worries, I'll take youse over and introduce you to everyone.'

Ruby was truly amazing to watch. Without even pausing for breath, she had taken Olivia's arm and seated her at the kitchen table then proceeded to fill the kettle.

'How are you finding it—a bit bewildering?'

'Just a bit,' Olivia conceded.

'Oh, we're a strange lot, that's for sure. The other nurses took one look and ran. Didn't even see the week out.' She eyed Olivia carefully.

'Well, I'm here for a lot longer than that, I can assure you,' Olivia responded with more conviction than she felt.

'Yep, I reckon you are. But a word of advice from an old chook who's been around the yard a while.' She leant over the kitchen bench and, despite the fact there was only the two of them, spoke in a theatrical whisper. 'Don't go letting the doctor upset you. Clem's bark is far worse than his bite.'

Although curious, Olivia felt she really shouldn't be discussing her employer.

'He seems very nice,' she answered noncommittally, though she secretly hoped Ruby would elaborate. Olivia didn't have to wait long!

'Oh he's golden. He snaps and snarls now and then but I just picture him as a spotty young teenager. I don't tell him that, mind, I just say ''Yes, Clem, no, Clem,'' and wait for his mood to pass—it soon does.'

'Everyone has their off days.'

'Of course, but he's got worse. It's to be expected, mind, with all he's been through. He's far too busy, and now with this new hospital and everything. I just don't know how he does it. He's always had a temper, but since Kathy passed on…' She blew her nose loudly on a hanky she'd fished from somewhere in her very ample bosom. 'Tragic, there's no other word for it.'

Olivia looked on, fascinated. This woman never stopped talking though she was busy all the while. The breakfast dishes were now washed and back in their various cupboards and the bench had been wiped down.

'It must be difficult for him,' Olivia agreed. 'He's very young to be a widower.'

'Whoever said only the good die young wasn't wrong. A real living angel was Kathy. And he's not coping. I don't care how many times he tells me he's all right—I know he's not.'

Olivia tried to steer the conversation. It really was getting too personal. 'I hear it's very busy at the surgery.'

'Tragic,' Ruby muttered, then, blowing her nose again, she stuffed the hanky back into her cleavage. 'Oh, the surgery's busy all right. Far too much work for the one doctor. It will be great when we get the hospital. A lot of the locals are opposed to it but they'll soon come round. They're just scared of change, and they'll be wary of you, too,' she added, 'with that English accent and your city ways. But youse'll soon win them over.'

'I hope so,' Olivia answered glumly.

'Of course you will,' Ruby reassured her. 'Now, come on, sweetie, we can't be here gossiping all day. You don't want to go making a bad impression.'

Walking over to the surgery, Ruby linked her arm through Olivia's. Really, Ruby was getting more maternal by the minute. Of course, just to add to Olivia's nerves, the waiting room was full. As they entered the chattering stopped and Olivia felt every face turn to her. Smiling tentatively, painfully aware of a deep blush spreading over her cheeks, she wanted to turn and run. Sitting at the desk was a middle-aged, harassed-looking woman with frizzy grey hair that had never seen conditioner.

'Thank goodness you're here,' she said as a welcome. 'I'll just let the doctor know.'

'Now, just settle a minute, Betty.' Ruby blocked her desk. 'There's always time for an introduction. This is Sister Olivia Morrell and, Sister, this is Betty. She's the receptionist here and chief cook and bottle-washer.'

'Isn't that a fact?' muttered Betty. 'I'm sorry, Sister. It's lovely to meet you, and not a moment too soon—the place is fit to burst as usual. Clem's needed over at the Hudsons. Apparently the old boy had another turn,' she added in low tones to a very attentive Ruby.

Olivia was sure that Betty shouldn't be discussing the patients with the housekeeper, but she was obviously in for a few surprises. The bush telegraph would appear somewhat similar to the hospital grapevine, and that took some beating. Even the switchboard staff had apparently known about Jeremy and Lydia.

'Anyway,' said Betty with a smile, 'we'll get there.' She nodded as a young woman came out of what appeared to be the consulting room. 'I'll take you through to Clem.'

As Olivia walked in, she noticed how much smarter Clem looked than on their first meeting. He was wearing beige trousers and a navy sports jacket, and a tie was sitting awkwardly on his thick neck. His black curls were smoother and she caught a whiff of cologne as he stood up and once again shook her hand warmly.

'Good morning, Livvy. It's good to have you on board.'

Olivia winced but Clem didn't notice.

'I did want to take some time to show you around but, as you can see from the waiting room, we're pretty full on.'

'That's all right, I'll manage,' she replied in what she hoped was an enthusiastic voice.

'Good girl.'

Olivia winced again as he nodded appreciatively. She didn't have to be a genius to see that Clem wasn't particularly politically correct.

'I'm sorry to throw you in at the deep end but I see from your résumé that you can suture, which is an absolute luxury for me. I've never had a nurse here that can stitch and, frankly, I've never had the time to teach them.'

'As long as the wound is examined by you before and after I suture, that's fine.'

Clem nodded dismissively. 'Well, in the treatment room I've got Alex Taylor. He's gashed his hand on some barbed wire while mending a fence. I've had a look and there doesn't appear to be any nerve or tendon damage, but the wound in itself is quite jagged and dirty and will need a lot of cleaning and debriding. If you could get started on him, that would be a great help. Buzz me when you're finished or if you've any concerns.'

'Right…' Olivia hesitated. 'I'll get started, then.'

'Good. He also needs a tetanus shot,' Clem added, more as an afterthought, then, picking up his fountain pen, started to write on a patient's file in a huge, untidy scrawl. Olivia stood there, not sure where to go. He hadn't exactly given her a guided tour of the place.

'Was there anything else?' he asked, without bothering to look up.

'Er, no,' she replied hesitantly. He obviously wasn't going to hold her hand. Perhaps Betty could show her where the treatment room and the equipment was. But back in the waiting room Betty was looking even more harassed than before. The phone was ringing incessantly, while she tried to force an uncooperative piece of paper into the fax machine. Oh, well, she'd just have to find her own way.

Alex was infinitely patient.

'No worries, Sister,' he said, adding reassuringly a little later, 'Take your time, Sister, I'm in no hurry.'

Olivia bustled about, trying to find suture packs and local anaesthetic. Finally, with her trolley laid out and her hands scrubbed, she was ready to start.

'Right, Alex, I'm with you now.'

'Right you are, Sister.' The elderly man nodded.

Olivia examined the wound carefully. Clem was right. It was indeed a nasty cut, very deep with untidy jagged edges and very dirty. After waiting for the local anaesthetic she had injected to take effect, Olivia once again inspected the wound, this time more thoroughly. The tendon and its sheath were visible, but thankfully intact.

'Alex, everything looks all right in there. I'm just going to give it a good clean and then I'll stitch it up. You shouldn't feel any pain, but if it does start to hurt you be sure and tell me.'

'Very good, Sister.'

Olivia was quite sure he wouldn't. Alex hadn't even let out a murmur while she'd injected the anaesthetic. 'Dr Clemson said you were repairing a fence?'

'Yep. The sheep were getting out and wandering off. I was gonna wait for me grandson to fix it, but he's away at uni till the holidays and I can't be doing chasing the stupid things. I'm too old for that.' He went on to tell Olivia about his farm and how his grandson was studying agriculture. She encouraged the conversation to take Alex's mind off his hand. Anyway, it was interesting to hear what he had to say.

'He's forever coming back from uni, full of new ideas and notions about what he wants to do with the land.'

'And does that worry you?'

''Struth, no,' Alex answered firmly. 'I'm all for progress. Mind, I'm too set in me ways to be changing things myself. But as for the young fella, he can do what he likes as far as I'm concerned. Farming's big business now it's a science.' He laughed. 'It'll all be his one day and I'm just glad he wants it. Not many young folk stay now. You just look at Clem. He wanted to stay in the city and carry on his work with the children.'

'But he came back,' Olivia ventured, curious despite herself at the insight into her boss. She had finished cleaning the hand and debriding the dead tissue. Aligning the edges, she started to suture.

'Old Dr Clemson—Clem's father—went to pieces after his wife died. His health started to fail. Clem came back to help out. He's a good sort, not like his brother Joshua—he didn't even make it in time for his own mother's funeral. Anyway, then the old fella died, God rest him. By then, though, young Clem had fallen in love with Kathy, and she would never have considered leaving here. She loved Kirrijong and it loved her.' Alex winced slightly and Olivia wasn't sure whether it was from pain or emotion.

'Is that sore, Alex? The anaesthetic is starting to wear off, but I'm just about finished now.'

'I'm all right,' he said, then continued his tale. 'Kathy belonged here, and for a while so did Clem.'

'What do you mean?'

'Well, he's busy with building the hospital and he's flat out here, but I don't reckon his heart's in it. I know he's grieving and I reckon the place has just got too many painful memories for him. I reckon we'll be lucky if he stays.'

Olivia's eyes suddenly misted over. Poor Clem. She knew all about painful memories and being alone. But if Jeremy had died? To totally lose someone… She wondered how Clem even managed to get up in the morning. At that moment she heard Clem walk into the room. He stood over her as she tied the last knot, surveying her work. The bitter tang of his cologne was a heady contrast to the chlorhexidine solution she was using on Alex's wound. Acutely aware of his closeness, her hand trembled slightly as she snipped the silk thread. Clem let out a low whistle and shook his head.

'You've made a rod for your own back Livvy. I couldn't have done a better job myself. You'll be doing all the suturing now. Right you are, then, Alex. Keep it clean and dry, and I'll see you again in a week. Here's a script for some antibiotics—that's a nasty cut and we don't want it getting infected. Any problems in the meantime and you're to come straight back.'

Alex rolled up his sleeve as Olivia approached with his tetanus shot. 'Right you are, Clem.' He got up from the trolley and added, 'I hope you don't go scaring this one off—she's a diamond.'

Olivia blushed but Clem laughed.

'I'll try not to.' He shook Alex's good hand and reminded him once again to return if needed.

'Bye, then, Sister. Thanks very much.'

'No, thank *you* Alex, for being so patient.' She smiled warmly at him and hoped all her patients would be as pleasant.

The rest of the morning passed in a whirl of dressings, recording ECGs and taking blood. An old lady eyed Olivia dubiously as she sat her down and produced a tourniquet.

'Clem normally takes my blood. I've got very difficult veins, you know.'

Taking a deep breath, Olivia forced a smile and assured the woman she knew what she was doing, adding, 'Dr Clemson is so busy this morning he didn't want to keep you sitting around, waiting for him, when you've probably got far better things to do.'

This seemed to appease her and grudgingly the woman offered her arm. Thankfully the needle went straight in.

Finally the last of the patients had been dealt with. Despite this, Betty still had to shepherd out a group of ladies from the waiting room who were conducting an impromptu mothers' meeting. Firmly closing the door, Betty let out an exaggerated sigh. 'They'll be wanting me to serve them tea and biscuits next. Come on, Sister, it's time for lunch.'

Leading Olivia through the surgery to the private part of the house she took her into the lounge room. Again, it was beautifully furnished, the walls lined with books, heavy drapes blocking out the harsh midday sun. Kathy must have used her talents in here as well. In one of the huge jade leather chairs, which clashed ravishingly with the dark crimson rug, sat a fat ginger cat. In the other chair, looking equally relaxed, sat Clem. His tie loosened, he was working his way through a large pile of sandwiches.

'Come in, come in. Ruby's done us proud as always— help yourself,' he said, offering her a plate. 'Don't wait to be asked or there won't be anything left. Isn't that right, Betty?'

Always conscious of eating in front of strangers and still full from her large breakfast, Olivia picked gingerly at a huge roast beef sandwich Betty had cheerfully put on her plate.

'Coffee, Sister?'

'Thank you, Betty, and, please, it's Olivia, remember.'

'Cream and sugar, Sister?' she asked, completely ignoring her request.

Didn't anybody here use the right name?

'No, just black will be fine.'

Clem raised his eyebrows. 'I'd suggest you tuck in, Livvy, we've got a busy afternoon ahead of us. I don't know what time we'll finish.'

'But I had a huge breakfast,' Olivia protested, then, seeing the expression on their faces, she hastily took a bite.

A talk show was on television, wives confronting their husbands' mistresses. That was all she needed.

Betty was lecturing her on the benefits of thermal underwear for night calls. 'It can be cold at night if you have to go out in a hurry,' she said, looking disapprovingly at Olivia's skinny legs. A psychologist on the television show was banging on about how wives often let themselves go after they got married. Jeremy had certainly accused her of that and they hadn't even made it up the aisle!

'I'm quite sure Olivia wouldn't be seen dead in thermals. Isn't that right?' Clem teased.

Olivia thought glumly of the small fortune she had spent on sexy underwear in an attempt to resuscitate her and Jeremy's dying sex life. All to no avail. 'Dr Clemson—Clem,' Olivia said curtly, 'as friendly as you've all been, I'm sure you wouldn't expect me to discuss my underwear—or was there something in my job description I didn't read?'

Betty coughed nervously; the television blared out the merits of keeping an air of mystery in the bedroom. Clem merely threw his head back and laughed loudly.

'Good for you. We're far too familiar here. Come on, we've got work to do.' And picking up the half-eaten sandwich left on her plate, he took a huge bite. Olivia watched distastefully and stood up.

'And if I'm not being too personal,' Clem said with more than a hint of sarcasm, 'may I suggest you go and put on some sunscreen and a hat? Half my house calls seem to be done in the middle of a field. Some insect repellent might be useful, too.'

Outside, he handed her the keys to a large black four-wheel-drive.

'This is yours, but I'll drive today, give you a chance to

get your bearings. Just put the petrol on my account at the garage.'

'Wonderful.' That was a relief. She had been beginning to wonder if 'transport provided' might mean a bus pass.

'Before we head off I'll just show you the set-up.' He opened the back door. 'As you can see, I've got all the back seats down. It's better to keep it like that so if the need arises you can transfer someone supine. There's a camp-bed mattress rolled up in the corner there, with a pillow and some blankets.' He opened up a large medical emergency box. 'I'll run through the box. Pay attention— you don't know when you might need it.'

Olivia bristled. She was only too aware of the importance of the equipment Clem was showing her—he hardly needed to tell her to listen.

'All the usual emergency drugs and intravenous solutions, all clearly labelled—giving sets, needles, syringes.' He took out each piece of equipment in turn, gave her a short lecture on its use and then replaced it. Olivia stood there, silently fuming. While she appreciated him showing her the contents, he was talking to her as if she were a first-year nursing student. 'An intubation kit,' Clem stated as he held up a plastic box clearly marked INTUBATION KIT.

'Is it?'

Clem chose to ignore her, instead painstakingly going through the various tube sizes and the appropriate ages they would be used on. Olivia automatically picked up the laryngoscope and checked that the bulb was working—it would be no fun attempting to put an intubation tube down an unconscious patient's throat if the light didn't work.

'There's spare bulbs here, but check it weekly. Have you ever intubated a patient before?' Clem enquired.

'Yes, several, but only in a controlled setting. Mr Dean insisted his senior nursing staff knew how, just in case. Anyway, it helps assisting doctors if you've done it yourself.' She thought for a moment. 'But I've never intubated anyone without supervision.' Clem heard the note of tension creep into her voice.

'And hopefully you won't have to. You can always bag them until help arrives, but who knows what can happen? At least you know your way around the kit. You can have a go, that's got to be better than doing nothing and watching someone die.' Olivia nodded glumly, not for the first time wondering just what she had taken on.

'Now the defibrillator. It's pretty standard, you can run a three-channel ECG off this model—'

'I've used that type before,' Olivia interrupted.

'Here's the on-off switch,' Clem continued, blatantly ignoring her again. 'Keep it plugged in overnight to charge it, but just run the cord through the Jeep window into the garage wall. Are you listening? I hope you're taking all this in,' he snapped rudely.

'I've used a defibrillator before—this model, in fact. I know what I'm doing.'

'I'm sure you do,' he said through gritted teeth, 'but when I ring you at one in the morning to come and assist me in an emergency, I need to be sure you know exactly where all the equipment is and how it works. It's no good you driving off in a hurry and leaving the bloody defibrillator still charging on the garage floor.'

'Obviously not,' Olivia retorted. She was nervous enough about her new responsibilities, without him treating her like the village idiot. 'I'm grateful to you for showing me things, but I really don't need a total re-train. If I don't know or understand something then I'll ask.' She stood there resolutely, staring defiantly into his angry, haughty face, awaiting his wrath, but it never came.

'Well, just make sure you do,' he said after what seemed an age. Turning his large back on her, he deftly replaced the equipment.

With her face burning, Olivia made her way to the passenger seat. She knew she had been right to stand up to him. He had to treat her, if not as an equal, at least with some respect.

Climbing into the driver's seat, he started the ignition. 'We'll go the back way. It's a short cut but don't use it till you're comfortable with the Jeep.' And without looking over once, he gave her a run-down on their first patient. 'The first port of call is the Jean Hunt, for her postnatal check. She's just had her fourth baby. A son after three daughters…young Sam. He's six weeks old now.' Clem skilfully guided the car around the tight bends.

'Oh, yes,' Olivia recalled. 'Dougie mentioned them. They must be thrilled.'

'Not exactly,' Clem replied grimly. 'Everyone's thrilled except Mum.'

'Oh, dear.'

Clem finally glanced over at her, realising she understood the situation.

'Exactly.'

Olivia remembered only too well the tearful mums on the maternity ward, trying desperately to appear happy to relatives and wondering why on earth they'd been feeling so miserable and unable to cope.

Clem continued, 'After an extremely long and exhausting labour with a difficult posterior presentation, young Master Hunt entered the world quite healthy, screaming his head off, and he hasn't stopped since. A complete contrast to the girls, who were the most placid little sheilas you could imagine. Alicia, the youngest, actually had to be woken for her feeds for the first couple of months. Not only does Jean have a husband and three other children to cope with, she's also dealing with a never-ending stream of well-wishers bringing little blue gifts and telling her how delighted she must be feeling.'

'Poor thing,' Olivia sympathised. 'How's his weight?'

'Borderline. He's gaining, but not as much as I'd like.'

Olivia thought for a moment.

'Could he have reflux?' she suggested.

Clem shrugged. 'I really don't think so, though I have considered it. I've seen a lot of reflux babies but Sam just doesn't quite fit the picture. I think it's more Jean.'

'Is she breastfeeding?'

'Trying to, but I'm going to suggest she puts him on the bottle today.'

Olivia couldn't believe what she was hearing. How behind was this place? Everyone knew you encouraged breastfeeding.

He looked over again. 'What's wrong, you don't approve?' Clem parked the car and turned around to face her.

She looked at him properly for the first time, and realised just how attractive he really was. 'It's not a question of whether I approve or not. I was taught to promote breast-feeding, that's all. To give in after such a short time seems strange to me.'

'Look, I do see your point. Breast is best and all that, but only if it's working. When it isn't, the bottle is fantas-tic.'

Olivia opened her mouth to argue but he cut her short.

'There's no breastfeeding mothers' support group here, no lactation consultant to call in, just the help you and I can offer. You may have only done a morning here, but you can surely see how stretched we are.' He held up his hand to silence her as she again attempted to put her point. 'Let me finish, then you can have your say.'

Olivia snapped her mouth closed and folded her arms.

'I've been round nearly every day since Sam was born, but there's not much more I can do. He's healthy, he's just hungry. For whatever reason, breastfeeding just isn't work-ing this time. Anyway, Jean's far more experienced than you or I—after all, she's successfully fed three children. It's a bit like taking snow to the Eskimos, offering her advice on her feeding technique.'

Olivia grudgingly nodded.

'And as chauvinistic as it may sound to a liberated young woman like yourself, Mr Hunt will be back from a hard day's work at the farm this evening. He'll want to come back to a tidy house and a meal. It doesn't mean he loves her any less than the sensitive twenty-first century men you may mix with, it's just the way it is here. And I can tell you now that Jean isn't going to take a stand for sisterhood and to heck with routine.'

Olivia digested his speech. She actually understood far more than he realised. She herself had desperately wanted to start a family as soon as they'd got married. But as with their elusive wedding date, Jeremy had wanted to wait, for what she hadn't been quite sure. The thought of Jeremy coming home to a messy house, a crying baby and a hysterical mother made her realise he wasn't the modern, liberated man he liked to think he was. Taking her silence as dissent Clem went further.

'I could prescribe anti-depressants or tell her to hang in there till things improve, but I'm not prepared to do that, at least not this early in the piece. That's not the kind of medicine I practise.'

And despite the fact she had indeed only worked a morning with him, Olivia knew that already. It was obvious from the adoration of his patients that he was a wonderful caring doctor. Still, she wasn't prepared to give in that easily. 'I still think you should go in there with an open mind,' she said defiantly, but, watching his face darken, wished she'd held her tongue. She probably wouldn't last the week out, like her predecessors.

'May I suggest something?' Clem said slowly.

'Of course.' Olivia nodded weakly. Perhaps he was going to tell her to remember her place.

'Maybe it should be *you* that goes in to the house with an open mind. In fact, why don't you decide what Jean should do?' he suggested.

'And if I don't come down on your side, you'll simply override me,' she retorted.

Clem shook his head. 'You don't know me very well. Of course, I could override you but I won't. It's your call.' He picked up his doctor's bag, effectively ending the conversation, and got out of the vehicle. Striding to the front door, Olivia had to half run to keep up with him. Knocking firmly, he turned. 'Remember, an open mind.'

Jean Hunt opened the door still in her dressing-gown, her hair unbrushed, her eyes red and swollen from crying.

'Oh, Clem, I'm so glad you're here. He's been screaming all morning.' She ushered them through to the family room, apologising for the mess. The house was in chaos. Toys littered the floor and piles of washing lay over the chairs and sofa. The morning's breakfast dishes were still on the breakfast bar. 'Please, sit down,' she said to Olivia, removing a pile of nappies.

Clem peered into the crib. 'He's asleep now.'

'Yes, but it won't last.' Her eyes brimmed. 'Can I get you a cup of tea?'

Clem turned to Olivia. Taking her cue, she jumped up.

'I'll sort out the tea. Why don't you let Clem examine you while Sam is asleep?'

Clem nodded appreciatively.

'He'll be awake before you know it. Six weeks old and he's hardly slept for more than two hours at a time. The girls were so easy—I just don't know what it is I'm doing wrong. Brian's so thrilled at having a boy, he just doesn't understand…' Jean's voice broke and her shoulders shook with emotion.

Clem, towering over her, put his arms around her heaving shoulders and spoke softly. 'Come on, Jean. Let's go through to the bedroom and I'll do your postnatal check, then we'll sit down over a nice cuppa and try to sort something out.' Gently he led her away.

After switching on the kettle, Olivia hastily did the breakfast dishes and wiped down the benches. The family room wasn't dirty, just untidy. She put the toys back into their box and started to sort out the laundry, folding the nappies into a neat pile and placing the rest into the groaning ironing basket. The place looked a lot better, and by the time Clem retuned she had made the tea.

'Jean's just getting dressed.' He raised his eyebrows 'You've been busy.'

Jean was eternally grateful. 'Sister, you didn't have to do that.'

'No problem, Jean. I'm glad to help.'

While they drank their tea, Jean, in a faltering voice, told them her problems. 'If I could just get a decent sleep and the house in order I'd be all right, but Sam takes for ever to feed. Then, when I finally get him off, no sooner have I put him down than he's awake and screaming again. I'm at my wits end.' She ran her fingers through her unwashed hair.

'Does Sam have any long sleeps at all?' Clem asked.

'Sometimes, at about five, which is useless for me. The girls are home from school then, wanting their tea, and then Brian gets in. As the girls go off to bed up gets the little fella, and that's me for the rest of the night, trying to keep him quiet so that Brian can get a good sleep.'

'Could Brian get up to him for a couple of nights, at the weekend perhaps so you could get a break?' Olivia volunteered. 'Perhaps if you expressed some milk?'

Jean shook her head. 'He's up at five a.m. to go to the

farm. It's the same at weekends—the cows still need milking. I can't expect him to be awake at night with the kids.'

Olivia finally realised the woman's predicament. Just then Sam stirred and let out a piercing cry, which made them all jump. It was amazing just how much noise a small baby could make. Clem picked up the infant as Jean started to weep.

'What's wrong with him, Clem?'

'Put him to your breast, Jean, and let me see you feed him.' Olivia spoke calmly, and Clem handed Sam to his mother. The irate baby arched his back and butted against Jean's breast, searching frantically for and finding her nipple. He latched on and mercifully relaxed. Making little whimpering noises, he suckled hungrily.

'Very good, Jean, you're doing wonderfully,' Clem encouraged. 'Just try and relax.' At that point Sam let out a furious wail and the angry protest started again.

Jean was just about at breaking point. 'What's wrong with him?' she screamed above the ear-splitting shrieks of her son.

Olivia walked over and gently took the baby from the distraught woman. The baby snuffled against her. Olivia felt his hot, angry little face against hers, breathing in the familiar baby smell. Rocking Sam, gently trying to soothe him, she contemplated Jean's situation. For all her knowledge and training she had no real experience. Here was a woman who had borne four babies to her nil. She had a husband and children to care for and a house she was proud of. The well-rehearsed platitudes of 'persevere' and 'things will get better' seemed woefully inadequate. Olivia could see what was wrong. Jean had plenty of milk but she wasn't letting down, probably because she was too tense. Appearances mattered, and to tell this woman to ignore the housework and concentrate on the baby, to get a take-away and not worry about dinner, would be like speaking a foreign language. Heck, there wasn't a burger bar for two hundred kilometres.

Clem watched Olivia closely as she rocked the baby. Sam rooted hopefully and, finding her finger, sucked hungrily, but again there came the same wail of frustration.

'He's hungry, Jean,' Olivia said.

'He can't be. I fed him just an hour ago. You saw me just try—that's not what he wants.'

Olivia gently but firmly explained about the letdown reflex. 'It's automatic in some women, as it was for you with the girls. But anxiety, tension, lack of sleep—any one of these can affect it. It's a vicious circle. The more Sam cries, the harder it is for you to relax and for your milk to get through. Have you considered trying him with some formula?'

'But breast milk's best—everyone says so,' Jean protested.

'A contented mum and baby are what's important. Anyway, giving him a bottle now doesn't automatically mean you have to give up on breastfeeding. Perhaps after a couple of feeds and a good sleep you'll be ready to do battle again. You could maybe give him a bottle at night and concentrate on breastfeeding in the day. There are lots of options. Even if he does end up on the bottle, you've given Sam your colostrum in the first few days, which is full of antibodies, and he's had six weeks on the breast. You've done very well.'

'What do you think?' Jean turned to Clem.

'I totally agree with Livvy.' He stood up. 'I've got some formula samples in the car. Why don't you make him up a bottle and we'll see how he goes?'

Half an hour later a much happier Jean cuddled her satisfied son. Young Master Sam made contented little noises.

'Feeling better now?' Clem enquired.

'Much, but I'm a bit disappointed.'

'Well, don't be,' Olivia said firmly. 'Like I said, it might be a different ball game tomorrow. But whatever you do, don't go getting stressed—just enjoy each other.'

'Thanks ever so.' She looked over at Olivia. 'You've both been wonderful.'

'We haven't finished yet.' Clem darted outside and returned with a huge casserole pot. 'Ruby's forever trying to fatten me up. There's more than enough here to feed the family, Jean.' He took Sam from her and put him gently into the crib. 'Now, the place is tidier, the baby's asleep and dinner's taken care off. You get to bed.'

'I should get some ironing done,' Jean protested, but Olivia quickly jumped in.

'Don't you dare.' She shooed her down the hall.

'I wouldn't argue with Sister Morrell if I were you, Jean. I've a feeling she'd win. Now, off to bed, Doctor's orders. We'll see ourselves out.'

Back in the car Clem praised her. 'You did a great job in there.'

'Only because I listened to you first,' Olivia admitted. 'I shudder to think of the mess I'd have made if you hadn't forewarned me.'

'I think you're being a bit hard on yourself,' he said kindly. 'We'll need to keep a close eye on Jean, make sure things are improving—she's on a short fuse at the moment. Let me know if you're worried about her.' He turned and smiled. 'It's good having you on board, Livvy.'

As she opened her mouth to correct him he started the engine. Oh, what was the point? She might just as well get used to it.

The rest of the afternoon passed quickly. In each home they were made welcome. Despite Clem's sometimes brutal honesty and arrogant assumptions, it was obvious the patients all adored him. Everywhere they went the patients insisted on making a cup of tea. As if he hadn't had a drink all day, Clem gratefully accepted and listened as they chatted. Finally, armed with a bag of lemons and some lamingtons, they had finished the rounds.

'For a day's work well done, I'll buy you dinner. It's time for you to visit the local hotel.'

'But we can't. I'm in my work clothes,' Olivia wailed. The thought of having to talk to him socially terrified her.

'I'm not intending to get you drunk, I can assure you, but it's nearly seven already and I'm sure you're about as keen to cook dinner as I am.'

Driving into the main street, he parked and escorted her straight into a bistro. Gorgeous smells wafted from the kitchen and Olivia realised how hungry she really was. Again Clem was greeted like a long-lost friend.

'G'day there. The usual, Clem? And what about the young lady?'

'An orange juice, please.'

Clem remembered his manners and introduced her. 'This is Olivia Morrell, the new sister at the practice.'

'Pleased to meet you, Livvy,' the landlord greeted her cheerfully. Casually holding her elbow, Clem led her over to a table by the window and went back to the bar to fetch their drinks. Olivia gazed out of the window at the miles of land stretched out before her. The road continued far into the horizon. It was magnificent. She wished she were here with Jeremy. It had been so long since they'd been away together or even out for a meal, just the two of them. There had always been work, or a function to attend. Perhaps if she'd insisted, or just gone ahead and booked a weekend away, maybe they could somehow have prevented the mess they were in.

'Daydreaming?'

Olivia jumped as Clem placed their drinks on the table. 'I was just admiring the view.'

'Yes it's pretty spectacular,' he agreed. 'As are the pies

here. I took the liberty of ordering for you. They do the best steak pie I've ever tasted.'

'Sounds marvellous.'

Conversation was surprisingly easy. He was very good company, with a wicked, cynical sense of humour. Olivia felt herself start to relax as he told her tales of the locals. The pie, as promised, was spectacular, the sauce rich and spicy. Mopping her plate with a second bread roll, she felt Clem staring at her.

'What?' she said, hastily putting down her roll.

'Nothing. I'm just glad you're enjoying the food,' he remarked.

'And why shouldn't I be? It's delicious.'

Clem surprised himself at how much pleasure he took in watching her unwind. For the first time since they'd met she was actually looking at him for more than ten seconds when he spoke. The constant fiddling with her earrings or hair had stopped. He decided to broach a question he had been wondering about. 'You said last night your "ex-fiancé". Was the break-up very recent?' Those stunning green eyes frantically looked over to the bar as if in a silent plea for help, her hand immediately shooting up to her earrings.

'Yes.' Olivia replied reluctantly.

'Were you engaged for long?'

'We were together five years, engaged for two.'

Clem let out a low whistle. 'Ouch,' he said simply, and took a drink of his beer. For a second she thought the conversation was over but he wasn't letting her off so easily.

'He's not exactly a fast mover. Why weren't you married?' he probed.

Olivia sighed, wishing he would just drop it. 'We were happy the way we were, there wasn't any need to rush,' she stated, bringing out the old platitudes she had used on her friends and parents so many times in the past.

'Rubbish,' Clem said rudely. 'I have a theory about couples in long engagements and so far I've always been right.' He paused. 'Do you want to hear it?'

'Not particularly, but I've a feeling I'm going to.'

Clem grinned and continued. 'One is desperate for the commitment, the other is holding out, but both pretend a long engagement is what they want. It's the same with couples who live together—there's always one holding back. Am I right?'

He was, of course, damn him, but she certainly wasn't going to let him know as much.

'Actually, no, you're not. Jeremy's been under a lot of pressure recently. We were waiting till he made consultant. There wasn't time to concentrate on a wedding as well.'

'Well, I'd have made time,' Clem insisted. 'I'd have snapped you up years ago.'

It was an innocent statement, made entirely in the context of the conversation, but for some reason Olivia felt herself start to blush. Clem didn't seem to notice.

'So what does he think about you being out here?'

'He doesn't know.'

'You're not some fugitive on the missing persons list, are you?' The tone of his voice made her look up and she was relieved to see he was smiling.

'He's a bit too busy with his new girlfriend, I would think, to be looking for me.'

Clem took a long drink of his beer. 'So one call from Jeremy and I could lose the only decent nurse this town has seen in months.'

'I'm more responsible than that,' Olivia retorted quickly. 'I'm not just some puppy dog that can be summoned. I've accepted the job and I'm aware of my obligations.'

'Whoa.' He raised his hands.

'Anyway,' she continued, 'as I've only been here a day, aren't you judging me rather hastily?'

'On the contrary. I believe in first impressions, though I must admit I was wrong about your eating habits.'

Olivia gave him a questioning look but he didn't elaborate.

'Kathy always said I knew at a glance…' He took a hasty sip of his drink and then in a soft voice he continued, 'Kathy was my wife. She died,' he said simply. Now it was his turn to avoid her gaze.

'I heard. I'm so sorry. How long ago?'

'It will be two years in a few months, but the way it feels it might just as well have been yesterday.' He drained his glass. 'Hold onto your heart, Livvy, because you only get hurt in the end. I sometimes wonder if the pleasure of being in love is worth the pain.' He gave her a rueful smile. 'Listen to us two lonely hearts getting maudlin.' The carefree shift in his tone did nothing to disguise the sadness hanging in the air. 'Can I get you another drink?'

Olivia reached for her purse. 'No, it's my turn. I'm going to have a coffee.' Like her, he obviously didn't want to talk about his loss. The difference was, she was too polite to push it. 'Can I get you one?'

Clem shook his head.

'Another beer, then, or a cup of tea perhaps?' she offered.

'Olivia, sit down a moment. There's something I must tell you,' Clem said in a serious voice. She tentatively sat down. What on earth could it be?

'You must promise not to tell any of the patients this. If it were to get out, so many people would be offended.'

Olivia nodded nervously. Whatever was he going to say? She'd only known him five minutes.

He leant over the table, taking her hand and drawing her nearer, looking around to make sure nobody could hear. Leaning forward, she listened intently.

'I hate tea. Absolutely loathe the stuff, and every day I'm forced to drink gallons.'

'What?' Olivia looked up at him, startled. Was that it? Throwing his head back, he started to laugh, so loudly, in fact, that a few of their fellow diners turned around, smiling, to see what was so funny. Unperturbed, he carried on until finally she joined in. It had been so long since she'd truly laughed and, what's more, she marvelled, it felt wonderful.

CHAPTER THREE

SITTING at her kitchen table, Olivia attempted to pen a reply to Jessica's letter. A niggling sore throat which had been troubling her for a couple of days seemed to have come out in force. Pulling a face as she downed some soluble aspirin, Olivia reread Jessica's letter. Although apparently still full on with Lydia, Jeremy was pestering Jessica to find out where Olivia had moved to. She took some solace when she read how awful he was looking—black rings under his eyes, unironed shirts, creased suits and snapping at everyone. Which was most unlike Jeremy, who saved his mood swings for the home front. At work he was calm, unruffled and totally pleasant to one and all.

Perhaps he was actually missing her, realising what a terrible mistake he'd made. What if he did get in touch? Could she take him back after all he'd put her through? Olivia knew the answer should be no, yet a part of her couldn't let go. He had been her first real relationship, her first and only lover. The reason she had left her family and friends in England and travelled to the other side of the world. Letting go just wasn't that easy.

She had been in Kirrijong a month now. The locals were starting to accept her. Alex had returned to have his sutures removed, bringing her a bunch of proteas and several bottles of home-made tomato sauce. Her fridge and pantry groaned with the weight of home-made wines and chutneys, nectarines and lemons. They waved as she passed in her black Jeep and had started to make appointments to see her without Clem. It felt good to be liked and wanted. Yet each night she crept into the huge wooden bed and, while hating herself for being so weak, longed to feel Jeremy's arms around her, ached for the warmth of human touch.

It was Wednesday and she wasn't due on duty till eleven. Normally Olivia arrived early anyway, there was always more than enough work to do, but she had allowed herself the luxury of a lie-in and the chance to catch up on some letters. She hadn't been feeling herself at all lately. Initially Olivia had assumed it had been the pressure she was under, but now, with this niggling throat and persistent headaches, she began to suspect she was coming down with the same flu that seemed to be sweeping the rest of the town. Yelping as she noticed the clock edging past ten-thirty, Olivia dressed quickly. The morning had caught up with her.

Breezing into the surgery bang on eleven, she smiled confidently at the now mostly familiar faces.

'Morning, Betty. Are these for me?' Picking up a pile of patients' files, she started to flick through them.

'Yes. One's for stitching—he's out the back. And there's an ECG that needs doing—Clem wants it done as soon as you arrive. And a word of warning—he's not in the sunniest of moods this morning.'

Olivia raised her eyebrows. So she was finally going to see the legendary dark side of the good Dr Clemson.

'He came in like a bear with a sore head this morning and then, to make matters worse, her ladyship arrived.'

'Her ladyship?' Olivia enquired, not having a clue whom Betty was talking about.

'Oh you haven't had the pleasure of meeting his lady friend, Charlotte, have you?'

'His lady friend?' Olivia recalled the first night she had arrived in Kirrijong, when Clem had failed to meet her. Funny, although she'd heard what Dougie had said, by the way Clem had spoken about Kathy she'd just assumed there was no one else. Anyway, it didn't matter to her who he went out with, of course it didn't, Olivia thought firmly. She was just surprised, that's all.

'If you can call her a lady.' Betty lowered her voice. 'What he sees in her I'll never—' She coughed suddenly and started to shuffle some papers. 'Speak of the devil.'

Clem held open his door and Olivia felt her jaw drop for there, walking out of his office and looking completely out of place in a doctor's surgery in the middle of the bush, was six feet in heels of absolute drop-dead gorgeous sophistication.

Dressed in an immaculate white suit, her skirt at mid-thigh revealing the longest bronze legs imaginable, Charlotte Ross sauntered over to the desk, tossing her raven black mane. There was arrogance about her, an air of superiority, that, Olivia guessed, came when you were that beautiful. She looked straight through Olivia and Betty and picked up the telephone, barking orders at Dougie who doubled as the local taxi. She shook a cigarette out of her packet. Olivia felt her temper rise. Surely she wasn't going to light up here? Charlotte obviously had some discretion, though, and put the cigarette back in the pack.

'Thanks, Clemmie, I'll see you this afternoon,' she purred in a voice quite different from the one she'd used on Dougie.

Clem nodded. 'Fine. I'll see you then,' he answered. Charlotte had obviously done nothing to cheer him up, judging by the murderous expression on his face.

Catching sight of Olivia still standing there, holding the patients' files, he turned to her. 'So you finally managed to get here, then?' he barked.

'I beg your pardon?'

'You're late,' Clem announced to the waiting room.

'Sister's been here a good ten minutes…' Betty soothed.

'She's getting you to make excuses for her now, is she?' he demanded of poor Betty.

Olivia couldn't believe what she was hearing. She looked around the now silent waiting room at the expectant faces. 'If I might have a word in your office, Dr Clemson,' she said in as steady voice as she could manage, given the circumstances.

'I'm too busy, and so are you. You've already kept the patients waiting quite long enough as it is. I'll deal with you later.' And disappearing into his office, he left Olivia quite literally shaking with rage.

A deep, throbbing voice with the hint of a fake American accent broke the silence. 'I'm going to wait in the lounge. Call me when my taxi arrives,' Charlotte ordered. Tossing her hair again, she waltzed out of the surgery, though not before she'd managed to smirk at Olivia.

Fuming, Olivia got through the rest of the morning. How dare he talk to her like that, let alone in front of the patients? The atmosphere progressively worsened as the day continued, with Clem barking orders and constantly buzzing her on the intercom. 'Do this. Fetch that. Where are the results for this patient?' Olivia did as she was told, for the time being. The last thing she wanted was another scene in front of the patients. It was fruitless, as well as unprofessional.

'But if he thinks he's getting away with it he's wrong. As soon as surgery is over I'll let him know exactly what I think of his behaviour.'

'You'll just make things worse. Let it pass, he'll settle down soon,' Betty pleaded.

Finally the last patient had been dealt with. Olivia made herself a cup of coffee and took a half-hearted bite of an apple. Sitting at her desk, she started to write up her notes. It seemed that no matter what you did in nursing these days it produced a never-ending pile of paperwork to be completed. A shadow over her file told her Clem was standing at the desk, but she didn't look up. She certainly wasn't going to make an apology easy for him.

'I would have thought you'd had plenty of time to eat this morning, judging by how late you were.'

Well, she evidently wasn't going to get an apology. Olivia looked up from her notes. Clem's face looked down at her, so hostile she could hardly believe the change, but she refused to be intimidated. 'I most certainly was not late this morning. I was due to start at eleven, which I did. It's now two forty-five and I'm working through my break.'

'How very noble,' he said sarcastically.

That really was the limit. So she had been warned of his black unreasonable moods. So he was up to his neck in work. So the man was a widower. If he thought she was going to scuttle into the corner and hide like Betty, he was wrong. She'd had enough of irrational mood swings from Jeremy to last her a lifetime. She certainly didn't need it from him. 'No, Dr Clemson, it isn't noble, merely necessary. The files have to be written up and I have to eat. I am human after all, although judging by the way you treated me this morning I doubt you either noticed or cared.' She watched his face darken with rage. If he'd been angry before, he was really mad now.

'And what exactly,' he said menacingly, sitting down opposite her, 'is it that you don't like about my behaviour?'

Olivia took a deep breath. Oh, well, she might as well let him have it. She obviously wasn't going to be here for much longer. 'I don't like being spoken to like a naughty child, particularly in front of the patients. If you have a problem with my work, discuss it with me in your office. I also don't like you taking your beastly temper out on me.'

'Anything else?' he snapped.

'Yes, actually, there is.' She was gaining momentum now. 'I most definitely don't appreciate being told I'm late for work, or you implying that I'm taking excessive breaks, when the truth is I'm working way over the hours you specified in my contract. I don't mind working late, every night if necessary. I don't mind coming in early. However, if I'm due to start work at eleven and I have no indication that you need me earlier, don't get angry with me for not being here. I'm not a mind-reader.' Her temper had bubbled to the surface.

'Well, that's obvious,' he replied. 'Because if you could read my mind you'd be ringing up the unions, claiming unfair dismissal. I hadn't realised you were so militant, Sister.'

Olivia stood up. She'd had enough of this ridiculous conversation. 'Are you sacking me, doctor? Because if you are just say so and I'll be straight out of here.'

Clem got up. Despite her height, he was still a good head taller than she was. Olivia stood there, her face defiant. He wasn't going to intimidate her.

'That would seem to be your standard answer to any criticism or confrontation. But where are you going to run to this time? You've exhausted Victoria and New South Wales. Perhaps you should cross the border and see how you go in Queensland—until the next time someone pulls you up, that is. Still, there's always the Northern Territory.'

He was poisonous. That was the utter limit. How dare he drag her personal life into this? How dared he make such unjust assumptions about her? Stunned by his contemptuous remarks, she stood there, her face white, literally shaking with rage. What on earth could she say to that? He opened his mouth to speak but Olivia found her voice.

'Don't.' She put her hands up in front of her. 'Don't you *ever* speak to me like that again.' And something in her voice told him he'd totally overstepped the mark.

'Livvy…'

She shook her head. Whatever he was going to say, she

didn't want to hear it. There were no excuses to justify that outburst.

'Just get on with your work. I'm going on a house call, you can page me if you need me. I don't know how long I'll be.' The contempt in his voice had gone but his arrogance remained. Refusing to look at him, she stood there quite still as he haughtily left the surgery.

Only when the door had safely slammed behind him did Olivia promptly burst into tears. Clem's dramatic exit was ruined somewhat when he had to return to retrieve his car keys. Seeing her sitting at the desk, weeping, a huge wave of guilt swept over him. To have reduced this proud, troubled woman to tears gave him no pleasure. His apology was genuine and heartfelt.

'I've made you cry. I'm sorry.'

It was Olivia's turn to be difficult. 'Don't give yourself the credit.'

'I can be so pig-headed at times. I really didn't mean it.' He handed her a tissue from the box on the desk, which she accepted with a sniff.

'I'm not crying about you. I've come up against far more arrogant doctors than you in my time.'

'I'll try to take that as a compliment.'

Olivia managed a faint smile.

'If it's not just me that's upset you, who has?' The gentleness in his voice touched her. He sat on the desk, putting a tender hand on her shoulder, troubled by how fragile she felt. 'I know I'm not your favourite person after today's episode but I'm here if you want to talk.'

Olivia felt her anger evaporate. She so badly wanted to talk, to share, and Clem did seem genuine in his interest. Perhaps a man's opinion would offer some insight.

'A friend wrote this morning. It would appear that the object of Jeremy's desire still isn't me.' Clem didn't respond and she continued tentatively, 'I took some refuge in the fact that he looks awful, hoping that perhaps he's missing me after all. But who am I kidding? It's probably all the sex that's exhausting him.'

He smiled down at her, not moving his arm. 'What's she like?'

Olivia tried to describe Lydia objectively, fighting back the image of the scarlet woman with six-inch nails and a cleavage to die for. 'Well, I'd like to call her a bimbo, but she's actually very clever. She's his intern. Jeremy's a surgical registrar,' she explained. 'She's also very…' Olivia hesitated '…pretty. All boobs and behind, blonde hair, baby blue eyes.

'I never saw it coming,' she went on. 'Lydia's the antithesis of what Jeremy usually likes. She's scatty, disorganised, but apparently she made him feel "needed".'

'Not exactly the "burn your bra" type, then?' Clem said dryly, and Olivia managed a shaky smile.

'She makes me feel like a frigid spinster, yet I was the one engaged to him.'

'You're hardly relegated to the desperate and dateless pile yet,' Clem reasoned. 'You're gorgeous.'

'Jeremy didn't seem to think so.'

'Jeremy sounds like an idiot,' he stated, but feeling her body tense under his hand he realised he was on the wrong track.

'He's just confused,' Olivia said defensively.

'Maybe, but he doesn't have the right to hurt you like this.'

'He's hurting, too.'

Clem doubted this. He had met more Jeremys in his career than he cared to remember. So pumped up by the instant adoration and authority a white coat gave them, they actually felt they deserved their affairs. It didn't matter who got hurt in the process, just as long as they got what they assumed was their right. And in this case Olivia was the victim.

Clem's face hardened and his grip involuntarily tightened on her shoulder. For Jeremy to have reduced this strong, eloquent woman to tears and self-doubt made him churn inside. He hoped Jeremy got what he deserved. Olivia wriggled away uncomfortably. 'I'm fine now. Thank you for listening.' The mask was back on, her guard up.

'Look, Olivia, I'm always here if you want to talk.'

Olivia shook her head and blew her nose loudly.

Cursing himself for his poor handling of the situation, he remained seated and tried to revive the conversation, determined to be less antagonistic. 'Why don't I come over tonight and we can talk properly?'

Olivia shook her head. 'No, but thanks, anyway. I'll be all right now.' She picked up her pen. The conversation was over. Clem hesitated, as if about to say something. Olivia's pen paused over the file, his hand moved to her face and, picking up a loose curl that had escaped, he smoothed it behind her ear. The seemingly innocent gesture caught her completely unawares.

'I'm not taking no for an answer. I'll bring dessert.'

He left the surgery, this time closing the door gently behind him. Olivia sat there, stunned. How on earth had that just happened? A few moments ago he had been the second most loathsome man to walk this earth and now she was having dinner with him. Putting her hand up to her face where he had touched her, she felt her burning cheeks, then, firmly shaking her head, she set back to work.

Finally the last of the files had been written up, and after packing her bag with various bandages, dressing packs and solutions Olivia headed into town to make her own house calls. There were only a couple of dressings that needed doing and one postnatal visit. Which should, she reasoned, leave her with plenty of time to have a long bath and prepare a nice dinner for herself and Clem.

It was a pleasant drive into town, and Olivia took her time. Approaching an old Queenslander-style home, she admired the immaculate garden with an abundance of flowers that had obviously been lovingly tended. An elderly woman on the veranda waved to her as she passed and Olivia cheerfully waved back, relishing the laid-back friendliness of this tiny slice of Australia. But the woman kept on waving and, just giving herself time to indicate, Olivia swerved the Jeep and bought it to a hasty halt. Jumping down, the hot afternoon sun's glare made it impossible to see the woman. Holding her hand up to shield her eyes, Olivia called out.

'Is everything all right?'

The elderly woman came into focus. Breathless from running, her lined face was full of concern. 'I thought you were the doctor. I saw the Jeep,' she gasped. 'I've been trying to call him. It's Harry—he's got these chest pains. I called an ambulance, he's really crook. Please, help.'

In no time Olivia helped the lady into the passenger seat and, executing a hasty U-turn, crunched the gears and sped the short distance up the drive and back to the house. The journey was all it took to glean that the lady was called Narelle and was Harry's wife. Coming to a sharp halt, Olivia was tempted to go in first and assess the situation, but she kept a cool head and instead quickly opened up the back of the Jeep, grabbing the emergency pack. Despite its considerable weight, she ran into the house.

The drapes were pulled and after the brightness of outside it took a couple of seconds till she could see in the cool dark room, but one look at the elderly man's grey, sweaty face was all she needed to know the trouble he was in. Slumped in a large armchair, he was obviously in a lot of pain. Olivia turned on the oxygen cylinder, her moist palms making it difficult to turn the lever. Gently she placed an oxygen mask over his face.

'Harry, I'm Olivia Morrell, Clem's nursing sister. Show me where the pain is.'

A shaking hand came up to the centre of his chest.

'And does it go anywhere else?' He shook his head. Realising it would be too much exertion for him to speak, she addressed Narelle as she hastily attached the cardiac monitor. 'When did the pains start?'

'About half an hour ago. He was just pottering in the garden. I told him it was too hot to be out there.'

'Has he ever had anything like this before?'

Narelle shook her head. 'Nothing. He's as strong as a mallee bull is our Harry.'

'No angina, high blood pressure, breathing problems, diabetes?' Olivia ran through a list of various medical complaints.

'Nothing. He just has a flu shot once a year.'

'How old is Harry, and is he allergic to anything you know of?'

'Sixty-eight and, no, he's not allergic to anything.'

Olivia scribbled down Clem's mobile number. 'Narelle, try Clem on this number.'

'I have been. I got it from the answering machine at the surgery but he's out of range. I left a message with his paging service. I've been trying to get hold of Betty but she's not home.'

So she really was on her own.

'It's his heart, isn't it, Sister? Oh, God, he's not going to die, is he?' Narelle started to panic, her voice rising to a crescendo, and Olivia knew she had to keep her calm. Any upset would only further distress Harry.

'Get me a small glass of water. I'm going to give Harry some aspirin.' The simple instruction was all it took to stop the woman's mounting hysteria, and she dutifully nodded.

But before Narelle even had time to turn for the kitchen the situation suddenly intensified as Harry's condition deteriorated rapidly. His eyes rolled back into his head and he slumped further into the chair. Deftly Olivia felt for his carotid pulse. Unable to palpate it, she glanced over at the monitor, which confirmed her fear—Harry had gone into cardiac arrest. Olivia gave him a hefty thump on the chest in a bid to kick-start his heart.

'Narelle, help me get him onto the floor,' she ordered, but Narelle was completely hysterical. There was no point in trying to calm her down. That would have taken time and that was what she was fighting against. Dragging him down to the floor by herself, trying to block out Narelle's desperate screams, Olivia worked quickly but methodically.

Having hastily attached the ambu-bag to the oxygen, she inserted the small curved tube that would keep Harry's airway open and enable her to give him the essential oxygen he so desperately needed. Then she rhythmically pumped his chest. Her cardiac massage was practised and effective, even managing to stop Narelle in her tracks as the regular bleeping of Harry's heart emitted from the monitor. But as soon as Olivia stopped, so too did Harry's heart, reverting instead to the chaotic and ineffective fibrillation that showed up as an erratic, squiggly line on the monitor. If Harry were to survive he needed more advanced lifesaving measures. Tearing open the defibrillator pads with her teeth as she systematically bagged him, Olivia charged the monitor and placed the pads on his chest.

Narelle was now all over Harry, shaking his limp shoulders, kissing his grey cheeks, begging him not to die.

'Narelle, stand back. I need to shock him.' Despite the firmness of her tone and the obvious direness of the situation, Narelle ignored her pleas, and Olivia was left with no choice but to physically drag the hysterical woman off her dying husband and practically throw her onto the couch.

She left Narelle there, sobbing piteously, as she applied the paddles and shocked her patient. The squiggly line remained. Olivia gave him a couple more breaths of oxygen and massaged his chest as she waited for the defibrillator to recharge to a higher setting. Shocking him for a second time, she held her breath and watched the monitor.

Her natural nursing instinct meant that her desire for this stranger to live was heartfelt and genuine, but the thought of being left alone with Narelle and a body if the resuscitation was unsuccessful was also on her mind as she watched the flat line on the monitor with mounting trepidation. But just as Olivia was about to recommence her resuscitation, the monitor flickered as it picked up Harry's heartbeat again. It was slow and irregular at first, but gained in momentum until his output was good and he had started to groan and thrash about, disorientated and in obvious pain. Olivia replaced the ambu-bag with an oxygen mask and lowered her face to his.

'It's all right, Harry,' she said in his ear, her tone gentle and soothing. 'Your heart went into a funny rhythm, but it's beating normally now. I need you to lie very still.'

Harry nodded faintly while Narelle, noticeably calmer but in shock, muttered something about going to fetch water.

Olivia reached for her mobile. She didn't have any choice. Her hands were shaking so much she could hardly manage the tiny keys, but luckily she got straight through.

'Melbourne City Hospital.'

Olivia swallowed hard. 'This is Sister Olivia Morrell.'

'Sister Morrell, it's good to hear—'

'I'm out bush with a critically ill patient. I need some urgent medical advice. Can you put me straight through to Tony Dean?' It was an instruction, not a question and for once Switchboard didn't argue. In an instant she heard Tony Dean's welcomely efficient voice.

'Olivia, where are you?'

She relayed her address with the help of a much calmer Narelle.

'I've got a sixty-eight-year-old man, no previous. Half an hour of chest pain. His ECG showed ST elevation. He went into a VF arrest. I've shocked him twice, and got him back, but…' Olivia glanced over to the monitor, alarmed at the sudden irregularity of his heart rhythm. 'He's throwing off a lot of ectopics. His heart rate's around 45. I'm worried he's going to arrest again. I'm trying to get hold of Clem, his GP, and an ambulance has been called, but that could take ages.'

'You're working for Jake Clemson?'

To Olivia the question seemed entirely irrelevant, but she knew Tony Dean too well to make a smart reply. He wouldn't be wasting time with niceties. 'Yes.'

'Well, that means you'll have everything you need in an emergency pack.'

'But I can't just go ahead and give him drugs without—'

'Yes, you can. This is a life-threatening situation and you're liaising with an emergency consultant.' He spoke very clearly and Olivia knew without a doubt that Tony Dean would face head on any medical legal consequences that might arise and would defend her to the hilt.

'Give him a bolus dose of lignocaine—that will help with the ectopics—and start a sodium bicarbonate infusion. He needs some morphine for pain. You know what you're doing, Olivia. You know the scene, and you've done it a thousand times. Just pretend you're in Casualty with a very incompetent junior doctor and you have to tell them what to do.'

And that was exactly what she did—and it worked. Suddenly she was in complete control, running the show. Looking down at Harry, she gave him a wink. 'You're going to be all right now.' And when Harry managed the tiniest wink back Olivia just knew that he really was.

Tony Dean stayed on the phone, organising the air ambulance from his end, leaving Olivia free to deal with her patient. When the road ambulance arrived she confidently said farewell to Tony, knowing Harry was in the best hands now. The crew worked efficiently alongside Olivia, ensuring Harry was pain-free and stabilising him for his transfer to the base hospital. Through it all Narelle held Harry's hand, whispering words of love and encouragement. Betty had arrived and was outside awaiting the air ambulance. The entire place, in fact, was a picture of quiet efficiency when Clem burst in, somewhat breathless.

'I came as soon as I heard.'

Picking up the ECG tracing, he squeezed the old man's hand.

'G'day there, Harry. What's been going on?' he asked Olivia.

'A myocardial infarction.' Clem nodded and Olivia continued, 'He arrested about five minutes after I got here. I shocked him twice and he reverted to sinus rhythm but he was throwing off a lot of ectopics. I liaised with Tony Dean as I couldn't get hold of you. I gave him a bolus of lignocaine, 5 mg of morphine and a sodium bicarbonate infusion. The ambualnce officers also gave—'

'Anything for nausea?' Clem interrupted.

'Some Maxolon, and I—'

Again Clem interrupted her. 'Good. I'll arrange an air ambulance.'

'It's on its way. They should be here soon.'

'We should give him some aspirin.'

'He's had that.'

For a second Olivia was worried she might be in trouble. Tony Dean, she had no doubt, would back her, but Clem?

He was an unknown entity. But the appreciative smile that crept onto his worried face answered her nagging doubts.

'I didn't need to rush, then, did I, Harry? Livvy had it all under control. It looks like you've been in the best of hands.'

'She's been marvellous,' Narelle enthused. 'Sister, I'm so sorry. I was no help. I just panicked when I saw him like that, I didn't know what to do. Sister had to drag me off him,' she explained to an attentive Clem.

'The air ambulance is in sight,' Betty shrieked from the doorway, destroying in an instant the calm aura that had prevailed. The flurry of activity continued until Harry was safely on his way to the coronary care unit at the base hospital and his niece had arrived to drive Narelle there.

'All in a day's work,' Olivia reflected, as she packed up her box and carefully disposed of the needles and syringes she had used into the small yellow sharps container. Afternoon rounds still had to be done and any earlier intentions of a gourmet meal soon disappeared once she finally made it home and surveyed her fridge.

Not for the first time since arriving at Kirrijong Olivia yearned for the convenience of a local take-away or even a decent deli. She hadn't arrived home till six-thirty and, as it was Ruby's day off, by the time she'd had a quick tidy up it was nudging seven. How she longed to throw a ready-made lasagne in the oven and spend an hour in the bath and put on some make-up. Instead, she hastily browned some mince and threw in some of Alex Taylor's home-made tomato sauce, praying that it would be as good as Alex had promised.

Gargling with asprin for the fourth time that day, she pondered whether to get Clem to take a look at her throat. Perhaps she needed antibiotics.

A quick shower and she faced the mirror. The usually

sleek red hair had curled from the shower steam and framed her flushed face in a wild mass of Titian ringlets.

'What am I doing?' With a jolt she realised she was treating this more like a date than a simple meal between two colleagues. The aspirin wasn't helping much. Her cheeks were burning and every bone in her body ached. Resting her hot face against the cool, smooth mirror, she started to calm down. So maybe she did fancy him, just a bit, and who could blame her? He was undeniably good-looking and working so closely…

'Stop it, stop it,' she reprimanded herself. Hadn't that been one of Jeremy's excuses? She was just being stupid. Anyway, who needed the complications? 'Not me, that's for sure,' she reminded herself firmly. He was her boss, no more, and anyway hadn't she vowed she was off men?

For the first time in years she left off her make-up and pulled on some denim shorts and a plain T-shirt. She certainly didn't want him to think she'd made any effort. If only Olivia had known that when Clem arrived, bringing with him a bottle of red wine and a tub of wickedly fattening double chocolate chip ice cream, his startled expression wasn't, as she assumed, one of disapproval.

Instead, as she opened the door he caught his breath in amazement at the stark contrast to the sophisticated, glamorous woman he was becoming so used to. The sheer natural beauty that radiated from her was truly terrifying; she looked about eighteen. The gorgeous riot of curls that fell in a wild tangled mass onto her slender shoulders gave a warm glow to her face. Without make-up her features were so much more delicate. Clem very nearly flung the ice cream and wine at Olivia and beat a hasty retreat to the safety of his own house. How, he tried to fathom, could he not have noticed how truly beautiful she was?

But he didn't run. He marched through in his usual arrogant way, muttering something about the 'bloody mozzies', and started poking about her kitchen drawers, trying to locate the corkscrew. Olivia added the pasta to the boiling water and busied herself stirring the sauce and cutting up some bread. Finally, just as the small talk had run out, the pasta was ready, and with the aid of a couple of glasses of wine the conversation started to flow. Of course, they talked shop. Olivia noticed how Clem's face lit up when he spoke about children. Many times she had marvelled at his skill to calm the most terrified child or distressed baby.

'I called in on Jean Hunt today. Young Sam is going great guns. She's still breastfeeding, with the odd bottle in the evening. Jean's singing your praises. You should call in, you won't recognise her. Perhaps you could do Sam's twelve-week assessment.'

'I will.' She nodded. Gradually he was handing over more and more to her and she revelled in it. She was already doing the weekly antenatal clinic and was thrilled to be using her midwifery skills, awaiting with anticipation the next delivery, which he had agreed would be hers. Despite her earlier trepidation, she wasn't nervous at the prospect. She couldn't have asked for a better assistant than Clem—he was a paediatrician after all. 'Don't you miss it? Paeds, I mean.'

'Definitely. There's something so rewarding about looking after children. They're so amazingly resilient and uplifting. Even the sickest ones manage to give you something back—a smile, a picture. You're never lonely when you're on the kids' ward.'

He spoke with such passion Olivia couldn't help but probe further. 'Have you ever thought about taking it up again?'

'I think about it every day,' he answered with simple honesty.

'Then why don't you?' It sounded straightforward

enough, but Clem stared at his plate and then looked up at her with a smile she was sure was false.

'Isn't that the six-million-dollar question?'

They moved through to the lounge for dessert. Olivia felt very decadent. Any meal at Jeremy's had always been eaten at the table so as not to mark the furniture. So instilled was this into her, even now she ate her morning toast alone there. Scraping the tub, he offered her the last of the ice cream. Olivia declined. 'No, you have it.'

He shook his head. 'I couldn't eat another thing. That was fabulous, Livvy. Is there no end to your talents?'

'Well, actually,' Olivia confessed, 'I can't take credit for dinner. The pasta is courtesy of Mrs Genobile for dressing her varicose ulcer and the sauce is from Alex for suturing his hand.'

Clem laughed. 'The patients have really taken to you.'

'I've taken to them,' she said honestly. 'The patients here are a lot more appreciative on the whole than the ones in Casualty. Mind you, when you're not waiting six hours on a hard trolley to be seen perhaps it's easier to be gracious.'

'I admitted I missed paeds, now it's your turn. Do you miss it?'

Olivia thought back to her work in Casualty. The teamwork, the comradeship. No matter how busy or how tragic the situation there was always time for each other, whether it was a sympathetic chat or a sudden burst of zany hysterics to lighten the mood. It seemed a world away and suddenly she was hit with such a huge wave of homesickness it threatened to drown her. She wondered if she'd ever be amongst them again. She nodded. 'I miss it a lot. That's not to say I'm not happy here,' she added hastily. He was her boss after all. 'But, like you, I think I'd found my niche, career-wise that is. But Jeremy…' Her voice trailed off, not wanting to bring him up again. She was tired of trying to defend him to Clem.

'Go on,' he insisted.

'I'm sorry I keep going back to Jeremy. You'll think I'm using you as an unpaid counsellor.'

He brushed aside her apologies. 'Talk to me, Livvy, I mean really talk. It might do you some good to let it out.'

'I don't want to sound pathetic.'

Looking into his meditative eyes, Olivia felt hypnotised. He had a way of looking at her that somehow seemed to bring her usual barriers of reservation crashing down, and amazingly she felt herself start to open up.

'There's really not much to tell. The same old story—I loved him and thought he loved me. Then I found out he was seeing someone else. He's living with her now. That was the one thing I held back on. Sure I stayed there more often than not, but I wouldn't move in with him. Not until we were married. Maybe I should have.' Olivia shifted uncomfortably, unaccustomed to sharing such intimacies. 'You surely can't want to hear this. You've enough problems without mine.'

'Let me be the judge of that.'

So she told him, well, bits. Choking on the words as she recounted some of the crueller things Jeremy had said to her, things she could hardly even repeat to herself. And he listened—not judging, not criticising, just listened—and topped up her wineglass, and for the second time in their short history he gave her a tissue.

'The strangest part was right at the end, after he'd said every hurtful thing imaginable and I'd handed in my notice and moved into Jessica's. He did a complete about-turn and asked me to come back to him. To start again and forgive and forget.'

'And what did you say?'

'Nothing. I took this job.'

'Were you scared you might relent?' His insight was amazing. Olivia nodded.

'Five years is a long time, and we really did have some good times. I didn't get engaged lightly. To me it was a heartfelt commitment. Part of me doesn't want to throw it all away. Maybe he has changed and learnt his lesson. Perhaps I should give him another chance. But part of me thinks he's blown it. I don't think I could ever really forgive him, ever really trust him again. It's over.'

Clem took her hands. 'Livvy, I hear you when you say it's over, but reading between the lines I can't help thinking you're considering taking him back. I'm sure if it's what you really want then you'll get back with Jeremy, but think hard. You know the saying, "Be careful what you wish for, it may come true." Yes, he might say he's changed and he might mean it for a while. But if he's serious about getting you back, what's he doing, living with Lydia? Shouldn't he be doing his damnedest to show you he's changed?' Clem's face was only inches away, his voice lulling her.

'That's what my mum says, but he really isn't as bad as I've made him out to be,' Olivia replied, suddenly defensive. 'I'm hardly objective, a woman scorned and all that.' She laughed bitterly.

'All I know,' he said gently, still holding her slender hands, 'is that when I had Kathy here, no matter what the circumstances, my main concern above all else was her. Love is about trust. It should make you feel secure, happy and content. Love should make you feel loved. It would have never even entered my head to look at another woman no matter what our problems, and we had our share, I can assure you. But we were a team.'

Olivia saw his eyes mist over and his beautiful full mouth fight for control. She wanted to comfort him but she didn't know how, scared that if she put her arms around his shoulders he might think she was coming on to him. Damn Jeremy, she thought. He had left her so twisted and screwed up she didn't even know how to respond to a friend in anguish.

'Does time heal at all?' she asked. And they knew her question was meant for them both.

'Well, "they" tell me it does. And sure, I'm not the wreck I was in the first few months after Kathy died. There's an old retired doctor in the next town, Dr Humphreys, and there's many a time he had to take over as I was in too much of a state to carry on. But gradually I pulled myself together and, apart from the occasional lapse, I'm in control or appear to be. But not an hour goes by when I don't think of her. Yesterday I went into the basement to find something and I found an old jumper of hers. I could still smell her…' His voice broke. 'Every night I get into bed and there's a huge space where Kathy should be.' His hands covered his face and Olivia was sure she could see the glimmer of tears between his fingers. 'She was too young, Livvy, she shouldn't be dead.'

Olivia sat there frozen, scared to speak in case she started crying, scared to touch him and, more alarmingly, scared of the feelings he stirred in her. In a stilted voice to hide the wave of emotion she felt, she searched for an answer to his dilemma. 'Have you considered moving away, starting afresh, getting away from all the memories?' Olivia felt a jolt inside—the thought of him leaving horrified her. Taking a gulp of wine, she forced herself to focus on the conversation and try to ignore the sudden shift in her feelings towards him. She would analyse them later.

'Well, there's a can of worms.'

'What do you mean?'

'My father's dream was that I'd take over from him as the town GP. Between my brother Joshua and me, I was the safer bet. While Joshua was off backpacking around Asia, calling himself a photographer, I was up to my neck in medical books. It was all I ever intended to do. But after medical school I did my hospital internship and I literally fell in love with paediatrics.

'I was doing very well. I'd just completed my exams and had been made registrar when Mum died suddenly and Dad literally fell to pieces. A case of history repeating itself. I came back to help out and that's when I fell in love with Kathy. Dad just faded away, he died of a broken heart. Kathy never wanted to leave here, but that's another story.'

He stopped talking suddenly and took a long drink. 'I think that's quite enough about me for one night and as for you, young lady, you look as if you're about to drop. Are you sure you're feeling all right?'

Olivia sensed there was a lot more he wasn't telling her. 'Oh, I'll be fine. Just a bit of a sore throat.' That was an understatement. Her throat was killing her.

'I think you'd better get off to bed—doctor's orders.'

'Oh, well, in that case…' She smiled and stood up. Their eyes met and held. Olivia caught her breath, watching transfixed she saw his pupils dilate as his face moved towards her. She could feel his rough chin, feel his mouth on hers. It wasn't a long kiss, just a gentle, unrushed, goodnight kiss, but it held promise and a passion Olivia was scared to interpret. She swayed slightly. Clem caught her wrist.

'Hey, you're really not well.'

'I just stood up too quickly.' She tried to catch her breath, wondering if she'd misread the kiss for he was talking quite normally, apparently unaware of the effect he'd had on her.

'Why don't you take tomorrow off?'

Olivia shook her head. 'I'll be fine, honest.'

'Well, at the very least have a lie-in. Come in a bit later—we'll manage.'

'I couldn't do that. I've got this frightful boss, you see. You just wouldn't believe the fuss he makes if—'

'Hey, hey.' He laughed. 'I really am sorry about this

morning. I can't promise it won't happen again, though, but I will try. I don't ever want to make a promise to you and break it. I always keep my word.'

She knew he was talking more about Jeremy than this morning's incident, and the strangest thing of all, considering her total distrust in men, was that she really believed him.

'I'm sure you do,' Olivia replied.

He moved towards her again, all the time gazing deeply into her eyes. This time there was no mistaking his intention. He was going to kiss her properly. She could feel her pulse pounding in her temples as his warm hands tenderly cupped her face, igniting a passion that, however unexpected, was welcomely received.

But before his full, sensual lips met hers the urgent sound of his pager rudely interrupted the sensual spontaneity of the moment. Its incessant tones took a few moments to register and Olivia opened her eyes abruptly, shaken by what had taken place. Trembling, she sat down as he picked up the phone and punched in a number.

'Do you know what time it is?' The abruptness of his voice made her look up. Clem never spoke to his patients like that, only his staff, she thought cynically. 'Look, Charlotte, it's been a long day. I'm tired.' He looked over at Olivia and rolled his eyes.

Olivia managed a small smile but her mind was whirring. Charlotte. She'd forgotten about her, and now here she was, trying to get hold of Clem at eleven o'clock at night. They must be an item after all. Feelings of shame swept over her. Had she inadvertently been doing to Charlotte what Lydia had done to her?

Clem dropped the phone back into the cradle. 'Look, I'm sorry. I'm going to have to rush off.'

'Nothing serious, I hope?' She was fishing now, secretly

hoping—and feeling cruel for doing so—that his answer would indicate that Charlotte was unwell—a patient.

'No. Just some personal business,' he answered evasively. 'Thanks for dinner.'

There was her answer.

Her composure completely restored, Olivia stood up. 'It was my pleasure. Goodnight, Clem. See you at work.'

The intimacy had faded in an instant.

As he got to the door he turned. 'Look after that throat,' he said, and then he was gone.

Closing the door behind him, Olivia let out a sigh. That had been far too close for comfort. If Charlotte hadn't rung when she had who knew what could have happened.

Taking a couple more aspirin, Olivia crawled into bed. For a moment she closed her eyes and allowed herself the luxury of remembering the feeling of being held in Clem's arms. It had been so long since she had felt wanted. So long since a man had looked at her with lust instead of loathing, compassion instead of contempt.

'No!' She banged her fists on the bed. Clem would be with Charlotte by now. Men—they were all as bad as each other, and she wouldn't let herself forget it again. As far as she was concerned, this night simply hadn't happened.

Turning off the light, she finally drifted off into an uneasy sleep.

CHAPTER FOUR

HAD Olivia been even remotely worried about facing Clem she didn't have time to dwell on it, for the bedside phone awoke her from a restless sleep in the early hours. Fumbling, she picked up the receiver. Knowing the call would be work-related, it forced her mind to concentrate as she flicked on the bedside lamp.

'Livvy, it's Clem. I know I said the next one would be yours but it happened in rather a rush.'

Instantly she was awake, reaching for her pen and notebook in case he was going to give her an address, as she tried to make sense of what he was saying.

'Did I wake you?' he barked.

She glanced at the bedside clock. 'Well, it is two in the morning. Is everything all right?'

'Helen Moffat just delivered, three weeks before her due date,' he explained. 'It was very quick. The baby seemed fine at first, but now I'm just a bit concerned. She's not holding her temperature and her blood sugar is a bit low. I don't want to overreact and get an ambulance, but I do think we ought to keep a closer eye on her. Could you open up the surgery and set up the incubator? I'll bring her over.'

'Sure. I'll be right there.'

Jumping out of bed, Olivia dressed quickly. She might as well put on her uniform as she was obviously going to be there a while. Pulling a comb through her hair, now even more wild and curly, she twisted it into a knot and expertly tied it on her head. She brushed her teeth, put on a slick of lipstick and ran the short distance to the surgery.

The incubator only needed plugging in, as it was always

made up and ready for any such emergency. Clem had said the baby's blood sugar was low so she prepared a paediatric burette and had a flask of dextrose in case the infant needed an infusion.

There was no doubt that the treatment room was impeccably equipped. In fact, many of the monitors here were more up to date than the ones she had used in Casualty. Olivia knew Clem fought tooth and nail to ensure his patients were given the best health care, despite the fact there was no hospital within easy access.

Sure, the town got behind him and arranged fund-raisers for various pieces of equipment, but from what she had seen and heard, a lot came from Clem's own pocket. He was undoubtedly on a good salary—the sheer volume of patients and procedures he undertook assured that—but he certainly didn't rest on his laurels. Instead, he pumped a lot back into the practice and on nights like this it showed.

Unsure if the mother would be coming, Olivia turned down the most comfortable of the patient trolleys and put on the fan heater, despite the warmth of the night.

Her throat was hurting in earnest now. Opening the drug cupboard she took out some aspirin and swallowed them without water.

'Caught you red-handed!'

Olivia swung round, aghast. Surely Clem didn't think she was stealing drugs? He stood in the doorway, dressed in the same clothes he had left her house in, carrying the newborn wrapped in a huge bundle of blankets.

'They're aspirin,' she said tersely, holding out the silver wrapping for him to inspect, then colouring when she saw Clem was laughing.

'Don't be so paranoid,' he teased, then in a more concerned voice added, 'Is that throat of yours no better?'

'It's nothing for you to worry about, though I had better put on a mask—this little lady has enough to contend with without my germs. Where's Helen?' Tying the paper mask, she walked over. Clem had a slightly euphoric manner about him, which at first she put down to too much Charlotte. But remembering her time on a labour ward, she realised with disquieting relief that his mood was more likely to be elevated from the delivery.

'At home. I gave her pethidine, not realising this little lady was going to make such a rapid entrance. She had a good cuddle with the babe while I stitched her, but I think she deserves to sleep it off in bed rather than on one of our hard trolleys.' Clem grinned as she peered into the swag of blankets. 'Livvy, at this ungodly hour anyone else would be wearing jeans and an inside-out T-shirt, yet you manage to look as if you're ready for a day's work. Do you sleep in your uniform?'

'I like to look smart. It's better for the patients,' she replied primly.

'Well, as your patient's only an hour old, I'm sure she'd forgive you if you weren't looking your best. I bet under that mask you're wearing lipstick.'

He was right, of course, but she wasn't going to let him know. 'Don't be silly,' she chided, lowering her eyes, glad the mask was covering her face. She really was useless at lying.

'Well, say hello to Kirrijong's newest resident. Isn't she gorgeous?' Gently he placed the baby in the incubator and unwrapped her. She really was a beautiful baby with an angry look about her pink face which seemed to say, Would you please just leave me alone?

'She's a bit jittery,' Olivia observed.

'It was a very quick labour. I think she's a bit stunned, and she's not very big. Five and a half pounds,' he added. Olivia tried to convert the figures in her head as she pricked the baby's heel to measure her blood sugar. 'Don't make me feel old,' Clem winced. 'Two and a half kilos.'

'That's better.'

'What's her sugar now? I gave her some dextrose back at the house.'

'Four.'

'Fine. We'll check it again in an hour.'

Olivia checked the baby's temperature with the scanner. 'Her temp's still a bit low.'

Clem nodded. 'I'm sure she's fine, though. A few hours' rest in the incubator will do it. We'll check her obs hourly. If she doesn't hold her temp and sugar I'll get her admitted, but I don't think there's any need at this stage. She doesn't need any more glucose for now but we'll push the feeds. There's some sachets of formula and bottles here.' He looked over at her. 'And before you tell me off, Mrs Moffat has already had a nurse and is coming over to feed the baby first thing in the morning. It would seem she's as keen on breastfeeding as you are.'

'I wasn't going to say anything,' Olivia retorted.

'I know. I'm only playing. Why don't you go back to bed, grab a couple of hours while you can?'

Olivia shook her head. 'No. Why don't you? I'll be fine. I'm up now anyway. I'd never get back to sleep.'

He was about to argue, but the thought of bed was far too tempting. 'Are you sure? We could take it in shifts. If I'm back by six you could go home, have a rest and then start a bit later.'

Olivia nodded, for a moment tempted to remind him of yesterday's temper tantrum, but she knew he felt awful enough already, without her rubbing it in.

'You're a godsend, but call me if you're at all concerned. I'm only down the hall.'

Preparing the bottles, Olivia tried not to dwell on the fact that Clem was lying on a bed only a matter of metres away. While it was very reassuring medically speaking, Olivia tried to ignore the pleasantly disturbing feelings the thought evoked. Resolutely she turned her mind away—that was one path she was definitely not going to be taking. Instead, she focused all her attention on the new baby, which was definitely far safer.

Olivia really didn't mind staying up. Making herself a cup of coffee, she settled into the reclining armchair they often used for older patients who were having a dressing and couldn't make it onto the trolley.

She had done her midwifery training at twenty-one, but more for a feather in her cap than any great vocational yearning. It had certainly come in useful on the odd occasion, but at that young age the agony of birth, the swollen breasts and hormone-induced tearful moods had seemed so alien.

Now, however, as her biological clock had started to tick more loudly, she could appreciate so much more what it was all about. Despite her aversion to the labour and post-natal wards, she had always loved the nursery. Loved looking at the tiny newborns, sucking on their fat fists, with nothing to worry about except their next feed, their whole lives ahead of them.

She recognised, too, that adrenaline rush Clem had obviously had from the delivery. Bringing a new life into the world. There was nothing more intimate or magical than that. Maybe it was something she could think about. Perhaps she could do a refresher course and this time around really enjoy midwifery.

She had checked the baby's obs and given her a feed by the time Clem came back, his black hair tousled and his clothes rumpled. 'Thanks for that, I really needed a sleep. How has she been?'

'Good. Her sugar was just on three. I've given her a bottle and her temperature's normal. She seems fine, but the feeds exhausted her. Were Helen's dates right? She's acting just like premmie.'

'I'm sure that's it. Mrs Moffat didn't want to go to the base hospital for a scan so I had to go by her dates. I think the baby's probably more likely thirty-five or -six weeks, than thirty-seven weeks gestation. She's just going to need a lot of small, frequent feeds and be kept warm. We'll keep an eye on her for the rest of the morning, and if she has any further episodes I'll get her admitted.'

'Do you want a coffee?' Olivia offered.

'I'll get it. You go and grab some shut-eye. Don't bother coming in till ten.'

'But you'll need to shower and change. Who'll watch her?' Olivia asked.

'I'll get Betty to come in early, she can keep an eye out. It's not as if the baby's very sick. Rest assured, if there are any problems Betty won't hesitate to pull me out of the shower. She's done it before.'

Olivia raised her eyebrows. 'Now, there's a picture I don't want to dwell on—Betty dragging you out of the shower!'

Clem laughed. 'Betty didn't seem to mind, though I was rather embarrassed, I have to admit. Not because Betty saw me naked, more in the sure knowledge that the whole of Kirrijong would hear about it in all too graphic detail.'

Olivia laughed with him. 'I'll be off, then.' She hesitated for a second. Her body ached for her bed, yet a part of her was reluctant to leave the cosiness of the temporary nursery and Clem in this good humour. Still, what else could she do? There was no reason for her to stay. No logical one anyway.

Her morning shower did nothing to refresh her, but despite feeling awful Olivia dragged herself to work. Her throat felt like sandpaper and every joint in her body ached. She didn't want Clem thinking she was being slack or, more to the point, she didn't want him thinking she was remotely affected by the events of the night before. She needn't have worried. His pleasant mood had evaporated and the night's happenings were evidently history. And that's the way you want it, she reminded herself firmly.

Baby Moffat was fine and slept peacefully. The surgery was unusually quiet and the morning dragged on endlessly, broken only by the occasional blood test and the baby's obs and feeds. Olivia took the opportunity to attack the chaotic cupboards in the treatment room and attempt to get them into some sort of order, but her heart wasn't really in it. Finally, at eleven, Clem checked the baby over and allowed her to go home to her parents, with strict instructions and regular home visits.

Listlessly Olivia washed down the incubator and prepared it for its next customer.

'Are you sure youse should be here?' Betty enquired gently.

'I'm fine,' Olivia replied with more conviction than she felt.

Betty bustled about, tidying magazines and watering the wilting plants. 'Fine, my foot. Youse should be in your bed. I can go and tell Clem—he'll understand. He's very good if his staff need a sickie.'

'No, don't,' Olivia replied, a little too sharply. Betty raised a quizzical eyebrow. 'I'll speak to him myself. I might give afternoon rounds a miss, and catch up tomorrow.'

'Well, if you're sure. I'm finished for the day but it's no problem for me to tell him before I go.'

'No,' Olivia replied firmly. 'You go home, have a good afternoon.'

As Betty fetched her bag Charlotte appeared, just as beautiful as the day before. Olivia flushed, unable to meet the other woman's eyes.

'Can I help you?'

Charlotte almost imperceptibly screwed up her tiny nose. Olivia was positive that she'd had a nose job.

'Where's Clem?' Charlotte asked Betty, completely ignoring Olivia.

'He's in the study,' Betty answered tartly.

Charlotte flounced off, leaving behind a heavy scent of expensive perfume, but as she got to the doorway she turned around and for the first time finally addressed Olivia. 'You could fetch Clem and I some coffee.' And with that she strode off, leaving Olivia standing open-mouthed, staring at her very trim departing backside.

'Ooh, she brings out the worse in me, that one. I dunno what the doctor sees in her,' Betty fumed.

'She and Clem are an item, then?' Olivia had to know.

'It would seem so. Nothing official, like. But she's forever ringing him up and dropping in, and I know they go out when she's in town. They used to date before Clem started courting young Kathy. She must be turning in her grave now that vamp's back on the scene. Not that it's any of my business who he sees, but I tell youse this much—the day she moves in I resign. The thought of seeing that sour face every morning would put me off me cornflakes.'

'But she's very beautiful.' Olivia didn't want Betty to even get a hint that she could be remotely interested in Clem.

'No, sweetie, beauty is from within and that one is as hard as nails. The grief of losing Kathy has turned him if he can't see what a nasty piece of work she is.' And muttering furiously, she bustled off.

Olivia was glad to see the back of her. While she could happily listen for hours on end to Ruby's endless tales and scandals, there was something about Betty's incessant gossiping that irritated her.

Olivia knocked at the study door. Clem looked up surprised when he saw her carrying in the laden tray.

'You didn't have to do that. You're not the housekeeper.'

Charlotte didn't say anything, just sat there puffing on her cigarette.

'You look awful,' Clem stated bluntly.

'Thanks very much,' Olivia muttered.

'Let me take a look at you. We'll go down to the surgery.'

'There really isn't any need. If it's all right, though, I'd rather go home. I've no urgent house calls, and you said you wanted to check on baby Moffat yourself. I can catch up tomorrow.'

'We'll see how you are first. I really think you ought to let me take a look at your throat.'

'I'd rather just go home,' Olivia answered firmly, aware of Charlotte's exaggerated yawn.

'Very well. But go straight to bed and if you feel any worse I want you to call me.'

Olivia nodded and thankfully left the stuffy confines of the study.

Emptying the contents of her handbag onto the bedroom floor, Olivia, with a thermometer under her tongue, searched frantically for some aspirin. 'Some nurse you are,' she muttered to herself. It was no use. She would have to go back to the surgery and get some, but the thought of facing Charlotte and Clem together unnerved her. The chemist's was only a fifteen-minute drive. If she left now she could be there and back in bed within half an hour. Looking at the thermometer, she was alarmed to see how high her temperature was. Oh, well, there was nothing else for it. Grabbing her purse and keys from the floor, she ran out to the Jeep.

Olivia decided to take the short cut Clem had shown her when she'd first arrived. It was along an unsealed road and would eventually take her out at the turning for town. That way, at least Clem wouldn't see her driving off. She was supposed to be sick after all.

'This is ridiculous,' she scolded herself as the four-wheel-drive bumped along the rough terrain. 'Behaving like some fugitive when I'm only nipping out for some aspirin.' A nagging voice told her she was in no fit state to be driving but she didn't realise it was the fever that was making her act so rashly. Clinging to the wheel, she wished she'd taken the main road. Clem had managed to make it look so easy, but in her present state she wasn't up to advanced driving skills.

Suddenly the vehicle spluttered, jolting a couple of times, and then stopped. Frantically she turned the key in the ignition—nothing. With mounting panic she pumped her foot on the accelerator—still nothing.

'Damn, damn,' Olivia cursed as she checked the fuel gauge. It read empty. She let out a small wail of horror. Of all the stupid things to have done. She had always been so meticulous. What was happening to her? First running out of aspirin, now petrol—and here of all places. She pictured her mobile telephone lying useless on the floor at home, along with the rest of her handbag contents. Gripping the steering-wheel, she fought to regain control. 'Don't panic,' she told herself firmly. 'Think.' It was no big deal. She could walk to the garage. It couldn't be that far.

Getting out of the vehicle, Olivia eyed the endless road ahead. There was no way she could walk it—that would take for ever and in her present state she simply wasn't up to it. Perhaps she should just wait. Surely someone would come along soon. But who? Clem had said that practically no one used this road. What if she were to cut through the bush? That would take ages off the journey and would bring her onto the main road. She couldn't just sit here and do nothing. Olivia tentatively stepped off the road and into the scrub. It wasn't that dense and if she just kept heading in the right direction she would be there in no time. Once on the main road someone would give her a lift.

Purposefully she walked, ducking branches, the eerie silence broken only by her own breathing and the snapping of twigs as she stepped on them. Suddenly something warm brushed her leg and Olivia let out a scream. A possum, which had been happily feasting on some berries until she had disturbed him, stood there frozen with fear. For a second he stared at Olivia with terrified eyes and then shot up the nearest tree. The incident was over in seconds, but it was all it took to unnerve her, and in that instant she lost her bearings.

For a few minutes she wandered in circles, frantically trying to find a familiar landmark, something she recognised, but it was useless. Finally, overwhelmed and exhausted, Olivia's legs gave way and she lay on the rough forest floor. How could she have been so stupid? She was really in trouble now. Who was going to find her? No one even knew she was out here. Clem thought she was safely tucked up in bed. Even if he did somehow notice that she was gone, he was hardly going to come out looking for her, let alone here.

Her face was burning, her throat so swollen she could hardly swallow. Olivia could hear the kookaburra's laughing in the treetops. Laughing at her for being so silly to think she might get Jeremy back, laughing at the stupid city girl who had got herself well and truly lost.

The hours limped by and finally her eyes grew too heavy to keep open, the urge to sleep, just for a little while, tempting. Perhaps she would wake up with renewed energy and start again. But she resisted the urge, terrified of waking up only to still be here. As night drew in, though, too scared to stay awake and listen to the animals' shrieking, Olivia gave in to temptation and let sleep wash over her.

How long she lay there she wasn't sure, but the sound of footsteps woke her. 'Over here,' she croaked, terrified her voice would desert her and she might be missed. A torch shone brightly in her face, making her put her hands up to shield her eyes from the sudden light.

'What the hell are you playing at, you bloody idiot?' There was no mistaking Clem's angry voice.

She felt so ill and cold, and totally, utterly, humiliated. 'I'm sorry, I didn't feel well,' was all she could manage to rasp.

'So you drove off into the middle of nowhere and went for a bush walk?' Clem demanded.

Her head was spinning, sweat drenching her. 'I went to get some aspirin.' Olivia tried feebly to explain.

Clem, relief and fear making him shout, realised this wasn't the time to be reprimanding her. This woman was sick. 'It doesn't matter now,' he said more gently. 'Come on, Livvy, let's get you home.'

And suddenly it all hit her. Whether it was because of her raging temperature, or the weeks of agony Jeremy had put her through, or a deep-rooted longing for her family in England, a huge surge of loneliness and desperation hit her like a bolt of lightning and she let down the guard she had fought so hard to keep up. 'What home?' she croaked. 'I haven't got a home. Nobody wants me.'

'Hush now.' Clem cradled her in his arms. 'Things will seem better soon.' He stroked her sodden hair, drenched with sweat, and rocked her gently. Feeling his strong arms around her and the solid weight of his body, for a moment Olivia leant against him, breathing in his familiar scent, allowing herself to be comforted. Gradually the panic in her subsided.

'I'm sorry. I'm fine now,' she gasped, mortified at Clem seeing her like this.

'You're anything but fine.' He fiddled around with a two-way radio and gave some garbled message about locating and retrieving. With horror Olivia realised he was talking about her. There was a search party out after her.

'I ran out of petrol,' she attempted again to explain.

Clem shook his head. 'You never, ever leave your vehicle. If Laura Genobile hadn't been out riding and seen the Jeep, who knows what could have happened to you?' Seeing her sitting there utterly defeated, the anger in Clem, borne from fear, evaporated and he scooped her up in his arms. 'I'll lecture you later.'

She insisted on trying to walk and he half dragged her through the bush, but her legs were too weak and soon gave way. Clem lifted her up and with no strength left to argue, there was no choice other than to let him carry her what was, in fact, just a short distance to his car. Laying her on the back seat, he gently lifted her head and gave her a drink of water and then drove her back home.

Dougie and Ruby were waiting anxiously, and ran out to meet them as Clem carried her into her house. 'Oh, Livvy, where on earth have you been? We've been so worried,' came Ruby's anxious voice as she hovered nervously, while Clem gently lowered her onto the bed.

'She just popped out to get some aspirin,' Clem replied dryly, but the sarcasm in his voice wasn't wasted on Olivia. 'I'm just going to examine her. Perhaps you could find a nightdress, Ruby.'

Olivia sat up, determined to retrieve her dignity and horrified at the thought of Ruby holding up one of her skimpy nightdresses for all to see. 'I'd like a bath first if you don't mind.'

Clem sighed. 'How did I guess that you'd have to argue?' He sounded irritated. 'Very well. Ruby, perhaps you could run a bath, not too warm, and then help her into bed. I'll get my bag and a couple of things from the surgery, then I want to examine her properly.'

After her bath Olivia sat lamely on the edge of the bed, wrapped in a huge towel. The exertion had completely depleted any remaining strength she might have had. Ruby peeled away the towel and Olivia attempted to cover her naked breasts with her arms.

'This is no time for modesty,' Ruby fussed.

Even in her semi-delirious state she managed to feel a glimmer of horror as Ruby lifted her arms and dressed her in a huge, gaudy, pink and purple floral nightdress. 'Where did that come from?' she croaked.

'I prepared your room. Your nightdresses wouldn't cover a sparrow. I didn't want youse feeling embarrassed in front of Clem so I fetched a few of mine—there's some more in your top drawer.' Ruby rubbed Olivia's hair dry vigorously with the towel. 'Right, sweetie, into bed with you.'

Thankfully, she slipped her aching body between the cool crisp sheets and laid her burning head on the soft pillows. She knew she must look an absolute fright, but for the first time in her adult life she couldn't have cared less about her appearance. Remembering her earlier hysterics, Olivia lowered her eyes in embarrassment as Clem entered the room.

'That's better.' He smiled. 'Thank you, Ruby. Perhaps you could make Livvy a warm, milky drink with a bit of sugar. Dougie has just gone to sort out the Jeep.'

'I've put everyone to so much trouble. I'm so sorry.'

'There, there, sweetie.' Ruby's fat hand held Olivia's slender one. 'Don't go getting upset. We're just all glad you're safe. You had us so worried.' Closing the door as she left, Olivia held her breath as Clem walked over to her, sure he was going to scold her, but he didn't say a word. Popping a thermometer into her mouth, he picked up her slim wrist and took her pulse. Olivia glanced up shyly at him.

'One of Ruby's passion-killers?' he said, looking at the

fluorescent gown that smothered her. The sudden unexpected humour caught Olivia by surprise and a small smile flickered over her pale lips. The thermometer wobbled. Taking it out of her mouth, he glanced at it but she couldn't read his expression. Gently he felt her neck. 'When did you start to feel unwell?'

Olivia thought for moment. 'Well, I've been under the weather for a while. I put it down to stress and a new job, but over the last few days I've been feeling a lot worse. I think I've got the flu.'

'I'll decide what's wrong with you,' he stated firmly. 'Your glands are huge. Let me have a look at your throat.'

Olivia obediently opened her mouth, wishing Ruby had let her brush her teeth.

'Ugh,' he said. 'No wonder you feel awful. Now, pull up your nightie. I need to examine your abdomen.'

'But I've got a sore throat,' Olivia protested weakly.

'Livvy, I'm a doctor. Would you feel more comfortable if I asked Ruby to come in?' he offered.

'No, of course not.' It wasn't that she didn't trust him, far from it. She was just all too aware of her painfully skinny body. She had always been on the thin side, but since she had broken up with Jeremy the weight had fallen off her.

Clem helped her to sit up and deftly removed the pillow, gently lowering her till she lay flat on the bed. His large hands gently probed her stomach. Olivia lay there, every muscle in her body rigid, mortified at the embarrassment of it all.

'Relax, Livvy, please,' he urged. 'Are you tender there?'

'No.'

'Or there?' He pushed again.

'No,' she lied.

'Livvy, please, relax your muscles—you're making it impossible for me to examine you. How about there?'

Olivia winced slightly. 'No!' Hastily she pulled down the awful nightdress and sat up. 'Look, I'm fine, I tell you. Now, if you'll just give me some aspirin and let me sleep, I'll be all right.'

'No, you won't.' Replacing the pillow, he held her shoulders and gently eased her back. 'It will need to be confirmed by a blood test, but I'm pretty sure you've got glandular fever.'

Olivia relaxed onto the pillow and closed her eyes. In a funny way it was actually a relief. So that's what was wrong with her. At least it explained the exhaustion and lethargy. At least there was a reason for the ever-threatening tears. She wasn't losing her mind after all, just struggling against a nasty viral infection. Clem let her digest the news and then continued. 'I was attempting to examine your abdomen for any enlargement of your liver or spleen. You certainly don't make things easy.'

An awful thought suddenly occurred to Olivia. 'I couldn't have infected any of the patients, could I? What about baby Moffat?'

Clem smiled. 'Unless you've been going around town kissing your patients passionately there's nothing to worry about. And if you have,' he added teasingly, 'we'd better have a long talk.'

Not the patients, just the doctors. She blushed as she remembered the previous night. Thank goodness Clem's pager had gone off when it had. Clem must have read her mind, but it didn't take an Einstein to guess what she was thinking.

'I had it myself when I was a student, so I know how rotten you must be feeling,' he said lightly, but the inference was there—she couldn't have given it to him anyway.

'So, what now?' Olivia asked, but she already knew the answer.

'Bed rest, bed rest and more bed rest, and not just because of the glandular fever. I believe you're emotionally exhausted as well as physically, and until you rest and get your strength back you're going to keep picking up every bug around. I'll move you over to my house, where it will be easier for Ruby and I to keep an eye on you.'

'No,' she answered quickly. 'I'll manage fine here.'

'Are you listening to a word I say, or are you just deliberately being difficult?' Clem asked, exasperated. 'Livvy, you have glandular fever. It isn't going to go away in a couple of days, you need to be looked after properly.'

'I said I'll manage,' Olivia replied with as much strength as she could muster.

'Look.' He appeared to relent. 'If you really can't stand the idea of having me looking after you, then perhaps I could arrange for transport to take you back to Melbourne. Is there someone who can care for you there?' Clem felt cruel, saying this, but it really was the last card he had left up his sleeve to play against this most unwilling patient.

Olivia lay there, defeated. Who, indeed? She couldn't dump herself on Jessica again, and all her other friends had jobs and families—they didn't need an emotional wreck with glandular fever to land on their doorsteps. And Jeremy? That was almost laughable. Perhaps she'd end up sharing a house with him and Lydia. Olivia turned her troubled eyes to Clem and shook her head. If she'd expected a look of sympathy she didn't get one.

'Well, then, it looks as if you're stuck with us. I'll compromise, though. You can stay here on the strict condition that you ring if there's the slightest problem, and that Ruby and I can drop in freely. At the first sign that you're doing too much I'll carry you over to the main house myself. Understood?'

Olivia nodded glumly. She wasn't exactly inundated with options.

'Good. Now, try and get some sleep. I'm going to fetch

some paperwork from home and then I'll be back. I'll be in the lounge all night if you need anything.'

Olivia opened her mouth to object. He couldn't stay here. He had surgery in the morning and she knew he had hardly slept last night. Then, remembering his threat of carrying her over to his house, she thought better than to argue. Clem was quite capable of bundling her up in these blankets and taking her over there right this minute. 'Thanks,' she muttered, though not very graciously.

'Now, is there anything I can get you?'

Shaking her head, she watched as he walked to the bedroom door. 'Clem?'

He turned. She wanted to say thank you, for finding her, for caring. And to say she was sorry for all the trouble. But she was scared she might start to cry. What was it about this man that brought her usually hidden emotions bubbling to the surface? 'Could I have another milky drink?'

He gave her a wide smile. 'Oh, no, what have I done? They say nurses make the worst patients.'

For the next forty-eight hours Olivia's dreams were as erratic as her temperature. Jeremy would appear in bed next to her, his lithe, taut body as beautiful as it always had been, whispering endearments, telling her how much he loved her. She would turn and reach out for him but then the door would open and Lydia would be there, carrying huge syringes and saying, 'Trust me, I'm a doctor.' Her husky voice would fill the room. Panicking, Olivia would reach for Jeremy for reassurance, for help, but he would lie there, laughing.

'How could I not want her, darling? Look at yourself— did you really think I would choose you?'

She would wake up screaming, drenched in sweat, desperately trying to escape the hypodermic that Lydia bore, fighting against them both. Within seconds dear Ruby would appear, as solid as a rock, in a vast dressing-gown, her hair in a net. The room would be flooded with light and Olivia would sob into the huge bosom, wishing Ruby were her mother. 'There, there, sweetie, it was just a dream. No worries, just a horrid dream,' the familiar Aussie voice would say. Ruby would stay with her then, dozing in the chair, and Olivia would lie there listening to Ruby's gentle snoring, praying for the morning so she could say she'd got through another night.

By the fourth night her temperature had long since subsided, yet the nightmares stayed. She awoke at two a.m. gripped with the same panic and fear that had haunted her since Jeremy had gone. Jeremy—where was he? Why wasn't he lying there next to her? And then it dawned on her that she was alone and he was with Lydia. This wasn't a nightmare she was having, this was sheer, living hell.

She longed for her mother, longed for the vast oceans that separated them to miraculously disappear and Mum to be there to somehow make things all right like when she was little, to promise things would seem better in the morning. But her mother was in England, as unattainable as Jeremy. The tears fell then, and she didn't fight them, just let the great shuddering sobs that convulsed her body come, doing nothing to hold them back.

Suddenly the light flicked on and she felt comforting hands massaging her shoulders, gently stroking her hair. 'It's OK, Livvy, let it out.'

Olivia froze. Where was Ruby? This was Clem she was weeping on. Abruptly she turned onto her back, pulling the covers up to her chin. 'I'm all right, it was just a dream.' She could feel his solid weight on the bed next to her, feel the warmth of his leg against hers through the thin sheet. What did it matter that it was Clem? At least it was another human being.

'Come here,' he said softly, and opened his arms to her.

She lifted her body slightly and, unresisting, allowed him to pull her towards him, enveloping her in his embrace. His strong arms wrapped tightly around her fragile frame and he held her securely, rocking her gently as she wept, never admonishing her, not once telling her to calm down, until finally the sobs subsided. Clem eased her back onto the pillows, tenderly wiping away her tears with the corner of the sheet. 'You've been through one hell of a lot, but things will get better.'

'Do you really think so?'

'I know so,' he said with conviction. She searched his face. He seemed so positive, so sure, and she badly wanted to believe him. Even before he moved she sensed his departure. As he stood up she felt the coldness of the sheet against her leg without him there.

'Please, don't go.' The words were out before she could stop them.

'I'm not going anywhere, I'm right here.' And sitting himself in the bedside chair, he leant over and turned out the light. 'Try to get some sleep. I'm here if you need me.'

Aware of his powerful presence, comforted by his regular breathing, gradually she drifted off and had the first peaceful sleep she'd had in weeks.

'Clem said you could have a bath today.'

Olivia winced as Ruby flung open the bedroom curtains. The bright morning sun flooded the rumpled bed. She looked around the room, her eyes coming to rest on the chair where Clem had slept, desperately trying to remember what she had said. How could she have let him see her in that state? How could she have lowered her guard like that? It was as if she'd been to a wild party and had a frightful hangover without the pleasure or excuse of champagne. Burying her head under the sheets Olivia frantically tried to piece together just what she had told him. She could vaguely remember the word Jeremy coming up too many times and a speech about her mother, and then pleading with him not to go.

'Oh, God.'

Ruby was over in a flash. 'Livvy, are you all right? Should I fetch Clem?'

'Oh, no, please, don't.' Even the thought of facing Clem made her blush from her head to her toes. Getting up slowly, Olivia made her way gingerly to the bathroom on legs that felt like jelly. Ruby placed a pile of towels and yet another flannelette creation on the vanity unit.

'I'll be right outside. If youse get dizzy call me straight away.'

'I will, I promise.'

Slowly she lowered herself into the huge enamel tub and wallowed in the luxury of the hot, bubbly water. She massaged conditioner into her hair and lay back, letting the water lap over her body. Deliberately she blocked all thoughts of Jeremy and Clem out of her mind, and just relished the moment.

'C'mon, now, sweetie, you don't want to overdo it.'

Exhausted from her exertions, Olivia sat obediently as Ruby dried her hair a few minutes later. 'I think I've got some cotton pyjamas in the dressing-table drawer,' Olivia ventured, crossing her fingers as Ruby scrabbled through her drawers. Sure enough, there they were, under a pile of lingerie.

'I'll go and fix you some breakfast while you get changed, but no hanging around—pyjamas on and then bed.'

Feebly she ran a comb through her hair and tied it in a high ponytail secured with a white scrunchie. Catching sight of herself in the mirror, she screwed up her face at the pale, drawn reflection that stared back. Realising she must be approaching death not to even want to put on make-up, Olivia acknowledged there were some absolute essentials in life and liberally sprayed her wrists and neck with her favourite perfume. Feeling refreshed but exhausted, gratefully she crawled back into the fresh bed Ruby had made up. She soon bustled in, carrying a tray.

'I've made you some toast and scrambled eggs. Now, there's freshly squeezed orange juice, with just a squirt of lemon. Be sure and drink it all, youse need your vitamin C.'

Olivia looked at the laden tray and felt a huge lump in her throat. Dear Ruby, she had made such an effort. She had even picked some anemones from the garden and arranged them in a tiny vase. 'I'll try.'

'You'll do more than try,' Ruby insisted. 'I used to squeeze the oranges and lemons for poor Kathy—she reckoned that was what got her through the mornings.'

The piece of toast in Olivia's hand dropped to the plate. She stared at the untouched orange juice. She knew it was none of her business, but she just had to know. 'What was she like—Kathy?'

The question stopped Ruby in her tracks. Taking a deep breath, she sat on the bed beside Olivia. For a while she didn't say anything, just stared out of the window, then she finally turned.

'She was the best,' she said in an unusually subdued voice. 'I remember her as a little 'un always smiling. She always loved Clem, long before he even noticed her. I remember when he started to date that Charlotte. Kathy's mum told me she cried the whole night through. Then the next thing I heard they were together and I've never seen a couple happier. They loved each other so much. Not that they were gushing or anything like that. It was just so obvious to everyone. They didn't need to tell you, it just showed in their faces. Clem's never been the same, and I don't think he ever will be. There's this sadness in his eyes, always there. He's always thinking of her.'

'How did she die?'

'Cancer. A wicked disease, it's no respecter of age or beauty.' Ruby wiped away a tear that spilled down her fat, rosy cheeks.

'Was she very beautiful?'

'She was a real beaut, our Kathy. Didn't need make-up, she was beaut inside and out. We all loved her. I used to come and sit with her near the end if Clem had to go to an emergency or when we could persuade him to have a sleep. Not once did she complain or worry about herself, just Clem—how he'd cope, who'd look after him. She never once said, ''Why me?'''

Olivia felt the hot tears spill now onto her own cheeks. The two women sat there for a time, both locked in their own private thoughts. Finally Ruby stood up. 'C'mon, Livvy, eat your breakfast now, sweetie. I'll get on.'

Half-heartedly Olivia pushed the toast around her plate. The tears that fell unchecked were for Kathy, the beautiful woman she had never met. Kathy. So cruelly robbed of time, taken for no apparent reason from the people she loved. And they fell for Clem, too. A good man, who didn't deserve this—to be left alone to pick up the pieces without his beautiful wife by his side.

CHAPTER FIVE

GRADUALLY Olivia regained her strength. Ruby, ever dili-
gent, petted and fussed over her like a broody hen, coaxing
her to eat the huge meals she prepared, letting her ramble
on endlessly and shooing out visitors when she felt it was
getting too much.

Not that she had many—a couple of her regular patients
dropped in, bearing fruit and chocolates. Iris Sawyer, the
retired practice nurse, had been a couple of times, but despite her insistence that the surgery was coping and Olivia
should concentrate on getting well, the visits only served
to make Olivia feel even more guilty. Iris should be enjoying her retirement, not covering for her. Betty seemed to
feel it was her duty to visit daily and fill Olivia in on every
last piece of gossip she could glean from the surgery. Olivia
found the visits exhausting and was always relieved when
Ruby appeared at the bedroom door and suggested Betty
join her in the kitchen for a cuppa.

The only person she looked forward to seeing was Clem.
He was good company and never demanding. He would sit
on the edge of her bed and chat idly about his day or the
patients. Sometimes he would bring over the plans for the
new hospital, asking her advice on the layout. It was nice
to be involved and he always took her suggestions seriously.

'You've just shot our budget for another five grand,' he
would say with a laugh as she overhauled the resuscitation
area or moved the nurses' station. Other times he would
just sit in the armchair and write his notes, the silence never
awkward. Sometimes Olivia would drift off to sleep, only

93

stirring when he left as he gently tucked the blankets in around her and put a cool hand on her forehead to check her temperature. He had never told her off about the stupidity of her actions, but she felt a lecture was only a matter of time.

One afternoon as Clem flicked through a medical journal Ruby burst through the bedroom door, her face hidden behind a huge bunch of yellow roses.

'These just arrived for you, Livvy. They must've cost a fortune, there's no florist in town, they had to be sent by courier.' She practically tossed Clem the mail she had collected and then, blatantly indiscreet, hovered by the bed as Olivia, her hands shaking, opened the tiny envelope.

'They're from Jeremy,' she said in an incredulous voice 'How did he know I was sick?'

'That's my fault, I'm afraid.' Ruby at least had the grace to blush. 'He rang a few days ago. He sounded nice and so concerned and I knew how youse was missing him and all.'

'But how did he know I was here?' Olivia asked, bewildered.

'Tony Dean probably told him,' Clem answered logically, without bothering to look up from his mail. 'And I wouldn't be too hard on Ruby. I nearly rang Jeremy myself when you did your disappearing act. You do realise, don't you, that he's on your résumé as your emergency contact?'

Olivia chose to ignore the question and its obvious implications, tears welling in her eyes as she read the card. 'He's coming to see me. He wants to talk.'

'Well, he'd better step on it. If the time his flowers took to get here is anything to go by, you'll be disgustingly healthy and back at work by the time he arrives.' There was no mistaking the harshness in Clem's voice, though all the while he spoke he carried on reading his mail, not even glancing at Olivia or her flowers.

'Don't be like that, Clem. It would have been hard to organise the delivery,' Ruby reasoned, seeing the disappointment flicker in Olivia's eyes.

'I just can't believe he's coming all this way to see me.'

'Neither can I,' Clem replied dryly, then in a gentler tone added, 'Just don't get your hopes up, OK?'

Olivia nodded.

'I'm going for a walk. I'll pop in later this evening.' He stood up and stretched, yawning without bothering to cover his mouth, his untucked shirt lifting with the movement just enough to reveal a glimpse of his muscled stomach. Olivia turned away, suddenly embarrassed.

'You're going already?' She couldn't hide the disappointment in her voice.

'I need some fresh air and I'd better go and check on the builders. There are a few things that need to be sorted—anyway, I expect you've got a bit to think about.' He gestured towards the flowers and then sat down on the bed. His dark eyes turned to her and Olivia felt her pulse rate rise. It was as if he were staring right at her very soul. Shaken, she looked away. Her soul really wasn't up to scrutiny at the moment. 'Please, Livvy, be careful.'

Unable to speak, desperately trying to keep her breathing even, it was all she could do to nod dumbly at him. In that instant she knew beyond a shadow of a doubt that her rising pulse rate and flushed cheeks had nothing to do with the glandular fever. It wasn't only Jeremy she had to be careful about. There was no hiding from it—she felt far more for Clem than she had ever dared admit, a physical attraction so strong she could almost taste it. As he left, gently closing the door behind him, Olivia lay back on the pillow, bewildered and confused at the feelings that coursed through her. The scent of Jeremy's roses seemed to overpower the room, clashing with the lingering musky traces of Clem's aftershave.

'Ignore him, pet. He's in a bad mood because he got a letter from his brother Joshua. He probably wants Clem to send him yet another blank cheque. Youse just enjoy your flowers. He sounds sound like a fine young man, that Jeremy.'

'He had an affair, he's still living with her,' Olivia reminded the elder woman, who had heard the whole story time and again.

'Happen he made a mistake. My Dougie was no angel. Many a tear I shed over his dalliances, but once we were wed, well, he's never looked at another woman,' Ruby said as she tucked in Olivia's bedspread. 'Now, try and get some rest.'

The phone by the bed rang shrilly. Ruby had just gone out.

'Hello.'

'Olivia, darling, is that you?' There was no mistaking the husky voice on the other end.

'Jeremy,' she gasped incredulously. 'I just got your flowers.'

'Sorry I took so long in sending them, but I've been caught up at the hospital.'

In just one short sentence he had incriminated himself. Wasn't his roster always his excuse? If he'd just stayed quiet she could have gone on believing that the flowers had simply been delayed. It was as if a huge alarm bell had sounded in her head.

Be careful, Olivia warned herself, echoing Clem's words from just moments before.

'What can I do for you?' Olivia spoke slowly, playing for time so she could decide how to handle the situation.

'Darling, don't sound so formal. I'm ringing to see how you are, of course. I've been so worried. Tony Dean said you were out bush in Kirrijong of all places, and then I finally track down a number and some old biddy tells me you've got glandular fever. I've been trying to speak to you for ages, but every time I ring some proprietorial bush quack tells me you're resting. I hope they're looking after you all right. Has he checked your liver function and—?'

'I'm being looked after beautifully,' Olivia answered curtly. Far better than you would have, she wanted to add, but she simply wasn't up to a row.

'Oh, well, good. I just wanted to make sure. Some of these country doctors can be a bit old-fashioned—they don't always keep themselves up to date. I just want to know you're getting the correct treatment.'

'Don't be so pompous,' Olivia snapped. How dared he make out Clem was some sort of backwater hick?

'Let's not argue, sweetheart,' he soothed. 'Right now I'm far more interested in finding out when you're coming home.'

Olivia nearly dropped the phone. He was talking as if she might have been delayed at the shops. 'What about Lydia?' She heard his sharp intake of breath.

'You leave her to me, Olivia. I miss you. I was an idiot to ever let you go. I need you, darling.' His voice dropped and slowly, caressingly he whispered endearments, using all the phrases of old that had never failed to win her around.

She lay motionless on the bed, listening, her knuckles white as she gripped the telephone. How did he do it? He had treated her so badly and yet she could feel herself weakening. There was something about his manner, a desperation creeping into his voice that made her think that maybe, just maybe he had changed.

She closed her eyes and for an instant Clem's face flashed into her mind, but she resolutely pushed it away. She mustn't confuse the issue. Clem had Charlotte and, anyway, this was five years of her life they were talking about. Surely that must count for more than some idiotic notion she had only entertained for literally five minutes.

'Are you and Lydia completely finished?' Even before he replied she knew there would be a flood of excuses.

'Darling, she's harder to get rid of than a red wine stain,' he drawled.

'Have you tried salt?' Olivia quipped, but Jeremy wasn't to be deterred.

'Just tell me you're coming home and I'll have her out of here in five minutes flat. She's absolutely obsessed with me, you know. I'm not just making excuses. She pursued me relentlessly, just never let up. I know I should have been stronger, but I was so stressed, what with this interview coming up and us going through a rough patch.'

Her mind whirred. What rough patch? As far as she'd been concerned, there hadn't been any major problems, just the usual dramas Jeremy was so good at creating. No relationship was perfect all of the time. Surely if it had been that serious he should have come to her, tried to work things out, before jumping into bed with Lydia. 'I don't want to hear excuses, Jeremy.'

'Of course you don't. You're not well, I understand that, but things will be better now. We can work this out. Just come back home. I really miss you, darling.'

'It has nothing to do with whether I'm well or not,' Olivia retorted sharply. 'And anyway I've got obligations here.'

'What are you talking about?' Jeremy answered, irritated and somewhat taken back by her refusal. This wasn't going to be as easy as he'd anticipated.

'I've got a job here. I can't just up and leave on a vague promise that you'll get rid of Lydia.' Her voice was rising. How dared he assume she'd drop everything and rush back into his arms?

'What about me?' he wailed like a selfish five-year-old. 'Aren't your obligations to me? I am your fiancé after all.'

'Ex,' Olivia stated resolutely. 'You relinquished your rights when you went to bed with Lydia. Don't try to turn this on me.'

Realising he was on the wrong track, Jeremy changed his tune. 'Olivia, calm down. Please, don't upset yourself. Obviously we can't sort this out in one telephone call, but surely five years together is worth fighting for?' Taking her silence as a positive sign, he continued, 'I was hoping to tell you this over a bottle of champagne but, given the circumstances, I'll tell you now. I know it will cheer you up.'

Olivia lay there, exhausted. What now? Wasn't this enough to be going on with?

'I got it, sweetheart,' he purred into the phone. 'I've been offered the junior consultant position. We're on our way, darling, you and me together. Mr Felix can't wait till you're well enough to go out for a celebratory meal. Things really are changing.'

So that was his plan. Jeremy wanted to dispel any rumours of relationship difficulties to his new boss. And though it would never be said in so many words, wasn't Jeremy now expected to have a wife on his arm at the never-ending round of functions they would have to attend? Was that why he wanted her back? She lay there, not saying a word, just listening to his endless stream of platitudes.

'Don't write us off, Olivia. I made a mistake, sure, but we've had five years together, we can't just let it go. I've been doing a lot of thinking and I've decided you're right. Perhaps it is time to set a date, and then we can start a family, put all this mess behind us.'

He was good. She had to give him that. The sugar to sweeten the bitter pill. Wasn't a baby the one thing she had desperately wanted? But not like this, not a patch job to save a crumbling relationship. She thought of Jean Hunt and how she had fought so hard to keep it all together. What if she had a difficult baby like young Sam? Jeremy would be out the door in a flash.

With every ounce of self-control she could muster, Olivia spoke in clear, even tones. 'Jeremy, the last thing I ever wanted was this "mess", as you call it. It was your doing. Do you really think I'd just come back and marry you after what you've put me through?'

'Olivia, please! Just listen—'

'No, Jeremy, *you* listen. Thank you for the flowers, thank you for ringing up to see how I'm doing, and congratulations on your promotion. Now, if you'll excuse me, I'm very tired.' And leaving him spluttering, she hung up and then promptly removed the telephone receiver from the cradle.

Over the next few weeks Jeremy rang regularly. More often than not Olivia let the answering machine take his calls but she occasionally picked up. To his credit Jeremy did seem genuinely sorry for the pain he had caused and it was obvious that he missed her, but Olivia deliberately kept the conversations light, too exhausted for another confrontation. Clem, on the other hand, became more and more distant. Still kind and considerate, he seemed rather formal. It was as if their brief intimacy had never happened and, indeed, Olivia sometimes wondered if she had imagined the whole thing.

Christmas was looming, but this year it held no excitement for her. It only served to ram home her loneliness. She thought glumly of the hospital balls that she was missing, the parties and celebrations. Ruby bustled into town with Olivia's shopping list and she listlessly wrote a few cards, but that was about as exciting as it got.

Late on one particularly long, boring afternoon Jeremy

rang while Clem was visiting. Instead of politely leaving the room, he stayed and carried on writing his notes. Not to be intimidated, and curious about Clem's reaction, Olivia carried on the conversation but Clem didn't appear remotely fazed. Damn him, Olivia thought. She might just as well have been talking to her mother.

Jeremy, on the other hand, unused to such a friendly audience, carried on chatting. Then, as if sensing another man's presence, for the first time Jeremy began to talk more intimately. His husky tones did nothing for her but, catching Clem's eye, Olivia blushed furiously and started to giggle. Clem rolled his eyes, obviously not remotely impressed by her behaviour. Hastily she concluded the conversation.

'You didn't have to hang up on my account,' Clem said curtly as she replaced the receiver.

'I didn't.'

'How's Jeremy?' he asked dryly.

'He seems fine,' Olivia answered noncommittally.

'And Lydia?'

'What do you mean?' How cruel of him to bring her up Olivia thought.

'Well, not so long ago she was the object of Jeremy's desire and the reason for your misery. I just wondered if she was still on the scene.'

She didn't respond. Maybe the phone call had got to him after all.

'You seem a lot better. I was thinking you could go for a little walk tomorrow. It will do you good to get some fresh air.'

Olivia nodded eagerly. It would be great to get out and blow away some cobwebs. 'When can I go back to work?'

'Easy.' He smiled. 'Let's see how you go tomorrow. There's a nice little track that takes you to a clearing by a creek, it's pretty spectacular. Ruby will give you directions, and mind you listen to them. No short cuts, please.'

Olivia blushed. 'I really am sorry about that.'

'I know, and I hate nagging, but just because it's pretty out there don't be lulled into a false sense of security. Looks can be deceptive. You've escaped a nasty situation once—next time you mightn't be so lucky.'

For a second she wasn't sure if he was talking about Jeremy or the bush.

'Take a mobile just to be sure. Please?' he added as she opened her mouth to protest. Grudgingly she nodded. Considering how her previous expedition had turned out, she was hardly in a position to argue.

Ambling through the bush next day, following Ruby's instructions to the letter, Olivia found the clearing easily. Dear Ruby, she had packed her the most the most spectacular lunch and smothered her in factor fifteen sunscreen and the biggest hat. 'Don't youse go getting heatstroke,' she had warned her, waving her off like an anxious mother.

Her weeks in bed had seen spring give way to summer. It was as if the world had been put on fast forward. Pulling back an overgrown bush, she turned into the clearing and Olivia caught her breath in wonder. A flock of rosellas, startled by the intrusion, flew off momentarily, only to return seconds later and adorn a huge coral gum tree, their green and red feathers decorating the old gum spectacularly, like a native Christmas tree.

A tiny stream, its level low from the unforgiving droughts, trickled by and life blossomed around it, the grass lush and green and dotted with flashes of vibrant colour from wild flowers, the bushes laden with berries, a stark contrast to the sunburnt, barren landscapes that had become so familiar. It was a tiny slice of heaven, and just the place to do some serious thinking.

Hungry from her walk, Olivia tucked into her sandwiches. Gradually the birds, which at first had eyed her so suspiciously, gave in to temptation and tentatively approached the crumbs she threw. Surrounded by beauty, she lay back on the grass, closing her eyes against the bright afternoon sun. Now her mind didn't turn automatically to Jeremy. Instead, it was Clem that filled her senses.

She wrestled with her thoughts, trying to fathom what on earth had happened. It was a question she had been trying to avoid. Clem. Sure, she knew patients often mistook their feeling of gratitude for something else. Was that what had happened to her?

Perhaps it was because he had been there for her and could empathise. He understood where she was coming from, knew how lonely the world felt when you came into an empty house at the end of a hard day. He rolled over in bed at night to reach for Kathy the way she had for Jeremy, only to be confronted by a cold, empty space. He, too, had suffered loss, and one far greater than hers.

But then again he had Charlotte. And that hurt. It hurt far more than she liked to admit, and it had nothing to do with how much she didn't like the woman. Just the thought of him with Charlotte made her stomach churn. Had she felt that with Jeremy and Lydia?

Just a few weeks ago she would have given anything to have had Jeremy begging her to come back. She was flattered by his attentions, of course. Proud of him for making consultant as well. After all, he had worked hard enough for the promotion. But what of his proposal? Wouldn't he now expect her to play the part of the consultant's wife—intimate dinner parties, the tennis-club set? Wouldn't he be even more insistent she give up work, with the incentive of a baby and his promise to be faithful if she complied?

All these things she would have done without question and, no doubt, enjoyed, but his infidelity had not only torn apart their relationship, it had forced her to examine herself. She did deserve better. Of course she was pleased that he hadn't just written them off and their engagement hadn't been a total farce. But what was it that Clem had said? That love should make you happy, content and secure. Jeremy had taken all those things from her. At the moment she didn't know what love felt like. The tears had dried up weeks ago and been replaced by a kind of numbness, a hardness that was alien to her.

Packing up her backpack, she emptied the last of the crumbs onto the grass, grateful to Ruby and Clem for letting her in on such a magical place.

Though Olivia had dreaded it, Christmas in Kirrijong turned out to be the happiest she had spent in Australia.

'I didn't know Jeremy was a horticulturalist,' Clem quipped when he arrived on Christmas morning and saw the red roses which had duly arrived the day before.

'What do you mean?'

'Well, his knowledge of flowers is truly amazing! Yellow and then red roses—how exciting! Good God, Livvy, did you really spend five years with him?'

And for the first time she didn't try to defend Jeremy. Instead, she merely laughed as the flyscreen opened and Ruby and Dougie barged in.

'Happy Christmas!' Ruby gathered her into a bear hug while Dougie struggled in with trays of food.

'Happy Christmas!' Olivia laughed, and it really was.

Ruby had embroidered some cushions and Olivia stared in wonder at the tiny delicate stitching, amazed that she had gone to so much effort. Ruby in turn shrieked with delight when she opened her chocolates and smellies.

'My favourites, Livvy. How did you know?'

'You bought them, remember?' Olivia replied warmly, as Ruby yet again enveloped her in a hug.

Clem bought her a compass and a pack of flares, which raised a few laughs, and a huge bottle of her favourite perfume. 'I saw your supplies were getting low,' he said gruffly. He caught her eye and they shared a tiny smile when he opened the jumper Ruby had bought on Olivia's behalf—garish red and green diamonds emblazoned the front.

'Livvy said for me to get youse a pen but I reckoned that you needed a couple more jumpers for those night calls,' Ruby explained with a beaming smile.

They had a barbie in the garden and much later, when they'd settled down to play Monopoly, all cheating shamelessly, Jeremy's inevitable phone call felt to Olivia more like an intrusion than a welcome diversion.

Finally, when the day had ended and Olivia had fallen exhausted but contented into bed, the only thing that had been missing, she reflected, had been mistletoe.

CHAPTER SIX

'THERE is absolutely no need for this. I'm perfectly well. I just want to go back to work.'

'Livvy, do I really need to remind you that you've had glandular fever? I need to examine you thoroughly before I even consider letting you return,' Clem replied, exasperated.

'Well, I'd rather you didn't.' The words came out too harshly, and instantly Olivia regretted her tone. But better that than let him know how she felt. How could she even begin to explain to this impossibly difficult man, who thought she was completely hung up on Jeremy, that her dreams were, in fact, constantly of him, and there was nothing remotely decent about them? It was as if her mind, jaded from self-control and reasoning by day, by night surfaced and took flight, visiting territories alien and uncharted but full of illicit promise.

She could hardly let him examine her. Apart from everything else she was painfully aware of her body. Never voluptuous, the glandular fever had managed to obliterate most of the few curves she'd possessed. Clem might have already seen her at her absolute worst, but she still had some pride. There was no way she was going to let him see her emaciated body.

Running his fingers through his shock of jet hair, Clem threw his pen down on the desk. 'Livvy, you're impossible but, of course, my opinion doesn't count.' He sighed and looked at her pleadingly but she wouldn't relent. 'Obviously I can't force you to let me examine you, but I can refuse to let you back to work till it's documented you're medically fit.'

Olivia frowned. That was something she hadn't considered.

'Look, old Dr Humphreys is coming to town on Tuesday for a consultation. He still has a few old faithfuls that he visits and I'm sure he'd be happy to see you. In the meantime, if you trust me enough, will you let me take your blood? We can at least check your liver function and if that's normal and Dr Humphreys agrees, you can start work again. Very part time, mind you,' he added sharply, ignoring her eager nodding. 'And at the slightest sign you're overdoing it I'll sign you off for a month, and don't think I won't.'

'Fine. And, no, I won't overdo it.'

Rolling up her sleeve, he picked up her arm, frowning slightly in concern. She had gone from being slender to downright skinny. His long fingers traced a vein, then gently he flicked her almost translucent skin to bring the vein to the surface. His dark curls fell over his forehead and Olivia noticed the tiny lines around his eyes as he squinted, concentrating.

She resisted a sudden urge to run her free hand through his hair. She closed her eyes, but he filled her senses. She could smell his aftershave, hear his regular breathing, feel his body close to her. If she fainted now, at least she could blame it on the needle, she thought, for a brief moment revelling in his closeness. Charlotte, Charlotte, Charlotte, she chanted to herself. It was a mantra she found herself repeating at the most inappropriate moments, like now. This really had to stop.

Clem coughed gruffly. Labelling the bottles, he spoke with his back to her. 'You need to put on some serious weight. I'm going to prescribe you a supplement meal drink. I want you to take it three times a day on top of your regular meals. I'm also going to order an iron screen. I suspect you're anaemic.'

He turned around and suddenly he wasn't the doctor any more. 'You need to look after yourself, Livvy. I mean really look after yourself and not expect too much. This really isn't the time to be trying to sort things out with Jeremy. You need a bit of peace. If he puts too much pressure on just tell him to back off. Don't play games with your health.'

Touched by his concern and confused by her feelings, so scared he might read the desire in her eyes, she purposefully rolled down her sleeve and nodded.

'Don't worry, I'll be fine.' It was safer to dismiss him.

Old Dr Humphreys took her blood pressure and listened to her chest. He must be well over seventy, Olivia thought, and had the concentration span of a two-year-old.

'Well, Dr Clemson was right. You are seriously underweight. How are you feeling?'

'I'm fine,' Olivia replied with more conviction than she felt. 'I'm just horribly bored and desperate to get back to work.'

'I don't know, you young sheilas, always wanting to work. Well, if youse feel well enough I can't see why not. But any worries, I want you to come straight back.' With shaking hands he went through her notes. 'You're a tad anaemic but the supplement will correct that. Your liver function's normal now, which is good. I'll just take a look at your stomach.' The telephone interrupted him. 'No, Dr Clemson will want those results, Betty. No worries, then.' He replaced the receiver. 'Now, where were we? That's right, I was about to look at your throat.'

Olivia didn't bother to correct him. Instead, she obediently opened her mouth as he gave her throat a cursory glance. He really was losing the plot. Just the sort of doctor Jermey had been worried about.

'Well, everything seems in order. I'll arrange another blood test in a month's time to check your iron levels. In the meantime, just take things slowly.'

'I will. Thank you.'

'No worries.'

Leaving the surgery, she walked slap-bang into Clem.

'Everything all right?' he asked.

'Everything's fine. I'll be back at work tomorrow.'

'Why not take the rest of the week off? Start after the weekend. We'll manage.'

'Dr Humphreys said I could start straight back, there really isn't anything to worry about. I'll just do mornings, like we agreed.' Determined to resist his attempts to keep her at home, her voice became more insistent.

'He examined you properly?' Clem demanded, refusing to budge.

Olivia evaded the question. 'Clem, please, you're carrying on like a headless chook.' She darted around him and out of the door. Stopping briefly, she smiled reassuringly. 'I'll see you in the morning.'

For all her efforts to get there, the exhilaration of being back at work soon wore off. If she had been expecting a welcoming committee, or at the very least to be eased into things, she couldn't have been more mistaken. Though the patients were delighted to see her and genuinely concerned about her health, they still wanted to be seen quickly. Clem was at his bloodiest, constantly snapping and downright rude at times, and though Olivia managed to escape most of his wrath, he certainly didn't seem intent on making her first day pleasant.

Olivia spent the afternoon in bed, not waking till the evening, amazed at how exhausted a few hours in the surgery had left her. For a moment she lay there, thinking about Clem. He really was the most complicated man. One moment he was gentle and caring, but he could change like the wind. Part of her was furious at him for treating her poorly on her first day back, while on the other hand she couldn't help but be concerned about his erratic behaviour. These weren't the childish tantrums Jeremy was so good at throwing. Clem's moods seemed to run far deeper. He was a good man, you could just tell. Time and again she had marvelled at his compassion. He never took the easy route to lighten his load.

She thought of baby Moffatt. It would have taken far less effort to have simply called an ambulance and had the baby admitted, and in these days of liability, safer, too. Instead, he had thought of the parents, the strain it would have placed on them, the distance that would have separated them from their newborn and had taken it all on himself. That wasn't the cool, distant man she had seen this morning.

Kathy's death was obviously still affecting him deeply. There was room for compassion and understanding. She hoped Charlotte had what it took to reach him.

Though not hungry, Olivia forced herself to cook some supper and listlessly ate it, knowing she desperately needed to put on some weight. Her clothes were all falling off her and, though never busty, what little she had seemed to be receding at the rate of knots. Taking the revolting meal supplement through to the lounge, Olivia flopped in front of the television and flicked through the channels. There was a good film just starting, a real weepy. Just what she needed. It would do her good to have a real cry over someone else's awful love life.

Just as the film climaxed the doorbell rang. Olivia was in floods of tears, of course. 'Damn.' She went to press the pause button and then remembered it wasn't a video she was watching. Oh, well, she had seen it before and knew it had a happy ending. If only real life was so easy.

There, standing in the doorway was Clem. 'I needed to see you to explain. Your first day back and I behaved appallingly. I've made you cry again after I promised I wouldn't.' He looked completely exhausted and, Olivia guessed rightly, slightly inebriated.

'You didn't make me cry. I was watching a film,' she stated firmly. 'And anyway you didn't promise, you just said you'd try not to. Sit down.' She gestured to the sofa. 'I'll get us some coffee.'

Clem did as he was told but as she turned and headed for the kitchen he reached for her hand, pulling her back to face him. 'I didn't come here for coffee, Livvy. I came to talk. I know I've had a bit too much to drink, and for that I apologise, but I know what I'm saying.' He let go of her hand and for a second she stood there, not sure what to do, uncertain what she might hear, her hand tingling from his touch.

'And what is it you're saying, Clem?' she asked finally. He looked up, his eyes filled with despair and something else she couldn't interpret.

'That I'm worried about you, Livvy, and I don't think Jeremy's very good for you.'

'Well, that's really not for you to decide. But if it makes you feel any better, I had rather worked that one out for myself.'

'Good. You deserve better, like what I had with Kathy. She died two years ago today.'

Putting his face in his hands, Olivia watched, mortified, as a tear slid between his fingers. 'Oh, I didn't realise. I'm so sorry.' So that was what this was all about. His black mood and now this drinking to blot out the pain. She could feel his grief, sense his utter loss. Taking a couple of deep breaths, he composed himself and leant back in the chair, his fingers fiddling aimlessly with the heavy gold band on his wedding ring finger, the pain etched in his strong features so intense it made her want to weep with him.

'I'm so confused. Part of me just wants to lie down with her, but the other part wants to get on with my life. I'm so torn, Livvy.'

Olivia resisted the urge to put her arms around his shoulders and simply cry with him. Maybe it would help but she couldn't be sure.

'I know she would want me to pick up the pieces,' Clem continued. 'She told me so herself. We talked about it once and she said it would break her heart if she thought I was destined to a life of grief and pain alone. I said all the right things, of course. That I'd be all right and she didn't have to worry, but I never thought it would really happen and definitely not so soon. I didn't think I was ready to move on. I certainly wasn't looking for another relationship, then before I knew it…' He was rambling now, but she let him talk without interruption. Better out than in. 'I just feel so damn guilty, and I took it out on everyone, including you. I didn't mean to be so rude. It was just easier today of all days. It's not the day to be making progress.'

Olivia shrugged. 'Perhaps it is. Maybe by talking, by letting things out, you've taken a step in the right direction.'

'I guess so. I've been dreading today and it lived up to my worse expectations. I was thinking about you, and I couldn't bear how I'd behaved, how I'd treated you on your first day back, so I came over to try to explain.'

Her heart went out to him. In the depth of his grief he still had taken the time to come over to apologise and explain his actions. Taking a deep breath, Olivia followed her instincts, battling with her usual reserve. She went over, sitting beside him on the couch. This time she didn't hold back, this time she knew how to respond, and she tenderly put her arms around him as he poured his heart out.

'I just don't know if I'm ready to start again. Part of me is so lonely and it would feel so good to be loved and held, yet part of me says it would be unfaithful to Kathy.'

'Has there been anyone else since Kathy?'' she asked gently. For a moment he didn't answer and she held her breath, terrified she might have intruded too far and equally scared of his answer.

'What do you think?' he answered slowly.

For a moment she sat there quite still. It was a silly question after all. Six feet three, every inch a man. As if he wasn't sleeping with Charlotte. What man wouldn't? So here he was on the anniversary of his wife's death, beating himself up because he'd met someone else. She wanted to scream that Charlotte wasn't good enough, what on earth was he doing with her? But knew she would be speaking out of jealousy. Clem needed a far more objective opinion and, for whatever reason, he had come to her for it.

'Just because you're moving on with your life, it doesn't mean you love Kathy any less. Maybe the time for grieving is over. That doesn't mean you have to forget Kathy. There's enough room in your heart for someone else. Falling in love again doesn't have to detract from the love you shared, and in time you'll work it out.'

She felt him relax against her and she longed to bury her face in his dark hair, to kiss away the pain and tears and somehow make everything all right, but it wasn't her place. All she could do was be there for him.

'You can talk to me, Clem. I'm a friend as well as a colleague, and I hope I always will be. You don't have to bottle things up, it's good to get these things out.' Blindly she continued, almost repeating what he had once said to her and praying she didn't put a foot wrong, ignoring the pain that seared through her as she battled with the image of Clem and Charlotte together in bed.

Feeling his shoulders tense beneath her arm, she knew she must have said the wrong thing.

'You still don't get it, do you?' He read the confusion in her eyes. Shrugging her off, she knew she had lost him. 'Perhaps I will have that coffee after all,' he said flatly. The moment was gone.

Waiting for the kettle to boil, Olivia tried to make sense of the jumbled emotions that coursed through her, and yet despite the confusion her thoughts were amazingly lucid.

Had she fallen in love with Clem? Was it possible to love someone you knew so little about? Sure, she knew Clem was a widower and a kind and caring doctor, and undoubtedly over recent weeks he had become a good friend. But they had never had a relationship, never shared any intimacies bar one kiss, and as intoxicating as it had been to her, it didn't add up to much in the scheme of things.

Yet didn't this man fill her dreams and stir her emotions in a way she had never thought possible? Weren't her feelings amplified around him—a smile, a laugh, a tear, a sob when he was around? Why, he just had to look at her the wrong way and her temper, so usually well in check, would bubble to the surface. With just the faintest brush of his lips she had felt giddy with longing. If Charlotte hadn't paged him that night....

Charlotte! Just thinking her name brought Olivia to her senses. She had no right to even be entertaining such thoughts. And anyway Clem was in the lounge, grieving for Kathy. Even if she could somehow wave a magic wand and make Charlotte disappear, she still had to face the fact that he deeply loved Kathy and always would. Beautiful, forever young Kathy, whose only sin had been to die too soon. How could she ever live up to that?

Carrying the drinks through, she saw Clem sprawled out on the sofa sound asleep. Taking a doona from the blanket box and a pillow from her bed, she tucked them in around him as gently as Clem had done for her countless times during her illness. For a moment she gazed at him, taking in the dark eyelashes fanning his cheeks, his beautiful full lips slightly apart. Lucky, lucky Charlotte. The urge to touch him was irresistible. Tiptoeing forward, she leant over him and gently kissed him on the forehead.

'Goodnight, Clem. Sleep well,' she murmured softly.

He stirred slightly as she crept out. Flicking off the lamp she made her way the short distance to her own room and lay on the bed, concentrating on keeping her breathing even, unable to relax, so conscious of Clem asleep nearby and so scared of what the future held.

It seemed she had only just drifted off when she heard the front door close. Climbing out of bed, she padded through to the lounge. The doona and pillow were now neatly folded on the sofa. Wandering through to the kitchen to make a coffee, Olivia saw a note from Clem on the table. She didn't read it straight away, but forced herself to wait until she was back in bed with a coffee by her side. With a trembling hand she unfolded the paper, wondering what he would have to say in the cold light of day.

'Thanks for listening last night, though I can't recall much of what was said. I don't make a habit of getting drunk and crashing on young women's sofas. (Not recently anyway.) I really think we need to talk.
Clem
P.S. You really ought to keep some aspirin in the house.

Olivia laughed at the last line and then reread the note. Whatever did he want to talk about? He had said it all last night. Clem had needed a friend and confidante and she had been there. Despite his popularity, Clem, Olivia realised, had no one he could really talk to. You couldn't imagine Charlotte talking about anyone but herself for more than five minutes, and at the end of the day, despite their affection for him, every one of Clem's local friends was also his patient.

Olivia realised how lucky she was for, although they were on the other side of the world, her parents were always there when she needed them, if only on the other end of the telephone. Clem's family consisted of his brother, and from what Olivia had heard Joshua wasn't exactly family-orientated. If anyone had had an excuse for drinking too much, Clem had had one last night.

CHAPTER SEVEN

'COULD I get James another drink of water, please?'

'I'm a receptionist, not a waitress,' Betty muttered to Olivia. 'That's the third drink they've asked for. You'd think she'd have given him breakfast before they came.'

'It might be nerves. He's not waiting for me to take his blood, is he?' Olivia enquired, looking over at the woman sitting anxiously with her young son.

'No, he's waiting to see Clem. They haven't even got an appointment. I warned Anne that they'll have to wait ages to be seen and now she's making me suffer, like it's my fault. I've enough work to be going on with, without providing a running buffet.'

Her whining voice seemed particularly grating this morning. Olivia shot her a withering look. 'It's not as if you're rushed off your feet. Clem hasn't even arrived yet,' she pointed out.

'Well, I'm going to ring him if he doesn't come soon. I'm fed up with the patients moaning at me about how long they have to wait, yet as soon as they're speaking to Clem it's all sweetness and light.'

For once Clem was late in. Not that Olivia needed him to start her day as there was an endless queue of patients waiting for various tests and dressings. She couldn't help but feel sorry for Clem when he arrived. The waiting room was packed and, given the fact he had spent a night fully clothed on her sofa, he couldn't be feeling his best. She couldn't be sure, but Olivia thought she caught the faintest hint of a blush on his deadpan face as he bade her good morning.

Betty was at her most irritating, trying to hurry Olivia along and juggle her list. 'Mrs Addy has been waiting an hour for her blood test. Why are you seeing James Gardner first? He's not even on your list.'

'Because he doesn't look at all well,' Olivia replied sharply, leading him through to the treatment room. That was an understatement. He looked as if he was about to pass out. Even if he just lay in a screened-off area till Clem could take a look, at least she could do some obs and keep an eye on him.

Scanning his notes, she saw that James was nearly ten years old and, apart from the usual childhood illnesses, he had always been healthy. Carefully she checked his heart rate and respirations, which were slightly raised. Popping a thermometer into his mouth, she noted that his lips were cracked and he looked dehydrated. 'You're not feeling the best, are you, mate?' She smiled sympathetically at the boy. 'I'll just ask your mum what's been going on.'

He nodded his agreement.

'Mrs Gardner.'

'Please, call me Anne.'

'Anne, how long has James been unwell?'

'A few days. I thought it was some twenty-four-hour bug he'd picked up from school so I kept him home, but he's getting worse. He's at the toilet every five minutes, though I'm not surprised—he's drinking heaps. I think he might have a urine infection. He didn't want to come to the doctor, they get embarrassed at this age.'

Olivia nodded. 'I know. But you're obviously unwell, James. The doctor's used to this sort of thing. It's best to get it sorted.'

'There's something wrong, I know it. I'd never normally turn up without an appointment. Betty was really put out, but I could hardly wake him this morning, Sister.'

'Don't worry about Betty. You're his mum, you know if

your child is sick. I'll just take his blood pressure and I'll get Clem to come and have a look.' And then I'll strangle Betty, Olivia fumed to herself.

'I don't want to jump the queue. I don't mind waiting,' Anne said.

'He needs to be seen,' Olivia said matter-of-factly.

James's temperature was normal but Anne was right—there was definitely something going on. Wrapping the cuff around his arm, Olivia leant forward, subtly smelling his breath as she took his blood pressure. With dismay she knew her hunch was right—there was no mistaking the classic pear drop scent, all too familiar from her years in Casualty.

'James, your blood pressure's fine, but if you don't mind I'm just going to do a finger-prick test to check your blood sugar. It will only sting for a second.'

'No worries,' he mumbled, hardly flinching as she pricked his finger. His mother watched anxiously.

His blood sugar was so high she couldn't get an accurate reading. It was a textbook case of diabetes—the unquenchable thirst, the acetone smell on his breath.

'I'll just go and get Clem.'

Betty was really flustered now. 'Mrs Addy was the first patient here,' she said. Mrs Addy was also her sister-in-law, Betty failed to mention, and obviously expected a few favours.

'I'll see her when I can, not when you tell me,' Olivia snapped, furious with Betty for making the Gardners' wretched morning just that bit harder for them. 'Is Clem with a patient?'

Betty, realising she might have overstepped the mark, adopted a more professional manner. 'He's just finished with a patient, but he's on the phone. I'll buzz him and let him know you're coming.'

Such was her concern for young James, Olivia actually

forgot to be embarrassed as she walked into his office, but when she realised Clem was on the phone to Charlotte, nerves caught up with her.

'Look, Charlotte, I'm really snowed under.' He motioned to Olivia to sit as he attempted to finish the conversation. 'I'll see you tomorrow when you get here, and don't worry.' Clem rolled his eyes upwards. 'OK, we'll sort that out later. Drive carefully.' Putting down the phone, he gave her a rueful smile. 'I bet you're feeling a lot better than I am this morning.'

'Probably,' she replied lightly, 'but I've got a James Gardner in the treatment room who, I can guarantee, is feeling worse than you. He was waiting with his mum to see you, but he looked so awful I took him in the treatment room to do some obs. I noticed his breath smelt of ketones so I took a blood glucose. It's off the scale.' Clem stood up. 'He actually doesn't look too bad, considering just how high his glucose is.'

'What have you told him?'

'Nothing yet. Anne knows he's sick but she seems to think it's a urinary infection. It's going to be a shock.'

'Poor kid.' He shook his head. 'Good pick-up, Livvy.'

For some reason she found it impossible to take a compliment from him. 'Hardly. You'd have to be blind to miss it,' she replied, embarrassed but flattered.

He caught her arm in the doorway. 'Many would have let him wait. You're good at your job, Livvy, good at what you do. Don't sell yourself short.'

Yet again Olivia marvelled at his tact and skill with patients. After examining James thoroughly, he somehow managed to sum up the gravity of the situation to James and Anne without alarming them.

'You definitely need to go to hospital, James. Your sugar's very high and you'll need some treatment to get it back to normal. The medicine you need is called insulin, and for now it has to be given in a drip.' He gave him a wide smile. 'You're going to have to wait for that ride in the helicopter, mate. You're sick, but not that sick. We'll get the treatment started and then Livvy and I will look after you till the ambulance gets here. How does that sound?'

James nodded. He was too sick to care, and hardly batted an eyelid when Clem inserted the intravenous cannula. Anne seemed to feel the pain for him.

'He'll be all right, won't he?' she asked, trying desperately to stay calm in front of her son.

Clem beckoned her over to the door out of earshot of James, who lay half-asleep on the trolley. 'He's going to be fine. But he's going to have a lot to deal with. Once he's stabilised he's still going to need the insulin. Do you know about diabetes?'

Anne nodded. 'My sister has it. She has to inject herself twice a day. Will it be the same for him?' she asked, fighting back the tears.

'Yes,' he replied, and Olivia knew that the truth, however brutal, sometimes just needed to be told. 'And it will be hard for James to accept that,' Clem continued, gently but firmly. 'We're going to have to help him realise his diabetes is completely manageable, and that it isn't going to stop him leading a full and active life. He will be all right,' he reiterated. 'Once in hospital, as well as treating him medically, they'll educate James and you all about diabetes. By the time he comes home he'll be telling me what to do—and I'm only half joking.'

Anne managed a wobbly smile and then started to cry. 'I'm sorry. It's just such a shock.'

'Of course it is,' Clem said gently. 'The ambulance will be despatched from the base hospital—it will probably take a couple of hours. Would you like me to ring Andy for you?'

Anne shook her head. 'No, I'll ring and tell him myself, but thanks, Clem.'

Clem had a word with Betty, now the picture of concern, and she ushered Anne into Clem's room so she could speak to her husband in private.

Walking over to Olivia, he gave a wry smile. 'She thanked me, can you believe it? Hell, this is a lousy job sometimes.'

Olivia didn't say anything—she knew he was right.

'I think we'd better start an insulin infusion here. Ideally I'd like to wait till he's admitted, but as that's going to take a while I think it would be safer to get things under way. Are you happy with that?'

Olivia nodded her consent and set about preparing the insulin in a saline and potassium infusion. In no time everything was under control and Olivia carried on with her other duties while keeping a watchful eye on James. The ambulance took nearly two hours to arrive but James's condition didn't deteriorate—in fact, his sugar started to come down. However, he still needed close observation and it was a relief when he was safely on his way.

Olivia enjoyed being busy. It was actually nice in some ways to have such an acute patient. It was like being back in Casualty, but the morning completely exhausted her. She didn't need to be asked twice when Clem popped his head around the door on his way out to home visits to suggest she leave all the paperwork till later and go home and rest. 'There's nothing here that can't wait. You try and have a sleep this afternoon. Don't forget how sick you've been.'

'I won't.' As he went to leave, Olivia knew she couldn't just let him walk away without checking he was all right. 'Clem.'

He turned in the doorway.

'How do you feel?'

He shrugged slightly. 'Nothing that a good night's sleep won't fix,' he answered, too casually.

Olivia nodded, not wanting to push. 'You know where I am.'

Clem nodded. 'I've really got to go. I've got a house call right on the outskirts and it's going to take me ages to get there. But thanks.' He smiled. 'For everything.'

Boosted by their conversation, Olivia decided to at least sort out the paperwork. Some she could take home and maybe do this evening. Betty was bustling about, straightening magazines, determined to stretch her hours so she could claim overtime. The phone ringing finally gave her something to do, yet she still managed to complain about it. Olivia collected up the last of the files and flung her bag over her shoulder.

'A cup of tea, Sister? Clem just rang. He forgot some tablets so he's on his way back. I thought I'd make a brew.'

Olivia suppressed a smile, thinking of Clem's revelation about hating tea. 'No, thanks, Betty. I'm finished here. I'm going home.'

Even before she heard the frantic banging on the surgery door, some sixth sense told her the sound of running footsteps on the drive were those of someone in real trouble. With lightning speed she ran to the door and undid the bolt. A young man who couldn't have been more than twenty stood there, breathless, his face etched with fear and panic. 'She's in the car. She's having it.'

And Olivia knew this was no first-time father getting over-excited.

Betty let out a moan of horror when she saw the man. 'Young Lorna, but she isn't due for months yet.'

Grabbing a wheelchair from the entrance, Olivia raced over to the car. 'Lorna Hall, is it?'

He nodded. She remembered Lorna from the antenatal

clinic. She hadn't seen her for a while but she'd be no more than twenty-six weeks gestation.

'She's in agony, the contractions just keep coming.'

She could hear the terror in his voice. 'What's your name?'

'Pete.'

'OK, Pete, you just stay calm and follow my instructions.' Olivia steeled herself. Taking a deep breath, she opened the car door. Keeping her voice as calm as possible, she greeted the terrified Lorna and briefly examined her. The forewaters were bulging and Olivia knew that if her waters broke the baby could be here in seconds.

'I want to push,' she screamed.

'Not yet,' Olivia said firmly. That was the last thing she wanted her to do. If she could just get them inside the surgery, at least there she had some equipment. It looked as if this baby was going to need all the help available. She looked anxiously over her shoulder. Where the heck was Betty when you needed her? Then she steadied herself. Betty would do the right thing, of course. She'd be ringing Clem to tell him to step on it.

With Pete's help they managed to get Lorna into the wheelchair and rushed her inside. She was trembling all over, her toes curled with the effort of not pushing. Inside, Betty and Pete lifted Lorna onto the examination couch while Olivia hastily pulled on some gloves. She made a mental note to later praise Betty for her efforts. Not only had she rung Clem but also Iris Sawyer and she had managed to plug in the resuscitation cot and open the emergency delivery pack. Lorna started to scream in earnest and Olivia knew this was it. This baby was coming, ready or not.

'I've got to push.'

'OK, Lorna, just hold on a moment longer.' She turned to Betty.

'Go and get the Doppler. It's on my desk.' Betty shook her head. 'Doppler?' Olivia could hear the apprehension in her voice and knew she had confused her. 'I don't know what you mean.'

Olivia forced a reassuring smile. She knew she had to keep Betty calm. 'I use it in my antenatal clinics. It's like a microphone attached to a speaker, to hear the baby's heart,' she said, and mercifully the penny dropped.

'Oh, yes.' Betty rushed off and returned seconds later.

Olivia squirted some jelly on Lorna's abdomen and, having felt the baby's position, she placed the Doppler and listened for the heartbeat, the microphone magnifying the sound for all to hear. Everyone relaxed for a second as a heartbeat was picked up—everyone, that was, but Olivia. The heartbeat was dangerously slow and dipping lower during the contraction. The baby was in foetal distress and the low rate told Olivia there wasn't much time. This baby needed to be born and quickly.

Slipping an oxygen mask over the young woman's face, Olivia explained in reassuring tones what she was about to do. 'You breathe normally. The extra oxygen you're getting will help your baby. I'm going to break your waters. It won't hurt, I promise. You'll just feel a gush.'

Deftly she grabbed the tiny hook-like instrument and ruptured the membranes, knowing this would expedite the birth. The liquor was stained with meconium, which was normally the baby's first bowel movement after birth. The fact the baby had passed this was another sign it was in danger, and if it were to inhale the meconium at birth it could run into all sorts of problems.

'I've got to push,' Lorna screamed.

Betty took Peter's arm. 'You wait outside, pet.' She led him away.

'No, Betty, Pete should be here.'

Betty turned and looked imploringly at Olivia.

'Lorna needs him,' Olivia said firmly, while nodding in understanding. Things certainly didn't look good, but this was his child and he had every right to be there. Apart from anything else, she needed every pair of hands available. 'Pete, hold Lorna's hand, and get her to follow my instructions.'

He did as he was told and much more, guiding and coaxing his terrified wife, drawing on an inner reserve that people somehow found in times of desperation.

Listening to the baby's heartbeat, this time Olivia knew there was no chance of Clem making it back in time. If she didn't get the baby out it would be too late. For a second she felt panic rise in her. But only for a second. It was as if she were on autopilot, in some ghastly, complicated birth video that she had watched in her midwifery training—except this time she was the co-star and poor Lorna the heroine. She'd broken the waters. Lorna had to do the rest.

For a second Olivia eyed the shiny stainless-steel forceps and thought about what Clem would do if he were here. He would probably use them. After all, if this baby wasn't born quickly it didn't stand a chance. But she didn't have the qualifications or experience, and in the wrong hands they could be lethal. Resolutely she looked away. It was up to her and Mother Nature. Despite the other people in the room, never had she felt more alone.

'Lorna, when the next contraction comes I want you to push as hard as you can, right into your bottom. I want you to really push hard,' Olivia repeated. 'Just concentrate on that, and don't stop till I tell you.'

Lorna nodded, then the pain took over. 'It's coming again.'

'Right, push. Come on, push hard.' They all encouraged her. Pete, oblivious of his wife's nails digging into his forearm, coaxed her, demanding that she keep on pushing.

'I can't,' Lorna screamed.

'Yes, you can, you're doing marvellously. Keep pushing. The harder you push the sooner your baby will be here,' Olivia encouraged, as the tiny head emerged. She swiftly suctioned the tiny nose and mouth so the baby wouldn't inhale the meconium when it took its first breath. Deftly she felt around the baby's neck and with dismay she realised the umbilical cord was wrapped around it.

'Don't push,' Olivia said firmly.

'But I have to.'

'No, Lorna. You mustn't. I want you to blow instead, like you're blowing out a candle. Don't push,' she reiterated, for if Lorna pushed now the cord would tighten around the baby's neck. Pete took over, telling his wife exactly what to do, leaving Olivia free to deal with the baby. Swiftly she grabbed the clamps and clamped and cut the cord. The infant's colour was ghastly.

'Lorna, I want you to push now.'

Lorna flailed exhausted, against the pillow. 'I don't need to, I'm not having a contraction,' she said faintly.

'You still have to push—your baby needs to be born.' For a split second their eyes locked and it was all it took to relay the urgency of the message. With her new maternal instinct Lorna somehow found the strength to push. Her young face purple from the exertion and pain, she pushed for all she was worth and when it was all too much Pete inspired her to push some more.

Olivia delivered the tiny baby and, leaving Betty and Pete to look after Lorna, she glanced at the clock as she rushed over to the resuscitation cot, the tiny form grey and limp in her hands. Laying him down, she again swiftly suctioned his tiny nose and mouth, and with infinite relief she saw him make the tiniest respiratory effort but his breathing was far too slow and irregular. Using her stethoscope, she listened to his heart, alarmed at its slowness. The baby's extreme bradycardia combined with his minimal respiratory effort meant that he wasn't being anywhere near sufficiently oxygenated, and Olivia was left with no choice but to commence a full resuscitation. With the ambu-bag she gently pushed oxygen into his lungs and massaged the tiny chest with her fingers, counting the compressions in her head as she willed the baby to respond.

'Why isn't it crying? Why isn't my baby crying?' Lorna begged, while Pete tried to reassure his wife.

'Sister's doing all she can. It'll all be all right, Clem's here now.'

Olivia didn't have time to acknowledge Clem's arrival but she had never in her life been so pleased to see anyone. He took over the respirations as she continued to massage the chest.

'What was his one-minute Apgar?' asked Clem, referring to the initial assessment Olivia had made of the baby. A score of three or less indicated a gravely ill infant.

'Two.'

'How long's it been?'

Olivia looked at the clock and for a second she thought it had stopped. Had it really only been three minutes since this tiny little boy had come into the world? It felt like an hour. 'Three minutes. Oh, come on, baby, breathe, please.'

Time seemed to take on no meaning as the world ran in slow motion. The baby's heart rate picked up, which meant she could take over the respirations while Clem, with great skill, managed to insert a line into the umbilical cord and administer lifesaving drugs directly into the baby's system.

Suddenly Olivia felt the faintest resistance in the ambu-bag. She saw his rib cage flutter and rise as his lungs expanded on their own. His flaccid limbs started to move, his tiny fists clenching. He started to cry, not the normal, lusty scream of a healthy newborn but a tiny wail like a mewing kitten. But it was a cry nonetheless, and the tension in the room lifted slightly. He was by no means out of the woods but at least they were heading in the right direction.

Olivia attached him to a multitude of monitors as Clem went off to briefly check on Lorna. Gently Olivia stroked the tiny infant's cheek. He might have got off to a lousy start in life but he did have some luck on his side. His GP was a fully qualified paediatrician after all. Clem was back in a moment.

'How's Lorna?'

'Terrified, of course, but Iris is here and she's very good. They heard him cry and I've briefly told them what's going on. I'll explain more when I know myself. Now, let's see how he's doing.' They looked at the array of monitors. 'What did you make his five-minute Apgar?'

'Seven.'

Clem nodded in agreement. 'Which is a good pick-up.' He listened to the newborn's chest. 'He's struggling and his oxygen saturation's low. Put him in a head box and we'll see if they improve.'

Olivia nodded. The baby was using his accessory muscles and grunting with each exhausting breath. He looked like a tiny washed-up frog.

'Betty's ringing the emergency transfer team, but it will be a while till they can get here.'

'Where will he be going?' Olivia asked as she set up the equipment that would enable the baby to receive a higher concentration of oxygen.

'Melbourne or Sydney, wherever there's an intensive care bed.'

Betty appeared and, unable to tear her eyes away from the tiny newborn, relayed her message. 'I've got the emergency transfer team on the line.'

'Thanks, Betty.' Clem nodded to Olivia. 'I'm going to get some much-needed advice from them and then I'll be back, but if there's any change tell Betty to come and get me straight away.'

Olivia nodded without looking up—there really wasn't any time for niceties.

Betty stood there, frozen. 'I've never seen one as small,' she said in a choked voice. 'But he's so perfect.'

One of the monitors was causing Olivia some alarm, and she didn't respond to Betty's comments. The baby's oxygen saturation level, never particularly good, was now starting to fall. She checked the probe attached to his tiny foot and the flow level to the oxygen head box. All the equipment was working perfectly. 'Betty, tell Clem his oxygen saturation has dropped to 80 per cent and is falling.'

'Eighty per cent,' Betty repeated, and rushed off.

Clem returned within a moment. 'The transfer team is mobilising—they've got a bed for him in Sydney. We were just debating whether to intubate yet or wait for them to arrive, but as his sats are falling they said to go ahead now.' A tiny muscle was flickering in his cheek, the only sign that this was causing him any concern. Apart from that detail, he looked as impeccably cool and in control as always. 'Set up an intubation tray, please, Livvy.' He gave her a reassuring smile. 'Don't worry, I did a stint in anaesthetics before I came to practise in the middle of nowhere.'

Olivia smiled in what she hoped was a reassuring manner. Despite Clem's apparent confidence, she knew he must be apprehensive. It was one thing to be competent at emergency anaesthetics, and he would obviously get practice out here, but a baby this tiny was a totally different ball game. Poor Clem. Still, they had no choice.

'Betty, take Pete and Lorna into another room. Stay with them and ask Iris to come in here.' He paused for a moment. 'Actually, you stay here and tell Iris to stay with Lorna. Livvy, move the phone over here. There's an anaesthetist on the line and he's going to talk me through in case I need any help.'

Betty held the receiver to Clem's ear as Olivia assisted Clem with the procedure. Thankfully the intubation went smoothly and in no time the baby was connected to the respirator. Through it all they were guided by the experts in Sydney. Again she realised how well stocked Clem had the surgery. Most of the drugs and equipment that the neonatal doctors recommended they had, and so were able to follow the instructions almost to the letter without having to make do. This baby really was being given every opportunity.

When his condition had stabilised, and on the advice of the transfer team, they wheeled Lorna and Pete in to finally see their baby. Olivia bit hard on her lip, fighting back tears as Lorna, with shaking hands, reached into the portholes and touched her tiny son. Pete held her shoulders as tears streamed down his face.

'It's all right, baby, Mummy's here,' Lorna soothed her son, gazing in wonder at the tiny hands she held, no bigger than her fingernails.

'He looks so tiny,' Pete said in a gruff voice. 'So fragile and helpless.' He stared at the monitors. 'All this equipment?'

'I know the monitors look frightening,' Olivia explained gently, 'but they're all helping him and giving us the information we need. None of them are hurting him.'

'But he was crying before. Why isn't he now? And why has he got that tube down his throat?' Lorna asked shakily.

Clem had already explained what each of the monitors and tubes were for, before he'd bought them to see their son, but obviously in their anguish it had been too much to take in. With infinite gentleness he explained again. 'That tube is helping him to breathe. You're right. He was crying, and he was breathing on his own, which is a very good sign. We chose to do this because his little lungs are too small to cope at the moment and he was getting exhausted. This machine will do the breathing for him and give him a chance to rest.'

'He'll be all right, though? He'll make it, won't he?' Lorna was inconsolable and unfortunately there were no guarantees.

'He's got a long battle ahead of him, but he's going to a great hospital. The emergency transfer team is coming here to get him and I'm constantly in contact with the specialists in Sydney. They'll be here soon. We're doing everything we can.'

'Can I go with him in the helicopter?' Lorna asked.

'That's not up to me, Lorna. The transfer team will have to decide,' Clem answered gently. 'There's not much room on board with all the staff and equipment. It will have to be up to them—they know best.'

Lorna started to cry in earnest, completely overwhelmed. 'He's just so small…'

Clem nodded. 'He's pretty tough, though, and he's made it over the first hurdle. With expert care he'll have the best possible chance.'

Pete cradled his wife in his arms. 'He's got a chance, Lorna. Clem says so. That's enough to be going on with for now. Let's just be grateful for that.'

The wait was interminable but finally the sound of the helicopter heralded the arrival of the emergency team. They wheeled in a huge incubator equipped with everything the baby would need to get him safely to Sydney. Olivia could only stand back and marvel at their skills. They handled the tiny baby so expertly and confidently, attaching him to their equipment, assessing his condition each step of the way.

They were there for well over an hour, ensuring he was completely stable before they transferred him, all the time reassuring his parents. They even took a couple of Polaroid photos, one of the baby and the other of Lorna and Pete next to the incubator, holding their tiny son's hand. Pete's parents arrived as Olivia was helping Lorna, stunned and exhausted, into the helicopter, but there was no time for them to see their newborn grandson. The baby's needs had to take precedence.

'Give these to Pete,' Lorna said in a shaking voice, handing Olivia the Polaroids. 'He can show them the photos.'

Impulsively Olivia reached over and hugged Lorna tightly.

Lorna clung on, grateful for the human touch but completely unaware how out of character this was for Olivia. 'Thank you, Livvy, thank you,' she said tearfully.

As the helicopter left, carrying its precious load, Clem turned to Pete. 'Are your parents going to drive you to Sydney?' Clem asked.

Pete nodded, tears coursing down his cheeks as he gazed at the photos.

'Well, take it steady,' he said, as practical as ever. 'The last thing Lorna needs is for you to be involved in accident. I'll ring the hospital later, see how he's doing.' His voice wavered slightly. 'Chin up, mate.' Clem shook Pete's hand. 'We'll all be thinking of you.'

As they waved off the car, watching it crunch its way down the gravel path to whatever the future held for them, Olivia finally broke down. Clem said nothing, just pulled her into his arms and let her cry. Finally, as the sobs subsided, he lifted her chin to make her look at him. 'Not the ideal first delivery, but you did a fantastic job.'

'If I had just got him out sooner, but the cord—'

'Don't do that to yourself. You did absolutely everything anyone could have done. Any hope he's got is because of you, so don't beat yourself up with what ifs. You gave him a chance.'

Olivia nodded, glad he understood. She knew she couldn't have done anything differently, but she just needed to hear it. His arms still around her, he looked down.

'You look completely done in.'

'It's been an exhausting day.' Olivia wriggled away, suddenly conscious of his embrace. 'Where's Betty?'

'Off to tell the whole town, no doubt. She's a terrible sticky beak.'

Olivia was about to agree, then remembered the wisdom Betty had shown when it had been needed. 'She really helped in there.'

'Why do you think I keep her on? I know she's a lousy receptionist but her heart is in the right place and she does come up trumps when you need her. I'm very choosy about my staff. That's why your predecessors didn't last.'

'Really?' Olivia frowned 'The agency gave the impression they left because...' Her voice trailed off. She could hardly repeat what Miss Lever had said about him.

'Because I was moody and difficult?'

Olivia shuffled uncomfortably. 'Something like that.'

'And is that how you find me?' he enquired.

Olivia thought for a moment.

'Yes,' she answered truthfully. 'Though not in the way I expected. I mean, you're a very good doctor and a wonderful boss...'

'But?'

'But nothing that would make me want to pack up and leave, unless, of course, I didn't want to be here in the first place.'

'Exactly. You've got it in one. A lot of people seem to think they'll come out here for a bit of a holiday and, as you know, it couldn't be further from the truth. At the end of the day, to the people here we're all they've got medically speaking. It's an awesome responsibility.'

'I know, and it terrifies me. I have to remind myself

sometimes that I ran a busy casualty department, and that I'm used to making difficult decisions and I am up to this. But sometimes, like today, I realise that we're alone at the front line. In Casualty there was always someone to confer with, someone's opinion there for the asking. I don't know how you do it. It must get pretty scary sometimes.'

'It does and that's the very reason I only keep good staff. I'd rather struggle on alone than with someone who isn't up to it. Take today. Betty is a receptionist—that's all she's paid for. Sure, I give her a few perks and sometimes I think it's more than she deserves. But just as she's seriously getting on my nerves and I think it's time I put my foot down and had a word, she outshines herself like she did this afternoon. It makes the incessant personal calls and sticky-beaking look rather irrelevant.'

Olivia understood. Betty really had been marvellous.

'So when some young nurse arrives, and straight away asks where the local hotel is, running out the door on the stroke of five and taking the phone off the hook at night, I have no compunction about being as moody and difficult as my reputation allows. You, on the other hand are the complete opposite. We work pretty damn well together.'

Olivia took this all in, touched by his praise but embarrassed as well. 'So why are you still so moody and difficult with me, then?' she teased, shrugging off his compliments.

He didn't answer. Instead, he stared at her for what seemed an eternity. Finally she dragged her eyes away. Clem cleared his throat. 'I don't know about you, but I could do with a stiff drink and I don't fancy fielding questions from concerned locals down at the hotel. Anyway, I want to ring the hospital later see how he's getting on.' He gestured to the private part of the house. 'Will you join me?'

Olivia hesitated, torn. It was certainly tempting to spend the evening with him but, given her feelings, she wasn't sure it was appropriate. But surely a drink with a friend after the afternoon they'd had wasn't unreasonable, and anyway she wanted to be there when he rang the hospital. She looked down at her soiled clothing. 'I'll go home and have a bath and change first. There wasn't exactly time to put on an apron.'

Clem smiled, noticing for the first time the mess she was in. 'Fair enough. I'll wait for you to come over before I ring.'

Olivia nodded. She knew how he felt. Neither wanted to be alone if the news was bad.

CHAPTER EIGHT

UP TO her neck in bubbles, Olivia tortured herself by going over and over the events. Oh, she knew what Clem had said and hoped it was true, but if only she'd had more experience. Was there *anything* she could have done differently?

Getting out the bath, despite a huge fluffy bathrobe and the warm evening, Olivia couldn't stop shaking. She suddenly felt light-headed. Clutching the bedside table, she sat down on the edge of the bed, waiting for the dizziness to pass. Maybe the bath had been too warm, Olivia reasoned as she relived the birth for the umpteenth time. Perhaps there *had been* something more she could have done, and Clem, knowing how hard she had tried and how upset she was, didn't want to make her feel worse. Of course not, she admonished herself. Clem was a wonderful teacher. If there was anything to be learnt from today he would have told her, no matter how hard it might be to hear. Still, an incessant voice kept nagging, maybe she could have done better.

She dressed slowly, pulling on some denim shorts and a white cotton blouse. A niggling pain in her shoulder made putting on her make-up more of a chore than usual, but without it her complexion was so pale, and Clem would only start nagging about her being back at work. The phone started to ring as she picked up her keys and grabbed a bottle from the fridge. The answering machine could get it. She didn't have to explain where she was going to anyone.

Clem greeted her warmly. 'I was starting to think about calling out the search party again.'

'Am I ever going to live that down?' Olivia grinned, offering the bottle she had brought.

'Not if I have any say in it.' He looked at the bottle 'Champagne. Are we celebrating?'

'To toast my first delivery in Kirrijong.' He caught the flash of tears in her eyes. 'It might not have been as I planned, but he deserves to have his head wet. It's still a miracle.'

'Oh, Livvy.' He swept her into his arms. 'Of course it's a miracle. That little tacker has touched us all—he's a fighter. Come on, we'll have a drink and then we'll ring to see how he's doing.'

He led her through to the lounge and sat her down. It was a room she had her lunch in every day and yet by evening light and without Betty it felt completely different. The heavy drapes were drawn and the gentle lighting illuminated the welcoming warmth and intimacy of this beautiful home. As Clem popped the cork he shot her a wary look. 'Your liver function test was normal?'

'Perfectly.'

'I still wish you'd let me check you. Nothing against Dr Humphreys. He was a fine doctor.'

'Was' being the operative word, Olivia thought, but didn't say anything. 'How's the hospital going?'

'Painfully slowly. That's two patients today who really needed it. Of course, Lorna and the baby would have been transferred anyway, but it would be nice to have an anaesthetist and a few more pairs of hands. Not,' he added, handing her a glass of champagne, 'that we didn't cope admirably, but I'm tired of coping, and constantly being on call makes it impossible to relax. Take yesterday. I had to ask Dr Humphreys weeks in advance to cover for me because I knew I'd need a night to myself, what with Kathy's anniversary and everything. Not that I was planning to get plastered, I hasten to add. That rather took care of itself. I really am sorry.'

'Clem, please, don't apologise. There's really no need and, anyway, you really weren't that bad.' She changed the subject. 'So, when do you think it will be up and running?'

'Another couple of months. I'm going to start advertising for staff.'

'Do you think you'll have much luck?'

Clem looked at her thoughtfully. 'There shouldn't be too much trouble. It's a different kettle of fish, recruiting for a country hospital compared to a GP practice. The incentives will be pretty good and there'll be a lot of experience to be gained. At least they won't have to ship every remotely interesting case off to the base hospital. The serious ones will still go to Melbourne or Sydney, but that's pretty standard.' He paused, as if about to say something.

Olivia waited. He had never formally offered her a job there, and she had just assumed that there would be one. Still, it would be nice to be asked. Clem didn't say anything, just reached over and refilled her glass. He obviously had other things on his mind.

She put her hand over the top of the glass and some champagne trickled through her fingers. 'That's plenty, thanks. I haven't had a drink in ages it will go straight to my head.'

Clem stood up. 'A fine host I am. You haven't eaten dinner, and I'm the one insisting you eat regular meals and fatten up. I'll fix us something now.'

'Please, don't. I'm honestly not hungry.'

He ignored her, of course. 'Just wait there. Put on some music, make yourself comfortable.'

He disappeared into the kitchen and Olivia eyed his music collection. It was far more familiar than the highbrow operas Jeremy pretended to listen to, and at least his stereo system looked user-friendly and Clem actually had cassettes. Jeremy's was all CDs and digital everything. It looked like a flight deck in a Boeing 747.

Settling on a hits mix she smiled as he entered.

'Dinner will be twelve minutes, according to the box.' He picked up the cassette holder Olivia had chosen. 'Now there's a blast from the past.'

'It reminds me of my wild youth.'

Clem raised an eyebrow. 'Really, Sister Morrell?'

'No, but I sometimes wish it had been.'

'Well, you sit there and reminisce about what could have been and I'll ring the hospital.'

Olivia nodded. She had been waiting for him to ring but had been too terrified of what the outcome might be to suggest it herself.

He was back within a few moments. 'He's stable.'

She let out a sigh of relief and Clem continued, 'There's been no major dramas since he left us, all his vital signs are as good as can be expected.'

Olivia digested this, but the question that was eating at her had to be asked. 'What about…?' She hesitated, unable to get the words out.

'Brain damage?' He asked the question for her. 'Livvy, you know it's far too soon to even begin to answer that. It could be weeks, months even, before they know.'

Oh, she knew that, knew all the statistics and that brain injury wasn't always immediately apparent, and she knew that there was still a lot to happen that could influence the outcome, but it wasn't enough. She turned her huge green eyes on him. 'But what do you think, Clem? What's your own opinion?'

Clem put down his glass. He knew she felt guilty, and with absolutely no reason. It was just part of the job. If you cared enough you got involved. 'I think,' he said slowly, 'that the little guy and Lorna and Pete have a struggle on their hands. No baby born at twenty-six weeks gestation sails through. If he comes out of this totally unscathed it will be a miracle. But miracles do happen, we saw that today. His one-minute Apgar was awful, but he was resuscitated very effectively and he picked up quickly—that counts for a lot. He looked in pretty good shape for such a premmie by the time the transfer team got here. I think we can be cautiously optimistic, and confident we did all we could and did it well.

'Hell.' Clem stood up suddenly. 'I forgot about the dinner.'

He returned minutes later with a vast pizza. 'I hope you like them crusty.' He laughed as he cut the pizza into generous slices. They knelt at the coffee-table, eating the pizza from the serving plate. Despite her earlier protests, Olivia realised she was hungry after all and tucked in unashamedly. About to reach for her third slice, she felt Clem staring at her.

'What are you staring at? Have I got something on my face?'

'Relax, I was just thinking how other woman must hate you. No matter what you eat, you never gain an ounce.'

'Nerves,' Olivia quipped. 'I'm just a bundle of them. It's probably just as well my life's in such a mess. The day I'm actually content I'll probably pile on the kilos and end up with hips you could—' Suddenly, and she never knew quite how it happened, Clem put a finger up to her lips and she knew the time for talking had ended.

'Livvy, look at me.'

She sat there quite still as he gently lifted her chin and slowly she raised her eyes to meet his. It was like looking in a mirror, seeing the burning desire she felt reflected in his, and she was finally in no doubt her feelings were reciprocated. Her heart was racing, her breathing speeding up, making her breasts rise and fall rapidly. He hadn't even kissed her yet, but the effect of this handsome, sensual man close up was more intoxicating than any champagne.

Sensing her consent, driven by his own desire, Clem moved his face towards her and teasingly showered her face then her neck with tiny butterfly kisses. Her eyes closed, her lips parted, she drowned in her senses, the bitter tang of his aftershave, the sweetness of his lips on her smooth skin.

Finally his mouth found hers and hungrily he kissed her, desperately forcing her lips apart with his tongue. He tasted of champagne and decadence and danger. She could feel the rising current that surged between them, hear their hearts beating in unison, and she revelled in it.

The distance from the living room to the bedroom was quickly negotiated and gently he laid her on the bed, all the time kissing her as if he couldn't bear to let her go. And she didn't want him to. Her ardour rising with each gasping breath, she could feel his hard, muscular body pushing against her slender frame. Instinctively she arched her body towards him, inflaming the fire that burnt between them. Expertly he undid her blouse and gasped as his searching hands encountered the gentle swell of her ripe breasts, a delicious contrast to her slender body.

With a gentle moan he buried his head into the velvet softness of her bosom, his tongue enticing her hardening nipples. One tender hand stroked her neck, while the other slowly, deliberately moved down, and Olivia knew she wanted him to go on, ached for him to go further.

'Are you sure, Livvy?' His eyes locked with hers and she nodded her consent.

'I'm sure,' she murmured, her voice not wavering as she gazed into his eyes. 'What about…?'

Gesturing to the *en suite,* he went to climb out of bed, but she gently pulled him back. 'No. I'll go.'

She darted into the bathroom, grateful for the chance to

gather her thoughts. She wanted that brief moment. Gazing in the mirror at her flushed cheeks and bright eyes, her lips red and full from the weight of his kiss, she knew that she had never been surer of anything in her life. Rummaging through his cabinet, she found the tiny foil packages and, ever the nurse, checked the expiry date on the back. A gurgle of laughter escaped from her lips as she realised that here she was, probably doing the most reckless thing she had ever done in her life, and the pedantic, efficient side of her was checking dates!

Making her way back to the bedroom, she gazed at Clem's outstretched body lying on the bed. Her heart was in her mouth but she couldn't help but gasp in admiration at the sight of him. Taut muscles subtly defined by the gentle bedside lamp. The silky shadow of ebony hair over his broad chest tapering into a fine line along his toned abdomen, edging downwards as if directing her to the very pinnacle of this beautiful man.

For once she had no reservations, no qualms, no self-doubt. Slowly, seductively she made her way to the bed. Kneeling astride him, she bent her head, her Titian curls tumbling onto his chest, her supple lips tenderly, teasingly exploring his torso. Boldly descending his rigid abdomen, relishing his scent, savouring the delicious salty tang of his skin on her lips, aware of her power as a woman.

She heard his sharp intake of breath as her lips moved lower still, teasing him until he could take it no more. In one supple movement Clem sat up, his strong arms engulfing her, laying her down on the rumpled sheets, the need to be inside her surpassing everything.

And then they were one, locked together in a rhythmic embrace that transcended all else, their bodies in blissful unison, driving each other on to a zenith that was as pure as it was magical.

Lying there, their bodies entwined, slowly the world

came back into focus—the ticking of a bedside clock, the ceiling fan delivering a welcoming gentle breeze on her warm, flushed skin. But just as suddenly as their intimacy had ignited it seemed to die. Olivia sensed his detachment even before he said a word.

'Clem?' Her voice was questioning, anxious, and his response did nothing to allay her fears. With a deep sigh he rolled onto his back and gazed at the ceiling, breaking the physical contact.

'Livvy, oh, Livvy.' His voice was deep, thick with emotion. He turned onto his side, propping himself on his elbow, and gently picked up her hand. 'I shouldn't have rushed you.'

Olivia shook her head. 'But you didn't. I thought it was what we both wanted?'

'It was, it is…' But it sounded to Olivia more as if he was trying to convince himself than her.

'Then what's wrong?' she demanded.

'Nothing's wrong, I just think we need to talk. Livvy, I never want you to regret a moment of our time together. I never want to hurt you, and without wanting to sound mercenary I won't let myself be hurt again.'

'What makes you think I'd hurt you?' she asked, bewildered.

He pulled her hand up to his face, his lips gently brushing her slender fingers. 'There was an engagement ring here not so long ago. We've both got so much emotional baggage I just think we should have cleared a few things up first, before we went this far.'

Suddenly she felt stupid. Acutely aware of her exposed breasts, she sat up and grabbed at the bedspread, pulling it around her. Never had she felt more vulnerable.

'There's no need to explain,' she said haughtily. 'I mean, I'm sorry if I forced you.' She knew she was being cruel, but she wasn't feeling very gracious. He had initiated things, he had asked her over and made love to her, and now he was calling a halt, telling her to slow down. Didn't she have any say here?

'Livvy, please, don't get upset. Just let me explain. You know I want you. It's just…'

'Just what?' Her voice was rising now. Olivia swallowed hard a couple of times. She wouldn't lose it here. The day had been bad enough without this. How dare he land this lot on her? 'Just that you thought you were ready, but now you're not sure? Or just, you thought I was? Well, I've got news for you, Clem. Make your mind up a bit earlier next time. I'm not a tap you can just turn on and off, I'm a woman!' In one movement she stood up, grabbing at her carelessly discarded clothes. In an instant he was beside her.

'Livvy, stop it.' His voice was firm without being harsh as he pulled her into his arms, holding her body stiff and unyielding against him. 'God, what did that bastard do to you? All I said was that we needed to talk,' he murmured into her hair, gently stroking her, gradually rekindling the intimacy and tenderness the night had held until finally she relented, relaxing against him, allowing herself to be comforted.

'All I was trying to say,' he repeated gently, 'was that we need to talk.'

'I know, I know.' She buried her face in the warm shelter of his chest. Olivia knew she had overreacted, and she knew he was right—they did need to talk, but not now. Jeremy, Kathy, Charlotte—they all had to be addressed, but surely it could wait?

She nodded, nestling into him. 'I know we do but, please, Clem, not tonight.'

Tenderly he drew her back onto the rumpled bed and back into his arms.

'I'm sorry I upset you,' he said softly. 'My timing can be lousy sometimes.'

'Oh, I don't know about that,' said Olivia huskily, running her long fingers lazily between his muscular thighs, boldly taking him in her hands and guiding him gently towards her. 'Your timing seemed perfect to me.'

Wrapped in his arms she slept so soundly even his pager didn't disturb her. Clem awoke her with a tender kiss.

'What time is it?'

'After one. I just got paged. Elsie Parker's taken a turn for the worse. There's not much I can do but I think it would help the family if I was there.'

Olivia nodded. Elsie Parker was in her late sixties and at the end of a long battle against ovarian cancer. 'Poor things. Is there anything I can do?'

Clem shook his head. 'I don't know how long I'll be. You go back to sleep, you look exhausted.'

'I'm all right, but I think I'd better go home. I don't really fancy waking up to find Ruby trying to make your bed.'

Clem laughed. 'Good point. The minute Ruby finds out, the whole town will know. It would be nice to get used to the idea ourselves first.' He squeezed her thigh through the sheet. 'You don't mind?'

Olivia shook her head 'No, you go.'

'I'll see you home.'

'Clem, I live two minutes away I can get there myself. Go and see how Elsie is doing—she needs you now.'

He smiled appreciatively and gave her a hurried kiss before he left. She lay there for a few moments after he had gone, remembering their love-making, her body tingling just at the memory of his touch, until finally, reluctantly she left the crumpled bed where they had finally found each other.

CHAPTER NINE

A SUDDEN violent spasm in Olivia's stomach awoke her. Retching, she just made it to the bathroom in time, a cold sweat drenching her. Leaning over the sink she rinsed her mouth from the tap and caught sight of herself in the mirror. Her face was pinched and pale, perspiration beading on her forehead, her eyes dark and sunken. She peered at her reflection. Imagine if she had stayed the night at Clem's—it was hardly a face to wake up to.

Gradually the pain eased to a dull ache and she made her way gingerly back to her bed. She looked over at her alarm clock—it was just after five. Surely the pizza would have been all right? It was only a frozen one, and it wasn't even as if she'd had a lot to drink—she hadn't even finished her glass of champagne.

Olivia drifted into an uneasy sleep, only to be awoken what seemed like seconds later by the sound of her alarm. She was no hero and under absolutely any other circumstances there was no way she would have even considered going into work. But given the developments of the previous night, what else could she do?

The thought of ringing Clem and saying she was too sick to come in was incomprehensible. He would misinterpret it as embarrassment or guilt. Their relationship was just too fragile and vulnerable to jeopardise at this tender stage. No. The music had to be faced. It was Friday. If she could just get through the morning then she'd have the whole weekend to recover and, anyway, she'd had far too much sick time already.

The pain in her shoulder made putting on make-up even

147

more difficult. Slapping on a great deal of foundation and blusher, she managed to look almost normal and made it to the surgery just ten minutes late. Thankfully, there were no patients waiting for her.

Betty greeted her warmly, obviously buoyed by the experience they had shared. 'Have you heard how the baby is? I wanted to ask Clem, but Mr Heath was already waiting and got in first.'

'Clem rang the hospital last night and they said he was stable. I would imagine he'll ring again this morning when he's got a minute. I'm just going to go into the treatment room to catch up on yesterday's files. Would you call if any patients come for me?'

Betty nodded. 'Would you like me to bring you in a coffee?'

She was obviously in the mood for a chat which was the last thing Olivia felt like, but she suddenly felt guilty, remembering how badly she'd needed to go over and over the birth. Betty must be feeling the same.

'Thanks, Betty, that would be lovely. Oh, and, Betty, I meant to thank you yesterday but I never got the chance. Your help was invaluable to me and I'm sure Lorna and Pete would say the same. I know Clem was pleased with you.'

'I did nothing,' replied Betty, blushing to the roots of her hair.

'Of course you did. Your actions bought us some time, which was what we were fighting for. What's this?' she added, pointing to a large jar on Betty's desk.

'I've organised a collection for Lorna and Pete—they'll be struggling, having to stay in Sydney. It's got off to a great start—everyone in the hotel chipped in.' The jar was crammed with notes and coins already, and the baby wasn't even twenty-four hours old.

Olivia felt a huge lump in her throat. Everyone was finding it tough here, the drought was really biting, and yet they still managed to chip in, sure in the knowledge that others were worse off. Only last week they had arranged a huge convoy of trucks to take feed for the cattle up in Queensland, knowing that if they thought they were struggling here, the situation was dire further north. It was just one huge family and Olivia felt privileged to belong. She dug into her purse and added a fifty-dollar note to the collection.

'That's very generous,' Betty said. Olivia gave her a small wink.

'Jeremy can afford it,' she joked, thinking of the car she had sold to get her here.

Betty giggled and even Olivia laughed. Maybe she would make more of an effort with the receptionist.

'We're going to have a working bee next weekend to fix up the house for them. Poor Pete had only got round to buying the paint—they just moved in last week. I know you've been sick and we don't expect you to help with the house, but maybe youse can knit something?'

Olivia nodded weakly. She had never held a knitting needle in her life. 'Of course.' She made a mental note to write to Jessica, and ask her to send a little matinée outfit. She could always tear out the label. A wave of nausea swept over her. 'I'll get started on those notes,' she said weakly, escaping to the treatment room. Betty was far too pleased with the praise to notice Olivia's rapid departure.

As she sat at the desk the words blurred in front of her. This was ridiculous—there was no way she should be at work. Maybe she had overdone things, what with the glandular fever and then all the drama of yesterday. Clem would understand. After all, hadn't he insisted she take it easy and tell him if there were any problems? She would simply tell him that she wasn't feeling well, and be totally professional but friendly. Her plans were to no avail, though. Walking out into the waiting room, she promptly collided with Charlotte, who practically shoved Olivia out of the way in her haste to get to Clem's room.

'I need to see Clem immediately!' she barked at Betty.

'He's in with a patient,' Betty retorted sharply. 'I'll let him know you're here as soon as he's finished.'

'I don't care if he's in with the Queen of England,' Charlotte snarled. 'I need to see him this instant.' It took all of Olivia's tact and even more of Betty's strength to block the door and prevent her from barging in on Mr Heath's prostate examination. Clem opened the door, enraged.

'What the hell's going on?' he demanded.

'I need to see you, Clem. Now,' Charlotte begged loudly, but in a far more endearing tone.

Clem, realising he was obviously not going to be able to calm Charlotte down without attending to her, looked over at Olivia. For an instant she felt a blush rise as she remembered the last time their eyes had met. 'Would you mind checking Mr Heath's blood pressure? If that's all right tell him I'll ring him at home this afternoon. Give him my apologies.' Clem's voice was totally calm, as if this type of intrusion happened every day. He also looked disgustingly healthy, which ruled out the pizza being off.

Olivia nodded, suddenly irritated by this silly woman, who assumed she was so much more important than everybody else was. Clem turned to the drama queen.

'Charlotte, go and wait in my study. I'll be there in just a moment.' Charlotte, pacified now she had got her way, strutted off. 'Betty, would you hold my calls, unless, of course, they're urgent?'

'But what'll I tell the patients that are waiting?' she asked. For the first time Clem sounded irritated. Charlotte must have got to him after all.

'Tell them something came up. It's not as if they don't

know. After all, Charlotte's outburst was hardly discreet. Tell them what you like.' And he marched off.

'Perhaps they were made for each other after all,' Betty muttered furiously.

Olivia tried to appease Mr Heath as she checked his blood pressure.

''Struth, I wanted to ask Clem for a script for me heart pills.'

'I'll have him write it up and I'll drop it in to the chemist for you this afternoon. He really is sorry. Something came up and he had to rush off.'

'I may be old, Sister, but I ain't deaf. That blooming sheila Charlotte calls and he runs. I dunno, she doesn't care tuppence for anyone except herself. What he's doing messin' with her I'll never know. Kathy must be turning in her grave, knowing that madam finally got her claws in him.' He waved a gnarled, arthritic finger at her. 'Nothing good will ever come of it, I tell you. She should stay put in Sydney, the city suits her.'

Olivia smiled noncommittally and helped the old man down off the examination couch. Privately she agreed with every word. Charlotte. She was like an unopened red bill, stuffed hastily into your handbag. Something, no matter how hard you tried, you never really forgot, but at least until you saw it you didn't have to deal with it. Well, the time had surely come. The music had to be faced, but not here, not at work. The next opportunity she got she would confront Clem, ask him outright just what was going on between him and Charlotte. The truth must surely be better than this uncertainty.

Finally Charlotte appeared, tearful but a lot calmer. Oliva tried to hover, to hear any snippet of their conversation, but a patient arrived, waving a pathology slip under her nose, and as there was no one else waiting for her, she really had no choice but to get on with it. Clem walked Charlotte to her car, hardly part of the service.

Olivia tried to concentrate as she took Mrs Peacock's blood. Thankfully she had good veins and the needle went in without difficulty.

'Well, that was nice and quick. It makes a change to be seen straight away. Thanks for that.' She rolled down her sleeve. 'Are you all right, Sister? You look a bit peaky.'

'I'm just a bit under the weather, nothing to worry about.' Olivia gave her a smile. 'Those results should be back early next week. If there are any problems, Clem or I will call you.'

'No worries. Thanks, Sister. And you take care of yourself.'

Walking over to the window where the sharps bin was kept, Olivia carefully emptied the kidney dish into the receptacle. Cursing herself for not being able to resist, she stood on tiptoe and peeped out of the window into the car park. And instantly wished she hadn't, for she was just in time to see Clem gently embrace Charlotte. She was leaning against him, nodding. Olivia felt as if she had been stabbed. She watched as he opened the car door and Charlotte climbed into her sporty soft top—red, of course. She was predictable. Olivia just ducked in time as Charlotte sped off and Clem turned and walked back to the surgery. She certainly didn't want Clem to catch her spying on him.

'What on earth was I thinking, getting involved with another man, let alone another doctor?' she muttered.

Clem walked into the treatment room. He had no reason to be there unless he wanted to see her. He looked tired but smiled when he spoke.

'I'm really behind now. How are you this morning?' Gently he put his hand up to her cheek, but she pulled it down and turned away, unable to take this display of affection. There were questions to be answered first. 'Mr

Heath needs a script for digoxin. I said I'd drop it into the chemist for him this afternoon,' Olivia said tonelessly.

'Thanks for that. I'd better write it up now or I'll forget, and I've already messed him about enough this morning.' He looked at her quizzically and suddenly his voice was serious. 'Livvy, are you feeling all right? You look ever so pale.'

I feel pale, she wanted to scream. I don't know if it's my stomach aching or my heart and head for being so stupid. Instead, she replied in the same toneless voice, 'I'm fine, just a bit tired. How's Elsie Parker?'

'Still battling on. She's amazing really. I've increased her morphine and changed her anti-emetic, which hopefully will make her more comfortable. I'll go and check on her this afternoon.'

Betty appeared at the door. 'The natives are getting restless.'

'I'm coming now.'

Betty bustled away.

'Livvy?'

'What?' she snapped. Clem just stood there. She didn't look at him, she couldn't bring herself to. Whatever he had been about to say, he obviously thought better of it.

'Never mind, it will keep till after surgery. I've left my prescription pad in the study. Would you mind bringing it in to me? I'll carry on with the patients.'

'Certainly.'

It was a beautiful study. Heavy wooden shelves lined the walls, every inch crammed with books, ranging from medical encyclopaedias and journals to various classics and the latest blockbusters. His huge, untidy desk sent Ruby into hysterics, but Clem knew where everything was and could place his hand on what he needed in an instant. Olivia, however, was not privy to his chaos. She rummaged through the various files and pieces of paper, eventually finding the prescription pad.

Picking it up, her heart skipped a beat, for lying there under it was a pregnancy test card. The blotting paper still paling showed it was a fresh test. What's more, it was positive! Her hands shot up to her mouth, stifling the scream that welled inside as the test card clattered to the floor.

How could he? How could he have done this to her? How could he have let her into his bed, into his life? It all made ghastly sense now—that was what this morning had been about. As friendly as Clem might be to his patients, that had been no doctor's congratulatory hug she had witnessed them sharing, and Charlotte's behaviour certainly wasn't one of a normal patient. Had she needed any more proof, Betty bustled in, bearing the final nail in the coffin.

'There you are. He's screaming for his pad. As if we don't have enough to deal with, he's now decided to head off to Sydney tomorrow morning, so I'll be on the phone all day, cancelling his weekend house calls. I hope he's back by Monday or we'll be stuck with old Dr Humphreys for surgery. It's bad enough when he's on call. Don't go getting sick this weekend—he'll kill us all, he's that old.'

Listening to Betty's ranting, Olivia swallowed the bile that rose in her throat. 'Why's Clem going to Sydney?' she asked, trying desperately to keep her voice even.

'And youse are supposed to have the brains. That's where madam lives, remember? I hope he's not going to propose. I mean it, I'll give him one week's notice.'

Numb now, she made her way back through the patient area. Clem's office door was open, and without bothering to knock she walked straight in and gave him the pad without a word.

'Thanks,' he muttered. Looking up, he saw her face and quickly came around the desk. 'Sit down. You really are pale.'

'I said I'm fine,' she snapped, near to tears and determined not to let him see.

'You don't look it.'

'Well, I am. How's Charlotte?' He was smooth—not even a flicker of guilt marred his concerned expression.

'Much calmer. She's off to Sydney, thank goodness. I'm just about sick of her dramas.' He sat down on the desk and gently picked up one of her slim hands. Olivia sat there frozen, her lips white, anger welling up inside her, only to be drowned by a huge wave of sadness for what might have been.

'Livvy, we really need to talk.'

'So you keep telling me, but we never seem to get there.' She damn well wasn't going to make this easy for him.

'I know. Look, I haven't been completely up front with you. I wanted to be sure about something before I bothered you with it, but things have suddenly started to happen—shall we say, a rather unexpected turn of events?'

Olivia's jaw dropped. Was that how he saw Charlotte's pregnancy? Some minor inconvenience to an otherwise normal day? But Clem continued talking, seemingly oblivious to her reaction. I have to go to Sydney tomorrow morning, but I really need to speak to you before I leave.'

'You've got patients waiting,' she pointed out.

'I know. What about tonight? I'll take you out for dinner. We can talk. I won't get sidetracked, I really need you to say yes.'

He was almost begging her. It was Jeremy all over. What did he think he could possibly say to her? That he wanted them both? Or that the baby was a mistake? Hadn't he listened to a word she'd said about Jeremy? Did he really think she'd be so stupid all over again?

'What about Charlotte?' There, she'd said it. She held her breath, scrutinising his face for a reaction.

'What about her? I told you, she's gone, she won't disturb us.'

Suddenly she couldn't bear the sound of his voice. It was so kind, so convincing. Maybe she should go out with him, hear what he had to say. Aware she was weakening, Olivia stood up sharply. What did this man do to her? She needed to get out, to think things through. She was scared, so scared that she'd lose her head and accept his story, only to be tortured all over again. 'Actually, you were right. I don't feel well. I think I'm going to have to go home to bed.'

'What's wrong?'

'I've probably just been overdoing things. Look, I'll take a raincheck on dinner and grab an early night.'

'Let me have a look at you.'

He looked so worried, as if he really cared. Surely there must be some explanation. Maybe he and Charlotte had had a one-night stand for old time's sake. Maybe… No, she reminded herself firmly, don't make excuses.

'No.' She almost shouted at him. 'I just need a rest. If you'll excuse me.' And not even bothering to say goodbye, she rushed out of the surgery, only stopping to grab her bag.

When she got home Ruby was there, busily sweeping the floorboards and desperate for news on the baby.

'You're early. Come on, I'll put the kettle on and we'll have a nice cuppa. Youse can tell me all about the baby. The way Betty's carrying on, it sounds like she delivered it. She didn't, did she?'

Olivia shook her head. Normally she loved Ruby and didn't mind whiling away the hours with her, but right now she really needed to be alone.

'Ruby, I don't feel too good. I'm just going to go and lie on the settee. Do you mind finishing up?'

Ruby fussed over her, laying her down and fetching a

pillow, but Olivia could tell she was hurt by her dismissal. 'Come over tomorrow morning,' Olivia suggested. 'I'll fill you in then. I really am tired.'

Appeased, Ruby tucked a rug around her. 'I knew it was too soon for youse to be back at work. You rest there, pet, and I'll get out of your hair. Can I get you a drink?'

'No, but thanks.'

Ruby hesitated. She really didn't want to leave. She'd never seen Olivia looking so awful, except those first couple of days after she'd gone missing.

'Is there anything I can do?'

'You could light a fire. I'm frozen.'

'But it's thirty degrees outside,' Ruby exclaimed, then, seeing Olivia shivering on the couch, she did as she'd been asked. Expertly arranging the wood, she lit a match and fanned the tiny flame till the fire burned merrily. 'Shall I fetch Clem? You look worse than you did fifteen minutes ago.'

'Ruby, please, don't.'

Ruby looked unsure, but Olivia insisted.

'I mean it. He knows I'm sick. That's why I came home early. I just need to rest. Promise me you won't go dragging him over.'

'Well, if you're sure…' She hovered for a moment then reluctantly packed up her things. 'Call if you need me.' She departed.

Olivia lay there for how long she wasn't quite sure, but gradually the room grew darker. Only the light from the ebbing fire filled the room, casting long shadows. Gazing into the glowing embers, she searched for answers.

How could she have let it happen? The last thing she had been looking for had been another relationship. Hadn't she only come to Kirrijong to straighten her head and stop her making a foolish mistake? Now Jeremy felt more like a distant memory than the man for whom she had wept such bitter tears. Instead she had gone and fallen completely in love with Clem.

'I love him,' she whispered to the dying flames. And somehow acknowledging the truth out loud made her feel calmer. Perhaps in a couple of months she'd be over Clem, too, but Olivia knew better. This was the thunderbolt, the once in a lifetime the world spoke about. He had made love to her, tapped wells of passions never explored. Opened the gateway to a nirvana she hadn't realised existed.

Yet how could she love him when she obviously didn't know him? The man she loved would never have been kissing her, making love to her, if he had Charlotte, however unwelcome, waiting in the wings. The Clem she knew would never have asked her out to dinner tonight if he'd just found out he was to become a father, even if it was, as she guiltily hoped, a mistake borne out of a brief fling. The Clem she loved would face the music and to heck with the consequences. He certainly wouldn't have let Charlotte speed off alone to Sydney.

Olivia's mind whirred. She simply didn't understand. Perhaps she had totally misjudged him and fallen in love with a fantasy figure; maybe it was a classic case of a patient falling for her doctor, or even just a rebound, to get her over Jeremy. If that was the case it had worked, but somehow it had backfired, for the cure was more agonising than the original disease. None of these excuses gave her any comfort yet the cold, hard truth was worse. She loved him, full stop, end of sentence. No ifs or buts, just a whole load of questions.

Yet did it really matter how she or even Charlotte for that matter felt? Whatever mess he had got himself into, Olivia was sure it was a reaction to his grief. Clem wasn't free to love either of them. His heart belonged to Kathy. How could she, with all her hang-ups and insecurities, even begin to compare with a woman who had been so perfect, trusting and gentle, the antithesis of herself? The only thing Kathy had done wrong had been to die and leave him, and it wasn't as if the poor woman had had a choice about that. Clem had his beloved memories. The ultimate other woman. How do you compete with a ghost?

The dull pain in her stomach spasmed suddenly, making her catch her breath. Olivia lay there in agony for a moment until gradually it eased. She was frozen to the core—perhaps a warm bath would help, she decided.

Watching the bath fill, she leant over to get the bubble bath but the pain in her shoulder intensified. The same nauseous feeling of the morning engulfed her. A spasm in her stomach hit her again, so violent it forced her to her knees, doubling her up on the bathroom floor. Something was wrong, terribly wrong.

Olivia tried to stand but her legs were trembling convulsively. She let out a whimper of pain and terror as she collapsed to the floor. 'Oh, God, help me, please.' She couldn't move, but just lay there, listening to the sound of running water, watching helplessly as the water lapped slowly over the edge of the bath. She had to get help. Had to get to the phone.

Slowly, so slowly, inch by inch, she dragged herself along the floor. The pain was so overwhelming, her muscles so fatigued, she was tempted just to lie there and rest a while, to let the bliss of oblivion descend on her, but an inner instinct, coupled with her training, told her she had to get to the phone. Had to let someone know of her plight. If she gave in, stopped now, then that would be it. The phone cord was just within her grasp and with a final, superhuman effort she stretched her fingers and pulled at the wire, bringing the phone crashing to the floor beside her.

The numbers were swimming before her eyes. Concentrating, trying desperately to focus, she somehow dialled Clem's number, praying she wouldn't get the answering machine or his voice mail.

'Clem speaking.' His voice sounded so calm, so normal. It was hard to believe he was unaware of the agony that was going on at the other end of the line. She tried to call his name but the words wouldn't come, just a tiny gasp. 'This is Clem. Is anybody there?'

She heard the urgency in his voice. Anyone else would have hung up, assuming a wrong number or a hoax call, but as a doctor this terrifying scenario had happened before.

'Clem,' she managed to croak, then inwardly cursed herself. If she had only one word left in her, why waste it telling him his name? But the heavens were listening and thankfully he recognised her voice.

'Livvy, Livvy, is that you?'

The fact he recognised her voice and the knowledge that help was on the way gave her some strength. 'Help me. Please,' she gasped.

'I'm on my way. Just stay there and don't move.'

She couldn't reply. The phone fell out of her limp hand and she lay there motionless on the floor, her breathing rapid and shallow, her skin deathly pale.

Clem frantically grabbed his medical bag and sprinted the short distance to the house, hammering loudly on the door, berating himself for not bringing the spare keys. Racing around to the side of the house, he saw Olivia through the bedroom window. Lying there so pale and still, he thought she must be dead.

In one movement he kicked out the window and opened the latch, desperate to reach her. Beside her in an instant, he saw she was still breathing. The relief was so intense he closed his eyes for a second and struggled to stay calm, then his sheer professionalism took over.

Her pulse was rapid and thready, she was so pale she

was practically exsanguinated. She was obviously, to his trained eye, bleeding out from somewhere.

He rang Betty, misdialling twice.

'G'day. Betty—'

'It's Clem, I'm at Livvy's,' he barked. 'She's critical. 'Organise an ambulance. Tell them we're going to need an airlift as well and that I'll ring with the details as soon as I can. Get Dougie and Ruby to come over now and tell them to bring the emergency blood from the fridge. Betty, hurry or we'll lose her.' He hung up, not waiting for a response, knowing Betty would come good when it mattered.

His training and experience were so ingrained that he treated Olivia methodically, managing to insert a drip into her hopelessly collapsed veins and squeeze lifesaving plasma substitute into her.

Dougie and Ruby arrived, horrified by what they saw. Clem was leaning over Olivia's inert body, oblivious of the pool of water they were both in from the overflowing bath. Dougie ran and turned off the taps as Ruby rushed over with the blood.

'Tell me what to do.'

'Squeeze this drip through. I'll get another IV line started and get the blood into her. Don't move her—she may have fallen. I don't think so but I'll put on a cervical collar to stabilise her neck just in case.'

Betty, with wisdom and insight that defied her scatty nature, arrived then, dragging the portable oxygen cylinder. She was purple from the exertion.

Clem looked at her gratefully. 'Good work Betty.' He slipped a green oxygen mask over Olivia's face, and for a fleeting second her eyes flickered.

Frantically Clem grabbed her hand. 'Livvy, Livvy, it's all going to be fine. We're getting you to hospital now.' In desperation he turned to Ruby. 'Did you see her eyes move? Do you think she can hear?'

And in that second Ruby knew. This wasn't a doctor speaking, this was a frantic man. His face held the same intense pain she had seen two years before. How clearly she remembered the week before Kathy had died, when she had taken her final turn for the worse. Betty had come running then, too, with the oxygen.

She knew then that Clem loved Olivia. They all did. In the months she had been there they had all grown to love and care for this tall, awkward, icy woman who could be so uptight and distant one minute and as vulnerable as a child the next. To see her lying there now, so fragile and helpless... Oh, poor, poor Clem. It must be like waking from a nightmare, only to be plunged straight back into the same hell all over again. He couldn't lose Livvy, too. God couldn't be that cruel.

They all battled with their emotions as they watched her limp body. Dougie coughing noisily to cover up his tears, leaving when the road ambulance arrived to help Bruce prepare a landing pad and light the flares. Ruby stood, trying to stay calm, with her hand on Clem's shoulder as he knelt over Olivia, oblivious of the ambulance officers working around him.

Betty had no such reserve and sobbed openly. 'What happened, Clem? What happened?'

He shook his head slowly. 'I'm pretty sure she's got a ruptured spleen.' His voice was quiet, flat.

'But how?' Betty's hysteria magnified Clem's frozen calm. 'Did she fall?'

'I don't think so. Glandular fever can cause an enlarged spleen. Very rarely it ruptures. I think that's what has happened to Livvy.'

'She will make it, though, won't she? I mean there's things they can do for that?'

Clem shrugged, utterly defeated. 'She needs more blood. She needs surgery, preferably half an hour ago. We've done all we can. It's out of our hands now.'

It took just over an hour for the helicopter to arrive from the base hospital, but it seemed like an eternity. They nearly lost Olivia twice, but just as it all looked hopeless the whirring of the chopper blades seemed to inject some hope into them all. Even Olivia stirred slightly and opened her eyes. She tried to focus on Clem's face, and for all his intuition he mistook the love that somehow shone in her dull, sunken eyes as gratitude for finding her again.

'You're going to be fine. The helicopter's here now.'

She tried to shake her head. That wasn't what she wanted to hear. She wanted him to tell her he loved her, to tell him she loved him, even if it was all too late. She tried to speak, but her mouth wouldn't obey her and only a small gasp came out.

'Hush, Livvy, don't try to talk now. We're all here. Everything will be all right. You have to trust me.'

And despite all the questions left unanswered, all the uncertainty, she did, no matter what.

His beautiful strong face was the last thing she saw as once again oblivion descended.

CHAPTER TEN

THANKFULLY Olivia knew nothing of the helicopter ride to Sydney. In a no-win situation they bypassed the nearer base hospital, after being informed the theatres were in use and the intensive care unit was full. They all knew that if Olivia was to stand any chance of survival she would need the best intensive care available. Bag after bag of blood was squeezed into her *en route,* as Clem knelt on the floor holding her lifeless hands, terrified that if he let go then so might she.

As the city lights neared and the crew expertly prepared her for a speedy exit from the helicopter, he had no choice but to let go. Helpless, he watched as the doors opened and she was rushed away. He wanted to run after her, to shout to them to do their best, that they couldn't lose her, she was far too precious. But his voice was lost in the whirring chopper blades, and all he could do was make his way to the theatre waiting room. He had told them all he could about her condition, all they needed to know.

The fact he loved her didn't matter to them. Everybody was someone's child or parent, lover or friend. All life was valuable, and they would give Olivia their best shot, in the same way he did each day, the same way Olivia did.

While he was sitting in the lonely waiting room, drinking endless cups of revolting machine coffee, a receptionist came in and asked for details. Gently she tried to get information out of him, but all Clem could manage was Olivia's name and current address. He didn't even know her date of birth. He loved this woman with every inch of

164

his being and yet he couldn't even answer the most simple of questions about her.

'I'm sorry,' the receptionist answered, confused when he stalled on her date of birth. I thought you were the next of kin.'

'I'm her doctor.'

'I see,' she answered, still none the wiser. Doctors didn't normally pace the floors and cry openly over their patients, not to the receptionist anyway. 'Is there any way you'd be able get the information?'

He gave her Betty's number—she could pull out Livvy's résumé. 'I want to be informed the minute she gets out of Theatre,' he said, trying to regain his composure.

'Of course, Doctor.' The receptionist turned to walk out.

'She isn't just a patient to me, you know,' Clem called to her departing back, though why he had to justify himself to her he wasn't sure. 'I love her.'

The receptionist turned. She was used to grief. 'So I gathered. I hope things go well.' She smiled sympathetically. 'She's got the best surgical team on tonight. If it was my loved one that was sick, they're whom I'd want to be operating. Well, from what I hear anyway.' She blushed, suddenly remembering she was talking to a doctor.

'Thank you,' Clem said simply, glad that even though it had been to a relative stranger, he had at least acknowledged his love for Olivia.

The wait was interminable. Never had he felt so helpless. He knew, and yet couldn't bear to think of, the battle that would be going on in the sterile theatre. The wheels of bureaucracy would have swung into motion and by now Jeremy would have been contacted.

Jeremy. He had never met him, only spoken to him on the telephone, and yet he hated him with a passion. Hated him for causing Livvy so much pain. The bastard hadn't even had the decency to marry her yet he was listed on her résumé as the emergency contact. He was probably on his way now. Clem just hoped he had stopped to inform her parents in England.

His heart went out to them and the terrible events that would unfold when they picked up the phone and heard the devastating news. Would they all come? Was he going to meet the people who had made up Livvy's world before she'd come to Kirrijong? Beautiful, complicated Livvy.

Sitting in the bland waiting room, the television playing an old black and white film, he stared blankly at the screen. The film ended and a newsbreak followed. How could it not be the headlines? Why were they talking about some attempted bank robbery when his beloved Livvy was fighting just to stay alive?

Standing as he saw someone dressed in theatre blues approach, Clem tried to interpret the grim, weary face before she spoke, desperate for a clue.

'Dr Clemson.' She held out her hand and Clem shook it. 'I'm May Fordyce, the consultant surgeon on tonight. I operated on your patient.' The formalities over, Clem knew the news was coming and for a second he didn't want to hear it, terrified in case Livvy hadn't made it.

'She's more than a patient.' It was only fair to warn her. He didn't want the details to be too graphic.

Miss Fordyce nodded briefly. 'Your initial diagnosis was correct. She had indeed ruptured her spleen.'

'Is she…?'

'No,' she replied, but there was no jubilation in her voice. 'She made it through Theatre, but really I'm amazed she did. She's lost a lot of blood and she's had a massive transfusion. We're worried about disseminated intravascular coagulation.'

She waited for a response, for some recognition to flicker in Clem's eyes. Then she realised she wasn't speaking to another doctor but a scared and desperate fellow human being, and gently spelt the grim news out.

'You and the air ambulance team did a marvellous job of resuscitating her with fluids. When she arrived in Theatre we performed an urgent splenectomy. She made it through but she's critical. She's extremely weak and the volume of the blood transfusion is causing a lot of concern. We're having a lot of problems with her blood coagulation and we're trying to prevent her from going into renal failure. The next forty-eight hours will be crucial.'

A hundred questions flashed into Clem's mind, but for now the answers were immaterial. The need to see her, to touch her, surpassed everything. 'Can I see her?'

'They're just settling her into Intensive Care. I'll let them know you're waiting.'

For ten minutes he was allowed to see her. Just ten precious minutes. Gently he held her hand and told her all the things he had meant to say but somehow had never quite managed. Ten precious minutes where he told her just how much he cared and how happy she had made him, maybe without even realising it, and that he was sorry, so sorry that he couldn't have done more. Could she hear? There was no way of knowing but he knew that he had to say it now, for it might be his only chance.

Lovingly he arranged her long red curls. Walking over to the sink, he moistened a hand towel and wiped away a streak of blood that had splashed her cheek. 'You'd have me for breakfast if I left it,' he whispered gently into her ear.

'We need to do some obs.' The sister hovered by the bed. 'And she needs to rest.'

'I won't get in the way, I'll just sit here, if you don't mind.'

The Sister hesitated, not sure of this situation. Was he her doctor, friend or lover? Whatever he was, he seemed nice, and she felt it only fair to warn him. 'Her fiancé has flown in from Melbourne, he just arrived. Miss Fordyce is talking to him now. I expect he may want to sit with her.'

'Her ex-fiancé,' Clem stated bluntly but it was no use. In just one short sentence he had been relegated. For a moment Clem had the craziest notion to pick Olivia up and just run. He didn't want to leave, didn't want Jeremy or anyone else invading, but he didn't have any say here. And the hardest part to take was that he wasn't sure whether Livvy would have wanted him to.

Olivia was the talk of the intensive care staffroom. Two doctors in love with the same woman. One blond, with film-star good looks and a slick charm, who flirted with the staff and praised them for their efforts. The other dark and ruggedly handsome, but moody and picky, questioning every test result, checking the obs charts. Both as different as chalk and cheese, each with a bristling loathing of the other.

Over the weekend Olivia mercifully gradually stabilised and, defying all odds, by Monday was ready to be moved to a small side ward on the high-dependency unit, an array of wires and monitors still adorning her, each relaying its vital messages to the nurses' station. It was here that she started to drift back to the world. Her eyes heavy, she opened them slowly, flinching at the late afternoon sun that flooded the bed. Her throat felt dry and sore, as if it had been roughly sandpapered, her arm, strapped to the intravenous giving set, heavy and unfamiliar.

She felt a hand on her head and a familiar voice welcoming her back to the world.

'Darling, it's all right. You're coming to. Take it easy. You're in hospital but I'm here now and everything's going to be all right.'

'Be careful what you wish for—it might come true.' It seemed that Clem's prediction had finally come to fruition, for there, coming into focus, his blond hair white in the fluorescent light's glare, his face smiling down at her, was Jeremy. Battling with nausea and pain, she tried to make some sense, to orientate herself, the numerous drips and machines all so familiar yet so alien now they were attached to her own body.

'Jeremy?' she croaked.

'Yes, it's me. I'm here now and I'm never going to let you go again.'

'What happened?' she asked feebly.

'Your spleen ruptured. It would have been enlarged from the glandular fever. It's very rare but it happened. I just feel so guilty.'

He had a lot to feel guilty about. Olivia could recall that much.

'I should have come and got you sooner, never left you in the middle of nowhere with an out-of-date bush quack. I'm sorry, darling.'

Olivia didn't respond. Instead, she lay there, trying to piece it all together. With the benefit of hindsight, everything made sense now. That niggling pain in her shoulder, the dizzy spells. Her medical mind realised they had been signs she had been bleeding internally. The abdominal pain, which she had just assumed to be food poisoning, had, in fact, been her dangerously enlarged spleen leaking slowly, with the potential to rupture at any time. But with hindsight it was easy to diagnose. It had been no one's fault. She could hardly point the finger at Clem when she had point-blank refused to let him examine her, and she had avoided a proper examination with Dr Humphreys. Anyway, surely no one would have envisaged what was, after all, an extremely rare complication of a common viral disease.

So now here she lay, with Jeremy playing the part of the concerned fiancé to perfection, saying all the things that a few months ago she would have longed to hear. It was almost farcical. A more dramatic reunion she couldn't have dreamed of. Totally inappropriately, and to Jeremy's absolute horror, Olivia started to laugh. He jumped back as if he'd been shot.

'She's confused. It must be all the pethidine you've loaded her up with,' he barked at the entering nurse, the Mister Nice Guy routine quickly starting to evaporate.

Olivia drifted in and out of consciousness. Once when she opened her eyes she saw Clem gazing down at her. He looked exhausted. The tiny lines around his eyes seemed deeper and they shone with tears. She wanted so badly to talk to tell him how she felt, but she had just had a shot of painkiller and its effects were starting to take hold, the words coming out muddled and confused.

'Shh. Not now,' was all he said, and gently placed a finger to her lips. 'You rest.'

When she awoke she was sure she must have dreamed the encounter, for there beside her was Jeremy. 'Hello darling. You've been out for hours.'

'What time is it?'

'Nearly seven. I was just waiting for you to wake up. I'm going to head off to the hotel and get some dinner. It's been a long day.' So he was complaining now. It wasn't as if she had asked him to come. 'But I've got some good news. I spoke with your surgeon and she's going to arrange your transfer to Melbourne in a couple of days. Get you back on home ground and amongst familiar faces. That's just what you need.'

'And you wouldn't have to take any time off work,' she added sarcastically.

'Olivia, don't let's fight. I thought that was all behind us now.' He kissed her haphazardly on the cheek. 'I'll let the sister know you're awake—they want to change your dressing. I'd just be in the way. Goodnight, darling. I'll be here first thing.'

Olivia nodded feebly. She had to tell him he was wasting his time, but right now she couldn't deal with a scene. It could wait till tomorrow morning.

Expertly, Sister Jay changed her dressing. She was middle-aged and incredibly efficient, with a brisk, rather old-school bedside manner. Olivia lay there, staring at the ceiling, thinking of what she would say to Jeremy, as the sister completed her task and deftly tidied up the bedclothes. After checking Olivia's pulse, she gently patted her hand and for a moment her face softened.

'You're looking a lot better. You were pretty crook there for a while, gave us all a fright.' Bustling out with the trolley, she returned a moment later. 'Are you up to a visitor?'

Olivia nodded. What did Jeremy want now? But standing in the doorway was Clem. He looked as tired and as awful as she felt.

'You look like it should be you in a hospital bed.' She smiled.

'They've put me up in the doctors' quarters. It's not bad, but I'd forgotten just how noisy they could be. There was a wild party on Saturday night—it went on till four a.m.'

'Did you go?'

He knew she was teasing but he played along. 'Just for a couple of hours, but the girls were awful and the beer was warm.' He came and sat gently on the bed, careful not to make any sudden movement that might cause her pain. Tentatively he took her hand and it felt so natural she left it there. 'I've actually spent the last few days and nights loitering around the corridor, waiting for Jeremy to leave. I'm surprised I haven't been arrested. I needed to see you were all right for myself. I came in once but you were out of it.'

So he had been here after all. It hadn't been a dream.

'I know what time it is, roughly to the nearest hour, but what day is it?'

Clem smiled at her question. 'It's Tuesday.'

'And you're still here. Why?' Suddenly she remembered that Charlotte was in Sydney. Of all the stupid things to ask. He had been coming here anyway.

'That's what I wanted to talk to you about.'

It was all too much—she simply wasn't up to hearing it. 'Not now, please.' Pulling her hand away, she turned her head towards the window and stared at the bland beige curtains.

'You're tired, of course. You need your rest. Can I come and see you again?'

What was the point? But somehow she needed to hear some answers, no matter how much it hurt. She had to find out all the details, but not tonight. 'Jeremy's coming in the morning,' she said.

'I see,' Clem answered, and she could hear the defeat in his voice.

'But he won't be staying long,' she added. 'Perhaps around lunchtime?'

Clem nodded. 'I'd like that.' Gently he stroked her cheek, but she couldn't take it, too scared she might crumble. Instead, she turned her face back to the curtains.

'I really thought I was going to lose you,' he murmured.

For a second she wavered, desperate to feel his arms around her, but common sense won.

'Thank you for saving me,' she said tonelessly, and then felt awful, for despite everything else this man had saved her life. She turned and looked at him. 'Thank you,' she said with more conviction.

Clem gave her a quizzical look. 'I'll let you rest. Till tomorrow, then.'

Olivia awoke next morning to the sound of the breakfast trolley. The 'Hourly sips' sign above her bed had been replaced by 'Free fluids'. Never had a weak cup of insipid hospital tea tasted so good. Gradually the tubes and drips had been taken down and all that was left to show of her near brush with death was one small drain, a dressing on her stomach and one peripheral intravenous line.

Being a nurse had some advantages. She was now officially well enough to be moved down into the shared ward away from the nurses' station, but while the ward was relatively quiet they left her in the side room. Replacing the cup in the saucer, she contemplated whether to ask for a second, but knew she shouldn't push it. Strange how the simplest things gave the most pleasure. The orderly came and pulled back the curtains.

'You've got the best view in the hospital here.' A huge gum nut tree filled almost the entire window. 'Enjoy it. When you get moved it's the furnace to look at.'

With mounting trepidation she dreaded Jeremy's arrival. She didn't have to wait long.

'Morning, darling, you look better.' Jeremy waltzed in, looking as immaculate as ever. 'I might even talk to Miss Fordyce and see if they can transfer you today. It's not as if they're doing much for you now and, anyway, I'll be in the ambulance with you. I am a consultant surgeon after all.'

Olivia listened, silently fuming. Jeremy just assumed he could pick up and carry on exactly where he had left off. Didn't she have any say in this?

'Actually, I won't be going back to Melbourne.' The words tumbled out and Olivia held her breath.

'Why?' he answered, nonplussed. 'Were you ill in the night? Is there something they haven't told me?'

'No, Jeremy. It's something you didn't ask me.'

He stared at her, completely confused.

'You just assume that I've forgiven you. You just assume

that I'm coming home with you. Well, I'm sorry, it's not that straightforward.'

He was over to the bed in a flash. 'We've been over that. It's all over with Lydia. You know how sorry I am.'

She almost felt sorry for him. He was so spoilt, so used to unquestioning adoration that it hadn't seriously entered his head that she might not come back to him.

'It's not about whether it's over with Lydia or not. It's the fact it happened in the first place. Jeremy, I'm sorry, I just can't forgive and forget—it's over.'

Jeremy shook his head. 'No, Olivia. Don't do this.'

A student nurse appeared and started to take her blood pressure. Intimidated to be in the room with such a senior nurse and doctor, she kept blowing the cuff up too tight.

'For heaven's sake don't they teach you anything in nursing school?' Jeremy snapped.

'She's doing fine.' Olivia smiled reassuringly.

Once they were alone again, he begged her to reconsider. 'Please, Olivia, I've changed, I promise. Once we're married you'll see—'

'No! *You* did this to us, Jeremy. I would have always been faithful, I would have supported you in anything, but I can't get over your affair. It's just too big. It's over, Jeremy.' She saw the tears well in his eyes and she knew he was devastated.

'You might change your mind,' he begged.

'I won't,' she replied firmly.

Jeremy shook his head. 'There's someone else. That Jake Clemson. I knew it. What's been going on?'

'This has nothing to do with him,' Olivia answered sincerely, because it didn't.

'I don't believe you,' Jeremy stated bluntly. 'Are you two having an affair?'

'No,' she answered truthfully, though such was her honesty that she told him the painful truth. 'But we did sleep

together, once. It meant far more to me than it did to him—
he's involved with someone else. And, anyway, this has
nothing to do with Clem. It's about us.'

'Oh, I'd say he had a fair bit to do with it,' he retorted
angrily, then the rage in him seemed to die as he begged
her to reconsider. 'Please, Olivia,' he implored, but his
pleas fell on deaf ears. It was simply too late.

Even her name sounded strange now. He was the only
person who had called her 'Olivia' in ages. Even 'Livvy'
was underlined on all her medical notes, a legacy of her
admission when Clem had attempted to give her details.
The Olivia Jeremy had known didn't exist any more. In her
place was a stronger person, who would fight for her ideals.

'I'm sorry, Jeremy.' And something about the certainty
in her voice made him finally realise she meant it. For a
second the anger re-emerged and flashed over his face, but
it soon subsided into a look of total defeat.

'I'm sorry, too, Olivia. Sorry for everything.' He stood
there for a moment, taking in the enormity of the situation.
Finally realising what he had lost. 'Do you want me to go?'

She nodded, biting her lip to stop the tears.

'Can I ring in a couple of days? See how you're getting
on?'

Again she nodded and managed a faint smile. 'That
would be nice.' She meant it. Hopefully they could go
about this in a civilised way, remain friends even.

He left then, and Olivia turned her face and wept into
the pillow, knowing how awful he felt, knowing that despite Jeremy's actions he had loved her, but just not
enough.

Wiping away the tears, she let out a gasp. The old gum
was full of bright reds and greens. A flock of rosellas was
feasting on the tree. For a second she was transported back
to Kirrijong, sitting by the tiny stream, pondering her future. So what now? Where did she go from here? She

couldn't go back to Kirrijong. It would be torture, seeing Clem every day, knowing he was with Charlotte. Watching her blossom, ripe with pregnancy, heavy with Clem's child.

For a second she considered going back to Melbourne, but only for a second. Her time there was finished. It would take a stronger person than her to return there and work alongside her ex-fiancé. She could even return to England. Now that the panic was over her parents had rung, saying they would wait a couple of weeks till they flew out. Although longing to see them, she was actually grateful for the reprieve. She wasn't exactly bursting with places they could stay!

The uncertainty of her future was a problem that for now could wait. First she had to get this morning over with. Saying goodbye to Jeremy had been hard, but she had already expended most of her grief about their break-up. But saying goodbye to Clem, that was another matter altogether.

Sister Jay appeared in the doorway, carrying a familiar stainless-steel kidney dish.

'Time for your pethidine injection, and when that's taken effect I was wondering if you'd mind if Hannah, the student, gave you your blanket bath. She needs to be assessed, but she goes to pieces if anyone watches her. I thought she might feel less threatened if I left her to it, and perhaps you could let me know how she does?'

Olivia agreed, though she doubted whether the poor girl would be any less intimidated after Jeremy's outburst.

'That's fine, but I don't want the injection, thanks.'

Sister Jay checked Olivia's prescription chart.

'Are you sure? It's been a while since your last one and you're still written up for regular analgesia. The physiotherapist is coming later to sit you out of bed, which is going to hurt. Don't try to be brave. You've been through a lot.'

But Olivia was adamant. 'Really, I'd rather not.'

Sister Jay shrugged and left.

Her stomach hurt, it hurt like hell, but the pain was nothing compared to seeing Clem for what was to be the last time. She wanted a clear head for that. Wanted to be sure she understood everything he said. It was also imperative to her that she memorised his face. If she was going to live the rest of her life on dreams, she at least wanted them to be accurate.

Hannah clattered in, blushing furiously as she pushed a huge trolley laden with jugs and various pieces of linen and toiletries.

'I've come to give you a wash,' she ventured nervously.

Olivia's heart went out to the young woman. Nurses hated looking after other nurses at the best of times, and poor Hannah had drawn the short straw. Wincing with pain, Olivia leant over and opened the bedside drawer. Nothing, not even a comb.

Hannah set to work and Olivia lay there, pretending not to notice the tepid water splashing her face and trickling into her ears. Lying on her side as Hannah gingerly washed her back, she eyed the goodies on the trolley. Fern-scented talcum powder, pink carbolic soap—hardly the stuff to bring Clem to his knees. Not, she reminded herself firmly, that that was on the agenda.

'Just stay there. I forgot to get the lanolin cream for your pressure areas.' Hannah hastily covered her with a towel.

'Just a moment,' Olivia called. 'Hannah, I know it's awful for you, having to bathe me, and you're doing marvellously,' she added as the young girl's eyes widened, anticipating criticism. 'But what I really need, more than anything else, is to feel human again. Is there anything in the store cupboard that doesn't reek of disinfectant? And is there any chance of borrowing someone's mirror? I know I look a sight and obviously I didn't bring anything with me.'

Hannah started to smile. 'Are you expecting a visitor?' she asked perceptively.

It was Olivia's turn to blush. 'Well, sort of.'

'Then we'd better get you sorted. I shan't be long.'

Hannah returned moments later with her own make-up bag. 'When Sister Jay asks, I gave you the best blanket bath ever.'

'Absolutely. The best,' Olivia agreed as she rummaged through the bag. They even shared the same taste in perfume.

Hannah combed the knots out of her hair, while Olivia shakily managed a touch of mascara on her lashes and a dash of blusher. She knew she must still look awful but it was a huge improvement. Hannah had found what was probably the only hospital gown that actually had all the ties and didn't constantly fall off your shoulders. A quick spray of perfume and she felt close to human again.

'Thank you so much.'

'No worries.' Hannah smiled, confident now the barriers had been broken down. 'I'll just do your obs and then I'll leave you.'

For all her inexperience Hannah wasn't stupid. As she took Olivia's pulse, Clem arrived. Feeling her patient's heart rate suddenly accelerate, she knew it had nothing to with the operation. She quickly wrote down the obs and with an almost imperceptible wink she left them alone, gently closing the door behind her.

'How on earth do you manage it?' Clem laughed. 'You've been to hell and back and you still manage to come out looking gorgeous.'

'Hardly gorgeous,' Olivia replied lightly, 'but I certainly do feel much better today.'

'I've just been talking to some fans of yours.'

'Who?'

'Lorna and Pete. Our namesake is on the next floor.'

'Our namesake?'

'Baby Oliver Jake. He's doing very well.' Olivia leant back on the pillow.

'Oliver Jake,' she repeated. 'They didn't have to do that. He's doing well, you say?'

'Exceptionally. It's still very early days and there's a long way to go, of course, but all the signs look good. They want to pop down and visit you, but I said to give it a couple of days.'

Olivia nodded. Finally some good news.

'That would be nice. I expect I shan't be inundated with visitors. When are you going back?'

He sat down on the bed, achingly close. She so badly wanted to reach out and touch him, but kept her hands firmly beside her.

'That depends. I've managed to arrange a locum.'

'Dr Humphreys? Are you sure that's such a good idea?'

Clem shook his head.

'No, I've actually hired someone who's seriously considering the job of running the hospital. It's worked out well. It gives him a chance to see whether it's what he wants to do, and if it is, he can have his say in the final touches to the hospital.' He looked closely at her, watching her reaction as realisation struck.

'But I thought you'd be running it,' she said slowly, utterly confused.

'I know you did. That's what I've been trying to talk to you about.'

Her mind raced.

'I was actually coming to Sydney at the weekend to have dinner with an old friend and colleague, Craig Pryde— though I wasn't expecting to travel by helicopter,' he added.

Olivia stared dumbly at him.

'You know how I missed paeds?' he said gently.

Speechless, she nodded.

'Well, I've known Craig for many years. He's a paediatric consultant here at this hospital. He's going to be retiring next year, and his senior registrar just resigned unexpectedly. He's asked me to consider the position. When Craig retires I'd probably be offered the consultant's position. It's a great opportunity.'

Agonisingly slowly, realisation dawned. His future was moving on and she hadn't even been in the picture. Of course he would come here. Charlotte would never stay permanently in Kirrijong.

Olivia's pledge to concentrate and remember every word quickly went out of the window. Fighting just to hold back the tears as Clem went into detail, she was unable to take in the rest of what he was saying.

'So what do you think?' Clem concluded.

Olivia swallowed hard and forced her eyes to meet his, determined to retain at least a shred of dignity. 'It's a bit of a shock, I admit, but if you're sure it's what you want then go for it.'

She tried to sound pleased for him, to inject some enthusiasm, but it was asking too much. Maybe she should have had the pethidine after all.

'But this isn't just about me. I need to know how you feel.'

'Why?' she asked simply. Her feelings didn't come into it. Shouldn't he be having this conversation with Charlotte?

'Livvy, haven't you heard a word I've been saying?'

Olivia shook her head dumbly.

'I wanted to discuss it with you but it all happened so quickly and we never did seem to get around to having that talk. Then you were taken so ill. I've been trying to ask you to come with me. I know you've got Jeremy to consider and I didn't want to interfere, but I can't sit on the fence any longer. I know we haven't had much time together but surely you feel it, too?' His words tumbled out and for once he wasn't the strong, confident Clem she knew.

It was Olivia who spoke calmly. 'Jeremy and I are finished. We have been for ages. It just took a while for him to get used to the idea,' she said.

Hope flickered in his eyes then faded as he saw the look of confusion on her face. 'This surely can't be that much of a shock. You must know some of how I feel? I've been trying to tell you for long enough.'

'I know about Charlotte. The baby, I mean.' She held her breath.

'How?' he asked, bewildered.

'I found the pregnancy test card.'

'But that's got nothing to do with us.'

Olivia put her hands up to her ears, trying to block out the sound of his voice. She couldn't bear it. Couldn't bear to hear the excuses and lies. 'Oh, I'd say it had rather a lot to do with us, or maybe I'm just being old-fashioned. But I still think a baby needs a father. I thought we'd at least agree on that.' She stared defiantly at him, waiting for the excuses, the pathetic attempt at an explanation. She was stunned to see his look of incredulous shock change to one of anger—not the usual flashes of temper she had grown used to but a black rage that descended on his tired face. And what was even more disturbing was that she saw the disappointment in his eyes.

'You think it's my baby?' His lips were white, set in a thin line. 'How could you think that of me?' he rasped. 'How could you, Livvy? Is that the kind of guy you take me for?'

This wasn't a reaction she had anticipated. Agonisingly, realisation dawned. She had made the biggest mistake of her life.

'What else was I to think?' she answered defensively.

'Obviously you didn't think. You just assumed. Hell, I know you've been hurt, but how dare you tar me with the same brush as Jeremy?'

'I didn't want to,' she pleaded, 'but it seemed so obvious. Ruby said—'

'I don't care what Ruby said,' he replied sharply, trying desperately not to shout. 'I told you never to listen to her. Why didn't you ask me?'

'I did. I asked if there'd ever been anyone since Kathy.'

He looked at her perplexed. 'Go on.'

'And you said, "What do you think?"' she responded lamely, knowing how inadequate her excuse sounded.

'So it was easier to assume that I was sleeping around. "What do you think?" "What do you think?"' His voice was rising now. 'My heavens, couldn't you see what I was trying to tell you? Since Kathy died I haven't been able to focus, let alone look at another woman—until you, that is. That night when I came to your door drunk I was terrified. Terrified because I knew I'd fallen in love and you seemed so wrapped up in Jeremy. Terrified because I finally knew it was time to move on.'

'But you used to go out with Charlotte. Surely you can see why I thought—'

'Oh, please.' He stopped her flood of excuses. 'One town dance fifteen years ago does not constitute a relationship, unless, of course, you're listening to gossip,' he said nastily. Then, seeing her start to cry, he let up.

'Charlotte's baby has nothing to do with me,' he finally explained, 'save the fact it will be my niece or nephew. She's got herself mixed up with Joshua, my brother, and I've been acting as an unwilling go-between. She's here in Sydney now, hoping he'll relent and marry her. The poor kid, it will probably turn out an absolute horror with those two spoilt brats as parents.'

What could she say? To have been so terribly wrong.

'Sorry' just didn't seem enough. All this time he had been trying to tell her he loved her while she had been thinking the worst.

'So you never slept with Charlotte?' She hesitated, taking in the enormity of what Clem was telling her. 'I was the first since Kathy.' Their one magical night together was suddenly magnified. She felt privileged and also painfully guilty, for Clem had been right—they *had* rushed things. She should have known that it had been his first time since Kathy. She should have been aware that, despite the joy and tenderness they had shared when they'd made love, there would have also been some pain and recrimination for Clem. No wonder he had seemed detached after they'd made love. No wonder he had needed to talk. It was something she should have known.

Seeing Olivia lying there utterly desolated, Clem felt his anger evaporate. This was hurting her as much as him, and the last thing he wanted was to cause her more pain.

'Yes, Livvy, you were the first since Kathy, and I hope the last. I can never go through this again. I've loved you from the moment I met you. I wasn't looking—in fact, I nearly ran a mile—but I couldn't escape it. It's just taken a while for me to get used to the idea. I was so sure I was going to spend the rest of my life alone, and then you came along. For the first time in ages there was a reason to get up in the morning, a face I wanted to see, and someone's opinion I wanted to hear. And it terrified me.'

Olivia lay there, slowly taking in what he was telling her.

'I know it's asking a lot for you to move your life here so I can chase a dream job. And before you even think it, it's not a "consultant's wife" I'm after. It's you, Livvy, and it always will be. I know you're going to need some time to think about it but, please, hear me out first. I can be so bloody-minded sometimes and I know I can be unreasonable, but I truly love you. I'd never hurt you.' He ran a shaking hand through his hair.

She felt like the judge and jury listening to the closing argument.

'I want to marry you, take care of you and show you that love can be good. But, Livvy, if you can't trust me, if you're unable to believe in all we could be together, we should forget it now. I can't live under the shadow of doubt—it's not fair on either of us.'

And for once there weren't any questions that needed answers. Everything Olivia needed to know was there in his eyes.

She took a tentative step off the cliff edge she had been balancing on for so long. Away from the uncertainty of the past and into the future.

'I don't need time to think about it.'

The jury was back; the verdict was in.

He stood there quite still, and she saw the apprehension in his eyes disappear as she held out her hands to him. In a second she was in his arms where she belonged, where she felt safe and loved. Whatever the future held, it would be with Clem beside her to share in the good times and catch her when she fell.

His strong arms pulled her into his ever-loving embrace and his mouth, tentatively at first, met hers, and then he kissed her with such a depth and passion she thought he might never stop. Delighting in each other's touch, neither heard as Sister Jay entered. She coughed loudly and Clem reluctantly let Olivia go.

'I didn't realise you still had visitors,' she said in a proprietorial voice. 'Miss Morrell should really be resting.'

Clem stood up like a scolded schoolboy.

'I've just had a call from Admin,' Sister Jay continued. 'It would seem there's some mix-up with your paperwork.

With your next of kin being in England, whom should we put as your emergency contact?'

Olivia caught the glimpse of mischief in the elderly woman's eyes and turned her face to Clem as he sat back on the bed beside her.

'That would be me, Sister,' he said, taking Olivia's hands. 'Dr Jake Clemson, Ms Morrell's fiancé, assuming, of course, that she'll have me.'

Olivia, suddenly oblivious of their audience, answered him with a kiss.

Leaving them to it, Sister Jay gently closed the door and, sitting at her desk, started to fill in the form.

'Well?' said Hannah impatiently to her senior.

With a smile Sister Jay put down her pen. 'I think we can take it as a yes.'

* * *

Don't miss Carol Marinelli's latest novel,
In the Rich Man's World. *It's available now*
in Mills & Boon® Modern Romance™ wherever
Mills & Boon books are sold!

The Doctor's Runaway Bride

SARAH MORGAN

To Suzy
For encouragement, expertise and humour, and
for being the best editor a girl could have.

PROLOGUE

'*I CAN'T* marry him.'

Pale and shaking, Tia Franklin struggled with the zip of her sleek white wedding dress, sobbing with frustration when it stubbornly refused to budge.

'Tia, wait—you'll tear it—' Sharon, her best friend and bridesmaid, tried frantically to calm her down but Tia wasn't taking any notice.

'I don't care.' As if to prove her point, Tia jerked at the zip again, her sobs increasing as it jammed and the material ripped. 'What does it matter? I'm not getting married now, so I certainly don't need a dress.'

Sharon stood still, frozen with horror. 'Tia, the wedding starts in half an hour and there are one hundred and forty guests waiting in the church—'

'I don't care about that, either.' Tia finally managed to wriggle out of the dress and stumbled across the hotel room to her suitcase, which was already packed for her honeymoon.

She released the catch and grabbed the first outfit that came to hand, tears falling steadily down her cheeks as she struggled into a pair of silk trousers and matching jacket.

Sharon was still staring at her, open-mouthed with disbelief. 'What's happened? You were so happy—and no wonder. Luca Zattoni is every woman's fantasy. Rich, cool-headed, Italian, body to die for…'

Despite her tears, Tia lifted an eyebrow. 'I thought you were a happily married woman?'

'I am.' Sharon looked unrepentant. 'But there isn't a woman alive who wouldn't look twice at Luca. He's sex on legs, Tia.'

Sex on legs.

Tia felt her heart beat faster. And that was the reason for the current mess. She hadn't been able to resist the man.

Sharon sighed. 'Tia, the entire female population is green with envy. You're the one that he's marrying.'

Tia lifted her chin. 'Not any more.'

Thoroughly alarmed, Sharon bustled across to her friend and took her by the shoulders. 'OK, calm down. Take a deep breath. Copy me…' She breathed slowly, trying to set an example. 'Right. That's better. Now, then, tell me slowly, has something happened or is this just bridal nerves? I was nervous before I married Richard, you know. It's normal to be nervous. Especially for someone with your background.'

'It's not nerves.' Tia pulled away from her friend and rammed her feet into the first pair of shoes that came to hand.

Totally at a loss, Sharon backed away and turned towards the door. 'I'll fetch Luca.'

Dear God, no! That was the last thing she wanted.

'I don't want to see Luca!' Tia's head jerked up and the desperation in her voice stopped Sharon in her tracks. 'I can't. I just want to get out of here as fast as possible.'

'Tia…' Sharon let go of the doorhandle and tried to reason with her, her voice soothing. 'Just because things didn't work out for your parents, it doesn't mean—'

'What?' Tia slammed the suitcase shut and stared at her, tendrils of blonde hair escaping from what had once been an elegant chignon. 'What doesn't it mean? That it will all go wrong for me, too? My mother drank herself into the grave because she discovered that the man she loved—*the man she trusted*—had betrayed her. Kept secrets from her. Do you really think I intend to put myself in the same position?'

Clamping her teeth onto her lower lip, Tia walked back

across the room and swept her make-up off the dressing-table into her handbag.

'I don't understand.' Sharon looked blank. 'I know that your father had affairs, but—' She broke off, her eyes widening as she registered what Tia had just said. 'Are you saying that you think Luca is *having an affair*?'

Tia felt the pain, hot and fluid, pour along her veins.

'I don't know,' she said honestly. 'I think so. Maybe. He's certainly having a serious relationship with another woman.'

'No.' Sharon shook her head and gave an incredulous laugh. 'No! I don't believe it. I never saw a man more in love with a woman than Luca is with you. He's crazy about you.'

Tia closed her eyes and took steadying breaths.

If only…

'Trust me on this one, Sharon,' she said finally. 'Luca is not in love with me.'

'So, if he doesn't love you, why are there one hundred and forty people waiting for you to marry him, and why am I dressed like a green blancmange?'

There was a long silence and when Tia finally spoke her voice was little more than a hoarse croak.

'Because I'm pregnant.'

The room was suddenly deadly quiet. 'Tia?'

'That's the reason he's marrying me.' Tia gave a wobbly smile and blushed deeply. 'And before you say it, yes, I'm a midwife and I should know the facts of life, but somehow I forgot them when I met Luca.'

In fact, she'd forgotten pretty much everything the moment she'd set eyes on Luca.

Fundamental things like how to walk away from a man before things became serious.

The truth was that Luca Zattoni was the most overwhelmingly attractive male she'd ever met. Cool and confident and stunningly good-looking, the chemistry between them had stopped her brain from functioning from the moment they'd met.

And that moment was etched in her memory for ever.

She'd been backpacking around Europe and she'd arrived in Venice late at night. As she'd left the bus station, a group of young lads had started to bother her and she'd felt a rush of relief when a car had suddenly pulled up.

Luca had stepped out of the driver's seat, broad-shouldered and menacing as he'd strode towards the youths who had surrounded her, his glossy hair shining blue-black under the streetlamps. He was clearly a man who could handle himself in any situation and her tormenters had melted rapidly into the darkness, leaving the two of them alone.

So she'd been left standing next to an empty bus station, awkwardly muttering her thanks to this handsome Italian stranger whose dark-eyed scrutiny had made her feel decidedly light headed.

'It's late to be wandering the streets of Venice,' he observed, his gaze flickering over her backpack and resting on her sturdy walking boots. 'Can I give you a lift somewhere?'

He spoke in English and he had the sexiest voice she'd ever heard. Smooth, masculine tones tinged with enough of an Italian accent to make the blood heat in her veins.

Tia's heart was thumping so hard she thought it might burst through her ribcage. 'H-how did you guess that I'm English?'

'Not difficult.' His eyes rested briefly on her silver blonde hair and he gave her a smile that made her breathing stop. 'Hair the colour of yours is very unusual in Italy. As you will discover if you continue to walk the streets at this time of night.'

She was still staring at him like an idiot. 'I haven't found anywhere to stay yet…'

'Venice is generally a very safe city,' he told her, 'but a

woman like you shouldn't be walking around on her own this late.'

A woman like her…

Her eyes locked with his and something passed between them. A feeling so powerful that her knees weakened alarmingly.

His eyes held hers captive, drawing her in. 'I would be happy to show you around and help you find somewhere to stay…'

She knew that getting into a car with a stranger was foolish in the extreme, but this man didn't seem like a stranger and their relationship progressed so fast she barely had time to reason.

And then Tia discovered that she was pregnant.

She dragged herself back to the present, aware that Sharon was still staring at her, clearly taken aback by her announcement.

'And you think that's why he's marrying you?'

'I didn't at first.' Tia's voice shook as she told Sharon what had happened. 'I believed what I wanted to believe— that he loved me and that was why he was marrying me.'

Sharon bit her lip. 'So…'

Tia took a deep breath. 'But I've found out that he was just using me as therapy. It seems he was getting over an-other relationship.' She shook her head slowly as she thought back over the past few weeks. 'He only proposed because I told him I was pregnant.'

Sharon looked horrified. 'How—? What makes you think he's involved with someone else?'

'Because I just met her.' Tia dropped the bag and stared into the mirror. Her reflection stared back, her skin pale and streaked with tears. 'I nipped along the corridor to talk to Luca's mother half an hour ago, when you were in the bathroom. She was deep in conversation with a very stun-ning woman. Someone I'd never seen before.'

Sharon sank onto the nearest chair and stared at her with trepidation. 'And?'

Tia fiddled with the silk of her jacket. 'His mother was saying what a sad day it was. That he should have been marrying Luisa—that's her name, by the way.' She sniffed slightly. 'And that he was marrying totally the wrong woman for totally the wrong reasons and it would never last.'

Sharon gave a soft gasp and lifted a hand to her throat. 'And what did this Luisa woman say?'

'That she and Luca had been so close for so long that things had just become confused. And that she'd seen him and spoken to him and he'd said he would always love her…'

'No!' Sharon groaned and shook her head. 'I don't believe it. Not Luca.'

Tia gave her a watery smile. 'Why not Luca? Let's be honest for a moment. This has been one of the fastest romances on record. I met him ten weeks ago. We barely know him, Shaz.' Tia's voice cracked and Sharon squeezed her arm.

'Luca's not a teenager, Tia. He's an adult male who knows exactly what he wants out of life. I can't see him marrying someone unless he wanted to. Maybe he finished it—'

'No.' Tia rummaged in her bag for a tissue and blew her nose hard. 'No way would any red-blooded male finish with a woman like this one. You didn't see her. She was seriously gorgeous. And elegant. Nothing like me. When Luca met me I was backpacking, for goodness' sake! I'm so far removed from his usual style of woman that it's laughable. I'm a homeless, rootless waif who's terrified of commitment. Believe me, there's no contest.'

Sharon frowned. 'You forgot to add that you're also warm, funny and irresistibly pretty. Tia, men have been falling over themselves to get to you for years and you don't even see it. Trust me, Luca is crazy about you—'

'Novelty value.' Tia blew her nose again and tucked the tissue up her sleeve. 'There's obviously a shortage of blonde women in Italy. But I've come to my senses now, and I'm relieving him of his responsibilities. He can go back to the woman he loves. Come to think of it, he's probably never been away from her. Maybe that's why he was spending all that time at the hospital.'

'He's an obstetrician.' Sharon reasoned. 'You know they work hideous hours.'

'Do I?'

What evidence did she have that he'd been working? Only his word, and he seemed to be very selective about what he disclosed.

And she could never marry a man who wasn't completely honest with her.

She stood up, slipped on her coat and picked up her bags.

'Tia, wait!' Sharon hastily followed her across the room and caught her arm. 'At least talk to Luca about it before you leave. There might be a simple explanation.'

Tia shook her head. 'For telling another woman that he would always love her? I don't think so.'

'But—'

'He doesn't love me, Shaz. He was just doing the honourable thing by offering to marry me and I was really stupid to believe otherwise.'

Luca had never once said he loved her. Not even when she'd told him about the baby and he'd proposed.

Sometimes, just sometimes, from the way he'd behaved, she'd thought that maybe—

But she'd just been kidding herself.

'He doesn't love me.' Tia moved towards the door and Sharon grabbed her again.

'He's going to be furious, Tia.'

Tia shook her head slowly. 'I don't think so.' She gave

a painful smile. 'I think he'll be relieved that I've let him off the hook.'

Sharon looked at her anxiously. 'So what are you going to do?'

Tia checked that her passport was in her handbag. 'Take the first available flight back to England. With any luck you'll give me my old job back and I'll find somewhere to live…'

Sharon frowned. 'Of course you can have your job back, and you can stay with Richard and me, but—'

'No. I need to be on my own.'

Sharon bit her lip. 'But, Tia, Luca is a very traditional Italian male. Do you really think he's going to let you leave, knowing you're pregnant? He'll follow you—'

'No.' Tia gave a sad smile and shook her head. 'If we were already married, then maybe, but Luca is still a single man and he's free to lead his own life.'

Free to marry Luisa.

'It's over, Shaz, and I need to build a new life for myself.'

Without Luca.

CHAPTER ONE

SHE wasn't going to cry.

Tia clamped her teeth firmly on her lower lip and wondered if the day would ever come when she no longer felt like sobbing the whole time.

A soft sigh from the newly delivered mother by her side brought her to her senses and she stared down at the tiny bundle in her arms.

The child was beautiful.

Barely two hours old, dark lashes feathered her cheeks which were still slightly blotched from the rigours of birth. Lying passively in Tia's arms, she gazed placidly up at the world, her blue eyes slightly unfocused.

Tia felt her throat close.

'Isn't she perfect?' The proud mother gave a wide, self-satisfied smile and waited to be handed her daughter. 'I can't believe how beautiful she is. I mean, I always thought babies were supposed to be ugly.'

Ugly?

Tia stared down at the sleeping cherub, marvelling at the way nature had managed to produce everything in miniature.

No—the baby definitely wasn't ugly.

'She's beautiful, Mrs Adams.' Tia's heart beat faster as the baby made little snuffly noises and turned her head searchingly. 'And she's hungry.'

Work. Thank goodness for work. It was the only thing that distracted her from her own problems.

She tightened the blanket around the baby and looked quizzically at Fiona Adams. 'Are you ready to give it a try?'

13

'I suppose so, although I have to admit that I'm really nervous,' the young woman admitted as she settled herself more comfortably on the chair. 'Everyone says I'm mad, wanting to breastfeed.'

'You're not mad at all,' Tia said calmly. 'Breast milk is designed for babies and you're giving her the very best start in life.'

Fiona looked worried. 'I bet I won't have enough milk.'

'Well, your milk often doesn't come in for a few days after delivery,' Tia told her, 'but what you do produce is something called colostrum.'

'And that's good for her?'

Tia nodded. 'Very good for her. Packed full of protein and antibodies. Very high in calories, too. Are you comfortable like that?'

She'd settled Fiona in a chair with her back and her feet supported.

Fiona wriggled again and held out her arms. 'Yes. I really wanted to put her straight on the breast after she was delivered, but she was totally out for the count.'

Tia nodded. 'You had pethidine during your labour, and it can make the baby sleepy.' She placed the baby in Fiona's arms, positioning her carefully. 'That's right. We want her mouth to be opposite the nipple, just like that—perfect.'

Fiona stared down at her baby daughter. 'Does the position really matter?'

'Oh, yes. It's vital if you're not going to get sore and disheartened by the whole thing. Everyone thinks that breastfeeding is instinctive, but it isn't, you know.' Her voice was soft as she tucked the baby into a good position, moving Fiona's arm so that she supported the baby's shoulders. 'It's a skill that has to be learned like any other. That's great, Fiona. You can use your fingers to support her head—like that. Brilliant.'

She slipped a hand behind the baby's downy head and

gently moved the baby's mouth against the nipple, encouraging her to suck. 'Come on, sweetheart, take a nice big mouthful for me...'

'Oh!' Fiona breathed in sharply and then looked up, her eyes misty. 'She's doing it! I can feel it.'

'That's great.' Tia watched the baby closely, checking that she was sucking properly. 'You're both doing really well.'

'So is that it? I expected it to be more complicated than that.'

Tia smiled. 'Well, sometimes it is. And for the first few days it's a good idea to let someone help you put her on the breast so that we can check that she's feeding properly.'

Fiona stared down at her daughter with an awed expression in her eyes. 'I can't believe that it doesn't hurt. I always expected it to.'

Tia shook her head. 'It shouldn't hurt. Not if she's latched on properly.'

'And how do I know that?'

'Well, for a start there shouldn't be any pain,' Tia said, 'and also if you look down you can see that she's taken the whole of the nipple and some of the breast into her mouth. That's how it works, you see. The nipple goes right back as far as the soft palate and that's what makes her suck. Her lower jaw closes on the actual breast tissue and she uses suction to strip the breast of milk. You'll feel her feeding but it should never be painful.'

'And what if I can't make enough milk?'

Tia gave a lopsided smile. 'Well, that's where nature is very clever. It's all about supply and demand. The more you put the baby to the breast, the more milk you produce.'

Fiona gave a contented sigh and settled down to enjoy feeding her daughter.

'You have a very unusual name.' She glanced up at Tia with a curious smile. 'What's its origin?'

Tia pulled a face. 'It's short for Portia.'

Fiona lifted her eyebrows. 'As in *The Merchant of Venice*?'

Tia gave a nod and a rueful smile. 'My parents were actors.'

'It's a pretty name,' Fiona commented, breaking off as her husband walked into the room, a bag of coins and a sheet of paper clasped in his hand.

'Mike, look!' Fiona spoke softly so that she didn't disturb the baby. 'She's feeding!'

Mike Adams flopped onto the bed and grinned soppily at his wife. 'Clever girl. I knew you could do it.'

'It's her that's doing it, not me.' Fiona touched her daughter's downy head with her fingers. 'She's brilliant.'

'She knows what's good for her,' Mike said stoutly, and Fiona gave him a wry look.

'And you, too, of course. You can't get up in the night if I'm breastfeeding.'

'Oops. Caught out!' Mike smiled sheepishly. 'I'll do the nappies.'

Fiona smiled placidly. 'Too right you will. And the winding.' She frowned at her husband. 'You look really rumpled. As if you slept in your clothes.'

Mike gave a short laugh. 'Sleep? Just remind me what that is again. You may have been the one who had the baby, but I'm exhausted!'

'Poor thing!' Fiona laughed. 'So, who did you phone?'

Mike gave a groan and ticked them off on his fingers. 'Your mother, my mother, your sister, Pam and Rick, Sue and Simon and Nick Whiteshaw.'

'Oh, great, well done.' Fiona turned her attention back to the baby and then glanced at Tia. 'How long do I keep going for?'

'Until she stops feeding.' Tia gazed down at the baby, noticing that she was still swallowing. 'She's still guzzling away at the moment.'

'Do I have to give her both sides?'

'Always offer both sides,' Tia advised. 'But let her take all that she wants to from the first breast. When your milk comes in it's important that she stays on the breast for as long as she wants to because the milk changes during the feed.'

Fiona's eyes widened. 'Really?'

'Really.' Tia smiled. 'What the baby gets first is what we call foremilk—it's lower in calories and thirst-quenching. After that they drink hind milk which is much more filling. If you take them off the breast too soon then they miss out on the milk that fills them up.'

Mike blinked. 'Clever.'

'Very.' Tia nodded and helped Fiona remove the sleepy baby from her breast and wind her carefully. 'Have you decided on a name yet?'

'We've narrowed it down to three,' Fiona said with a chuckle. 'Mike's first choice is Georgia, mine is Isabelle and we both quite like Megan.'

'Megan Adams.' Tia tried it out, nodded her approval and took the baby from Fiona, snuggling her against her shoulder with an easy confidence that brought an envious sigh from the mother.

'You're so natural with her. Do you have children?'

'No.'

Not yet…

Suddenly Tia needed some air. She placed the baby carefully in the cot and drew the curtains back round the bed. 'Give me a shout next time she's ready to feed and I'll help you, Fiona.'

Forcing a smile, she hurried out of the four-bedded bay and back to the nurses' station, taking a long, steadying breath as she tentatively touched her still flat stomach.

Her heart stumbled and panic swamped her.

This wasn't the way things should have turned out.

She'd never wanted to bring a baby into the world on

her own. After her own experiences it was the last thing she would have wished on a child.

Taking a deep breath, she forced herself to think rationally. She'd cope, of course she would. Plenty of people did. Not everyone was like her own mother and there was no reason why she should be, but still...

Dragging her mind back to her work, she settled herself at the computer and updated Fiona's notes, glancing up as Sharon, in full professional mode as the unit sister, bustled up to the nurses' station.

'Are you still here, Tia?' She frowned and checked the clock on the wall. 'You should have gone home hours ago.'

Tia ignored her.

She didn't want to go home. She liked being at work. It took her mind off her problems.

'Baby Adams has taken her first feed nicely,' she told Sharon, her smile overly bright. 'I'm just updating the notes and then I'll go and check on Mrs Dodd if you like.'

'What I'd like is for you to stop pretending nothing is wrong.' Sharon lowered her voice and glanced up the corridor to check that no one was within earshot. 'Have you called him?'

'No.' Tia turned back to the computer, vaguely registering that Sharon looked slightly agitated about something. 'And I don't intend to.'

'But if he comes to you, you'd talk to him?'

'Sharon, I left the man standing at the altar,' Tia reminded her patiently, wondering why her friend was looking so nervous, 'and he's in love with another woman. There's no earthly reason why he would possibly want to see me ever again.'

'Except, maybe, that you're carrying his child,' Sharon pointed out quietly, her eyes flickering briefly down to Tia's flat stomach. 'Talking of which, how are you?'

Tia pulled a face. 'Oh, you know, sick, exhausted—apart from that, fine.'

Sharon didn't smile. 'You need to register with a doctor, Tia.'

Tia nodded and didn't meet her eyes. 'Plenty of time for that.' Not wanting to pursue the topic, she stood up and tucked her notebook into her pocket. 'Maybe you're right about it being time to go home. I'll see you tomorrow.'

Sharon looked suddenly flustered. 'Tia, wait, there's something I—'

'Not now, Sharon.' Tia interrupted her with a weary smile. 'I really don't want to analyse my love life any more tonight.'

She just wanted to go home and be on her own.

She walked through to the staffroom, changed her clothes and made her way down the stairs to the car park. The battered old bicycle that she'd found in the garage of her rented cottage was exactly where she'd left it.

By the time she'd cycled home she was exhausted, but the minute she saw the red Italian sports car parked outside the cottage her exhaustion vanished.

No!

Surely he couldn't be…

Opening the front door slowly, Tia walked through to the kitchen and pushed open the door, stopping dead as she saw the man lounging there, one powerful thigh resting on the kitchen table, his cool, dark eyes steady on her shocked face.

'Luca…' One hand reached out blindly for the wall as she sought support.

She really, truly hadn't expected to see him again. Certainly not now. It had been two weeks.

Two weeks, and somehow she'd managed to diminish him in her mind. She'd blanked out just how much his physical presence affected her, forgotten how his blatant masculinity and unshakable self-confidence made her weak at the knees.

'Tia.' Thick, dark lashes swept down over his eyes, con-

cealing his expression. He looked remote and unapproach-
able and she was suddenly totally unable to speak. Luca
always did that to her. He was the only man in the world
who rendered her completely tongue-tied.

She said the first thing that came into her head. 'How
did you know where to find me?'

'I called Sharon.' His eyes lingered on her pale face. 'She
gave me your address.'

Sharon?

'No.' Tia shook her head in disbelief but Luca's expression didn't change.

'Don't blame her. I didn't give her much choice. Let's
just say I was...' he paused and searched for the right word
'...persuasive.'

And Tia knew only too well just how persuasive Luca
Zattoni could be when he wanted to be.

That explained why Sharon had looked so uncomfortable
and guilty.

She glanced back towards the front door, still feeling
shell-shocked by his unexpected presence. 'But presumably
Sharon didn't provide you with a key?'

Luca lifted one broad shoulder dismissively. 'The sign
was still outside and the letting agent was very helpful once
I told him who I was. He seemed concerned about you
living on your own here. This cottage is extremely isolated
and you obviously aroused his protective instincts.'

It took a few moments for his words to sink in.

'The letting agent gave you a key?' She looked at him
incredulously. 'Is there anyone you can't charm, Luca?'

'Apparently.' A ghost of a smile touched his firm mouth.
'Or presumably you wouldn't have left me standing at the
altar two weeks ago,' he drawled, resting one lean brown
hand on his muscular thigh. 'We have a great deal to talk
about, *cara mia*.'

Her heart rate suddenly increased dramatically. 'We have
nothing to talk about, Luca.'

Certainly not now, after a long day at the hospital. Tia hadn't been expecting this conversation and she had no idea how she was going to handle it. Was she going to confront him with what she'd discovered? Or was she going to wait for him to tell her the truth about his past, which he should have done right from the start? She needed to be prepared before she spoke to him. She needed to feel strong and in control.

As it was, all she felt was…vulnerable.

'Nothing to talk about?' He straightened in a fluid movement and strolled across the kitchen towards her. 'First you take flight on our wedding day without the slightest explanation, and next you leave the country, go back to your old job and rent a cottage in the middle of nowhere. We could talk for a week and not cover even half of what we have to discuss.'

Tia's throat was uncomfortably dry. 'I left you a note.'

'Ah, yes…' Thick lashes lowered slightly to shield his stunning dark eyes. 'The note that Sharon delivered, saying that you had changed your mind about marrying me.'

Her heart gave a little flip. She hadn't expected him to follow her and she wasn't prepared for this confrontation.

'It wouldn't have worked, Luca.' Her knees trembled slightly but she forced herself to hold his gaze. 'We were getting married for the wrong reasons. We—we didn't know each other properly.'

She hadn't known that he was involved in a serious, long-term relationship with another woman.

There was a long silence while he studied her face, the expression in his dark eyes unreadable. 'So, just like that, you leave?' His tone was even. 'You decide this by yourself, with no consultation with me? No attempt to discuss whatever problem you think exists? *Dio,* is that normal behaviour for two people who were planning to marry?'

Tia's breathing quickened and anger gripped her. *He* was criticising *her*? This was the time to confront him about what she'd heard, but she wasn't ready to do that yet. She didn't want to say something she'd regret. She needed time to think through the best way of tackling the subject.

Anyway, it was his responsibility to tell her about his past, to open up and tell her the truth.

'When would we have had this discussion, Luca?' She took refuge in attack. 'You were always at the hospital.'

His black brows met in a frown. 'Is that what this is all about? My working hours? I'm an obstetrician, Tia. You should understand the demands of the job better than most women.'

Suddenly she didn't feel at all well. She'd woken early that morning, been sick repeatedly and now he was expecting her to dissect their relationship. It was too much.

Her eyes closed briefly and she took a deep breath. 'Do we have to talk about this now?'

'Yes.' His voice was a deep growl and she flinched slightly. She'd always thought that Luca was very controlled, but suddenly he seemed like a stranger.

Which was part of the problem.

They didn't really know each other. That fact had been brought home to her with shocking clarity on the day of her wedding. She should never have agreed to marry him, but she'd been so swept away by the way he'd made her feel…

'We can meet up tomorrow or something,' she suggested, hoping that she wasn't going to embarrass herself by being sick in front of him. 'Where are you staying tonight?'

'Staying?' One dark eyebrow lifted as if her question was wholly irrelevant. 'Here, of course.'

'No way, Luca.' She shook her head vigorously. 'This is my cottage.'

Luca straightened in a fluid movement and moved purposefully towards her. 'And you're expecting our child,

Tia.' He said the words with careful emphasis. 'Your place is with me.'

'With you?' Her heart started to gallop. With him? Surely he wasn't serious—not after everything that had happened. 'You're not seriously suggesting that we should still get married?'

'Hardly.' His tone was dry. 'You've made your feelings on that subject very clear.'

Tia blushed slightly and looked away. Leaving him at the altar had been a lousy thing to do, but at the time she hadn't been able to see an alternative. She'd just needed to get away as fast as possible.

'So what exactly do you want, Luca?'

There was a slight pause. 'You,' he said softly. 'You and our baby.'

'Luca, no!' Her voice was suddenly hoarse and her heart was beating faster than she would have thought possible. 'It's time we were honest with each other. Our whole relationship was a mistake. We were just—very carried away…this baby wasn't planned.' Tia decided that it was time to voice at least some of her concerns. 'A month ago when I told you I was pregnant, you couldn't escape to the hospital fast enough!'

He tensed and his mouth tightened. 'That's not true.'

'It is true, Luca, and you know it.' Despite her best intentions, she felt her voice wobble slightly and forced herself to stay calm. The last thing she wanted was for him to know how badly his reaction had hurt her. She had too much pride. 'You were horrified to learn that I was pregnant and don't try and deny it because I'm excellent at reading body language and yours was shouting at me!'

His dark eyes were suddenly wary and for the first time since she'd met him he seemed slightly uncomfortable.

'You misunderstood me. It's true that the news of the baby came as a shock at first,' he admitted finally, his voice quiet. 'I would be less than honest if I didn't admit that I would have preferred us to have more time together before we considered having children, but—'

'You don't need to make excuses. I know that you weren't pleased, and nothing can change that.' Suddenly Tia felt hideously sick and she took several deep breaths to try and settle her stomach.

An ominous frown touched his forehead. 'Tia, when you first told me that you were pregnant, I hadn't been to bed for almost forty hours,' he said, his dark eyes intent on hers as he paused only inches away from her. 'I was called to one difficult delivery after another. By the time I saw you I was dead on my feet. The news that you were pregnant came as a shock, I admit that, and I probably didn't react the way I should have, but...'

Her eyes challenged him and she tried to ignore the effect that his closeness had on her. 'So you're saying that had you had a good night's sleep you would have been delighted?'

His dark gaze swept over her. 'You need to calm down, *cara mia*. You're very emotional.'

'Emotional?' Her jaw dropped and she gaped at him. 'Of course I'm emotional. We had three blissful weeks together in Venice, but when we moved back to your home in Milan you changed, Luca. I barely saw you. You spent every available minute at the hospital. When I finally found time to tell you that I was pregnant, you reacted as though it was the worst news I could have given you and vanished to the hospital again. Then you came home and proposed. But obviously for all the wrong reasons. I think I have every right to be emotional.'

Especially in view of what she'd found out since.

He muttered something under his breath in Italian and raked long fingers thought his glossy dark hair. 'Tia, I have already admitted that my reaction was less than perfect—'

'Understatement,' Tia muttered. 'Major understatement.'

A muscle worked in his jaw. 'I think we both need to calm down and then start this conversation again.'

'No.' She shook her head vigorously, desperate to get rid of him. Being so close to him eroded her will-power. 'There's nothing more to be said. This isn't about the baby, Luca, it's about us. You and I. And the fact that our hormones got tangled with our common sense.'

Nausea washed over her and she lifted a hand to her mouth. Oh, help! She was going to be sick again. She was sure of it.

Luca frowned sharply and his long, strong fingers curled into her shoulders. 'What's the matter? Are you ill?'

'No,' she lied, steadying her stomach with a few deep breaths. 'I'm just not enjoying this conversation. I want you to acknowledge that we both made a mistake so that we can move on.'

His hands dropped from her shoulders and his face might have been carved from stone. 'We're having a baby, Tia. It's too late to talk about making mistakes. We need to plan for the future.'

'Luca, we don't have a future,' she said firmly, genuinely amazed that he'd even suggest such a thing. But it was because of the baby, of course. Whatever his initial reaction had been, he'd clearly decided that responsibility should come before personal happiness. 'If a relationship isn't right without a baby then it certainly won't be right *with* a baby. We're totally wrong for each other. Discovering that I'm pregnant doesn't change that. I understand that you're upset because I left you at the altar, but—'

'I don't care about that,' Luca said dismissively. 'That is in the past, but the baby is in the future and our future is together.'

Tia stared at him. Sharon was obviously right. Luca Zattoni was a traditional Italian male to the core.

He might have been shocked originally, but the concept of family and children was so important to Italians that she should have guessed that, once he'd had time to think about it, there was no way that Luca would just dismiss the fact that she was pregnant.

'I am not going back to Italy with you, Luca.'

'You still haven't told me why you left Italy in the first place,' he said through gritted teeth. 'I can't believe that you changed your mind at the last minute. If you had doubts, why didn't you discuss them with me? *Dio*, I went up to your room and found everything gone. How did you think I felt?'

Remembering just what had made her leave in such a hurry, she looked at him without sympathy. 'I expect it damaged your ego.'

He muttered under his breath and gave her an impatient glance. 'Tia, I left the need to protect my ego behind in childhood, but I would be less than human if the unexplained disappearance of my bride-to-be—*my pregnant bride to be*—didn't disconcert me somewhat.'

'I thought you'd be pleased that I'd gone,' she mumbled, rubbing her toe on the kitchen floor and refusing to look at him. Having him so close was unsettling to say the least. She couldn't look at the man without remembering how they'd been together…

'I wasn't pleased,' he said softly, his Italian accent suddenly very pronounced as he accentuated every syllable.

She lifted her chin, her expression defiant. 'If you missed me so badly, if you were really that worried, why didn't you follow me straight away?'

He tensed and hesitated for only the briefest moment. 'There were complications,' he muttered finally. 'Things I needed to sort out.'

Luisa.

Tia turned away, hiding her hurt, but knowing that she'd done the right thing not to marry him. She didn't want to be anyone's second choice.

'You haven't told me why you changed your mind.'

'I—I had second thoughts,' she said honestly, flicking her hair back and looking him straight in the eye. 'I suddenly realised that there were so many things I didn't know about you.'

Luca frowned. 'Like what?'

Flustered, Tia avoided his question. 'I don't know, but it was all so fast and I don't think you should get married without knowing everything there is to know about the person you're marrying—'

'Tia there are always things about another person that stays hidden,' he said, and she shook her head.

'Not when you've known each other for a long time. When people have known each other for a long time they're as familiar as old socks.'

He lifted an eyebrow and looked at her incredulously. '*Dio.* That is your idea of a stimulating relationship? To live with someone who is like a sock?'

'I'm just trying to say—'

'It's all right—I think know what you're trying to say.' He let out a long breath and shook his head slowly. 'Tia, the length of a relationship is not always an indication of its depth.'

His voice was suddenly quiet and her heart suddenly missed a beat.

Was he going to tell her about Luisa?

Luca's jaw clenched. 'It's true that our relationship moved quickly and was very intense—'

Intense?

That had to be the understatement of the year.

She'd been so totally overwhelmed by what had been happening between them that she hadn't bothered to think about the future.

'But we weren't suited, Luca.'

'No? If my memory serves me correctly, we were never able to look at each other without needing to rip each other's clothes off,' he drawled softly. 'I wouldn't exactly describe that as ''not suited'', would you? You were in my bed the same night we met.'

His blunt reminder of just how quickly they'd become intimate brought a flood of colour to her cheeks and Tia closed her eyes. He was right, of course. The physical chemistry between them had been frighteningly powerful. It had completely swamped her common sense, what little she'd had, and it had clearly taken his mind off his troubles with Luisa.

'There's more to a relationship than good sex, Luca,' she said quietly, dragging her eyes away from his penetrating gaze and trying to regain some semblance of control.

The mere brush of those long, strong fingers against her flesh made her tremble and she struggled to hide it from him.

Dear God, why couldn't she just tell him the truth? That she knew he'd met her when his other relationship had been in trouble. That she knew he was in love with another woman.

He was watching her closely. 'You think our relationship was just about sex?'

For her, no, but for him?

'We're different, Luca,' she said finally. 'I—I didn't realise how different until we lived together in Milan. Perhaps if I'd had a job...'

The temperature in the room dropped below zero.

'There was no reason for you to work.' His jaw tightened and his expression was grim. 'I gave you credit cards—you weren't short of money.'

That was true enough. The Zattoni family were obviously extremely wealthy. She'd never had access to so much money in her life. But she didn't really care about money.

'It isn't about money, Luca,' Tia declared emphatically, trying to make him understand something of what she'd felt when they were in Italy. 'When we met in Venice it was beautiful—romantic. But Milan...'

'Milan is not Venice,' he agreed quietly, his eyes fixed on her pale face. 'Milan is more of a business city than a tourist one. It's foggy in winter and muggy in the summer and the pollution is grim.'

'I felt suffocated there,' Tia admitted, 'but it wasn't really the place. It was *us*. You spent all your time at the hospital and I was lonely.'

'Lonely?' He frowned sharply. 'You had the support of my family. How could you have been lonely?'

Tia's eyes slid away from his. 'They hate me, Luca,' she told him. 'They think I'm the wrong sort of woman for you, and do you know what?' She forced herself to meet that unsettling dark gaze head on. 'They're right. I *am* the wrong sort of woman. You should have married someone sleek and elegant, someone who'd know how to spend your money…'

It was the nearest she'd got to telling him that she knew about Luisa but not by the flicker of an eyelid did he betray himself.

'My family do not hate you.' His expression was suddenly ominous. 'What possible grounds do you have for making such a statement?'

She caught the look of disbelief in his eyes and decided to tell the truth.

'Luca, I never saw them,' she told him quietly, 'apart from the weekends when you and I visited them together.'

He muttered something under his breath in Italian. 'You spent most weekdays with them. Shopping, lunching.'

Tia gave a wry smile. 'No, Luca. Check your credit-card bill. I never once shopped or lunched. They never invited me and, anyway, I wouldn't have wanted to. I don't like spending money that way. That isn't the sort of life I'm used to and they knew that, which is presumably why they never invited me.'

Anger flashed in his black eyes and Tia winced. 'They're very traditional,' she said quickly, wishing she'd never said anything. She certainly didn't want to turn him against his family. 'They knew I wouldn't have been comfortable spending days with them.'

Luca's jaw was tight. 'So how did you spend your days?'

Tia gave a sad smile. They'd been together for three months and only now was he asking that question.

'I stayed in the flat and read books,' she told him, 'or I went for walks.'

He was suddenly tense. 'Milan is not a great city for walking. Where did you walk?'

She shrugged. 'Wherever took my fancy.'

'And you wouldn't have had the first clue where was safe and where wasn't.' He closed his eyes briefly. 'That evening we met in Venice, you were pacing the streets at night on your own. Do you have a death wish?'

'No, but I like to live my own life, and—'

'Tia, you are a stunningly beautiful woman,' he ground out angrily, 'and your blonde head shines like a beacon. It is very unusual to see a woman of your colouring in Italy and you attract no little amount of attention. You were putting yourself at risk.'

Without any warning her heart turned over. He thought she was beautiful?

No, that just didn't make sense. She was as unlike Luisa as it was possible to be.

Before she had a chance to digest this piece of information, his hands closed over her shoulders like a vice. 'I will talk to my family about their behaviour and you will promise me that you won't walk around on your own at night again.'

'I can't promise and I don't want you to talk to your family. There's no reason to. It's in the past now.' Suddenly Tia felt exhausted. Too exhausted to talk any further. 'It was all my fault, anyway. I am so far removed from a perfect Italian wife it's laughable. Your family did what they thought was best and they were right. I'm the sort of person who needs space and independence. I'm not the sort of person who enjoys shopping, lunching and beauty salons.'

She swayed slightly and Luca's grip on her shoulders tightened.

'We shouldn't be talking about this now.' He scooped her up as if she weighed nothing, holding her firmly against his chest. 'You're not well. You look pale and worn out. You need to go to bed.'

Bed.

Just thinking about bed when she was held this close to him made her body start to tremble. She could feel the hard muscle of his chest through the fabric of his shirt and her fingers itched to touch him.

No.

'Put me down, Luca.' She wriggled in his arms and then groaned and buried her head in his shoulder as everything swam.

He ignored her efforts to escape, his expression grim as he negotiated the narrow staircase that led upstairs.

'Where's your bedroom?'

'It's none of your business,' she protested weakly, wishing that being in his arms didn't feel quite so good. But she fancied him so much that her whole body melted if he so much as looked at her. It wasn't just that he was stunningly good-looking. There was something about him, an air of confidence and power, that was incredibly sexy.

Dear God, did she have no sense of self-preservation?

How could she still feel this way about someone who didn't want her? How could her body still respond to him?

Luca shouldered open the few doors upstairs until he found what was obviously her bedroom and laid her gently on the bed.

'Our problem is that we are both too alike, you and I,' he told her, stroking the hair out of her eyes with gentle fingers and then checking her pulse. 'We are hot-tempered and stubborn. Why didn't you tell me that you felt ill? How long have you been in this state?'

Tia closed her eyes and fought back the waves of nausea. 'I'm not in a state. I'm just pregnant,' she mumbled, feeling drowsiness wash over her. She'd never felt so tired in her life. It was as if her body had turned off a switch and everything had shut down. She just had to sleep.

'Go away, Luca,' she murmured, fighting to stop her eyelids drooping. 'I want you to go home to Italy and leave me alone.'

She saw his eyes darken, knew she ought to finish the conversation but her body betrayed her, slowly drifting into sleep mode before she could resolve the situation. Her eyelids closed and she was dimly aware of Luca standing up and of having blankets tucked around her. Then darkness claimed her.

CHAPTER TWO

TIA awoke to the sound of rain thundering on the windows.

Remembering the evening before, she closed her eyes and gave a groan of mortification.

Luca.

She'd virtually passed out cold on the man. He'd carried her to her bed and…

Her eyes drifted to the clothes piled neatly on the chair in the corner of the room.

Her clothes.

Pushing back the duvet, she glanced down and saw that she was wearing one of Luca's old T-shirts. She ran her fingers over the soft fabric, her sensitive nose picking up his elusive male scent, the same scent that had wrapped itself around her on all those hot, steamy nights together.

The mere thought of his lean, brown hands touching her made her heart flip against her chest and a devastating weakness spread through her body.

Luca…

She'd never felt about anybody the way she felt about him.

And he must have undressed her last night.

Where had he stayed? Here? In the cottage? *Was he still here now?*

Tia sat up suddenly and swung her legs over the edge of the bed, anger bringing her to life.

How dared he?

How could Luca expect to stroll back into her life as if nothing had happened when he was in love with another woman? How dared he put her to bed and undress her? He was in no position to play happy families.

Her feet hit the floor and the sudden movement made her stomach churn.

She made it to the toilet just in time and retched miserably, wondering dully why any woman chose to get pregnant.

'You got up too quickly.' Luca's deep voice came from behind her and his long fingers lifted her hair away from her face.

'Go away, Luca.' She closed her eyes tightly, utterly humiliated that he should see her like this. Being ill was bad enough without having him witness it. 'I want some privacy.'

'I'm a doctor, *cara mia*,' he pointed out, his voice surprisingly gentle as he handed her a cool flannel. 'I see sick people every day.'

'I'm not people,' she said, wishing her stomach would settle. 'Leave me alone so I can die in peace.'

He murmured something in Italian and lifted her easily to her feet. 'You're not going to die. You have morning sickness. It should go by the fourteenth week.'

Tia slumped against the wall and looked at him with dull eyes. She was already twelve weeks pregnant. 'Another two weeks of this?'

He gave a faint smile, his dark eyes surprisingly sympathetic. 'Have you been sick much?'

'All the time,' Tia mumbled, and his smile faded as he switched into doctor mode.

'Do you have any pain when you are sick?'

'No.' She shook her head. 'Relax, Luca. I'm fine. Just pregnant.'

'You've lost weight.' His dark gaze raked over her slender frame and she looked at him, exhausted.

'Of course I've lost weight. The last few weeks haven't exactly been a picnic for me either, you know.'

'What has the doctor said about you?'

'What doctor?'

He frowned sharply. 'You haven't seen a doctor yet?'

She sighed. 'It's hardly been on the top of my list of priorities, Luca.'

'You should have had blood tests and a scan.' His eyes narrowed. 'When did you start your last period?'

'For goodness' sake!' She coloured, embarrassed by his question, and he muttered something under his breath and cupped her face in his hands.

'Tia, you are having my baby and I am a doctor,' he reminded her gently. 'You have no need to feel awkward. I need to ask you these things because I need to know that you are OK. Indulge me and answer the question. Please?'

'Twenty-fourth of July,' she muttered, feeling her cheeks heat again. They might have made the baby together but there was something about him that made her feel impossibly shy. 'Or, at least, that's what I think. I had some spotting a month later but not a real period. I worked out that I must be due on the 30th April.'

He nodded slowly. 'We need to get you booked in at the hospital and I want to send a urine specimen to check that you have no infection. It could be a reason for the vomiting.'

'Luca, I have morning sickness,' she said gruffly, strangely touched by his concern despite her mixed feelings towards him. 'It isn't hyperemesis.'

Hyperemesis gravidarum was a rare condition of pregnancy where nausea and vomiting were severe and could cause serious problems for the mother.

His expression was serious. 'Just how often have you been sick?'

'Quite a bit,' Tia confessed as she reached for her toothbrush. 'Usually whenever I'm tired. I suspect that you had a narrow escape last night. It's probably just as well you put me to bed early.'

He didn't laugh. 'Then you have to make sure that you don't get tired. It's your body telling you something.'

She brushed her teeth on autopilot and slowly sipped some water. 'Stop giving me orders, Luca.'

She put her toothbrush back in the cupboard and leaned her burning forehead against the cool glass of the bathroom cabinet. She felt terrible. She had to be at work in an hour and at the moment she could barely drag her body out of the bathroom. How did people get through nine months of this?

He held open the bathroom door and stood to one side. 'Go back to bed and I'll make you some breakfast.'

'Breakfast?' She shot him an incredulous look and put a protective hand on her abdomen. 'Are you some sort of sadist? Do you really think I'm hungry?'

'Food will help,' he reminded her gently, a glimmer of a smile touching his hard mouth. 'You're a midwife, Tia. You should know that eating something before you move in the morning can sometimes alleviate morning sickness. I'll fetch you some crackers.'

'There aren't any crackers,' she muttered, sliding past him, careful not to catch his eye. 'And stop ordering me around. You're not responsible for me. And while we're at it, you've got a nerve, undressing me while I'm asleep. And you had no right to stay the night.'

'You fell asleep in all your clothes,' he pointed out dryly. 'Hardly the most effective way of guaranteeing a good night's rest. And your prudishness is rather misplaced in the circumstances.'

Hot colour flooded Tia's cheeks. She knew what he was implying. That he knew her body better than she did. And it was all too true. The things that he could make her feel were scary.

'That was the past.' She said it to herself as much as him and started to walk down the stairs, holding tight to the bannisters to help support her wobbly knees. 'You no longer have the right to undress me.'

'I refuse to discuss this with you now.' His tone was

even as he followed her into the kitchen. 'Sit down and I'll
make you some breakfast.'

She gaped at him, sure that she'd misheard.

Luca was offering to make her breakfast?

Well, that really was a first!

As far as she could recall, Luca couldn't so much as boil
a kettle. He certainly hadn't done so in the three months
that she'd known him.

'I thought Italian men were totally undomesticated,' she
commented, watching with fascination as he yanked open
cupboard after cupboard and finally tried the fridge. This
was not a man who knew his way around a kitchen.

'*Dio*, there is nothing here! What were you planning to
eat?' His tone was incredulous as he stared into the empty
fridge. 'Thin air?'

'At least that won't upset my stomach,' she joked
weakly, shrinking slightly at the black expression on his
face. 'OK, there's no need to scowl. I haven't had time to
shop yet. I was going to do it on my way home from work
this evening.'

The minute she said it she could have bitten her tongue
off. Bother. She hadn't intended to tell him about the job
yet.

There was an ominous silence and Luca straightened up
from his exploration of the empty fridge, his smooth dark
brows locked in a frown.

'Work?' His eyes were suddenly cool. 'What do you
mean, you were going to shop on the way home from
work?'

She gave a long sigh. 'Luca, I'm going to be a single
mother. I need a job—'

The fridge door closed with a muted thud. 'You are not
going to be a single mother.'

'Luca…'

He walked towards her, his eyes flaming with anger and
his broad shoulders tense. 'And you do not need a job.'

'I need to support myself, Luca.'

'You do not need to support yourself,' he said with icy cold clarity. 'That is my responsibility.'

She took a deep breath. 'But, you see, I don't want to be your responsibility. I need to work.'

'No,' he contradicted her fiercely. 'You do not need to work.'

Tia looked at him sadly. 'Which just goes to prove my point that we don't really know each other. If you knew me, you'd understand. But the truth is that our relationship is nothing more than a wild affair that got out of hand. And now we need to move on. I've been offered my old job back, Luca, and I intend to take it. In fact, I've already taken it. I've been working at the Infirmary for the past ten days. I'm surprised Sharon didn't mention it when you had your little chat.'

'Well, she didn't.' Luca stared at her, a muscle working in his dark jaw. 'Now that I am here to support you, give me one good reason why you need to work.'

His arrogance made her defiant. 'I don't have to give you a reason for anything I do. You can't bully me, Luca.'

A flush touched his tanned cheekbones and he had the grace to look uncomfortable. 'It was not my intention to bully you, merely to try and understand—'

'It's too late for that now,' she said stiffly, and his mouth tightened.

'It is not too late,' he ground out. 'We are having a baby and we stay together. And you will not work while you're pregnant.'

Tia stared at him, fascinated that he seemed so totally unashamed of blatantly expressing such chauvinistic opinions. Hadn't the man ever heard of equality or political correctness?

'Plenty of women work when they're pregnant.'

'But not you,' he growled, raking long fingers through his hair, clearly hanging onto control by a thread. 'I refuse to allow you to risk your health and our baby's health when you don't need to.'

Tia had always known that Luca was very traditional, but his flat dismissal of her new job was starting to make her blood boil.

'Stop trying to run my life,' she said angrily, wrapping her arms around her body in a gesture of self-protection. 'I have to work, Luca. For all sorts of reasons that you wouldn't begin to understand. Except for the few months I spent in Italy with you, I've always worked and fended for myself ever since I was young. I don't need or want to be supported. Especially now I'm back in England.'

Glittering dark eyes rested on her pink cheeks. 'But now you're pregnant,' he pointed out, his voice lethally soft, 'and I assume the reason that you were ill last night was because you were working all day. Am I right?'

Tia flinched at his tone but nodded slowly. 'Perhaps, but—'

'And then came home and virtually passed out,' Luca pointed out, sarcasm evident in his smooth tones as he cut through her attempts to justify herself. 'Working is obviously going to do you and the baby a world of good.'

'I just don't understand you.' Tia stared at him, baffled by the strength of his reaction. 'All of a sudden you're thinking about nothing but the baby. But when I first told you, you barely reacted. What's changed, Luca? Is this baby really so special to you, or is it just that you're such a primitive, unreconstructed male that you can't bear other people to see the mother of your child working?'

'Other people's opinion is of no interest to me whatsoever,' he responded grimly. 'But to answer your question, yes, of course the baby is special to me. And if you'd given me time to get used to the idea and not run off like a child in a tantrum, you would know that already. We could have discussed it.' His gaze was distinctly cool. 'But talking about things isn't something you're very good at, is it? You prefer to run and hide.'

Because all her life she'd had no one to rely on but herself.

It was obvious now that the baby was the reason he'd followed her. Luca was Italian through and through, with all the family values of his ancestors. There was no way a man like him would let his pregnant wife leave. Even if he did regret marrying her.

She tried hard to pull herself together. She'd known that he didn't love her so why did it hurt so much that he wanted their marriage to work because of the baby?

'Like I said last night, the baby isn't the issue here,' she said stiffly. 'It's our relationship, Luca. We—we don't really know each other.'

His eyes locked with hers, his expression impossible to read. 'Then we will get to know each other.'

She looked at him with exasperation. 'Luca, this is ridiculous. We're completely wrong for each other.'

Not least because he was still in love with someone else. All right, he might be here with her at the moment but that was clearly because of the baby, not because he was in love with her. Had the man once mentioned the word 'love'? No.

'If we don't know each other,' he said smoothly, 'then how can you possibly know that we are wrong for each other?'

She bit her lip. 'I just do.'

'You're talking nonsense. One of the reasons we haven't talked much is because we spent the whole time making love,' he reminded her gently, and Tia's cheeks coloured at the look in his eyes.

It was absolutely true.

They'd been unable to spend time together without ending up in bed. Even when they'd returned from Venice and Luca had been working all hours, their physical relationship had sizzled with passion. Tired or not, where sex was concerned the man was one hundred per cent hot Italian.

There was a long silence and Luca's gaze roved slowly over her flushed cheeks and rested on her mouth. She knew that he was remembering those nights, too, and heat pooled in the pit of her stomach.

'There is a simple solution to all this,' he said softly, dragging his eyes back to hers. 'If you think we don't know each other, then we get to know each other.'

Tia shook her head. 'It's too late for that, Luca. You want someone to stay at home and keep house, someone who will happily spend your money and rely on you. I'm not like that. I've never relied on anyone in my life. I can't do it. I'm not the right woman for you.'

'You are having my baby,' he said steadily, his eyes never leaving hers. 'That makes you the right woman.'

Tia opened her mouth to argue and then noticed the clock on the wall and gave a gasp of horror. She was going to be late. Was that his plan? To make her so late they wouldn't want her working for them?

'I don't have time for this, Luca,' she muttered, standing up and making for the kitchen door. 'I'm going to have a shower and then I'm going to work. I don't know what time your flight back to Italy is but you can stay in the cottage until you go. Just post the keys through the door when you leave.'

Without waiting to hear his reply, she left the room, trying not to look at the grim set of his firm mouth.

It was obvious that Luca still had plenty to say on the subject but it was going to have to wait. She didn't intend to jeopardise her job for anyone.

She needed to work and she wanted to work, and no chauvinistic Italian was going to stop her. However much he made her knees knock.

*   *   *

Despite her worries about the time, Tia arrived early and the first person she saw was Sharon.

'Are you mad at me?'

Tia slung her bag into her locker and changed into her uniform. 'I should be.'

'But you're not?' Sharon looked at her hopefully. 'What happened? What did he say about Luisa?'

Tia turned the key in her locker. 'I didn't mention Luisa.'

'Why?' Sharon looked horrified and Tia stopped dead and let out a long breath.

'Because I want him to tell me himself, not just because he thinks he's been found out.' Her chin lifted. 'I don't want a relationship where we have secrets. Remember my parents? When my mother found out about my father's affairs she was devastated. She'd always trusted him.' Tia felt the familiar feeling of anger swell inside her. Anger towards the man who'd ruined her mother's life. 'I will not have a relationship with someone who keeps secrets.'

Sharon's expression was cautious. 'But what did he say? Did he just want to yell at you for leaving him at the altar?'

Tia frowned. 'Funnily enough, that hardly figured in the conversation. I'll say this for the man, he's a very cool customer. He seemed almost indifferent to the chaos I caused. He was more concerned with discussing the future.'

Sharon's eyes widened. 'So there is a future?'

Tia shook her head. 'Not as far as I'm concerned. He obviously wants to be around for the baby, but that's not enough for me.'

Sharon looked puzzled. 'Are you sure that's really the reason?'

'Of course.' Tia pulled herself together, dropped the locker key in her pocket and made for the door. 'I need to get on. Mrs Adams was about to feed the baby when I walked past so I said I'd help her. I'll do her check afterwards.'

'OK, thanks.' Sharon followed her out of the staffroom and Tia made her way to the four-bedded side ward.

'Hello, Fiona. How's the feeding going?'

'Really well.' Fiona looked up with a smile. 'Someone's helped me put her on the breast every time, but she seems to latch on really well and she only fed three times in the night. I thought that was pretty good.'

'Absolutely.' Tia leaned over the cot and stroked the downy head with a gentle finger. 'Were you a good girl for Mummy? Did you agree on a name?'

Fiona nodded. 'She's going to be Megan.'

'Nice. Well, in that case, Megan, it's time for breakfast.' She scooped the baby up firmly and handed her to Fiona, watching carefully as Fiona tried to put the baby on the breast herself.

'That's great, Fiona. You've both really got the hang of it.'

Tia stayed with Fiona until she was happy that the baby was feeding nicely and then moved on to help another new mother.

Before she'd even pulled the curtains around the bed, Sharon called her.

'Sorry, Tia, would you mind going up to labour ward to give them a hand? They've had six admissions in the last two hours.' Sharon rolled her eyes and walked up the corridor with Tia. 'Chaos. And, of course, they'll all end up down here.'

So Tia hurried to the labour ward and introduced herself to Nina, the midwife in charge.

'Would you mind looking after Mrs Henson for the time being?' Nina checked her notebook. 'She's only four centimetres and not coping well at all. We've bleeped the anaesthetist and he's coming to do an epidural. And do you mind having one of the student midwives in with you? She needs to get a few more deliveries.'

Tia nodded. Student midwives had to deliver a certain

number of babies under supervision before they were allowed to qualify.

Dawn Henson was a twenty-two-year-old woman, having her first baby, and one look at her face was enough for Tia to realise that she was terrified.

'The pain is so much worse than I imagined,' she gasped, her knuckles white as she grasped her husband's hand. 'I really, really wanted to have a natural birth but I don't think I can stand it. I feel such a failure.'

'You're not a failure, Dawn,' Tia said firmly. 'Labour isn't a competition. The pain is different for each individual and everyone copes in different ways. I think you've made a wise decision to have an epidural.'

Dawn bit her lip. 'But I didn't really want to have one. I'm terrified of having a needle in my spine. What if it goes wrong?'

'It won't go wrong.' Tia looked up as Duncan Fraser, one of the anaesthetic consultants, walked into the room. 'Here's the person to talk to. Dr Fraser will explain everything to you.'

Signalling with her eyes that Dawn was more than a little anxious, Tia busied herself getting things ready for the anaesthetist.

Duncan talked quietly to the couple for a few minutes, explaining the procedure and the risks involved, pausing while Dawn had another contraction.

'OK, I need to start by putting a drip in your arm.'

Tia handed him a wide-bore cannula and Kim, the student midwife, checked Dawn's blood pressure.

'All right, Dawn, I want you to sit on the edge of the trolley for me—that's it.' Tia helped her to adjust her position until she was as comfortable as possible and waited while Duncan scrubbed up.

He put on a sterile gown and gloves and positioned himself behind Dawn. 'All right, I want you to tell me if you feel a contraction coming so that I can stop,' he said quietly as he gave the local anaesthetic into the skin.

Duncan nicked the skin with the scalpel and introduced the Tuohy needle, advancing it cautiously towards the epidural space. He checked that the needle was in the right place and Tia watched Dawn carefully, knowing that even the slightest movement at this stage could result in a dural puncture with unpleasant consequences for the patient.

Fortunately Dawn remained still and Duncan quickly threaded the epidural catheter through the needle and withdrew the needle.

'All right Dawn.' Duncan glanced up briefly and then returned to his task. 'I'm going to inject a small dose of anaesthetic now.'

He gave a test dose and then taped the epidural catheter in place and attached an antibacterial filter to the end. Tia timed five minutes and then checked the blood pressure.

Satisfied with the reading, Duncan gave the remainder of the anaesthetic dose.

'All right, Dawn, Tia is going to need to check your blood pressure every five minutes for the first twenty minutes just to check that it doesn't drop.'

Dawn gave him a grateful smile. 'I can feel it working already—the pain is nowhere near as bad.'

'Good.' Duncan gave her a warm smile, talked to Tia about giving top-ups and then left the room.

Now that the pain had gone, Dawn's face regained some of its colour and she was a great deal happier.

'Will I still be able to push the baby out?'

'We'll certainly aim for that,' Tia told her, checking her blood pressure again and recording it on the chart. 'As you progress towards the end of the first stage of your labour, we'll let the epidural wear off so that you can feel to push.'

It was towards the end of her shift when Dawn started pushing and the baby was delivered normally, with the minimum of fuss. Tia quietly praised Kim who had performed a textbook delivery.

'I can't believe it's all over.' Dawn collapsed, exhausted, her face pale. 'I can't believe we've got a little girl. We've only thought of boys' names, haven't we, Ken?'

Her husband gave a shaky laugh. 'We'd better start thinking fast.'

Tia gave an absent smile, her eyes on the student midwife. The placenta wasn't coming away as quickly as it should and Kim was obviously concerned. Tia knew that with the use of oxytocic drugs and controlled cord traction, the third stage of labour—the delivery of the placenta— was usually completed in ten minutes in the majority of labours.

In Dawn's case they were well past ten minutes and Tia was well aware that there was a danger of bleeding if the placenta was retained.

'Stop using cord traction,' she instructed Kim in a low voice. 'There's a risk that the cord might snap or the uterus might invert.'

Tia pressed the buzzer to call for help and then palpated Dawn's abdomen. If the uterus was well contracted then it could mean that the placenta had separated but was trapped by the cervix.

Outwardly calm, still making small talk about the baby, Tia gently palpated the uterus with her fingertips. Instead of feeling firm and contracted, it felt soft and distended and her heart gave a little lurch.

She massaged the top of the uterus with a smooth, circular motion, careful not to apply too much pressure.

'Is something wrong?' Dawn looked at her with tired eyes and Tia gave her a reassuring smile, noting that she seemed very pale and restless.

'Your placenta isn't separating as quickly as it should do,' she said carefully, 'so we'll just get the doctor to take a look at you. Nothing for you to worry about, Dawn.'

Sharon entered the room seconds later, her eyebrows lifted questioningly.

'I think we may have a retained placenta here. Can you bleep the senior reg?' Tia asked quickly, and Sharon nodded immediately.

'Will do.'

'Put the baby on the breast, Kim,' Tia instructed quietly, and the student immediately did as requested, understanding that the action of breast feeding could help the uterus contract. Tia tried to rub up a contraction and just as she was starting to feel seriously worried the doors slammed open and Sharon hurried in, closely followed by—

Luca.

Tia's heart kicked against her ribs and she turned incredulous eyes to Sharon who merely shrugged helplessly, indicating from her expression that she didn't know what was going on.

Luca barely gave her a second glance, instead striding straight to the bed and introducing himself to Dawn. Tia immediately snapped back into professional mode, her personal feelings towards him temporarily forgotten. Now wasn't the time to question his presence.

'It seems as though she has a retained placenta,' she told him quickly, 'She delivered forty minutes ago. The uterus is atonic. I've tried to rub up a contraction, we've put the baby to the breast.'

Luca started scrubbing, firing questions at her over his shoulder. 'Has she emptied her bladder?'

'We've just catheterised her,' Tia told him, 'and we've got everything ready to set up an IV.'

'She's had an epidural?'

Tia nodded. 'Yes, but it's wearing off.'

'Let's top it up immediately and bleep the anaesthetist. I want her transferred to Theatre,' Luca instructed, turning to his SHO who was hovering. 'Can you sort out the epidural top-up and the IV, please, Dr Ford? Take blood for haemoglobin and cross-matching.'

Despite the emergency, the glamorous, dark-haired SHO couldn't stop sneaking looks at Luca, and Tia found herself grinding her teeth as they moved Dawn into Theatre.

Luca walked quickly over to the head of the bed and gave the frightened woman a reassuring smile.

'Dawn, your placenta does not want to come away by itself so I'm going to have to help it out,' he said quietly, his Italian accent giving his words a warm and attractive quality. 'You still have the anaesthetic in place so it shouldn't be painful, but if I hurt you in any way I want you to tell me immediately. We will work as a team, I promise.'

Tia watched with awe as he calmed both Dawn and her husband with his quiet confidence and then prepared for a manual removal of the placenta.

Tia bit her lip. She'd actually never seen a placenta removed like this before. She'd read about it, of course, but she'd never actually seen it happen and she was heartily relieved that Luca was there to take charge. There were stories of exceptional circumstances when a doctor couldn't be found and a midwife had had to undertake the procedure. Frankly, the thought made her shudder.

Sharon hovered at the back of the room, knowing that she could have a serious emergency on her hands.

'She has a partial separation,' Luca told the SHO as he examined Dawn. 'The fundus is broad, whereas it should be contracted, and she is losing some blood.'

Actually, that was an understatement, Tia thought anxiously. Dawn was now bleeding steadily and she watched as Luca covered his hand in antiseptic cream and introduced it carefully into the vagina, following the line of the cord which he held tight with his other hand.

Then he released the cord and transferred his free hand to Dawn's abdomen.

'I can feel the separated edge…' Luca's handsome face was a mask of concentration as he worked his fingers between the placenta and the uterine wall.

Tia watched, fascinated despite her anxiety for Dawn, noting that he used his free hand to press on Dawn's abdomen to prevent tearing of the lower segment of the uterus.

With a grunt of satisfaction, Luca rubbed up a contraction and gently removed his hand, dropping the placenta into a kidney dish. 'There. OK, we need to check that this is intact.'

Tia adjusted the light and they examined the placenta thoroughly to check that none of it had been retained within the uterus.

When he was satisfied that the placenta was complete Luca turned his attention back to the mother.

'Everything is fine, Dawn,' he said quietly, examining her abdomen again. 'Your uterus is well contracted now and the bleeding has stopped. We'll check your haemoglobin level but I don't think that the blood you have lost will cause you a problem.' He turned back to his SHO. 'Give her some more oxytocin and start antibiotics.'

'Yes, Dr Zattoni.' The SHO was gazing at Luca as if he was the answer to her prayers, and Tia was filled with a sudden insecurity.

It didn't matter whether Luca was in love with Luisa or not—he would always have women throwing themselves at him. And would he be able to resist them? She knew better than most that plenty of men wouldn't.

Men like her father.

Feeling sick at the thought she looked for an excuse to leave the room.

'I'll go and phone the ward,' she mumbled, desperate to get away from the sight of Luca talking to the glamorous SHO. In fact, she could have used the phone in Theatre but she needed some space to calm herself down.

Sharon was hot on her heels as she made for the desk. 'Look, I'm really sorry. Believe me, I had no idea—'

'It doesn't matter.' Tia sat down on the nearest chair and took several deep breaths.

Sharon looked at her anxiously. 'Prof told me he had a new senior reg, but I didn't bother asking the name and I didn't even know he was due to start today. When I rang Switchboard they just told me that a Dr Zattoni was on call—I had no opportunity to warn you.'

'It doesn't matter,' Tia repeated, feeling a rush of relief as her stomach calmed down.

Sharon looked totally confused. 'But he couldn't have arranged this overnight. Did he tell you last night that he'd applied for a job here?'

'No, of course not.' Tia's voice was gruff and her eyes were slightly too bright. 'He doesn't tell me anything, remember?'

Sharon shifted slightly and glanced back along the corridor. 'He's a damn good doctor, Tia—that was an incredible performance back there.'

Tia nodded, a slight frown touching her brows. She'd never seen Luca in action before and he'd certainly been impressive.

Hoping that Sharon would drop the subject, she picked up the phone and called the postnatal ward just to warn them that Dawn would be on her way shortly and to brief them on what had happened so that they could monitor her condition.

'Well, he's obviously not thinking of returning to Italy any time soon,' Sharon said quietly, and Tia looked at her.

'No.' She summoned up a smile for the sake of appearances, trying not to think about what it would do for her pulse rate to see Luca at such close quarters every day.

'Which means that he can't possibly be involved with Luisa.'

'Does it?' Tia closed her eyes and let out a sigh.

What a mess.

Sharon sat down on the chair next to her, her voice soft. 'He wants you, Tia.'

Tia gave a crooked smile. 'Or does he just want the baby. If it hadn't been for the baby, he'd have patched things up with Luisa, remember?'

Sharon sighed. 'Tia, you have to talk to him about it.'

'No.' Tia lifted her chin stubbornly. 'He has to be the one to talk to me.'

Picking up the phone to end the conversation, she called a porter to come and help with Dawn and finished completing her section of the notes.

Luca strolled up to the desk, his shoulders looking broader than ever under the white coat.

'Have you finished your shift?'

Tia stared at him defiantly, still furious that he hadn't told her that he'd be working in the same hospital as her.

'No.'

'Yes.' Sharon corrected her with a frown, glancing across at Kim. 'Kim, would you mind taking Dawn up to the ward? Tia's already spoken to them so they're expecting her.'

Tia stood up. 'I'll—'

'It's already past the end of your shift and you're exhausted,' Sharon said firmly, avoiding Tia's eyes. 'Go home.'

Tia almost growled out loud. She was more than ready to go home but she didn't want to go with Luca.

'All right.' She stood up. 'But I'll make my own way.'

Luca's jaw tightened but he said nothing in front of her colleagues, instead choosing to follow her into the staff-room.

'Luca, this is the female changing room,' she pointed out, trying not to notice just how good he looked with his powerful body planted firmly in front of the door.

He shrugged dismissively. 'I have something to say to you and I assumed you didn't want me to say it in public.'

She yanked open the door of the locker, unable to keep the sarcasm out of her tone. 'I'm amazed you want to talk to me at all. What's the point of having a conversation when one misses out important details like, "By the way, Tia, I'll be starting a new job in your hospital tomorrow."'

And that was just for starters. She knew only too well what other important fact he was keeping from her.

'I didn't mention it because I didn't know that I would be starting today,' Luca said evenly. 'In fact, I didn't know that I would be starting at all. I have had several conversations with the hospital but it was only confirmed this morning. It seems that they are in a crisis. Someone is off with food poisoning and someone else has taken compassionate leave. So, instead of starting in a week's time, I agreed to start immediately.'

'But you could at least have mentioned it,' Tia pointed out, her eyes blazing as she dragged her clothes out of her locker.

Luca frowned. 'Nothing was confirmed and we had other, more important matters to discuss, as I recall.'

Tia stared at him in exasperation. 'But you didn't even tell me that you were applying for a job in England, and yet you must have applied months ago.'

There was a long silence and a strange look flickered across Luca's handsome face.

'Just after we met,' he admitted finally, and Tia let out a disbelieving breath.

'And it didn't seem relevant to mention that either? Well, believe it or not, I like to know what's going on,' Tia said, stripping off her cotton bottoms and dragging on her jeans. She took hold of the hem of her top and then hesitated. 'Look the other way.'

Their eyes clashed and a sharp stab of electricity shot through her body and weakened her knees.

He clearly thought it was crazy to look the other way when he'd seen her naked more times than he could count.

'We don't have that sort of relationship any more, Luca,' she croaked, tightening her fingers on her tunic.

Muttering something under his breath, he turned his back, the tension visible in his broad shoulders.

She changed quickly and pushed her clothes into her bag. 'You can look now.'

'Thank you.' His ironic glance was at odds with his courteous tone and she looked at him warily.

'Now what?'

'Now we go home and finish the conversation we were having when you passed out on me last night,' he said softly. 'My car is in the car park.'

She slung her bag over her shoulder. 'Thanks, but I'll make my own way home.'

His mouth tightened into a grim line. 'On that contraption you call a bike? No way. You have been working all day and you are exhausted, Tia. I will give you a lift.'

She glared at him and then smiled sweetly. 'Will my bike fit in the boot of your car?'

Luca winced visibly at the thought. 'You can leave it here.'

'Overnight?' She shook her head. 'No way. Someone might steal it.'

'Steal it?' His incredulous tone and the lift of his dark eyebrows told her clearly what he thought of that suggestion. 'Tia, it is a heap of rusty metal. No one in their right mind would steal it.'

She opened her mouth to argue again and then closed it again. The truth was she *was* totally exhausted. She'd never felt so tired in her life and the thought of cycling the five miles home was almost laughable.

'All right.' She knew she sounded ungracious but she couldn't help it. 'We'll go in your car.'

'Good.' For a moment she thought she saw humour

gleam in his dark eyes but then it was gone and he held the door open for her. 'Let's go.'

They walked in silence out of the building. Just as they were crossing the car park, the glamorous Dr Ford dashed up to Luca, wanting him to check some trivial detail on a drug chart.

All Tia's fears flooded back. Was Luca interested in the woman? She was certainly attractive and she was totally ignoring Tia.

On impulse she slipped an arm through his. 'Hurry up, darling,' she whispered in her sexiest voice. 'I've been waiting to go home with you all day.'

Luca went still and she saw surprise flicker briefly in his eyes. And she could hardly blame him for that! She was pretty shocked herself. Whatever had possessed her? One minute she was keeping him at arm's length and the next she was ready to claw Dr Ford's eyes out...

Embarrassed and confused by her own behaviour, Tia gingerly released his arm and shrank quietly into the background as Luca turned back to the SHO, scribbled something on the chart and issued some brief instructions.

As Dr Ford walked back across the car park, Luca turned to her, his gaze uncomfortably penetrating.

'Well?'

'Well, what?' Still feeling embarrassed, Tia yanked the car door open so hard that she nearly removed it from its hinges.

One eyebrow swooped upwards. 'I need to spell it out?'

Tia glared at him. 'She was drooling all over you, Luca.'

He turned his head to watch the retreating woman and then looked back at her, his eyes narrowing. 'Dr Ford? You're imagining things.'

'Oh, come on.' Had he really not noticed? 'She's crazy about you and she's only just met you and she's probably the first of many. I suppose the whole hospital will be drooling over you by the end of the week.'

'Drooling?' The expression in his dark eyes was stunned. 'I'm a doctor, Tia, not some sort of sex symbol.'

Tia bit her lip. How had Sharon described him? *Sex on legs.*

Did he really have no idea how attractive he was to women?

'Think about it, Luca,' she mumbled. 'Was that really an important question she asked you or was she finding reasons to speak to you?'

He opened his mouth and closed it again, staring at her thoughtfully. 'She's my SHO, Tia.'

'You don't need to tell me that.' Tia gritted her teeth. 'She's been ogling you all afternoon.'

'Ogling?' His face was blank and suddenly he sounded very Italian. 'What is ogling?'

Tia tipped her head back. 'Staring at you, making eyes at you, flirting.'

'You're imagining things.' His tone was calm but his gaze was speculative as it rested on her face. 'She is my SHO. We have to speak to each other. We certainly weren't flirting.'

Had he really not noticed? 'She couldn't take her eyes off you, Luca.'

'And you were jealous.' His quiet statement was more than a little smug and her chin lifted.

'Jealous?' She gave a short laugh that sounded false even to her ears. 'Are all Italians as arrogant and self-confident as you? I wasn't jealous, Luca.'

Being jealous would mean that she wanted him—and she didn't, did she?

'You have no reason to be jealous,' he told her, carefully ignoring her comment about Italians.

She slid into the car and waited for him to start the engine.

'When you are angry, your eyes turn a very interesting shade of green,' Luca observed mildly, pulling out of the car park and onto the main road. 'I noticed it the first night we met when I made the mistake of trying to tell you that you shouldn't be hanging around a bus station at night.'

'I shouted at you, didn't I?' Tia shot him a sideways look that bordered on the apologetic. 'I'm not very good at being told what to do,' she confessed grudgingly, and he gave a laugh of genuine amusement.

'So I am beginning to learn.' An unbearably sexy smile tugged at the corner of his mouth as he glanced towards her. 'It certainly makes for an interesting and unpredictable relationship, *cara mia*.'

But did they have a relationship?

Tia got ready to argue but found she didn't have the energy. She shouldn't have agreed to help out by working the extra hours.

Maybe if she closed her eyes for just a few minutes she'd have enough energy to deal with Luca once they arrived home.

She had a feeling she was going to need it.

CHAPTER THREE

WHEN Tia opened her eyes again she was lying on the sofa with a blanket tucked around her.

'So you're finally awake.' Luca placed a mug of tea on the low table next to her and sat down on the end of the sofa. 'I must admit you're scintillating company when you're pregnant.'

She struggled to sit up, feeling decidedly groggy and disorientated. She had no recollection of how she'd got into the house. 'Did I sleep in the car?'

'Like a dead person,' Luca said dryly, his eyes scanning her quickly. 'Collapsing on me seems to be becoming a habit. It's a good job you don't weigh very much.'

Which was nonsense, she knew. Luca was incredibly strong and athletic—more than capable of lifting someone twice her weight.

'I'm sorry,' she mumbled, wishing that he wasn't sitting quite so close to her. She could see the taut muscle of his thigh under the material of his trousers and her throat closed.

She wanted him so badly it was almost a physical ache.

How could she still want a man who was in love with another woman? How could she still want a man who had kept such an enormous secret from her? How could she be in love with someone whose view of women seemed to be firmly set in the Stone Age?

Their eyes met and held and she felt her heart rate increase alarmingly. Then Luca stood up suddenly, his voice rough.

'I've made you something to eat.' He strode back into the kitchen and returned carrying a tray.

57

Tia stared in disbelief at the strange mass on the plate. 'Wh-what is it?'

He followed her gaze and shifted slightly. 'It's an omelette,' he said stiffly. 'I couldn't find a recipe book.'

A recipe book? For an omelette?

Staggered that he'd tried to cook something for her, Tia hid a smile, knowing that his male pride was at stake. After all, it wasn't entirely his fault that he was so undomesticated. From what she'd seen, it was his upbringing.

Whenever they'd stayed with Luca's family she had been appalled by the way they waited on him. No matter that Luca's sisters were both intelligent, they seemed not to question their role in nurturing their brother and Tia had spent more time holding a teatowel than a conversation.

But here he was, cooking for her. Or at least trying to!

She picked up a fork and started to eat.

'Does it taste all right?' His need for reassurance was so unlike Luca that she almost dropped the fork.

Was this really the same arrogant, self-assured man she'd known in Italy? It was the first time she'd ever witnessed him express doubt about anything. Was he really seeking her approval for something as simple as an omelette?

'It tastes great,' she said finally, unable to resist teasing him slightly. 'Better than it looks.'

After a moment's hesitation he returned the smile, his cheeks creasing in the way that made her heart stop. Luca Zattoni was without doubt the sexiest man she'd ever seen, and no matter what he did she would probably always want him.

The thought effectively removed her appetite and she put the fork down on the plate with a clatter and a shake of her head.

'I'm sorry, Luca, but I'm not really hungry,' she said quietly, her eyes sliding away from his. 'It isn't your omelette—really. It's…nice and I'm grateful to you but…'

He watched her steadily and for a wild, uncomfortable

moment she thought he must have guessed the reason for her sudden lack of appetite. But he merely removed the plate without comment, shifting slightly on the sofa so that he was facing her.

'In that case, this is as good a time as any to finish our talk. You've had a sleep, so hopefully we should manage it without you being sick or passing out.'

There was still a trace of humour in his voice but this time Tia didn't respond. Suddenly she did feel sick—but with misery.

What was she going to do? She'd thought that it would be easy to get over him. That he wouldn't affect her any more. But it just wasn't the case. One look—one smile— and she had serious trouble with her breathing.

She bit her lip, angry with herself. How had she ever let one man affect her as much as Luca? And so quickly. It was just a physical thing. It must be.

'I don't know what there is to talk about, Luca,' she said, concentrating on her tea and on not looking at him. If she didn't look at him it should theoretically be possible to keep her pulse rate within the normal range. 'I'm not going to marry you.'

'I'm not asking you to.'

Savage disappointment twisted her insides and she felt a lump building in her throat.

'Right.' She looked up at him and gave him a wobbly smile. 'So you agree that our relationship is over…'

He frowned. 'I agree to nothing of the sort,' he said, stretching out a hand and smoothing a stray strand of blonde hair out of her eyes. 'I merely said that I'm not asking you to marry me. Our relationship is very much alive.'

Her heart thudded against her rib cage. 'We were wrong to get involved so quickly, Luca.'

When he was still involved with someone else.

He sighed and something like regret flickered across his face. 'It's true that we could have taken things slower...'

It was the nearest he'd ever come to admitting to her that their relationship had been a mistake.

'Right,' she said shakily, trying to ignore the feeling of sick disappointment that he hadn't contradicted her. 'Well, there's nothing more to be said, is there?'

'On the contrary, there's plenty I need to say.' He stood up abruptly and paced across the room to the window, his shoulders tense as he stared into the darkness.

He paused and then turned to face Tia, his expression serious. 'I have thought carefully about what you said last night and I can see now that being in Italy wasn't easy for you. I was working much of the time and I accept now that my family may not have been as supportive as they should have been. I intend to speak to them about that.'

Tia's eyes widened. He was admitting that fault might have been on his side? For a man as autocratic and proud as Luca, that was quite an admission.

'Luca—'

'Let me finish.' He turned to face her, a light frown touching his dark brows. 'I'm sorry that you feel that I was never around, but there were certain factors which meant that I was at the hospital more than I would have liked.'

What factors? Luisa?

'And what about the baby? How do you really feel about the baby?' Her voice was little more than a croak and a smile pulled at his firm mouth.

'We both know that we made that baby the first night we met, *cara mia*.' His voice was suddenly soft. 'And I blame myself for that entirely. I should have had more control.'

Tia coloured. 'I was there, too. And I still can't believe I slept with you on the first night. I'd never—' She broke off and looked away, cursing herself for being so honest. *She'd never meant to tell him.*

'You'd never slept with a man before,' he finished gently. 'Did you really think I didn't know that? I knew almost from the first moment I met you. You were very inexperienced and naïve. It was one of the reasons I was worried about you wandering the streets at night. You are very independent and feisty but also very innocent, and it shows.'

'Oh.' Tia stared at him stupidly. 'I didn't want to tell you.'

He'd been so sophisticated and self-confident, so unlike the men—*boys*—she usually met.

'You are a stunningly beautiful girl, Tia, and there is an incredible attraction between us, otherwise perhaps I would have had the strength of will to take things more slowly. That night was unbelievably erotic,' he murmured softly, his eyes wandering slowly over her flushed cheeks, 'which is, of course, why we find ourselves in this position now.'

Her eyes moved warily to his and then slid away again. It was impossible not to be affected by Luca's looks, she thought helplessly. It wasn't just his eyes that reflected the raw nature of his masculinity, it was everything about him. The hard lines of his cheekbones, the dark shadow of his jawline.

She gave a small sigh, acknowledging the fact that no woman in her right mind would turn down the advances of a man like Luca. It was hardly surprising she'd lost all her morals and common sense. One look from those dark eyes and she'd been lost.

'We— I suppose we both got carried away,' she responded, and he gave a half-smile.

'I think that's probably a rather limp description of what happens between you and I, *cara mia*.' His eyes dropped to her mouth and she felt her heart rate increase rapidly in response to his gaze. 'I have a suggestion about our relationship.'

She licked dry lips. 'What?'

'You say that we got involved too quickly.' His eyes returned to hers and held them. 'That you don't really know me.'

'That's right.' Her voice was little more than a whisper. 'The physical side just overwhelmed everything.'

Including common sense.

His eyes darkened slightly and she knew he was remembering just how good it had been between them.

'You were very inexperienced so I can see how that might have been the case. So what I suggest,' he said roughly, 'is that we start again. Slow things down. Take time to get to know each other.'

She stared at him, her breathing rapid as she listened to him. He was seriously suggesting that they carry on their relationship?

What about Luisa?

'I—I don't know, Luca,' she said, raking her hair away from her forehead with shaking fingers. 'I need to think about it.'

'There's nothing to think about,' he said smoothly, walking back across the room and standing in front of her. As always, he was supremely confident and sure of himself. 'You yourself said that we don't know each other well enough, so let's put that right. Spending some time together will show us whether we can truly love each other or not. We owe it to our child to at least find that out.'

She winced at the cold brutality of his words. She already knew that he didn't love her, of course, but hearing him spell it out hurt more than she possibly could have imagined.

'Tia?' His firm tone made her glance up and she realised that he was waiting for her to say something.

And she didn't know what to say.

She loved Luca, she knew that, and she wanted to be with him, but not if he didn't want to be with her. Not if he only wanted their relationship to work because of the baby.

She lifted her chin. 'It wouldn't work.'

A muscle worked in his jaw and he took a deep breath. 'Think about it, Tia.' He glanced at his watch. 'You've had a long day and you need to get some more sleep now. Are you intending to work another early shift tomorrow?'

'Yes.' Tia nodded slowly, still trying to work out what she was going to do. She could ask him about Luisa, of course, but then she'd never know whether he would have told her himself given time.

'I'll take you to work,' he told her, the expression in his eyes suggesting that he wasn't going to take no for an answer.

'All right.' What choice did she have? Her bike was at the hospital.

His eyes narrowed. 'Now, go upstairs and relax in a warm bath. You need an early night or you'll be sick again.'

Too tired to argue, Tia slithered off the sofa and caught the blanket as it slipped to the floor.

'Are you planning to spend the night here again?'

'Of course.' His brows clashed in a frown, as if he was surprised that she should even ask the question. 'You're expecting my baby and you don't seem to be able to go through an entire day without vomiting and collapsing on me. There's no way I'm leaving you on your own.'

She stared at him, knowing that she should insist that he leave, but somehow unable to form the words. Having him in the cottage with her was strangely reassuring.

And unsettling.

'Well, if you're staying another night, you can use the spare room,' she said, knowing that she sounded ungracious but unable to help herself.

'Your generosity is overwhelming,' he drawled in response, but the corner of his firm mouth twitched slightly.

'I'll just remember not to stand up straight in the night or I'll be the one who's unconscious. The ceilings in this house are unbelievable. How tall is the average English man?'

Tia glanced at his powerful frame and then wished that she hadn't. There was nothing average about Luca Zattoni. He was overwhelmingly male, and aware of his own sexuality.

'Obviously the owner of this house wasn't very tall,' she said lamely, and he smiled. A slow, sexy grin that reminded her of all the reasons she'd fallen for him so heavily.

'Either that or he had a permanent headache. Goodnight, *cara*. Sleep well.'

Tia had trouble concentrating at work next day. All she could think about was Luca. He just seemed to take it for granted that their relationship would carry on.

'Is everything OK?' Sharon looked at her with concern. 'You're terribly pale, Tia.'

Tia summoned up a smile. She'd been sick again that morning but, fortunately for her, Luca had obviously still been asleep because this time she had the bathroom to herself.

'I'm fine,' she lied. 'Just a little tired. Where do you want me today?'

'On Postnatal for the time being. They're terribly busy, courtesy of all the deliveries yesterday.' Sharon moved closer and lowered her voice. 'Let's grab a coffee later if we get the chance.'

They didn't.

Tia didn't stop all morning, moving from one woman to another, performing daily checks and helping with feeding.

Fiona Adams was doing well and looking forward to going home.

'I'm just waiting for the paediatrician to come and check

Megan,' she told Tia with a smile. 'Then we're on our way.'

'That's great. And how's the feeding going?'

'Great. My milk has come in now and my boobs have trebled in size.' Fiona fished out an enormous bra from her bag and waved it at Tia. 'Look at that! Have you ever seen anything less sexy?'

Tia grinned. 'Well, it's not really designed to be sexy. It's designed to be practical and give you support.'

Mike, Fiona's husband, arrived at that moment, carrying a suitcase, and he laughed at the sight of the offending bra.

'You always said you wanted plastic surgery, love—now you know that all you needed was a baby.'

'All?' Fiona pretended to look offended. 'I'll have you know that your "all" kept me awake for most of the night. Did you bring the car seat?'

'Of course.' Mike looked at her patiently. 'Would I really have forgotten that? I couldn't carry everything at once, so it's still in the car.'

Fiona chewed her fingernails anxiously. 'It will be funny, being at home. Who will I talk to when I have a problem?'

'The community midwife will call until she's happy that you're fine and then there's the health visitor,' Tia told her, checking that she had all the telephone numbers. 'And if it's the middle of the night then you can always call us here.'

At that moment Megan woke up and started to yell.

'No!' Fiona stared at the baby, appalled. 'She can't possibly be hungry again! I've been feeding her for most of the night. She'll pop.'

'A breastfed baby doesn't always feed at regular times,' Tia reminded her, bending over the cot to scoop the baby up into her arms. 'Sometimes it might feel as though they're feeding non-stop, but don't forget that they regulate their own milk supply. The more they feed, the more you produce, so if she starts feeding a lot then you know that you're going to start making more for her.'

Fiona groaned. 'Well, there's no way I'm buying a bigger bra.'

'You can't. They don't come any bigger than that one,' Mike joked, his smile fading as he saw the expression on his wife's face. 'Sorry, sorry. You look great, love.'

Tia smiled and placed Megan gently in Fiona's arms. 'There you go.'

'Thanks.' Fiona's eyes misted. 'Look at that little nose.'

Mike bent over the pair of them and Tia made her excuses and left them in peace.

On her way out of the bay she bumped into Julie Douglas, the paediatric registrar.

'Baby Adams…?'

'In there…' Tia waved a hand. 'But they're having a SFM at the moment so I'd go and have a cup of tea.'

'SFM?' Julie looked blank and Sharon grinned as she sailed past.

'Soppy Family Moment. Definitely to be avoided,' she advised, grabbing Tia by the arm. 'Can you go and see how Dawn Henson is doing? The doctors are on their way round and last time I looked she was getting washed.'

Tia found Dawn back on her bed.

'How are you this morning?' She settled herself in the chair opposite and glanced into the cot. 'Fast asleep?'

Dawn rolled her eyes. 'At last. She's been awake virtually all night. If anyone wakes her up I'll strangle them with my bare hands.'

Tia grinned. 'That bad, huh?'

'How do mothers ever recover?' Dawn lay back against the pillows and closed her eyes. 'I'm shattered.'

Tia's smile faded. The woman did look tired. 'Tonight, why not ask the night staff to put her in the nursery for a few hours? They'll bring her to you when she needs feeding, but it just means that they'll settle her for you after the feed and you won't be woken by every snuffle.'

Dawn gave a wan smile. 'The trouble is, I'll be woken by everyone else's babies' snuffles. I've discovered that hospitals are not restful places.'

'That's true, but we can certainly give it a go.' Tia glanced up and felt her heart turn over as Luca strode down the ward with the rest of the team. 'I think the doctors want to take a look at you.'

Dawn struggled to sit up but Luca stopped her with a wave of his hand. 'Don't move. Just tell me how you feel.'

'All right, I suppose.' Dawn blushed slightly. 'A bit sore.'

Luca nodded and then questioned her quietly about her blood loss and asked if she'd had any pain.

Just as Dawn finished answering the baby woke and started to bawl.

'Oh, I don't believe it.' Dawn gave a horrified groan. 'I'd only just got her off. She can't be hungry.'

'Perhaps she just needs a hug?' Luca lifted an eyebrow towards Dawn, seeking permission to pick the baby up, and she nodded.

'Be my guest. I think my arms are too tired to hold her.'

Luca scooped the bawling bundle up carefully and tucked her expertly on his shoulder.

'Did you hear your mama?' His voice was deep and gentle as he spoke to the baby. 'She says that you cannot possibly be hungry, so maybe you just had a bad dream, hmm?'

Ignoring the rest of his colleagues, who were looking at him in amazement, he switched to Italian and talked quietly to the baby, his voice softening as the baby's eyes started to close again.

Within moments the baby was asleep again, lulled by his deep voice and the soothing touch of his hands.

Carefully he laid her back in the cot and smiled at the mother. 'Hopefully you can now have five minutes' peace.'

Dawn was wide eyed with amazement. 'How did you do that? Thank you.'

'Prego.' Luca inclined his head and then issued some instructions to Dr Ford who was looking as elegant as ever.

Tia watched them move on to the next patient and held back a sigh.

'He is truly gorgeous,' Dawn muttered, shifting herself into a more comfortable position. 'I tell you, I would have swapped places with my daughter if I could! I wonder what it would be like to have a man like that run his hands over you and speak to you in Italian.'

Tia stared after Luca's broad shoulders and felt her insides twist.

She knew exactly what it felt like.

Incredible.

'Tia?' Julie walked up, stethoscope looped around her neck. 'I've checked baby Adams and she's fine. As far as I'm concerned, they can go home.'

'Thanks.' Tia pulled herself together and went to check that Fiona was all set for her discharge.

She was, and she and Mike gazed proudly at their daughter, safely strapped in her new car seat.

'She looks so tiny in that.' Fiona's voice wobbled slightly and Mike gave her shoulder a squeeze.

'Yeah, and in no time she's going to be nagging you for make-up and trendy clothes, so make the most of it. At least at this age they don't run up a phone bill.'

Tia walked down the corridor with them and waited while they climbed into the lift.

'Are you off, Fiona?' Sharon bustled up and said her goodbyes and then grabbed Tia by the arm. 'Kettle's boiled.'

*   *   *

'What am I going to do?' Tia stared at her friend helplessly. 'He wants us to spend time together and get to know each other.'

Sharon spooned sugar into her coffee and stirred it thoughtfully. 'I'd say that's a good idea.' She dropped the spoon into an empty mug and picked up her coffee. 'Tia, you're crazy about the man. Stop looking for problems. Whatever did—or didn't—happen with Luisa, he's clearly chosen you. Accept that and move on.'

'But I don't know whether he's just chosen me because of the baby.'

'So ask him,' Sharon suggested. 'Maybe it's time you were honest. Tell him what you heard about Luisa and see what he says.'

'No,' Tia said flatly. 'If I have to ask him, I'll never be able to trust him again. He has to tell me himself.'

Sharon sighed. 'Tia, not everyone is a rat like your father.'

'No?' Tia's eyes were suddenly overly bright. 'But how do I know for sure? I don't find it easy to trust men.'

'I know that.' Sharon gave a wry smile. 'I didn't think that you'd ever get married—' She broke off and flushed, suddenly realising what she'd said. 'Not that you did, of course, but you nearly did—'

'Before I realised what a complete fool I was being.'

'You weren't being a fool,' Sharon said firmly. 'You love Luca, Tia.'

'Do I?' Tia closed her eyes for a second. 'Do you know, I'm not even sure of that any more.'

Sharon looked perplexed. 'Well, how does he make you feel when you're with him?'

'I don't know.' Tia shook her head. 'Breathless. Confused. Dizzy. Sick. Excited.'

Desperate.

Desperate for him to drag her into his arms and make love to her.

'To be honest, he has such a powerful effect on me physically that I can't work out how I feel about him,' Tia admitted finally. 'It's like being a teenager again. If he's even in the same room as me I feel weak.'

Sharon gave a smug, self-satisfied grin. 'You see? I always said it would happen like that for you. I always said that you'd be swept off your feet if you found the right man.'

The right man.

Was that Luca?

She'd certainly thought that he was but now, after everything that had happened, she wasn't so sure.

'How do you tell the difference between lust and love?'

Sharon pursed her lips thoughtfully and stared into her drink. 'Well, I suppose the answer to that is that you take lust out of the equation.'

'What do you mean?'

'You do what he says. Literally.' Sharon gave a little shrug. 'You get to know each other properly. You know, talking, long walks, laughter, dinner. But no bed.'

'No bed?' Tia looked at her stupidly and Sharon grinned.

'Tough one, huh? Personally I can't imagine living with a man like Luca and having no bed, but I suppose it does make sense in a sort of twisted way. It seems to me that all you've shared so far is passion and none of the other things that you share when you're developing a relationship with someone. Maybe if you knew him better you'd know whether he was the sort of person likely to have an affair.'

'It isn't always stamped on a man's forehead, you know,' Tia mumbled. 'My poor mother thought my father loved her, was faithful, and then—'

'Yes,' Sharon interrupted her quickly, 'but let's not think about that now. You're not throwing away the chance of a relationship with a man like Luca just because your father was less than perfect.'

'But—'

'Just give it a go, Tia,' Sharon advised. 'What have you

got to lose? If you decide that it isn't going to work, that you really can't trust him, then go your separate ways. You won't be any worse off for giving it a try.'

Tia stared at her. Wouldn't she?

Maybe Sharon was right. On the other hand, she had an uncomfortable feeling that the more time she spent with Luca, the harder it would be to let him go.

'But we're so different, Shaz,' she said simply. 'Even forgetting about the Luisa thing, we're different. For a start, he hates me working and you know that I need to work.'

'I think once he gets to know you, he'll understand why you need to work.' Sharon's face was suddenly serious. 'You say that you don't really know him, but how much does he really know about you?'

Tia felt her heart flutter in her chest. 'Probably not very much.'

Sharon nodded slowly. 'It strikes me that the pair of you have got too many secrets. Have you told him that you've always been scared of having children?'

'Hardly.' Tia gripped her mug tightly. 'He's Italian, Shaz,' she croaked. 'Italian men love children. How can I possibly tell him that I'm terrified of being a mother?'

'I think what's important is that you're honest with each other, and I really think that you need to tell him what you heard his mother and Luisa saying the day of your wedding.'

'No.' Tia shook her head stubbornly. 'Definitely not that. That is something that he needs to tell me himself.'

But would he?

CHAPTER FOUR

'YOU'RE very quiet,' Luca observed as he drove them both home. 'Are you upset?'

Upset and confused.

Tia glanced sideways at him and then wished she hadn't. Every time she looked at his mouth her stomach swooped in the direction of her shoes and she felt an almost desperate need for him to kiss her as only he could.

'This whole situation is such a mess,' she muttered, rubbing slim fingers over her forehead to ease the tension. 'We don't know each other, Luca.'

Luca's gaze didn't leave the road. 'And there is a simple solution to that, as we have already agreed. We get to know each other.' He turned into the lane that led to the cottage, pulled up and switched the engine off. 'Have you considered what I proposed earlier?'

The smooth Italian accent was enough to melt a polar icecap and she felt her heart start to beat faster. It had always been like that with Luca. One look, one word had been all it took to set her on fire. He hadn't actually needed to touch her to get a reaction, but when he had...

But could there really be more between them than a breathtakingly powerful attraction?

Or was Luisa the woman he really wanted?

'I—I don't know, Luca,' she said finally, her head starting to throb with the stress of the situation.

He nodded slowly. 'You are treating this like a major life decision, but perhaps you should look at it another way,' he suggested, his voice calm and level. 'Already you are expecting our baby. You owe it to our family to take some time to make this relationship work.'

Our family.

Tia felt a lump building in her throat. He made it sound simple and straightforward but, of course, it wasn't.

Living together as a family meant living with Luca—having him close to her all the time.

It would be torture.

'Why are you hesitating?' His voice was velvety smooth and she closed her eyes and gave a wry smile.

'Because the one word we haven't mentioned is love, that's why.' What he was describing sounded more like a business arrangement.

'Love…' Something flickered briefly in his dark eyes and then it was gone. 'Just because our feelings for each other aren't what they might be, it doesn't mean we can't live together amicably and create a stable family for our child.'

A stable family.

For a brief moment Tia's mind flitted back to her own childhood and in that instant she made her decision.

'All right.' She turned to face him, her mind made up. 'We'll do as you suggest and get to know each other better, but there are two conditions on my part.'

Luca's smooth brows twitched into a frown. He clearly hadn't been expecting conditions. 'Which are?'

She felt her heart thumping madly. 'Firstly, that you accept the fact that I want to work. No disapproving looks, no arguments, no atmosphere when I leave the house in the morning and end up working extra hours.'

His jaw tightened and his stunning eyes narrowed. 'And second?'

'Second.' She swallowed hard and looked away from him, bracing herself for his reaction. 'Second is no touching.'

A long silence stretched between them and eventually he spoke, his voice lethally soft. *'Excuse me?'*

Her eyes slid to his incredulous dark gaze and she took a deep breath.

'No touching. I can't think straight when you touch me Luca,' she said, the words tumbling out in a rush as she tried to explain herself. He was well aware of the effect he had on her physically so there was no point in being anything but honest. 'It's the reason we're in this mess right now. We need to find out whether we truly like each other and we can't do that if we're physically close. You can live in the same house as me but you sleep in the spare room.'

There was an ominous silence which stretched on and on. When he finally spoke his voice was raw.

'You are seriously suggesting that we live together but don't make love?'

Her heart was now thumping so hard she thought it might explode through her chest.

'Yes.' Considering the state of her insides, her voice was surprisingly steady. 'It makes sense, Luca.'

There was another long silence and she grew steadily more uncomfortable under his incredulous gaze. She realised now that she'd been ridiculously naïve to even think that a man as physical as Luca would agree to such a condition.

'All right.'

She gaped at him, wondering if she'd misheard. 'Luca…'

'If that is what you want, then we'll do it.'

Tia swallowed.

What she wanted…

She'd thought it was what she wanted but looking at his powerful shoulders and smouldering dark gaze she was beginning to think she must be slightly mad. What woman would ask a man like Luca *not* to touch her?

And she couldn't believe that he'd agreed to it. She shot him a suspicious look but his expression was unreadable. If he had another agenda then he was keeping it well hidden.

'And you won't make a fuss about me working?'

His mouth compressed. 'As long as you agree to restrict the hours you do and to let me buy you a car.'

She frowned. 'I don't need a car.'

'A car,' he interrupted her, his gaze steely, 'or you don't work.'

She could see that he wasn't going to give an inch and she gave a sigh. 'All right. Thank you. A car. But a small car.'

'A small car?' The tension seemed to leave him and his eyes shimmered with amusement. 'You are the first woman I have ever met who would choose to have a small car. The rest of your sex would be handing me brochures of glamorous sports cars at this point.'

His smile made her heart flip over. 'I don't want a glamorous sports car,' she told him. 'It's a waste of money.'

'Indeed.' His tone was dry and a smile flickered across his handsome face. 'Now, onto your second condition. No touching.'

The car suddenly seemed a very confined space and he suddenly seemed very, very male.

'It's true that the physical attraction between us is unusually strong.' His eyes dropped to her mouth and then lifted again to her wide green eyes. 'I can see how it has possibly overwhelmed other aspects of our relationship, so I agree to your second condition. No touching.' The corner of his mouth lifted slightly. 'Although I have a feeling it may not be easy.'

Tia gave a weak smile. She had a feeling that it wouldn't be easy either. Heavens, even now she was dying for the man to kiss her. It wouldn't be so bad if she didn't already know just what he could make her feel. But she did…

Luca touched her cheek gently and pulled the key out of the ignition. 'But any time you want to change that rule, let me know.'

He opened his door and she watched him unfold his six-foot-plus frame, her heart beating a steady tattoo against her chest.

Change the rule?

His straightforward admission that he still wanted her made her limbs tremble.

Not that wanting her physically meant anything, of course. Luca had already proved that he didn't need to be in love with her to enjoy an intense physical relationship.

But that wasn't enough for her.

She was going to get to know him, and then decide what the future held for them.

The following morning Luca took her to work without comment, although she could see from the stiff line of his jaw that he wasn't pleased with the idea.

'I'll be OK, Luca,' she said quietly as she undid her seat belt and fumbled for her bag. 'I wasn't sick this morning.'

He turned to her, his eyes serious. 'Tia, I'm not happy about you working, you know that. There is no financial reason for you to work and I don't really understand why you feel the need, but I gave you my word and I won't try and stop you. But if you are unwell, I want you to call me. Do you understand?'

She hesitated and then gave a nod. 'All right, but I think you're overreacting.'

'I'm Italian and an expectant father,' he pointed out, a smile touching his firm mouth. 'I'm allowed to overreact.'

Unable to resist the lazy warmth in his eyes she returned the smile, remembering that it had been his sense of humour that had first attracted her to him. That and his aura of strength.

'We still haven't really talked about this baby, Tia,' he pointed out softly as he parked and switched off the engine. 'Tonight I'll make us some dinner and we can discuss it properly. You wanted us to get to know each other better, so our feelings about the baby are a good place to start.'

Her heart gave a lurch. She wasn't at all sure that she was ready to discuss how she felt about the baby.

She had little chance to think about it, however, because Sharon grabbed her the minute she arrived on the unit.

'I need you on Antenatal. We've had an emergency admission from A and E.' She matched her pace to Tia's as they walked quickly along the corridor, talking as they went. 'They thought she had some sort of viral illness to start with, but now they think it's severe pre-eclampsia.'

Luca was at the desk, together with Dr Ford and Dan Sutherland, the consultant.

'She complained of severe headache and visual disturbances,' Luca was telling the team, 'and she's also had epigastric pain and vomiting. The casualty officer thought it was a virus to start with but was smart enough to do a pregnancy test.'

'She didn't know she was pregnant?' Dr Ford looked slightly disdainful and Luca flashed her a slightly impatient look.

'It would seem not.'

Dan Sutherland picked up the notes. 'Does she have many risk factors for pre-eclampsia?'

'A few.' Luca raked long fingers through his dark hair. 'First baby, overweight, family history according to the case officer—her mother had pre-eclampsia—and her blood pressure was already high.'

Dan frowned. 'How do we know that?'

'The casualty officer rang the GP to check on her history.'

Dan raised his eyebrows in surprise. 'Smart chap.'

Luca gave a wry smile. 'It was a woman,' he drawled softly, his eyes flickering back to the notes. 'She called me down to A and E because she was worried, I examined the patient and gave her a nifedipine capsule to chew because we needed something fast-acting. In my opinion she was—

and is—at very high risk of developing full-blown eclampsia.'

Dan nodded. 'All right, let's take a look at her. She's going to need one-to-one care, I should think.'

'Tia will be her midwife,' Sharon said quickly, pushing open the door and holding it while they all trooped into the room.

'Hello, Sue, I'm Dan Sutherland, the consultant and this is Dr Zattoni, my senior registrar, and Dr Ford…' Dan made the introductions as Sue Gibbs lay on the bed, clearly very ill. 'And you had no idea you were pregnant?'

Sue shook her head, slowly. 'None. My husband and I were desperate to have a baby, but in the end nothing happened so we gave up. I still can't believe I'm pregnant. Are you absolutely sure?'

Dan gave a brief nod. 'But it seems that you've developed a condition called pre-eclampsia, Sue. Which is basically high blood pressure of pregnancy. It can be dangerous if not controlled, so we're trying to bring your blood pressure down.'

'Will the baby be all right?'

'Don't worry about the baby,' Dan said immediately. 'The scan shows us that at the moment he's fine. His heartbeat is strong and he's still moving around. It's you we need to worry about.'

He motioned to Tia to take over with the patient and moved to one side with Luca.

'We need to give her an anti-hypertensive by infusion, do you agree?'

Luca nodded. 'And we need to catheterise her and monitor her output.'

Dan cast another look at the patient and then lowered his voice. 'I suggest you stay close.'

Luca nodded, understanding immediately. 'That was my intention.' He turned to Dr Ford. 'I want you to check U and Es, LFTs, urate and placental function and platelets. A falling platelet count and changes in clotting factors have been reported in many cases of pre-eclampsia. Tia, can you put her on a monitor and keep her on it for now?'

Tia nodded. It was obvious that they were very worried about Sue.

She monitored Sue's blood pressure regularly throughout the morning but despite the drugs it still crept upwards.

She slipped out of the room briefly to have a word with Luca, who was at the desk finishing a telephone call, Dr Ford by his side.

'Her blood pressure is sneaking up again,' she mouthed, and he nodded as he replaced the receiver.

'She is at a very high risk of developing full-blown eclampsia,' he agreed and Dr Ford frowned.

'But you've given her anti-hypertensives.'

'Anti-hypertensives do not alter the course of pre-eclampsia,' Luca reminded her. 'There is only one thing that will do that, which is?'

He paused, waiting for Dr Ford to answer, but she looked at him blankly.

'Delivery.' Tia broke the awkward silence, thinking that if the glamorous Dr Ford paid as much attention to her textbooks as she did to her make-up and her male colleagues, she might be a better doctor.

'Yes.' There was a warmth in Luca's eyes as they rested on her briefly and then he turned his attention back to his SHO. 'I'd like you to bleep Duncan Fraser, the anaesthetist, and warn him that we might need his services at short notice, and do the same with Paeds, please. I think we're probably going to need to get the baby out. And could you also call ITU and check their bed state?'

Dr Ford reached for the phone, her expression flustered for the first time.

Tia followed Luca back to the room.

Sue's husband, Eddie, was sitting on the bed, his face ashen.

'Will she be all right?'

'She is very ill,' Luca said honestly, 'but she is in the right place and we are doing everything we can.'

Eddie's face crumpled and Luca put a sympathetic hand on his shoulder. 'Come with me to the relatives' room,' he said quietly, 'and I can explain exactly what is happening.'

They left the room and Tia was alone with Sue.

She checked her patient's blood pressure again and then tensed. As she watched, Sue became suddenly restless, her head drawn to one side, then her body went into spasm and she started to fit.

'Damn!' Smashing her hand against the emergency button, Tia immediately inserted an airway, quickly disconnected the CTG machine and shifted Sue into a semi-prone position.

Grabbing the oxygen, she placed the mask over Sue's face, knowing that care of the mother was everything.

She heard footsteps outside the door and sighed with relief.

Reinforcements…

Luca came back into the room at a run, his eyes taking in the problem immediately.

'I want to give her magnesium sulphate,' he ordered, his voice calm and level as he delivered his instructions. 'Give her 4 g in 100 ml of normal saline over at least five minutes, and then I want an infusion rate of 1 g an hour for 24 hours.'

Tia prepared the drug and gave it to Luca to check.

'All right.' He gave the drug and glanced towards Dr Ford. 'Check her patellar reflexes every fifteen minutes, Tia, her resps should be more than sixteen a minute. Check every fifteen minutes and if it drops below that I want to know immediately. And let's keep an eye on her urine output.'

Duncan Fraser, the anaesthetist, hurried into the room at that point and Luca glanced up, his expression grim.

'We need to section her now.'

Duncan nodded. 'Let's get on with it, then.'

It was the fastest section Tia had ever seen, and in no time the baby was out and screaming with outrage.

'Sounds hopeful,' Luca commented, his eyes still on the wound. 'Julie? Give me some good news on the baby.'

'He seems fine.' Julie Douglas, the paediatric registrar, had the baby on the rescusitaire and was checking it over. 'Small, of course—I've warned Special Care to expect a new customer. How's Mum?'

'Not good.' Luca didn't look up. 'Someone, please, tell Eddie that he has a little boy. The man must be out of his mind with worry. Tia, can you do that?'

'Of course.'

Tia checked again that the baby seemed all right and then walked into the anteroom where Eddie was pacing, frantic with worry.

'Eddie, you have a baby boy,' Tia said softly, and he stared at her, ashen-faced and stunned.

'A boy?' He looked at her stupidly and then shook his head, rubbing a hand around the back of his neck to relieve the tension. 'Ridiculous, isn't it? We always wanted a baby, and now we've got one I don't really care. All I want is for Sue to be back to normal. How is she?'

'She's poorly,' Tia admitted, 'but she's getting the best possible care. Dr Zattoni is just finishing in Theatre and then she'll be transferred to ITU. You can go and see her when they've settled her down.'

'And the—my son?'

'He's beautiful.' Tia smiled at him. 'Very small, so he'll be in Special Care for now. The paediatrician is taking him up there now. Are you ready to see him?'

Eddie licked his lips. 'I don't know.'

Suddenly Tia made a decision. 'Wait there.'

She slipped back into Theatre and walked quickly up to

Julie. 'Can I take the baby for two minutes? If we wrap him up well…'

Julie stared at her. 'You want to take the baby?'

'His father doesn't know whether he's coming or going,' Tia told her quickly. 'I think he needs to see his little boy quickly. Just for a moment.'

Julie frowned. 'But—'

'Julie, will it harm the baby if he is well wrapped up for a few minutes?' Luca's voice intervened across the theatre. 'I agree with Tia that it is important. This family have had a terrible shock—they are not prepared for this baby at all. If we're not careful, we could have bonding problems.'

His dark eyes locked with Tia's and she knew what he was thinking.

If Sue died, would Eddie blame the child?

'It should be all right, I suppose.' Julie gave a nod and wrapped the baby, handing him carefully to Tia. 'Don't be long. He needs to be checked out in Special Care.'

'Hello, sweetheart.' Tia gazed down at the tiny features of the baby and her heart melted. He looked completely helpless. 'We're going to meet your daddy, so be a good boy and don't let me down.'

Someone opened the door to the anteroom for her and she slipped inside and walked across to Eddie who was sitting with his head in his hands.

'Someone to meet you, Eddie.' Taking a chance that her instincts were correct, she laid the tiny bundle on his lap and held her breath.

There was a long silence. Eddie stared wordlessly down at his baby son and then tears started to pour down his cheeks.

'He's beautiful,' he croaked, tightening his grip on the little bundle. 'So beautiful. How can I possibly blame anything so perfect? I still can't take it all in—we thought we couldn't have children.'

He rambled incoherently for a few minutes and Tia slipped an arm around his shoulder.

'He's beautiful, Eddie,' Tia said softly, feeling her own eyes fill as she watched him. 'A bit small, but the paediatrician thinks he's doing very well. I don't suppose you've thought of a name?'

'Oh, yes.' Eddie gave an embarrassed sniff and gazed down at his son. 'We always knew what we'd call a little boy. Harry.'

'That's lovely.' Tia's voice cracked and she cleared her throat. Maybe being pregnant made her more emotional than usual. 'OK, well, we need to get Harry up to the ward now…'

Julie was hovering in the doorway, keeping a close eye on her charge. 'Why don't you come, too, Mr Gibbs? You can stay with him while we settle him in and then go and tell your wife all about him.'

It was hours later when they finally climbed into Luca's car to drive home.

'I can't believe how quickly she fitted,' Luca said as he reversed the car out of his space. 'You had an airway in the room, ready? That was quick thinking.'

'In my pocket,' Tia murmured. 'It seemed like a good idea.'

'It was more than a good idea.' Luca flicked the indicator and pulled onto the main road. 'You're an excellent midwife. How on earth did you manage to put her in the recovery position by yourself?'

Tia shrugged. 'Panic, I suppose. I kept thinking that if Sue died, the baby would die, too.' She gave a sigh. 'Do you think she will die, Luca?'

He pulled a face. 'I don't know. She is certainly very sick but I hope that she will be all right.'

'You were fantastic,' Tia said softly, a flush touching her cheeks. 'Really fantastic.'

He glanced at her briefly and his gaze burned into hers. 'Thank you.'

They arrived at the cottage and Luca pushed open the door. 'What a day! Go and have a bath and I'll prepare supper.'

She stifled a grin. 'Another omelette?'

'No.' He shut the front door behind them and walked through to the kitchen. 'I'm the first to admit that my experience in the kitchen is limited but I arranged to have some shopping delivered today so there should be something simple in the fridge.'

She stared at him. 'You went shopping?'

Luca Zattoni? *Shopping?*

He gave a shake of his head and a wry smile. 'No. I didn't exactly go shopping. But I arranged for the supermarket to deliver.'

She blinked at him. 'What supermarket? And how could they deliver? We weren't in.'

A flush touched his hard cheekbones. 'Dan Sutherland's secretary ordered everything and I gave her a key to the cottage. She nipped here today so that someone was in when they delivered.'

Luca had arranged all that? The least domesticated male on the planet?

Tia was totally speechless and he gave her a gentle push. 'Go and have a bath.'

Without argument she wandered upstairs and minutes later she slid into a deep bubble bath with a contented sigh. She still couldn't believe that Luca had really gone to those lengths just for her. It was totally out of character.

Or maybe it wasn't.

Maybe it was just another indication that she didn't really know much about him.

Drifting away with her thoughts, she was still trying to make sense of it when the door opened ten minutes later.

Tia gave a squeak of embarrassment and slid under the bubbles as Luca strolled in.

'What are you doing? You promised—'

'I promised I wouldn't touch you,' Luca drawled softly, his eyes darkening as they rested on the gentle swell of her breasts. 'And I haven't.'

Not with his hands maybe, but with his eyes…

'I knocked, but you didn't answer. I wanted to check that you hadn't fallen asleep in the bath.'

'Well, I haven't,' Tia muttered, and he gave a slow smile.

'In that case, why don't you get dried and come down to supper?'

Not while he was standing there!

Suddenly she was hideously aware of every inch of her naked body and her eyes meshed with his. Oh, dear God, how had she ever thought she'd be able to keep the physical element out of their relationship?

He'd removed his jacket and undone his top button and she could see a hint of dark, curling chest hair at the top of his shirt. And she could remember exactly how his chest looked. How it felt under her eager fingers. The way his muscles curved, strong and sleek, and the way his body hair trailed downwards…

She swallowed and slid further under the water. She needed a cold shower, not a hot bath.

He handed her a towel and from the gleam in his eyes she was fairly sure that he knew exactly what she was thinking.

Damn the man.

How was she going to get dressed and eat supper without breaking her own rules? She was desperate for him to touch her.

But she'd made the rules and now she had to stick to them. No touching, she'd said, and he'd agreed.

It was going to be a difficult evening.

CHAPTER FIVE

WHEN Tia finally plucked up the courage to slink into the kitchen, she was amazed by what she saw.

Instead of relying on the usual harsh kitchen lights, Luca had found some candles and grouped them in the centre of the scrubbed pine table. The subtle, cosy lighting flickered across the room, revealing a tempting selection of mouth-watering dishes which he'd laid out on the table.

The atmosphere was romantic and intimate and she felt inexplicably shy. She really didn't know this man at all. It was like being with a stranger. The longer she knew him, the more he surprised her.

'I thought all you could cook was omelette?' She used humour to try and disguise just how confused she was feeling, and he returned the smile as he strolled across the room towards her.

'I haven't exactly cooked,' he confessed, glancing at the table with a wry smile. 'And we both know that my omelette was inedible.'

Another point in his favour. He obviously had no problem admitting when he wasn't good at something.

'Well, this looks fantastic.' There was a delicious-smelling soup, crusty bread and various cold meats and salads. Her smile was teasing. 'For an unreconstructed Italian male, you're obviously good in the kitchen.'

'I am very good in the kitchen, *cara mia*.' Suddenly the temperature of the room seemed to shoot up and his eyes gleamed wickedly. 'And so are you, if my memory is correct.'

'Luca, for goodness' sake…' She blushed deeply but couldn't look away from his compelling gaze.

'I was late home from work and I'd ruined your dinner.' His soft voice caressed her nerve endings. 'Do you remember that night, Tia?'

Of course she remembered that night.

The minute he'd walked through the door their dinner had been forgotten.

'Luca…' His name was almost a plea on her lips and she felt sexual heat curl deep inside her stomach.

He slid a hand behind her head and gently forced her to look at him. 'It has always been like that between us, has it not?' His voice was husky with desire and his eyes slid to her mouth.

For endless seconds they stood still, both battling against the physical force which drew them together, then Luca released her suddenly and stalked to the other side of the kitchen.

'I must have been mad to agree to the no-touching rule.' His voice was a frustrated growl and he dragged both hands through his black hair, his eyes stormy. 'Maybe I should check into a hotel until we decide that our relationship can move forward.'

Tia felt her heart lurch uncomfortably in her chest. Would it move forward? She wasn't sure.

'We were supposed to spend the evening talking,' she reminded him, a small smile of satisfaction touching her mouth as she registered his tension.

It was good to know that, physically at least, he wanted her as much as she wanted him.

'Talking.' The corner of his mouth quirked and he shrugged his broad shoulders. 'OK. Maybe if you sit at one end of the table and I sit at the other…'

Tia slid into a chair and concentrated on the food. Suddenly talking didn't seem as easy as it had sounded. She could barely keep her body functioning properly when she was in the same room as the man, let alone hold a conversation. She wanted Luca so much it was a physical ache.

'What shall we talk about?' Her voice came out as a squeak and she cursed herself as she read the gleam in his eyes. He was totally aware of the effect he had on her.

'You.' He leaned back in his chair at the opposite end of the table, thick, dark lashes shielding his expression as he watched her. 'You are a very private person, Tia. I want to know more about you. A great deal more.'

His speculative dark gaze made her feel like a dizzy teenager. 'There's not much to know,' she hedged, and he gave a short laugh.

'Tia, we are both in agreement that we have spent insufficient time talking. For example, I know nothing about your family. All you told me was that your parents died when you were young. Do you have no other family?'

She played with her soup self-consciously.

She really wasn't used to talking about her childhood.

'No.' She scrabbled in her mind for a change of subject. 'Unlike you, who are surrounded by family.'

He inclined his head in agreement, a rueful smile touching his firm mouth. 'A mixed blessing, as you've discovered.'

Tia glanced at him. 'I bet they're not too pleased that you've chased me to England.'

He gave a careless shrug. 'I have no idea what they think. I'm not in the habit of seeking their approval. My father died when I was twelve and I've been making my own decisions ever since.'

She stared at him, beginning to understand why he was so self-assured.

'I'm sorry,' she said quietly. 'That must have been difficult for you. How did he die?'

'Living life to the full,' Luca said wryly, his voice amazingly matter-of-fact as he described an event that must have had devastating consequences for a young boy. 'He was riding a motorbike. My mother thought that my father took too many risks for a man with children, and maybe he did…' He shrugged. 'I don't know. Fortunately his business was thriving and my uncles were able to carry on running it so she had no financial worries, but my mother·had always let my father make all the decisions and suddenly he was gone.'

'So you took over?'

He nodded slowly. 'I was barely more than a child myself, but that's exactly what I did and soon everyone expected me to make decisions for them.'

Tia tilted her head on one side, a smile touching her mouth. 'Are you trying to justify why you're so autocratic?'

'No. That's probably just a basic character flaw.' He gave an apologetic smile that was so sexy it made her stomach flip. He really was staggeringly handsome.

'But you made all the decisions in the family?'

He gave a dismissive shrug. 'I suppose so.'

Tia nodded. 'Well that explains a lot about you.'

'It does?' His dark eyes shimmered with amusement and she blushed.

'Well, if you're used to bossing your sisters and your mother then I suppose it's hardly surprising that you try and take over my life, too,' she said quickly, hoping that he couldn't read her mind. Her thoughts were positively X-rated! 'The trouble is, I've also been looking after myself since I was young and I don't need anyone to make decisions for me. It's probably why we clash.'

Luca's gaze sharpened. 'How young?'

She played idly with her knife. 'Eight.'

'Eight years old?' His voice was soft. 'That must have been very hard, *cara mia*.'

She gave a dismissive shrug. 'Maybe.'

He sighed and sat back in his chair. 'Tia, I'm fully aware that you change the subject every time I mention your parents.' His voice was gentle. 'Are you going to hide from me for ever, or are you going to trust me?'

There was a lengthy silence. He was right, of course.

She *did* hide from people and she always had. It was a defence mechanism that she'd developed over the years. And as for trusting him…

'Tia, if you want me to understand you, you have to start revealing some of yourself to me,' he said quietly, and she swallowed hard, acknowledging the truth of what he was saying.

'My parents were actors,' she said, quickly outlining the bare facts. 'They married very young—too young, I suppose. My mother was crazy about my father and she thought that he felt the same way about her.'

Luca's eyes were fixed on her face. 'But he didn't?'

Tia's mouth tightened. 'It would seem not. He had one affair after another and my mother started to drink. Too much.' She broke off and glanced at him briefly. 'She died when I was eight.'

He let out a long breath. 'And your father?'

Tia played with her spoon. 'My father made it clear that he couldn't look after me so I went into care.'

'Care?' He looked blank. 'You stayed with family?'

'There was no family,' Tia said simply. 'I went into foster-care and then a children's home while I waited for someone to adopt me. But they didn't.' She gave an overly bright smile. 'And who can blame them? You think I'm reckless now, you should have met me then. I was your average teenage nightmare.'

His gaze didn't falter and she knew that her bravado hadn't fooled him. 'So you never had a proper home? Family?'

'No.'

'That must have been difficult.' His voice was even, as if he knew that too much sympathy would be hard to cope with.

She stirred her soup slowly. 'Well, it made me very independent. It's probably the reason I don't take kindly to people telling me what to do,' she told him with a smile.

'I'm used to having to work things out for myself because I've always been on my own.'

'But you're not on your own now.'

She lifted her eyes to his and her heart squeezed tightly at the expression in his eyes.

'No…'

'But you are finding it hard, are you not,' he said calmly, 'to learn to trust another person? Presumably because of what happened to your mother and because you have been let down so many times in the past.'

'Yes,' she said honestly. 'I—I didn't think I'd ever be able to trust a man. Even now I'm worried that you—that you…' Her eyes slid away from his and she stumbled slightly over the words. 'Might be keeping all sorts of secrets from me.'

There—she'd said it. Now she just had to wait for Luca's response.

She looked at him, searching for signs of guilt or discomfort but she saw nothing but sympathy in his expression.

'Tia, you can trust me,' he said quietly, his dark eyes trapping hers. 'But I can understand that, with your experiences, my word is not enough to stop you worrying. Only time will do that. So let us tackle another issue. How do you feel about being pregnant? How do you feel about having my baby?'

Her heart thumped steadily as she looked into his eyes. Could she tell him the truth? That she was terrified? That she wasn't sure she'd be a good mother.

No.

She couldn't threaten the fragile peace that had settled between them by admitting that she'd never thought she'd get married or have children.

'I'm pleased about the baby,' she whispered at last, concentrating her attentions on the plate of ham in front of her. 'Very pleased.'

There was a long silence and she could feel his gaze sweeping her pale face.

'Are you sure? This isn't the time for secrets between us. I want you to tell me the truth.'

Secrets?

He was a fine one to talk about secrets when he still hadn't mentioned Luisa.

'I'm pleased,' she repeated firmly, poking at her food. 'What about you, Luca? How do you really feel now that you've had time to get used to the idea?'

'I still would have chosen to have more time alone with you,' he admitted, his accent almost unbearably sexy, 'especially in the light of what you've just told me, but I am very pleased, Tia. Very pleased indeed. I love children.'

Tia added some salad to her plate, her hands shaking slightly. Of course he loved children. All Italian men loved children, didn't they?

'But if I hadn't got pregnant? What then?'

He shrugged. 'Then we would have had more time to get to know each other properly. But it is pointless to dwell on what might have happened. We need to concentrate on the present. You still haven't seen a doctor. I want you to register with Dan.'

She opened her mouth to accuse him of being autocratic but then closed it again. Luca was right. Dan was easily the best consultant. Everyone knew it. And he was kind and approachable too. *Which helped when you were absolutely terrified.*

'I'll talk to him,' she offered, and Luca lifted an ebony brow.

'Just like that.' His mouth twitched at the corners. 'No arguments? No accusations of trying to run your life?'

'It just so happens that on this occasion I agree with you, that's all,' she said primly, and he laughed.

'Well, that is definitely a first. Maybe we're making progress.'

Maybe they were.

The next morning she was sick again and Luca was by her side in an instant. He murmured something soothing in Italian and held her until she finally collapsed against him, exhausted.

'Oh, Luca.' She felt pitifully sorry for herself and he tightened his grip.

'Remind me to be more sympathetic the next time a woman tells me she is suffering from morning sickness,' he said gruffly, wiping her face with a flannel and helping her to her feet. 'I never realised how awful it can be. Go back to bed for a few minutes and I'll bring you a drink.'

She did as she was told, knowing that she shouldn't be leaning on him but unable to help herself. She had to admit that for a very macho male, he was surprisingly undaunted by her antics in the bathroom.

He walked back into the room and she noticed for the first time that he was wearing nothing but a pair of loose-fitting tracksuit bottoms.

'I was still in bed when I heard you get up,' he said, intercepting her look and proffering an explanation. 'I'm not in the habit of wearing clothes to bed.'

She was well aware of that and the sight of his tanned, muscular chest was a tantalising reminder of what the rest of him looked like.

Incredible…

He had the perfect musculature of an athlete and she averted her eyes and took the glass of water he brought her with a murmur of thanks.

The bed sagged slightly under his weight as he sat down next to her. 'I don't suppose there's any chance I can persuade you not to work today?'

'None at all,' she said, putting the glass of water back on the bedside table. 'I feel much better now.'

'Right.' Luca rolled his eyes and gave a wry smile. 'Has anyone ever told you that you're difficult to handle?'

'Yes. Lots of times.' Tia swung her legs out of bed and reached for her dressing-gown, taking deep breaths to calm her stomach. 'Now, if you'll excuse me, I'm going to use the bathroom. Hopefully to wash this time.' She walked towards the door, deliberately avoiding looking at the powerful muscles of his shoulders.

The no-touching rule was becoming harder by the minute.

Luca drove her to the hospital and Tia found herself working in the antenatal clinic for the morning.

'Do you mind, Tia?' Sharon immediately apologised. 'I'm moving you around everywhere, I know, but I've got a midwife off sick and we've got a busy clinic. You should enjoy it—your Luca's working down there this morning.'

He was?

Tia's heart lurched uncomfortably. On the one hand, concentrating was difficult with Luca around but, on the other hand, she was intrigued to learn more about him as a doctor. What she'd seen so far had certainly been impressive.

She made her way to the clinic and introduced herself to the sister there.

'Could you do a booking visit?' Janet handed her a pile of notes and leaflets. 'First baby, she's down the end on the left. Karen King.'

The booking visit was the first time that the pregnant woman attended the hospital and it took longer than other appointments.

As Tia walked briskly along to the room she found herself looking for Luca and gave herself a firm telling-off.

Why, oh, why did he have such a powerful effect on her?

Pushing thoughts of him from her mind, she opened the door and smiled at the woman seated by the desk.

'Hello, Karen, I'm Tia.' She shook the other woman's hand and settled herself comfortably at the desk. 'This is your first trip to the hospital and this visit does take longer the others. I'm afraid I'm going to bombard you with questions.'

'I don't mind at all.' The other woman's eyes sparkled and she placed a protective hand on her abdomen. 'I've been longing for this appointment. You really feel you're pregnant once you've been to the hospital, don't you think?'

Her excitement and enthusiasm made Tia's heart twist. *Why didn't she feel the same way?*

'Then I gather you're pleased about the pregnancy,' she said, her voice slightly gruff as she opened the notes and pulled a pen out of her pocket.

'I've never been so pleased about anything in my whole life,' Karen said softly, her eyes shining with tears. 'I just can't believe we're going to have a baby. Nigel and I can't stop hugging each other. We've been trying for almost a year. I was really starting to think I wouldn't be able to have my own child and that's a terrible feeling for a woman, isn't it?'

Was it?

Tia stared at her. 'Well, I—'

'All your life you just assume you're going to have children,' Karen continued, 'and then you get married and you assume that you can choose to have a baby when you like, so you try and then nothing happens and it's as if your whole life is over. Do you know what I mean?'

No.

Tia swallowed hard. She didn't have a clue what the other woman meant. Her situation was the complete opposite to Karen's. All of her life she'd assumed that she wouldn't have children. That she would never want to have children. Then she'd become pregnant without even intending to...

'Well, I'm pleased you're pleased,' Tia said quickly, trying to move the consultation away from the emotional side. It was making her feel odd inside.

'How have you been?'

'Pretty sick,' Karen confessed, 'but I read somewhere that if you're sick it means that your hormone levels are high and you're less likely to miscarry. If I lost this baby I don't know what I'd do.'

She looked at Tia anxiously and Tia gave her a reassuring smile. 'You're fourteen weeks now, Karen, and you had a normal scan at twelve weeks. It's unusual to miscarry at this stage.'

Karen gave a shaky smile. 'I hope you're right.'

Tia checked Karen's menstrual history and estimated the date of delivery and asked questions about her obstetric history.

'This is your first pregnancy?' She scribbled in the notes as Karen chatted away, asking questions about Karen's general health and her family history.

'We're all very healthy,' Karen said.

Tia stood up. 'Great. OK, I need to do some tests. Weight, height, test your urine and take some blood. All very routine.'

When she'd finished the tests she sat down and discussed the options with Karen. 'What most people opt for is shared care,' she explained, 'so you visit your GP and community midwife for most antenatal checks and just come to the hospital for key visits. Then obviously you come here to be delivered.'

Karen nodded. 'I definitely want to have this baby in hospital. It's so precious, I wouldn't dream of having it anywhere else.'

She placed a protective hand on her abdomen again and Tia looked away quickly.

Why couldn't she feel like this woman? The truth was

she spent most of her time pretending that the baby wasn't there—*worrying about Luca*.

But she *was* pregnant.

Panic surged inside her and she stumbled to her feet, suddenly desperate to get away from Karen.

'I just need to arrange for you to see the doctor,' she said quickly as she made for the door. 'I'll be back in a moment.'

Breathing rapidly, her palms damp with sweat, she hurried out of the door and bumped straight into Luca who was walking past.

'Slow down!' His hands shot out and steadied her, his long fingers tightening on her arms as he held her firmly. 'What's happened?'

'Nothing.'

Except that she was having a baby and she didn't have any of the normal feelings.

Luca gave her a searching glance and then guided her into a nearby consulting room which was empty.

'Now, tell me the truth.' He stood with his back to the door, blocking her escape, his dark eyes locking onto hers. 'Something has upset you. What, Tia? Tell me.'

She shook her head, feeling totally foolish. How could she possibly tell him?

He said something in Italian that she didn't understand and closed the distance between her.

'Stop hiding from me.' He cupped her face in his hands and tilted her face up to his. 'You're as white as a sheet and you're shaking. I want to know what has happened.'

Luca's jaw was tense and she sensed that he was angry. With her? For being ridiculous?

'I—It's nothing, Luca,' she said quickly. 'But now you're here, I need you to see a patient in Room 2.' She pulled away from him before his nearness demolished her self-control.

Whatever had possessed her to impose a no-touching

rule? What she really needed now was to feel his arms around her.

'You know something, Tia?' His tone was conversational but his gaze was strangely intense. 'We could be married for a hundred years but we won't ever get to know each other unless you start trusting me with your feelings.'

Tia stared at him.

How? How could she do that? How did she know that he wasn't going to hurt her?

She just couldn't bring herself to take that chance.

'We've got patients waiting,' she croaked, and he gave a wry smile.

'Of course. This is the NHS. There are always patients waiting. We need to talk, Tia, but I agree that this is not a good time.' He stood to one side to let her pass him. 'Who is this lady you want me to see? Is she the reason you're upset?'

Tia walked briskly past him, ignoring his last comment. 'It's a booking visit,' she told him. 'First baby, no problems that I can see. She just needs a routine medical check.'

He followed her out of the room. 'Will you chaperone?'

Tia nodded and took him through to meet Karen.

He talked to her calmly for a few minutes about the baby and then examined Karen's heart and lungs.

'That all sounds perfectly normal,' he said finally, looping the stethoscope around his neck. He finished his examination, scribbled in the notes and then leaned against the desk.

'So…' His voice was warm and caressing. 'Tia has been telling me all about your conversation.'

Tia glanced at Luca with a puzzled frown. What was he talking about? She hadn't mentioned their conversation.

Karen laughed. 'I've bored her to tears,' she admitted with an apologetic smile. 'All I can talk about is this baby and how much I want it. I was absolutely desperate to get pregnant and I can't quite believe it's finally happened.'

Luca gave her a warm smile but his eyes rested on Tia. 'Having a baby is a wonderful thing,' he said quietly, 'although some women have very mixed feelings and that is very natural, of course.'

Tia's heart started to beat more rapidly. Was he addressing his remarks to her? Had he guessed how she felt about being pregnant?

'I don't have mixed feelings,' Karen stated emphatically. 'I'm completely delighted.'

Luca shifted his gaze back to the patient. 'Good.' He gave her a brief smile and stood up. 'You're in excellent health, Karen. You'll be going to your GP next but if you have any problems you know you can phone us.'

With a last smile he left the room, closing the door quietly behind him.

'Oh, that man is totally gorgeous,' Karen drooled as she pulled on her jumper. 'Can you imagine being involved with someone who looks like him? I'd be in a permanent state of faint.'

Tia coloured and Karen gave a gasp and clapped her hand over her mouth.

'Oh, no! You're not…' Her eyes widened and she gave a groan. 'You are, aren't you? And I've just put my foot in it.'

'It doesn't matter,' Tia reassured her quickly. 'And, anyway, you're right. He is gorgeous.'

Karen looked at her dreamily, embarrassment obviously forgotten. 'Does he speak to you in Italian?'

Tia laughed and closed the notes. 'Sometimes. But I don't usually understand a word of it, I'm afraid.' She changed the subject quickly. 'As Dr Zattoni said, your next appointment is with your GP, but you know you can always call us with any problems.'

'Thanks.' Karen stood up and patted her stomach. 'Do you think I'm crazy, being so excited?'

'No.' Tia managed a smile. 'Not crazy.'

Lucky.

If only her own attitude to pregnancy was so simple.

Tia watched Karen go with mixed emotions, then she worked her way through a steady list of patients and was relieved to stop for a breather when Luca caught up with her later that afternoon.

'Sharon called for you but you were with a patient.' He lowered his voice, aware that people were probably listening. 'She's invited us to supper this evening but I wasn't sure if you'd be too tired. I said I'd call her back.'

'I'd like to go.' Tia stroked her blonde hair behind her ear. 'What about you? You'd like her husband—he's a GP.'

He nodded slowly. 'I met him briefly at the wedding.' He gave a wry smile. 'But I have to admit that I didn't take much notice of him then. I'll tell her yes, but we won't stay late because you look exhausted again and you were so stressed earlier.'

'It's this pregnancy business,' Tia muttered. 'Tiring work.'

He frowned. 'Have you spoken to Dan yet?'

Tia's eyes slid away from his. 'Not yet,' she murmured, purposely vague. 'Give me time.'

'I'll give you time,' he said softly, 'but not too much time. Remember that, Tia. Either book yourself in or I will do it for you.'

Before she had time to accuse him of more male arrogance he turned on his heel and strode away, leaving her staring after him.

With a great effort of will she got on with her work and was forced to call Luca again when she examined a woman who was 32 weeks pregnant and discovered that the baby was breech.

'Does that matter?' Sally Clarke looked at her anxiously and Tia gave her a reassuring smile.

'Not at all, but we do refer breech presentations to the doctor.'

Luca walked into the room at that moment and Tia explained what she'd found.

Sally was starting to look anxious. 'I really don't want to have a Caesarean section,' she admitted. 'It's the one thing I dread. Will I have to?'

Luca shook his head. 'Not necessarily. We will need to keep close eyes on you but a vaginal delivery is sometimes possible. It depends on a number of factors.'

Sally bit her lip. 'Can you turn him around?'

'Not at 32 weeks,' Luca told her. 'He would just turn around again. But that may be an option in a few weeks' time. We'll keep an eye on you and maybe try turning him nearer the time of delivery.'

Luca ordered a number of tests and examined Sally himself.

'I really hurt under my ribs,' Sally grumbled, rubbing herself gently, and Tia smiled sympathetically.

'That's because his head is pressing on your diaphragm.'

She and Luca spent a long time with Sally and Tia made a mental note to try and be on duty when she delivered. She knew that many obstetricians sectioned breech presentations routinely, but clearly Luca was willing to consider letting her try for a normal delivery.

Her shift over, Tia decided to nip up to Special Care to see how little Harry Gibbs was doing. Everyone on the unit was keeping tabs on Sue's progress and were thrilled to hear that she was stable.

Harry was still in an incubator and Eddie was sitting in a chair next to him, reading out loud from a children's book.

'How's he doing, Eddie?' Tia peered into the incubator and Eddie closed the book with a sigh.

'Well, they tell me I've been lucky. Apparently he could have had all sorts of breathing problems, but he seems fine apart from the fact that his sats keep dropping. Whatever that means.' He gave her a rueful look. 'I've been swamped with so many medical terms in the last twenty-four hours that I've given up asking for translations.'

Tia smiled. 'If they're telling you that his sats are dropping, they mean that his oxygen saturation is a little low at times, which is why they're giving him the oxygen. But clearly he's doing brilliantly. Have you talked to Sue?'

'She's still unconscious,' he told her, 'but I sat by her all night. I talked about the baby. Said all the things we would have said together had we known she was pregnant.'

Tia slipped an arm around his shoulders. 'This has been such a shock, hasn't it? And you're coping so well.'

'I don't feel as though I am.' Eddie stared at his son. 'Do you realise, we haven't even got a cot at home?'

'Well, he won't be ready to go home for a while, so don't worry about that,' Tia advised. 'Just get through the next few days. You've got plenty of time to think about the detail. When did you last sleep?'

He looked at her blankly. 'I've no idea. Two days ago?'

'Why don't you go home?'

Eddie shook his head. 'No way. Not until I know Sue's going to be all right.'

Tia racked her brains. 'Wait here.'

She found one of the SCBU nurses and explained the problem. 'Is your parents' room free?'

They had a room available for parents with severely sick children.

The nurse frowned. 'It's free, but if we have a very ill baby—'

'Then Eddie will have to move out,' Tia agreed. 'But at the moment it's the only chance the guy has to get some sleep. Please?'

The nurse nodded. 'I'll clear it with Sister. Tell him to help himself.'

'Thanks.'

Tia gave the news to Eddie and helped him settle himself in the small but adequate bedroom.

Then she glanced at her watch and realised that Luca was probably waiting for her downstairs. And they were going to Sharon's.

CHAPTER SIX

The minute they arrived at Sharon's, Tia knew it was going to be a difficult evening.

Sharon was obviously dying for an update and barely waited until Luca was out of earshot before asking, 'Well?'

'Well, what?' Tia shrugged out of her coat and hung it in the hallway, one eye on Luca as he strolled through to the sitting room with Richard, Sharon's husband.

Sexual awareness poured through her veins as she watched Luca sit down on the sofa, stretching long, muscular legs out in front of him with the easy confidence of someone totally at ease with themselves.

He was on call and had dressed smartly in well-cut trousers and a black polo-neck jumper that accentuated his Latin looks.

'He's stunning,' Sharon muttered, following her gaze, and Tia pulled herself together, wishing she was better at hiding her feelings.

'Looks aren't important, Shaz.'

And she was fast discovering that there was more to Luca Zattoni than just looks. She'd learned more about him in the past few days than in all the weeks that she'd lived with him in Italy.

'I want to hear everything.' Sharon glanced after the men and then gestured towards the kitchen. 'Come and help me in here. We can talk in peace.'

Tia followed dutifully, her eyes flickering over the various pans boiling on the cooker.

'Can I do something?'

'Yes.' Sharon whipped a pan off the stove and placed it

on a mat. 'You can give me an update on your love life. The suspense is killing me.'

Tia shrugged. 'There's nothing to tell. We're fine.'

'Fine? What's that supposed to mean?' Her friend bustled around the kitchen, warming plates and draining vegetables. 'I've been worrying myself to death all week and all you can say is that you're fine? Elaborate! Are you talking? Are you sleeping together?'

'Shaz!' Tia glanced at the door and prayed that Luca wouldn't appear. She'd die of embarrassment! 'Of course we're not sleeping together. We're getting to know each other, remember?'

Sharon stared at her. 'And he was OK with that?'

'Yes, of course.' Tia smiled brightly, trying not to think about the level of tension that was steadily building between her and Luca. It was anyone's guess which one of them was going to explode first.

Sharon lifted a casserole dish out of the oven, obviously unsure what to say. 'And are you getting to know each other better?'

Tia shifted in her seat. 'Shaz, it's only been a few days.'

'But you weren't sure how you felt about him as a person.' Sharon popped a spoon in the casserole and tasted it. 'Do you like him?'

Did she like him?

Tia thought of the times he'd held her when she'd been sick, of the omelette he'd made and the way he'd slept in the spare room even though he must have been hideously uncomfortable. She remembered the candles and the shopping and the warmth he showed to patients and his obvious skill at practising medicine.

'Yes,' she said finally, her tongue licking her dry lips. 'Yes, I like him.'

'And has he mentioned Luisa?'

'No.'

It was the one black spot. He still hadn't been completely honest with her.

'Need any help, Shaz?' Richard stuck his head round the door and looked at his wife. 'We're starving to death ou here.'

'Don't rush me.' Sharon shot him a reproving look. 'You can carry the plates through if you want to help.'

The meal was superb and Luca gave Sharon a warm smile. 'This is excellent,' he said quietly, a smile playing around his mouth as he complimented her. 'Truly excellent.'

'Oh. Well…thank you.' Sharon blushed, flustered by the attention, and Tia watched Luca, her eyes resting on his jaw and then sliding down to his broad shoulders.

The need to touch him—to be touched—was becoming an overwhelming ache. She wanted to slip his shirt over the smooth skin of his shoulders and bury her face in his warmth and strength.

His gaze intercepted hers and she knew that he'd read her thoughts. Her heart thumping, she tried to drag some air into her starving lungs, heat flooding her body as she saw the raw desire flare in his eyes.

Sharon's voice broke the spell. 'So are you still being sick, Tia?'

Tia blinked and dragged her gaze away from Luca's aware of Richard's mild protest.

'Darling, we're eating,' he pointed out, his tone amused as he looked at his wife. 'And you never ask a pregnan person if they feel sick. It instantly makes them feel sick You're a midwife. You should know better.'

Sharon looked apologetic. 'Sorry.'

Luca smiled. 'Tia is coping very well with the sickness She is being very brave about the whole thing…' He paused slightly. 'Especially considering how frightened she is about having this baby.'

Tia's face lost its colour and her eyes flew to his. He'd guessed that she was frightened? How?

'She told you?' Sharon gave a smile of relief, oblivious to the tension simmering between her guests. 'Thank goodness for that. I told her you'd understand but she was completely convinced that, being Italian, you wouldn't want a woman who was scared of marriage and children. She has a serious commitment phobia does our Tia.'

Thank you, Sharon.

Tia closed her eyes and wished herself somewhere else. Now that Sharon had confirmed Luca's suspicions, what was there that she could say?

The conversation moved on but Tia was aware only of Luca's dark eyes resting on her from time to time and she knew that the subject was far from closed.

'So what's it like, practising medicine in the UK compared to Italy?' Richard topped up the wineglasses and the conversation shifted to more general topics.

While Luca and Richard debated the merits of various health systems, Tia moved the food round her plate, trying to work out what to say when Luca confronted her in private.

They were finishing coffee when Luca's bleeper sounded.

He pulled a face and went to use the phone, returning minutes later with an apologetic expression on his handsome face.

'They are concerned about a twin delivery,' he explained, reaching for his jacket and car keys. 'I have to go, I'm afraid. Sharon, thank you for a lovely evening. Tia?'

Tia stood up without argument, seeing a means of escape. If she left now, she'd be in bed asleep by the time he arrived home. *Which meant that they could postpone the conversation she was dreading.*

* * *

Several hours later Tia heard the sound of Luca's key in the door. She hadn't slept. Not even for a minute. Her mind was too full of what had happened at Sharon's.

And now Luca was home.

And ready to talk, no doubt.

Hearing his footsteps on the stairs she kept her eyes closed and tried to breathe steadily, knowing instinctively that he would come into her room.

The door opened and there was a long pause. Then she heard him walk across the room and the bed dipped as he sat down.

'Your parents may have been actors, *cara mia*, but they didn't pass on their talents to you,' he drawled softly, stretching out a hand and flicking on her bedside lamp. 'Has anyone ever told you that you are the master of avoidance?'

Tia burrowed deeper under the covers. 'I'm not avoiding anything,' she mumbled. 'I'm just trying to sleep.'

'Don't lie to me, Tia. You have been wide awake all evening, worrying about this conversation,' Luca said, his voice low and rough. 'I saw the expression on your face at dinner. You were horrified that I'd guessed how you felt. Horrified that I have managed to uncover a little part of what you are feeling. You are constantly hiding from me, Tia. Especially about this pregnancy. I need you to be honest with me.'

But was he being honest with her?

She lay still for a minute, feeling a lump building in her throat. 'All right.' She sat up suddenly, her fingers clutching the duvet tightly against her as if she was using it as a barrier between her and him. 'You want to know what I think of this pregnancy? Well, you're right. I am frightened. Actually, I'm terrified. I swore I would never get married and have children and suddenly—' She broke off, her breathing rapid, and wrapped her arms around her knees in a gesture of self-protection. 'I don't expect you to understand. I know that I'm nothing like any woman you've ever met before.'

'Well, that's certainly true.' He stroked her face with a gentle hand. 'But it's not true to say that I don't understand. I want to know exactly how you feel, Tia, and this time I don't want you to hold anything back. You say that you never wanted to get married and have children. Presumably because of your own childhood, no?'

Tia stared at him with dull eyes. She might as well tell him at least part of the story.

'As I told you the other night, my parents' marriage was a disaster,' she said flatly. 'My father had one affair after another—he seemed unable to commit to one woman. And then when Mum died I was passed around a string of foster-homes.'

Luca stroked a hand down her cheek. 'Did anyone try and arrange for you to be adopted?'

Tia gave a sad smile. 'Gawky, eight-year-old bereaved girls aren't that appealing. Everyone wants cute babies. And on top of that I had severe asthma as a child—no one wanted a child with an illness.'

He grimaced. 'So you ended up in a children's home.'

She nodded slowly. 'In the course of my childhood I met children who were the products of bad relationships, children who'd been abused and abandoned. Children who had no one to love them. It seemed to me that being a parent was an enormous responsibility. Probably the biggest responsibility that there is. I swore that I'd never do it.'

But she had. She was pregnant. Panic flooded her veins and her eyes flew to his.

Luca slipped his long fingers through hers and tightened his grip. 'It is true that being a parent is an enormous responsibility,' he said calmly, 'but most families manage to do an excellent job. Your past has given you a distorted view of the truth. Very few children end up in the position that you were in.'

'But for the ones who do…' Tia shook her head and her eyes filled. 'Do you have any idea what it's like? Knowing that no one wants you? It's the loneliest feeling in the world.'

Her voice was little more than a whisper and Luca muttered something under his breath and let go of her hand.

'You are not your parents, Tia.' His voice was gentle as he scooped her up and lifted her onto his lap. 'You are nothing like your parents. You will be a wonderful mother.'

'But what if I'm not?' She stared at him with wide frightened eyes. 'What if the baby is born and I don't love it?'

Having voiced her biggest fear, she closed her eyes and held her breath, waiting for his horrified reaction.

Instead, she felt his arms tighten around her. 'Is that what is worrying you? That you won't love it? That is a very common fear, you know that.' His voice was deep and very male as he soothed her. 'And some women don't love their babies immediately. I have known plenty of mothers say that they didn't instantly love their babies. For some people it is there straight away, but for others…' He gave a shrug. 'For others love must grow.'

Tia stared at him. 'Do you believe that?'

He nodded slowly. 'I know that you will love our baby.'

She swallowed. 'And what if I don't?'

Would he reject her?

He gave a half-smile. 'You will probably thump me for saying this, but you are very hormonal, *cara mia*, and you are expressing fears that most pregnant women feel at some time.'

Tia shook her head. 'That's not true. That woman in clinic today. Karen. She was so excited about it she made me feel ill. I don't feel like that, Luca. When I think about the baby I just feel panic.'

He said something in Italian and then switched to English. '*That* is why you were so upset today. I guessed as much.' His grip on her tightened reassuringly. 'It's early days, Tia. Karen had been planning a family for ages. Tha n't what happened with us. Our baby has come before we planned it and the baby isn't real to you yet. Stop worrying and trust me, Tia. Everything will be all right.'

She lifted her face and her eyes met his. The intensity of his gaze made her heart beat steadily against her ribs and he reached out and stroked a hand down her soft cheek.

He was going to kiss her.

She wanted him to kiss her. She wanted him to kiss her so badly.

His mouth hovered only a breath away from hers and she closed her eyes, her lips parting in readiness for his kiss.

Luca...

She waited in an agony of anticipation and then gave a whimper of surprise and disappointment when he lifted her firmly off his lap and tucked her back under the duvet.

'No touching,' he reminded her, his voice deep. 'We are getting to know each other, Tia, and I want that to continue. For the time being, we talk and nothing else.'

Without another word he walked out of her bedroom, closing the door firmly behind him and leaving her breathless with frustration.

How?

How could he have been so close to kissing her and resisted?

She groaned at the unfairness of it all. When she'd made the no-touching rule she'd had no idea that it would be this difficult to carry through...

Tia was working in clinic again the next morning when Luca found her.

His dark hair gleamed under the lights of the antenatal clinic and he looked strikingly handsome.

'I have arranged for you to have a scan,' he told her, coming straight to the point. 'You need to ask for an hour off.'

Tia gaped at him, outraged by his high-handedness. 'An what am I supposed to tell Sharon? We're rushed off ou feet.'

'I want you to see our baby,' he said calmly, clearl unfazed by her anger. 'You are pregnant, Tia, and you can carry on denying it.'

See the baby? What difference would seeing it make?

And was she really denying it?

Maybe she was.

Tia swallowed, her brain suddenly jumbled. Maybe tha was exactly what she was doing.

'All right.' She ignored the sudden fluttering of nerve in her stomach. 'What time is the scan?'

'Twelve o'clock,' he said immediately. 'I'll meet yo there.'

She nodded and watched him go with mixed feeling She knew that the hospital policy was to scan women : about twelve weeks, both to estimate gestational age an to detect any signs of foetal abnormality, but someho she'd managed to avoid thinking about it.

Until now.

Suddenly feeling very nervous, she went looking fc Sharon and asked her if she could take her lunch at twelv and then went back to her patients.

Clinic was incredibly busy but she managed to get awa at twelve and made her way to meet Luca.

Most routine scanning was carried out by a radiographe trained in all aspects of ultrasound, so Tia was surprised see Justin Lee, the professor of foetal medicine, waitin with Luca.

She knew that Professor Lee usually only scanned higl risk pregnancies and she looked at Luca with alarm in he eyes.

'I wanted the best, and I saw no reason to hide our re lationship,' he told her quietly, and Justin Lee extended hand and gave her a warm smile.

'We've all been following Luca's work on pre-term delivery with great interest,' he said. 'I read the last paper he had published and it's been a pleasure to meet him in person and even more of a pleasure to discover that his girlfriend is pregnant! I happen to have a free half-hour and Luca wanted me to do your scan. Is that all right with you?'

Tia nodded slowly. She could hardly refuse to be scanned by someone who was reputedly one of the country's leading foetal medicine specialists!

Justin settled himself on a stool next to the machine and Luca stared over his shoulder.

'This is a state-of-the-art machine,' Justin told him, and proceeded to give Luca the low-down of its capabilities, most of which was beyond Tia's comprehension.

She lay tense and unsmiling as Justin started to scan her, her mind suddenly clouded with panic.

What if something was wrong with the baby?

As if sensing her distress, Luca moved from his place by Justin's side and settled himself next to her, taking her hand in his and encouraging her to look at the screen.

'Watch this,' he urged, his deep voice velvety smooth. 'It's magic, Tia. Our baby.'

Our baby.

Reluctantly she glanced at the screen and her gaze was caught and held by what she saw. The image was so clear she gave a little gasp and Luca's grip on her hand tightened.

'That's an arm,' he told her, watching the screen as Justin carried on with the scan, 'and the head, can you see?'

Oh, yes, she could see.

Suddenly Tia felt as though someone was squeezing her heart.

Their baby...

'He's very active,' Justin said with a smile, pressing some buttons to take measurements.

'He?' Tia's voice was little more than a croak and she cleared her throat.

Justin gave her a smile. 'Not necessarily. I confess tha I'm horribly sexist and call all babies he at this stage.'

He made some notes and pointed out some other thing he thought would interest them. All too soon it was ove and Tia was slipping off the couch and fastening her shoes

She straightened up and for the first time in her preg nancy her hand crept to her stomach. Suddenly the fea went and she felt incredibly protective.

She only half listened while Justin discussed the result of the scan with Luca, her mind almost completely focuse on the living being she was nurturing within her body.

'I'll leave you two alone for a few minutes,' Justin said gathering up the notes and handing something to Tia.

'What's this?'

She stared down at the photograph in her hands and he vision blurred.

'It's your baby,' Justin said quietly, a smile in his voice 'Congratulations.'

He left the room, closing the door quietly behind him and Luca took the photograph out of her hands and place it on the couch.

'Does it seem so frightening now that you've seen him? His voice was deep and rough and she shook her hea slowly.

'No. No, it doesn't.'

He slid his fingers into her blonde hair and tilted her fac up to his.

'How did it feel, Tia, seeing our baby for the first time? His eyes were gentle. Huge tears welled up in her eyes an rolled down her cheeks.

'It was amazing,' she whispered, a smile breaking ou on her face. 'I hadn't really thought about the baby as person until today, but when I saw him wriggling around…

'It was very moving,' Luca agreed, brushing her tear away with a gentle hand. 'And now maybe it's time to te the people you work with that you are pregnant. At leas then they are less likely to take advantage of your good nature and overwork you.'

Tia nodded. Suddenly, instead of being an overwhelming problem, the baby was something infinitely precious, to be protected.

'I suppose I'd better get back to the clinic.'

'Don't forget to book yourself in with Dan,' Luca reminded her, and she smiled.

'Has anyone ever told you that you're overbearing?'

Luca gave a smouldering smile. 'You,' he murmured in a deep voice. 'Frequently.'

Just looking into his dark eyes made desire curl deep in her stomach and she forced herself to pull away from him and gather up her things.

She savoured the newly powerful feelings that she had for the baby, marvelling at the way they'd erupted from her heart with no warning. How could she have been so frightened of this baby one minute and so excited the next? It was like a miracle and she snuggled the tender feelings around herself like a blanket.

Suddenly all her fears had gone. She knew that she was going to love this baby because she already loved it. She'd fallen in love with it the moment she'd seen it, just as she had with Luca.

Luca…

It had been love at first sight.

The moment she'd seen him she'd known that he was the only man for her.

And now, the more she knew of him the more she loved him.

He'd known that she needed to see the baby. He'd known that once it had become real she would love it, and he'd been right.

And she knew that she was going to be a good mother.

*   *   *

Tia spoke to Sharon the next morning. 'I think it's time I saw a doctor.'

'At last.' Sharon put her hands on her hips and gave a nod of approval. 'Anyone in mind?'

'Luca wants Dan Sutherland.'

'Good choice,' Sharon said approvingly. 'He's the best there is. Not that you have any worries, with Luca hovering in the wings. He's excellent, Tia. He's got marvellous instincts. You should have seen him yesterday with this difficult delivery that we had. I've never seen anyone so skilled using the ventouse.'

Tia felt a flash of pride. Luca was a very skilled doctor, there was no doubt about that.

'I'll talk to the staff in clinic and see if they can arrange for Dan to fit you in right away.' Sharon picked up the phone and punched in the number, still talking to Tia. 'I assume this isn't something you're trying to keep secret any more?'

Tia shook her head, thinking of Justin Lee. 'Luca seems to be pretty open about our relationship...' She told Sharon about the scan and Sharon's eyes widened.

'Justin Lee did it himself? My, my, you were honoured.' She turned her attention back to the phone. 'Janet? It's me.' Quickly she outlined Tia's situation. 'So can Dan fit her in this afternoon?'

Tia waited while Sharon finished the conversation and replaced the receiver.

'No problem.' Sharon smiled at her friend. 'He'll see you at the end of clinic.'

'Thanks,' Tia said, getting to her feet. 'I need to get back down and do some work or poor Janet may not be so accommodating.'

'Don't overdo it,' Sharon said sternly and Tia gave a wry smile.

'You sound like Luca.'

'Do I? Well, he's bound to be over-protective.' Sharon

gave a short laugh. 'Obstetricians make notoriously para-noid fathers. Unless we keep an eye on him he'll probably have you sectioned at 37 weeks just to be on the safe side.'

Tia laughed. She and Luca hadn't actually got round to talking about the delivery yet.

She made her way back down to clinic and got on with her work.

Halfway through the afternoon she saw a woman who was thirteen weeks pregnant and had severe vomiting.

'I feel so awful,' the young woman confessed, her face pale and wan. 'I can't keep anything down and the minute I see someone else with food I'm sick.'

'You poor thing.' Knowing just how ill she'd felt herself, Tia was very sympathetic. 'Could you hop on the scales for me, Mary? I'll weigh you.'

Mary slipped off her shoes and pulled a face as she climbed onto the scales. 'I know I've lost weight,' she mumbled, glancing anxiously at the reading. 'My clothes are all baggy. I haven't even had to buy any maternity clothes.'

'You can step down now.' Tia checked her weight against the last reading and frowned. The weight loss was significant.

'Is it bad?' Mary gave a sigh and sat back down, obvi-ously feeling as ill as she looked. 'You can be honest—as I say, my clothes are falling off me so I'm already prepared for bad news.'

'It's not bad news exactly,' Tia said quickly. 'But we do need to check you over. I'll just fetch a doctor and then we can talk it through in more detail.'

She found Luca about to drink a cup of coffee and he gave a wry smile.

'I thought a coffee-break was too good to be true.' He stood up and lifted an eyebrow. 'What's the problem?'

She briefed him quickly and he followed her back along the corridor to see Mary.

'By the way, I've just been to ITU to see Sue Gibbs.' A look of satisfaction crossed his handsome face as he gave her the news. 'She's definitely on the mend. Her blood pressure is down and she's sitting up and talking. They're planning to take her to visit the baby later.'

Tia's eyes shone with delight. 'That's fantastic!'

Luca nodded, pausing as they reached the clinic. 'She was lucky she came into hospital when she did.'

'She was lucky she had you when she got here,' Tia said gruffly, and Luca gave her a keen look.

'You were the one who got that airway in while she was fitting, Tia.'

'Teamwork,' she said stoutly, and he smiled his agreement.

'Teamwork.'

They walked into the room to see Mary and Luca introduced himself and flicked through the notes. Then he examined her, carefully explaining everything that he was doing.

Halfway through the examination Dr Ford appeared, her eyes immediately locking onto Luca.

'Sorry I'm late for clinic, Dr Zattoni,' she breathed. 'I was watching Dan Sutherland section a lady with twins.'

'No problem.' Luca quickly updated her and then turned back to Mary. 'I know that this isn't what you want to hear, but you must spend a few days in hospital while we sort out this vomiting. We need to try and find a cause and we need to try and stop the sickness.'

'I thought the cause was pregnancy,' Mary muttered, and Luca inclined his head.

'That's true but sometimes there are identifiable causes. I want to run some tests.'

Mary stared at him. 'What for?'

He rested one muscular thigh on the couch and folded his arms across his chest, totally relaxed as he talked to his patient. 'I want to do thyroid function tests—sometimes excessive vomiting can be caused by thyroid or adrenal dysfunction.' He ticked the tests off on his fingers. 'I want to take some blood so that we can judge how much fluid we should be giving you, and I want you to have a scan straight away.'

Mary sighed. 'How long will I be in hospital?'

'Hard to say,' Luca said honestly, his shrug making him seem more Italian than ever. 'Do you have problems at home?'

'Not at home.' Mary pulled a face. 'At work. I'm a lawyer and taking time off for something like this is frowned on. In fact, my whole pregnancy is frowned on, to be honest. It's just a massive inconvenience to them.'

'And to you?' Luca's voice was soft. 'How do you feel about the baby, Mary?'

Mary paused. 'I thought I could have it all,' she admitted at last. 'I was determined to carry on as I always have, working fourteen hour days until the day the baby arrives, but I never imagined that I'd feel so awful.'

Luca was very still. 'And is your job so important to you?'

Mary seemed to think for a minute. 'Well, I always thought it was,' she said slowly, 'but when they're so unsympathetic, it makes you wonder what it's all for.'

'Pregnancy is a very special time,' Luca said quietly. 'You should take care of yourself.'

'Yes.' Mary nodded and gave him a wan smile. 'Perhaps you ought to have a word with my employers.'

'Willingly.' Luca was totally serious and Mary gave a sigh.

'Only joking. I'll have to face the music myself and tell them I need some time off.'

Tia compared Mary's story with Sharon's reaction to her own pregnancy. She was lucky that the people she worked with were so sympathetic and supportive. Obviously it wasn't the case for everyone.

Luca turned to Dr Ford and issued a stream of orders which left Tia's head reeling. 'Call the ward and admit her, please, and then get a line in and take blood for PCV, U and Es, TFTs. Make sure that the nurses know to chart all the losses and send a urine sample so that we can exclude a UTI.'

Dr Ford scribbled frantically on her pad. 'And shall I arrange a scan?'

Luca nodded. 'Please.'

He stood up and smiled at Mary. 'I hope that a good rest might be enough to sort this problem out. I'll pop and see you later tonight but stop worrying about work.'

Tia tried not to look at his broad shoulders or the powerful muscles of his thighs. Maybe if he'd never made love to her it wouldn't be so bad, but knowing just exactly what Luca could make her feel was starting to drive her to distraction. They'd come so close to kissing the night before, and if she hadn't made the silly no-touching rule she knew that they would have ended up in bed.

As far as she was concerned, the no-touching rule could finish at any time.

She was sure of her feelings and touching wasn't going to change them.

She was totally, utterly, crazily in love with Luca.

But he still hadn't told her about his past.

CHAPTER SEVEN

THE weeks leading up to Christmas were busy and Tia barely saw Luca at home. There was a nasty flu bug going round the hospital and consequently they were very short-staffed.

'You look exhausted,' she muttered one morning as she made them both a quick breakfast before they left for the hospital. 'Can't you take today off?'

'Unless I catch flu, there's no chance.' Luca curved a lean brown hand around his coffee-mug and gave a mocking smile. 'Dan's away this morning and I'm covering his theatre list as well as my own workload. Still, tomorrow is Christmas Eve and we have two whole days to ourselves.'

Tia's eyes widened and she shook her head, puzzled. 'But I'm working.'

'Not any more. Sharon and Dan put their heads together and decided that we need Christmas off,' Luca told her with a smile. 'So tomorrow we're going to buy a tree and do some shopping. We're having a proper family Christmas.'

A family Christmas?

Tia looked at him and swallowed hard. Normally she hated Christmas because she was either on her own or working.

'I—I don't usually bother with a tree,' she confessed, and he gave her a slow smile that made her insides churn.

'Well, this year you're bothering. We're buying the biggest tree in the forest.'

Caught up by his enthusiasm, Tia laughed. 'The ceilings are too low.'

He gave a careless shrug. 'So we cut the top off.' He

glanced at his watch and rolled his eyes. 'Come on, or we'll be late.'

Tia had to admit that his stamina was awesome. Despite the punishing hours he'd been working, he still looked relaxed and alert. If it had been her, she would have been in a coma!

'I'm looking forward to having two whole days alone with you. I'm sorry I haven't been home much lately.' His dark eyes were watchful and she shifted slightly under his gaze.

'It doesn't matter. I've been pretty tired, to be honest. I'm usually in bed by nine o'clock anyway if the baby stops kicking for long enough to let me sleep.'

He gave a slight smile and his eyes flickered down to her now rounded stomach. 'He is wearing his mama out and he hasn't arrived yet.'

'Yes.' She blushed slightly. Since that night when they'd almost kissed, he hadn't been near her.

They'd continued to talk and share confidences but he'd kept a distance from her and she didn't know what to do about it.

She'd set the rules but she didn't know how to tell him that she didn't want to live by them any more.

No touching.

She must have been mad. She wanted him to touch her so badly it was a physical ache.

Maybe he didn't want her any more.

Tia was spending more and more time on the antenatal ward where they were always desperate for staff. As it was Christmas, they discharged as many patients as they could, but they were still short-staffed which meant they had to close one ward and merge the antenatal patients with the postnatal patients.

'Another brainchild of the powers that be,' Sharon complained, after another argument with the hospital managers. 'Just because it makes sense on paper, it doesn't mean that it works in reality. Don't these people ever think about the emotional side of things? I've got women with high-risk pregnancies forced to be side by side with women who have just had bouncing, healthy babies. Talk about cruel!'

Tia gave a rueful nod. It *was* cruel and she'd seen the yearning in some of the women's eyes as they'd walked past the breastfeeding room.

Mary, the woman they'd admitted from clinic suffering from hyperemesis gravidarum, had spent several weeks in hospital being rehydrated before finally being discharged.

'It's such a wonderful relief to have stopped feeling sick,' she confided in Tia with a wide smile. 'I just hope it doesn't start again.'

'What happened with your job?' Tia helped Mary zip up her holdall and get ready for her husband, who was collecting her. 'Did they give you the time off?'

'With a great deal of complaint,' Mary said, with a sigh. 'I can see now that I'm not going to be able to carry on in with my current job when I have the baby. I thought that I could do both—you know, the nanny and the high-powered career—but it doesn't work, does it? Not if you want to see the child.'

'No, I suppose not.' Tia bit her lip as she looked at Mary, wondering what she was going to do herself. Luca had grudgingly accepted that she would work while she was pregnant but they hadn't discussed what would happen once the baby was born.

'It's funny how you change,' Mary said softly, slipping on her shoes and picking up her coat. 'I used to think that I wouldn't give up my job for anyone, but now I think that I wouldn't give up being with my baby for anyone.'

Tia nodded slowly. 'I suppose you just have to find an employer who is willing to be flexible.'

Mary laughed and smiled as she saw her husband walking onto the ward. 'Yes, well, that certainly isn't my lot! They're about as flexible as an iron rod. Thanks, Tia.

You've been really great this last few weeks. Thank Dr Zattoni for me, too, will you?'

Tia nodded and walked with her to the door. 'Take care now.'

She watched Mary go and then returned to the ward. Her day was incredibly busy and at three o'clock a woman was admitted with premature rupture of membranes.

'I felt this rush of water down my leg,' she told Tia, 'and at first I thought I'd wet myself—so embarrassing—but then I realised that it must be to do with the baby so I rang the labour ward. What happens now?'

Tia gave her a reassuring smile. 'We need to examine you to see what's going on.'

'But it will be a dry birth, won't it?' The woman looked at her with scared eyes and Tia shook her head.

'There's no such thing as a dry birth, Chloe,' she said calmly. 'That's an old wives' tale. Women used to think that if their waters broke early the birth would be dry, but your waters will always break before the baby is born, even if it's a last-minute thing. It doesn't affect your labour in any way. What it can affect is the health of the baby if your waters break a long time before you go into labour.'

Chloe's eyes widened as she struggled into the unflattering hospital gown. 'How?'

'The fluid around the baby is held in place by a membrane and it means that the baby is totally enclosed in a little bag,' Tia explained carefully. 'If your membranes rupture, the baby is theoretically exposed to germs from the outside world. The most important aspect of looking after you is to check that you don't develop an infection.'

She checked the notes and saw that Chloe was thirty-five weeks pregnant, but before she could examine her Luca arrived with Dr Ford and three students in tow.

'Mrs Hunter, I'm Dr Zattoni.' Luca shook Chloe's hand and gave her a warm smile. 'Could you tell me what happened?'

Chloe looked at him anxiously and repeated her story.

'And you have no pain? Nothing that makes you think you could be in labour?'

Chloe shook her head. 'Will you have to deliver the baby?'

'Not necessarily. A pregnancy can sometimes continue for several weeks without problems. Our concern is to ensure that an infection does not develop.'

Chloe nodded. 'Yes, that's what Tia told me.'

Luca's eyes flickered to Tia and she flushed under his warm gaze.

'All the signs are that the baby is well at the moment. We will do some tests right away and then make some decisions on the best way to manage things.'

Chloe looked at him anxiously. 'What sort of tests? Will I have to stay in over Christmas?'

Luca was noncommittal. 'Possibly. I need to examine you internally to take a sterile sample of the liquor—that is the fluid that surrounds the baby,' he explained. 'That will give us an idea of lung maturity—how well your baby will be able to cope if it is born early. Then I want you to have another scan, just to check that everything is still looking good with the baby.' He turned to Tia. 'What's her temperature?'

Tia nodded and gestured to the chart. 'It's normal. Thirty-six point eight. We'll check it four-hourly.'

'Good.' Luca gave a brief nod and then turned to Dr Ford and gave her some instructions, breaking off as his bleeper sounded.

He lifted it out of his pocket and grimaced. 'Labour ward. I'd better go.' He glanced at Chloe with a smile. 'Tia will arrange for you to have a scan and I will be back to examine you shortly.'

But he didn't reappear. Tia was about to bleep him when Phil Warren, one of the registrars from the other obstetric team, arrived on the ward to examine Chloe.

'Sorry about the delay. It's a nightmare on the labour ward,' Phil muttered in an undertone as he scrubbed and prepared to take the specimen. 'A woman has ruptured her uterus. Luca's trapped in Theatre.'

'What?' Tia stared at him in horror and disbelief. Rupture of the uterus was extremely uncommon in the UK. 'Was it a previous Caesarean section scar?'

Phil nodded. 'She'd already been admitted in labour but the doctor didn't spot it. It was Luca who suspected it— he's seen it before apparently. Anyway, he whipped her into Theatre just in time. She had a massive haemorrhage and it was touch and go with the baby.'

Tia stared at him in horror. 'What did Luca do?'

'Luca?' Phil gave a dry laugh. 'You know him. Mr Cool. He got the baby out so fast we didn't see his fingers move. Funny, really. Every other surgeon I know would have been at least a little tense in that situation but not Luca. He doesn't know the meaning of the word panic. The only slightly stressful moment was when he lapsed into Italian and no one had a clue what he was talking about.'

'And is the mother all right?'

Phil nodded. 'I think so. When I left, Luca had stopped the bleeding, but it looked as though he might have to do a hysterectomy.'

'Poor woman,' Tia said softly.

'Yes, but she's lucky that it was Luca,' Phil said. 'That was a tricky piece of surgery and he undoubtedly saved two lives. I don't think I could have done what he did. He's a bit of a hero on the labour ward today!'

Tia felt a glow of pride. The more she saw of him, the more she realised what a skilled obstetrician Luca was.

Later that afternoon she was moved to labour ward to help out and discovered that Sally Clarke, the woman with the breech presentation, had been admitted earlier in the day.

'Luca is still promising to deliver her vaginally,' Sharon

muttered as she went through the notes with Tia. 'If it was anyone but him I'd be protesting madly, but he's adamant and he does seem to know what he's doing. Can you go and assist? If things go wrong we'll need some extra bodies and, anyway, you know her, don't you? She was asking for you earlier.'

Tia hurried to the labour room and pushed open the door.

Sally was lying quietly, holding tightly to her husband's and as she listened to Luca.

'You have an epidural in place,' Luca told her, 'because don't want you to push at the wrong time.'

Tia knew that it also meant that he could use forceps if e needed to.

'I'm never, ever having another baby,' Sally wailed, gripping her husband so hard that her knuckles turned white.

He looked at Luca in desperation and Luca gave him a reassuring smile.

'Everything is fine, I promise you.' He examined Sally carefully and then glanced at Dr Ford. 'This is an extended breech—so that the presenting part is the buttocks. It is the most common type of breech presentation and much safer than a footling breech.' He gave Sally a smile. 'Sometimes they come out feet first and that gives us more of a head-che.'

Sally gave him a wavering smile, her trust in him clear to see. 'What if he gets stuck?'

Luca shook his head. 'He won't get stuck.' He was to-lly sure of himself. 'We know the size of the baby from he scan that you had, and we know the size of your pelvis om the X-rays.'

Dr Ford stepped closer, her arm brushing Luca's. 'Did he have lateral pelvimetry?'

Luca nodded. 'It shows the shape of the sacrum and ives accurate measurements of the anteroposterior diam-ers of the pelvic brim, cavity and outlet.' He looked at

Sally and gave a sexy, lopsided smile. 'This baby will fi
Sally. Trust me.'

He glanced at the CTG machine and placed a hand o
Sally's abdomen. 'You have another contraction coming—
I want you to push when I say.' His eyes flickered to Tia
'Can you chase the paediatrician for me, please?'

Tia slipped out of the room and called Switchboard
knowing that the delivery wasn't far away. She knew tha
lots of obstetricians chose to deliver all breech presenta
tions by Caesarean section because they were afraid of li
igation. It was typical of Luca that he'd allowed Sally t
have the delivery that she wanted. His experience and in
stincts had told him that a vaginal delivery should be saf
and he wasn't going to let other people's opinions dent hi
self-confidence.

She spoke quickly to the paediatrician who assured he
that he was on his way, and then returned to the room t
find that Luca had delivered the baby's buttocks and legs

Luca gently pulled down a loop of cord. 'It's importan
to avoid traction on the umbilicus or the cord might tear
he murmured to Dr Ford, 'but it is also important not t
manipulate or stretch the cord because it can cause spasm

Dr Ford leaned closer to Luca. 'What happens now?'

'The uterine contractions and the width of the buttock
will bring the shoulders down onto the pelvic floor,' Luc
told her, 'and then they'll rotate.'

He glanced up and smiled at Sally. 'You're doing bri
liantly. Nearly there.'

Tia watched as he grasped the baby by the iliac cres
and tilted it to free the shoulder.

'I need a towel.'

Tia had warmed one in readiness and she handed it t
him quickly.

Luca wrapped it around the baby's hips, improving h
grip and also helping to keep it warm.

As the anterior shoulder appeared he placed two finger

over the clavicle and swept them round to release the arm
and then grasped the ankles to free the posterior arm.

'Just the head to go, Sally,' Luca said quietly, infinitely
patient as he waited, refusing to hurry nature. 'I wait a
couple of minutes and the weight of the body will bring
the head onto the pelvic floor.'

Dr Ford looked at him with open admiration. 'How will
you deliver the head? Will you use forceps?'

'No.' Luca didn't take his eyes off the patient. 'It doesn't
really matter how you deliver the head as long as it's slow
and controlled. That's the vital thing to remember. Tia, are
you ready to clear the airway?'

'Yes.' Tia got ready with the suction and held her breath
while he grasped the baby's feet and, with gentle traction,
swept them in an arc over Sally's abdomen, allowing the
lower half of the baby's head to slip out.

She quickly aspirated the nose and mouth, making sure
that the air passages were cleared.

'All right, Sally,' Luca's voice was deep and controlled,
'I want you to take regular breaths while I deliver the rest
of the head.'

He took another three minutes to deliver the baby, allowing the slow release of pressures and tensions on the skull
before finally placing the bawling child in the arms of his
mother.

'You have a beautiful son,' Luca said huskily, a smile
playing around his firm mouth. 'Congratulations. And well
done. You were very brave.'

Tears spilled down Sally's cheeks and she reached out a
hand to Luca. 'Thank you,' she said, the words choked as
she battled with tears. 'If it hadn't been for you I know I
would have had a section and I would have hated that. You
made it special.'

Luca squeezed her hand. 'You're very welcome,' he said
quietly, stepping back as the paediatrician moved closer to
take the baby.

It was way past the end of her shift but Tia didn't want to leave until the placenta had been delivered and Luca had finished.

She wanted to go home with him.

As they made for the car park Dr Ford caught up with them and put a hand on Luca's arm, her expression warm.

'You were just amazing in there. There's so much I want to ask you. Shall we go for a drink?'

Tia almost gasped at the audacity of the woman but relaxed slightly as she felt Luca's arm slip round her shoulders, pulling her close to him. 'Not tonight—I've finished work and Tia and I are off until Boxing Day. There'll be plenty of time to answer your questions when I'm back.'

A warm glow spread through Tia's veins as his grip tightened. He was making it clear to Dr Ford that a meeting with her would be nothing but professional.

'Fine.' Dr Ford gave a bright smile that barely hid her disappointment and swung her dark hair over her shoulders. 'I'll see you after Christmas, then.'

'Indeed.' Luca took Tia's hand firmly and led her to the car. 'Get in before you collapse. You must be exhausted. You shouldn't have stayed for that breech delivery.'

Tia's expression softened. 'I like Sally and—' She broke off and blushed slightly. 'And I wanted to watch you.'

Mild amusement lit his eyes. 'Was I being tested? Did I pass?'

His lazy drawl made her blood heat and she struggled to keep her breathing steady.

Oh, yes, he'd passed.

'You were great,' she said gruffly. 'Most doctors would have just sectioned her to avoid the risk of litigation. Dr Ford was right. You were amazing.'

He gave a shrug. 'I don't think so. There was no reason why she couldn't deliver normally,' he said. 'She had a good-sized pelvis and the baby wasn't big, she had a normal volume of liquor, no pre-eclampsia and no foetal distress. It was perfectly reasonable to let her deliver on her own.'

'And what about the woman earlier, the ruptured uterus?' Tia turned to look at him. 'Did you have to do a hysterectomy?'

'No.' Luca shook his head and raked a hand through his hair. 'She was lucky. We managed to repair it.'

Lucky.

Lucky to have Luca.

'Luca…' She turned to face him, feeling suddenly impossibly shy. 'Thanks.'

He yanked on the handbrake and frowned at her. 'For what?'

'For not going for a drink with Dr Ford.' She swallowed hard. 'She's very attractive…'

'And why should that make a difference?' He lifted an eyebrow, his expression deadly serious. 'It's you I want, Tia.'

Did he?

Warmth spread through her veins and for the first time she was tempted to believe him. He certainly didn't behave like a man who was in love with another woman.

He gave her a slow smile and turned the key in the ignition. 'Come on, let's go home and get some sleep. We're going to have a busy day tomorrow.'

'How about that one?' Luca pulled the collar of his wool coat up and narrowed his eyes as he looked at the trees.

Tia picked her way over the muddy path and squinted at the price. 'Luca, it's a blue spruce! It costs a fortune.'

Luca shrugged indifferently. 'Do you like it?'

Tia looked at it again and tried to imagine it covered in delicate white lights. 'It's gorgeous, but—'

'Then we have it,' Luca announced arrogantly, looking around for the man who was helping haul the trees to people's cars.

Fifteen minutes later they were bumping down the forest track with the tree half hanging out of the boot of the car.

'I hope we don't meet a policeman,' Tia said, glancing back anxiously to check that the tree was still mostly in the boot. 'Is it going to fit?'

Luca nodded with his usual confidence. 'It will fit.'

It did. In fact, it was perfect, filling their cosy living room with a musky smell of forest and pine needles.

Tia fingered the needles with awe. 'This is a dream tree.'

'No.' He tucked his fingers under her chin and lifted her face to look at him. 'It's not a dream, Tia, it's real. Remember that.'

He bent his head slowly and brushed a kiss against her mouth and then paused, obviously fighting some internal battle.

She held her breath, wanting him to kiss her properly, but he released her suddenly and gave her a tense smile.

'Come on. We haven't started our Christmas shopping yet.'

The town was crowded and they were soon caught up in the excitement of Christmas, smiling at the groups of carol singers gathered on street corners and admiring the decorations in the shop windows.

They stopped at a small café to drink hot chocolate and eat sandwiches, and Tia's face glowed with excitement.

'You know something,' she said, her hands wrapped around her steaming mug of chocolate, 'this feels like someone else's Christmas.'

He sat back in his chair and gave her a puzzled frown. 'Someone else's?'

'Yes.' She broke off, her cheeks flushed, suddenly shy. 'I was always on the outside looking in at Christmas. It's one of those times of year that always seems to be perfect for everyone else. I know that it isn't, of course,' she said quickly, 'but it just seems that way when you're lonely. This is the sort of Christmas that I always envied everyone else for having. You know, the tree, the lights, sharing it with someone you—'

Dear God, she'd almost confessed that she loved him!

Luca was suddenly very still and when he finally spoke his voice was hoarse. 'Someone that you…?'

Tia's heart thumped steadily. 'Enjoy being with,' she said quickly. 'Someone you enjoy being with.'

His eyes searched hers for a long moment and suddenly he looked tired. 'Well, this year it isn't someone else's Christmas, Tia. It's yours and mine.'

As their eyes locked, her heart started to thump.

Suddenly she didn't care about Luisa or whether or not she'd been part of Luca's life before she herself had met him. Either way, she was entirely sure that the woman wasn't a part of his life now.

'Luca…' how could she tell him that she wanted to end the no-touching rule?

'Are you ready to go home?'

She nodded and wrapped her scarf loosely around her neck, dipping her head in its soft folds to hide her blush.

Back at the cottage, they lit a fire and decorated the blue spruce, smiling with satisfaction as they looked at the results of their handiwork.

Tia had found a holly tree at the bottom of the garden and had decorated the hearth with twists of greenery and berries.

'This is wonderful.' She smothered a yawn and stretched herself full length on the sofa, relishing the view of the tree. It was a fairy-tale Christmas tree, covered in tiny, delicate white lights and a few tasteful silver decorations. And under it were presents, gaily wrapped and tied with ribbons of various colours. She knew that Luca had put them there and she smiled at him gratefully. 'Thank you, Luca.'

'Prego.' A smile touched his eyes and he knelt down to tend to the fire, throwing on another log and giving it a prod.

His black jumper pulled across the powerful muscles of his shoulders as he leaned forward and his jeans were tight over his thighs.

Suddenly her throat dried and she swung her legs off the sofa and stood up.

'Luca…'

He put the poker down on the hearth and turned, his eyes darkening as they clashed with hers.

'Luca, I don't think… I— Would you—?' She broke off, blushing furiously but he rose to his feet in a fluid movement and walked slowly towards her.

She waited, breathless, for him to speak, but he didn't. Instead he stopped only inches away from her, his eyes still burning into hers. And then he lowered his head and covered her mouth with his, lifting his hands slowly and stroking his fingers down her cheeks as he kissed her.

His hands slid round the back of her head, angling her face so that he had better access to her mouth, and she felt the tip of his tongue slide between her lips.

Her body started to tremble and she kissed him back, her tongue tangling with his, her hands sliding under the wool of his jumper and settling on the silken smoothness of his hot flesh.

There was surely no one else in the world who could kiss like Luca.

She didn't feel him move, but suddenly she was lying on the soft rug in front of the flickering fire. They were both breathing rapidly and he stared down at her for a long moment, as if unsure about something.

Surely he wasn't going to change his mind? Not now…

'Luca.' She slid her hands further under his jumper, loving the feel of his hard muscles, loving his strength. Impatient to feel more of him, she pushed the soft fabric up his body and he sat back on his heels and dragged the garment over his head, throwing it carelessly onto the floor next to them.

Tia could barely breathe. Impatient for more, she lifted er hands and reached for his zip.

He smiled. A wicked, intimate smile that made her groan n desperation.

'Patience, *cara mia*.' He lowered himself onto her, care-ully supporting his weight on his elbows, and this time his iss was hot and purposeful, and she knew with a shiver f excitement that this was a kiss that was going all the vay.

It was like holding a flame to dry timber. Something nside her ignited and the flames spread, licking through er trembling, quivering body

Her hands slid behind his neck, drawing him closer, and er heart thudded uncontrollably as he kissed her with a avage passion.

Somehow the buttons of her dress were undone and he ragged his mouth away from hers, his breathing laboured, is eyes dark with need as he wrenched the dress down her ody. Frantic to feel him against her she used her legs to ick it away, her heart pounding as she felt his long, skilled ngers slip inside the elastic of her panties.

It had been so long…

His name on her lips was barely more than a whisper as e touched her intimately, as only he ever had, his fingers vorking a magic that left her shaking with need.

Impatiently she pushed his trousers down his hips, feel-ng the comforting weight of his muscular body press down n her as he parted her thighs. She felt his hard hands on er buttocks as he guided her closer to him and then he aused.

He said something in Italian that she didn't understand, esitating for just long enough to drive her wild with frus-ration.

'Luca, please…' She lifted her hips towards him and he ltered his position, entering her smoothly and slowly, with

none of the fierce desperation that had characterised thei
previous encounters.

But his touch was all the more arousing for its unusua
gentleness. Instead of slaking their need with driving force
he took her slowly, introducing her to an eroticism tha
she'd never known before. Hypnotised by the heat in hi
eyes, she gazed up at him, the incredible intimacy betwee
them making her breathless. In the past there had been a
edge of violence to their love-making, a mutual desperatio
that had driven them both wild. But this time his move
ments were slow and deliberate, building the excitemen
between them to an almost intolerable level.

Still holding his gaze, she slid her hands over his har
buttocks, urging him still closer, and she felt him mov
deep inside her, filling her and driving her towards com
pletion.

Then he lowered his dark head and his mouth closed ove
hers again, his tongue touching hers, tasting, seducing unti
she felt a throbbing need build inside her. As spasms o
pleasure convulsed her body she felt him tighten his gri
and knew that he'd reached the same pinnacle.

She held him tightly, her eyes squeezed closed as sh
tried to bring herself back to earth, tried to cope with th
turmoil of her emotions.

Despite all her efforts, tears stung her eyelids and sli
down her cheeks. He'd made love to her so gently, so pos
sessively, and yet he still hadn't said that he loved her.

Was he still thinking about Luisa?

'I'm sorry. Did I hurt you?' His rough voice teased he
sensitised nerve endings and she shivered as he rolled ont
his back, taking her with him.

'No.' She leaned her head on his muscular chest, tryin
to hide her tears, but he slipped a hand under her chin an
tilted her face towards him.

'If I didn't hurt you, why are you crying?'

What could she say? *Because I missed you? Because I love you and you don't love me?*

His arms tightened around her and she closed her eyes, revelling in the physical contact that she'd denied herself for so long. It was so good to be near him, to be held by him.

'You've never made love to me like that before,' she said, her cheeks growing pink under his steady gaze.

'Slowly, you mean?' He gave a wry smile. 'You and I were never very good at taking our time, but this time I was worried about the baby.' His gruff statement made her heart twist.

'You're an obstetrician. You should know better than anyone that making love doesn't hurt the baby.' So that was why he'd been so unusually gentle.

'You haven't answered my question.' He lifted a hand and stroked the tears away from her face, his eyes searching. 'I broke the no-touching rule, didn't I? Is that why you're crying? Are you angry with me?'

His unusual self-doubt touched her.

'No.' How could she possibly be angry? She'd wanted him as badly as he'd wanted her.

She just wished that he loved her.

A frown touched his smooth dark brows. 'Tia?'

How could she tell him the truth? That making love had just confirmed what she already knew. That he was the only man in the world she ever wanted to be with.

'I'm fine. Merry Christmas, Luca.'

The frown disappeared and he smiled. 'Merry Christmas.'

She closed her eyes and nestled against his chest, fighting back the tears again. She wasn't going to cry. She was going to enjoy the moment. All right, so Luca didn't love her, but he found her attractive and she was expecting his baby.

That would just have to be enough.

CHAPTER EIGHT

JANUARY was bitterly cold and Tia threw herself into he
work and concentrated on preparing herself mentally fc
the arrival of their baby.

Her relationship with Luca was becoming closer by th
day. And as for their love-making… She closed her eye
and felt her heart miss a beat. It was so spectacular that
was hard to believe that he really didn't love her. In fac
sometimes when they were in bed he was so tender wit
her that she could almost convince herself that he *did*.

Which was ridiculous, of course, she reminded herse
firmly, because he'd never once told her that he loved he
in all the months they'd been together.

Fortunately the weeks seemed to fly by and she had t
be fitted for a larger uniform to accommodate the growin
evidence of her pregnancy.

At work things were as busy as ever but Sharon wa
careful not to give her too heavy a workload.

'If you deliver early it will just be extra work for us
she teased one morning as they were sharing a coffee o
the postnatal ward. 'How are you feeling?'

Tia smoothed a hand over her swollen abdomen. 'Big
she admitted with a rueful smile. 'Big and clumsy. An
what's worrying me is how on earth it's going to com
out.'

She hadn't mentioned her fears to anyone but the thougl
of the labour was beginning to worry her.

But at least she was excited about the baby now. Eve
though she was a midwife and knew the theory better tha
most, she still devoured pregnancy magazines and read ev
erything she could get her hands on.

Sharon grinned at her. 'Is Luca anxious?'

'Luca?' Tia looked at her with surprise and then smiled.
You're joking, aren't you? When have you ever seen Luca
nxious about anything?'

'Never. You're right.' Sharon nodded agreement. 'He's
he coolest doctor I've ever worked with but, still, you are
is wife and obstetricians behave differently with their
vives.'

Tia frowned thoughtfully.

Was Luca anxious?

He certainly didn't seem to be. *Unlike her.*

Fortunately for Tia, the postnatal ward was very busy
nd she didn't really have time to dwell on her own
houghts and fears.

'he weeks passed quickly and she was halfway through an
arly shift in the thirty-third week of her pregnancy when
he felt a stabbing pain low in her abdomen.

She gave a soft gasp and stopped dead, clutching the
otes that she'd been about to return to the trolley.

The pain gripped her fiercely and then vanished, leaving
er tense and anxious.

What had caused it?

She rubbed a hand over the curve of her abdomen, trying
) be rational. Towards the end of pregnancy it was normal
) feel Braxton-Hicks' contractions, mild contractions that
nade the uterus tighten up and contract in preparation for
abour. She knew that sometimes they could be painful.

Was that what she had felt?

Should she call Luca?

Filing the notes carefully back in the trolley, she decided
) carry on with her shift and see what happened. It was
ound to be nothing. Maybe she'd pulled a muscle lifting
omething that she shouldn't have done. What else could
: be? She had at least another seven weeks to go until the
aby was due.

And she really didn't want to bother Luca with it. He'
only insist that she go home to rest and then she'd have t
leave Sharon and the others in the lurch.

As it was, she only had one more week at work and sh
knew that Sharon had been searching for a replacement.

Determined to carry on, she checked her notebook an
noticed that she still needed to do a daily examination o
Mrs Burn, a thirty-year-old woman who'd had a forcep
delivery during the early hours of the morning.

Putting her own problems to the back of her mind, Ti
walked through to the four-bedded ward which was on th
south side of the hospital. Despite the fact that it was sti
only March, the sun shone strongly through the window
making the room bright and warm.

'Morning, ladies,' Tia said cheerfully as she walke
briskly up to Mrs Burn. She noticed immediately that th
woman looked pale and tired. 'I've just come to do you
check, Lisa, if this is a good time for you.'

Lisa nodded slowly and tried to struggle into a sittin
position.

Tia frowned. 'Are you in a lot of discomfort?'

Lisa nodded, her eyes filling. 'I can't sit on my bottor
at all. It's agony. I know I'm being a wimp, but I can
help it.'

'You're not being a wimp,' Tia said immediately, he
expression concerned. 'Let me take a good look at you an
then we can decide what to do.'

Tia started out by examining Lisa's breasts, checking tha
they were soft and free from lumps, redness and sorenes
'How's the feeding going?'

'All right,' Lisa mumbled, 'although I can't sit up at all

'Has anyone showed you how to feed lying down?' Ti
satisfied herself that everything looked healthy and the
helped Lisa wriggle down the bed so that she could ex
amine the uterus. 'For a start, it's so much easier at nigl
just to feed the baby while you're still lying down, and

ou're sore down below it will help you not to be on your
ottom.'

Lisa shook her head. 'They've been so busy up here
ince I arrived. Someone did help me latch her on the first
ime but I've been trying not to bother them since then.'

'You don't have to worry about that. It's what we're here
or.' Tia frowned as she palpated Lisa's abdomen. She
new that, like most units, they were very stretched, but it
nade her uncomfortable to hear that Lisa had been reluctant
o ask for help.

Satisfied that the uterus was well contracted and not pain-
ul, she asked Lisa various questions and then checked her
erineum. What she saw made her wince. No wonder the
oor woman was in pain. She had developed a severe hae-
natoma of the vulva.

'Lisa, I can see straight away what the problem is,' she
aid quietly. 'You've developed a blood clot down below.
'm going to call one of the doctors and ask them to take
look at you.'

Lisa's eyes widened with anxiety. 'Won't it just go by
self?'

Tia hesitated. 'It might,' she said finally, 'but I have a
eeling that the doctors might want to sort it out for you.
'll just give one of them a call.'

She bleeped Luca and explained what had happened over
ne phone, breaking off for a few seconds as the stabbing
ain hit her again.

'Tia?' Luca's deep voice was sharp and concerned down
ne phone. 'Are you all right?'

She sucked in a breath and waited for the pain to pass.
'm fine,' she told him, changing the subject quickly. 'So
vill you come and take a look at Lisa Burn for me?'

'I'll be five minutes,' he said shortly, and she suspected
nat his haste was as much to check on her as the patient.
She was right.

He strode onto the ward in record time, his dark eye cloudy with concern as he walked towards her.

'She's in Ward 4,' Tia began, but he raised a hand and stopped her in mid-flow.

'I'll see Lisa in a minute. First I want you to tell me what's wrong. And don't say nothing because I know you well enough by now to know when you don't feel right.'

It was true.

From being someone who didn't understand her at all he now seemed to be able to virtually mind-read.

'I've felt a sharp pain a couple of times, that's all,' she mumbled, and his broad shoulders tensed slightly.

Maybe he was more anxious than he seemed to be.

He asked her some questions and then gave a sigh 'You're probably right that it's nothing,' he said, his eye scanning her pale face, 'but I would prefer that you went home.'

Her eyes slid away from his. 'I'm all right at the moment If it comes back, maybe I will.'

'Tia…' His voice was a low, threatening growl and she looked at him pleadingly.

'Luca, they're so short-staffed here, it would put a terrible strain on them if I went home. I'm not doing anything strenuous and, anyway, this is the best place to be if something is going to happen.'

She didn't voice her fear, but she was terrified of being at home on her own when the baby came. It didn't matter whether Luca loved her or not—when it came to the baby she trusted him implicitly.

'All right.' He relented, stroking her cheek with lean brown fingers. 'But try and rest as much as you can.'

'I promise.' Tia flushed slightly and her breathing quickened under his touch. 'Are you ready to see Lisa now?'

Luca nodded, his eyes clinging to hers for a long, very unsettling moment. Then he seemed to pull himself together.

'All right. Where is she?'

He examined Lisa and immediately agreed with Tia. 'It's haematoma. We'll observe it for a few hours and see if contains itself.' He glanced at Lisa. 'I suspect we will eed to take you to Theatre and evacuate the clot.'

True to her promise, Tia was careful not to do anything o energetic during the rest of her shift, and when Luca ame back onto the ward to check on Lisa for the second me, she was sitting down, talking to one of the mothers ho had just come back from Theatre.

She stood up instantly when she saw Luca and together ey had another look at Lisa.

'It's spreading,' Luca said immediately, his eyes quietly mpathetic as he looked at Lisa. 'I'm going to pop you own to Theatre, give you a small anaesthetic and get rid f this blood clot.'

'I'll make the arrangements,' Tia said at once, and busied erself doing just that.

Once she'd escorted Lisa down to Theatre it would be me to go home, but she wasn't at all sure that she really anted to go.

She hadn't felt the pain for a few hours.

But what if it came back and she was on her own?

She lingered on the ward for another hour and then de-ded that she was being ridiculous. After all, she could ardly stay at the hospital all night, could she?

Gathering her belongings from her locker, she said good-ye to the rest of the staff and made her way to the car ark.

Maybe a warm bath would relax her, and after that she uld prepare some supper for Luca.

t eight o'clock Tia was pottering around the kitchen in er dressing-gown when the phone rang.

It was Luca, of course, telling her that he'd be late.

She replaced the receiver and looked sadly at the casserole which was bubbling temptingly on the top of the cooker.

Every time she tried to cook him a nice meal he missed it, but there was nothing that could be done. She turned the heat off with a resigned sigh, helped herself to a portion and then dropped the plate with a clatter as a sharp pain ripped through her abdomen.

Doubled over and gasping, she struggled over to the kitchen table and flopped into the nearest chair, trying hard not to panic.

It was the same pain she'd felt periodically earlier in the day, only this time it was a thousand times worse. It was as if someone was using knives on her insides. Surely this degree of pain wasn't normal? She stroked a hand over her stomach, trying to relax herself, talking quietly to the baby. At least she was still feeling plenty of movements and she knew how important that was.

Suddenly she wished desperately that Luca was at home.

Should she phone him? She glanced at her watch, torn between the need for reassurance and guilt at disturbing him. The probability was that she'd be worrying him unnecessarily.

Maybe she'd just see how she felt in half an hour.

He'd promised not to be too late but he'd also mentioned that he had an emergency section to perform so she knew that he wouldn't be home for a few hours at least.

Tia frowned ruefully at the mess on the kitchen floor. What a waste of casserole! She really ought to clean it up but she was afraid that if she moved the pain might come back.

A glance at the clock on the kitchen wall told her that was only eight-fifteen. Just a quarter of an hour since Luca had called. Which meant that she needed to fill her time with something or she'd go mad.

Gingerly, still with one hand on her stomach, she stood up, waiting for the pain to tear through her again. Fortuately, it didn't. It was still there, lurking menacingly in the background, but instead of stabbing, it seemed to have settled down to a dull sawing that was more bearable.

She walked slowly through to the sitting room and lowered herself carefully onto the sofa, stretching out her legs and breathing steadily. She felt the baby kick against her hand and gave a soft smile. Whatever was happening, it was good to know that he was still all right.

She flicked on the television and became absorbed in a programme on dolphins, settling herself more comfortably on the sofa. Gradually her eyes closed and she drifted off, only dimly aware of the deep voice of the narrator in the background.

She awoke desperate for the bathroom and clumsily manoeuvred herself off the sofa and up the stairs.

The minute she opened the bathroom door she knew she was bleeding and icy rivers of panic trickled down her spine.

Dear God, no. Please, not that…
She needed Luca.

Even as she moaned his name she heard his key in the lock and she sagged with relief and called again, this time loud enough to be heard.

She heard the urgent pounding of his feet on the stairs and then he was beside her, his expression grim as he scanned her pale face.

'*Dio*, Tia—you are in pain again?'

She nodded slowly and straightened, trying to catch her breath. 'Yes, but that's not all.' She broke off and gazed up at him, her green eyes deep pools of fear. 'Luca, I'm bleeding.'

He wrenched his coat off and slung it unceremoniously over the bannister and then steered her towards the chair in the bathroom. 'Why didn't you call me?'

She shook her head and bit down on her lower lip, trying not to cry out. 'I fell asleep. Oh, Luca…' Tears of panic

and pain welled in her eyes and she looked up at him
desperate for reassurance. 'What's happening?'

'I don't know yet, but I soon will,' he promised her
crouching next to her, his voice strong and reassuring
'Trust me, *cara*. We need to get you to hospital. It will be
safer to examine you properly there. Will you be all righ
if I just go and call an ambulance?'

'No.' She grasped his arm and shook her head. 'No am
bulance. I don't want you to leave me. Can you take me
in the car? Please, Luca?'

He spoke rapidly in Italian and raked long finger
through his sleek, dark hair.

'How much are you bleeding?' He was virtually talking
to himself as he checked quickly, his mind obviously work
ing through the options. 'It's not too bad at the moment
All right, we'll go in the car. Can you stand up?'

She hesitated and then nodded, sliding to the edge of the
seat and standing gingerly, bracing herself as she waited
for the pain to tear at her insides again.

He lifted her easily in his arms, ignoring her protest tha
she was too heavy, and carried her down the stairs and ou
to the car.

'All right.' He accelerated away smoothly, driving a
quickly as he safely could. 'I want you to describe the pai
to me again. Where is it? How does it feel?'

'It's here…' Tia winced and rubbed a hand low over he
abdomen. 'Quite low down and it comes and goes.'

'Does it feel like labour?' Luca broke off and shook hi
head impatiently. 'Forgive me, that was a stupid question
You don't know what labour feels like. Try and describ
the pain, Tia.'

Tia looked at him helplessly. 'I don't know if I can
Stabbing, quite rhythmic—it feels as though something'
wrong.'

Luca stretched out one hand briefly and rested it on th
top of her abdomen. 'It doesn't feel as though you're hav

ng contractions. Everything will be fine, *cara mia*,' he said
oftly, 'but we do need to get to the bottom of the pain and
.'d rather we did that in the hospital to be on the safe side.
When did you last feel the baby move?'

'Just before you arrived.' She gave him a nervous smile.
He kicked me really hard.'

He nodded and put both hands back on the wheel.
Good.'

The trip to the hospital took less than half the usual time
and in no time at all she was on the labour ward.

'I want to examine your abdomen.' Luca helped her
move into the right position and adjusted her clothing to
give him access. 'OK, let's see what's going on here…'

His hands moved gently over her abdomen, a frown
ouching his handsome features as he examined her.

'The consistency of your uterus is normal. Is there any
enderness?'

'No—not really. It hurts but I don't think it's anything
you're doing.'

'I want you strapped to a monitor and I want to scan
you. Now.' Luca straightened up in a lithe movement and
glanced at Tia who was fighting back tears of panic.

Why, oh, why did this have to happen?

If anything happened to the baby…

She closed her eyes and tried to calm herself down. Luca
lidn't need her to fall apart.

Scanning her tense features, he pulled her into his arms,
alking soothingly in Italian before switching to English.

'Calm down. It will be all right.'

She stared up at him, her eyes frightened. 'If I lose the
oaby, Luca…'

He brushed her cheek with his knuckles. 'You won't lose
he baby.'

'What do you think is wrong?' She shifted slightly on
he bed, trying to find a comfortable position.

'I suspect you have a mild separation of the placenta,'

he said quietly, walking towards the door. 'We'll have a better idea once we've scanned you.'

Tia felt as though she'd been showered with cold water and her palms suddenly felt sweaty. *A separation of the placenta.* She should know all about that, but suddenly everything she knew seemed to have vanished from her head. All she could think about was that she couldn't bear the thought of losing the baby.

'I'm only thirty-three weeks pregnant, Luca,' she reminded him hoarsely, her words stopping him in his tracks. 'It's too early.'

'The baby is a good size, and you're only a day off thirty-four weeks,' Luca said firmly, turning as Sharon appeared at the doorway. He spoke to her quietly and then turned back to Tia. 'Let's try not to panic until we know what we're dealing with.'

Seconds later Sharon came in again with the relevant machines and Luca gave her a grateful nod.

'I want to scan her and then I want her on a monitor. And could you call Dan Sutherland? I'd like his opinion.'

'Well, he certainly owes you some time after all the clinics and Theatre lists you've covered for him this week,' Sharon said immediately, her eyes on Tia. 'Don't you worry. You're in the right place now and that baby of yours is going to be just fine.'

Tia forced back the tears that were threatening. She hoped they were right.

Luca scanned her carefully, checking the position of the placenta and looking for concealed bleeding.

'There.' He leaned forward and touched the screen with his finger to show Sharon what he'd noticed. 'The placenta is in the upper segment and I can see just a small concealed bleed. I want her kept on a monitor, Sharon.'

Tia licked dry lips. 'My placenta is coming away?'

Luca looked at her hesitantly. 'Yes. But it's only a small area—'

'Luca, I'm a midwife,' she reminded him in a croaky voice. 'Small areas can become big areas.'

He sat down on the bed next to her, taking her hands in his. 'Tia, now that we know what the problem is, we can deal with it. The baby is absolutely fine at the moment. He is still getting plenty of oxygen. We're going to admit you to the ward here and you're going to take it easy for a few days while we watch you.'

A lump grew in her throat at the thought of being on her own in a sterile hospital room.

She wanted to go home to their cottage.

'This is all my fault,' she whispered, placing a protective hand on her abdomen. 'The baby must have known that I didn't want it, but now I do, desperately, and—'

'Hush.' Luca's voice was firm but kind. 'Don't torture yourself. The feelings you had were perfectly normal. They certainly have no bearing on the fact that you're bleeding. You need to try and relax, Tia. Please.'

Tia took a shuddering breath and tried to pull herself together. 'I want to be at home—' She almost said 'with you' but stopped herself just in time. The last thing he wanted was her all over him. They were good friends and they had an amazing sex life, but that was it.

'Well, if you're worried about not seeing Luca, don't be,' Sharon said briskly, helping Tia back into the wheelchair. 'The man has a second home here in case you hadn't noticed. He can sleep in the spare on-call room on the ward if he likes.'

'Good idea.' Luca nodded immediately. 'I'll pick up some stuff later and move in until you're sorted out.'

The knowledge that he'd be close to her made her relax for the first time since she'd arrived at the hospital, and she gave him a grateful smile.

He might not love her but she certainly couldn't fault the way he behaved towards her. He was very attentive and caring.

'Right.' He rubbed a hand over his face and took a deep breath, obviously marshalling his thoughts. 'Let's get you up to the ward and then I want to do a haemoglobin, a coagulation screen and a Kleihauer test.'

Dan Sutherland strolled into the room at that moment, his expression concerned as he looked at Tia.

'What's been happening to you, then?'

Luca filled him in and Dan nodded slowly. 'Right. We really need to do a speculum examination as well. Would you rather I did that?'

Tia nodded, her cheeks flaming red. It shouldn't have been embarrassing to be examined by Luca but she knew that it would be.

Sensitive to her feelings, Luca mentioned something about fetching some blood bottles and strode out of the room, leaving her with Dan and Sharon.

'Poor chap.' Dan glanced after him, a sympathetic expression in his eyes. 'It's never easy, having someone you love as the patient. He looks so stressed.'

Tia was hardly aware of what Dan was doing as he carried out his examination. It was true that Luca was stressed, but she knew that it was because of the baby, not her. She knew just how much the baby meant to him.

'The bleeding is definitely from the uterine cavity,' Dan said finally, tearing off his gloves and tossing them in the bin. 'How far on are you? Thirty-three weeks—nearly thirty-four.' He frowned down at her notes, lost in thought. 'All right. Sharon, let's give her some dexamethasone because I have a feeling that this baby might decide to make an appearance early.'

Tia felt her heart lurch. She really, really didn't want the baby to come early. She wanted to have a normal, healthy full-term baby like everyone else. What had she done to deserve this? Why couldn't she have had the sort of birth that she'd read about in the glossy magazines?

Tears pricked her eyes and she cursed herself for being

so emotional. Before she'd become pregnant she'd considered herself to be a resilient person, someone who hardly ever cried, but today she felt as though there was a dam inside her, waiting to burst.

Sharon must have noticed because she waited for Dan to leave the room and then slipped her arms around Tia.

'You poor thing. You must be so worried, but try not to be, sweetheart. We'll sort you out. Have a good cry if you need to. It's mostly hormones, you know that as well as I do. And disappointment.' She nodded wisely, the gentle expression in her eyes showing that she'd understood everything that Tia was feeling. 'Everyone assumes that they'll have a normal pregnancy and delivery but it doesn't always happen that way.'

Tia sniffed and rubbed away the tears with the back of her hand. 'I don't know why I'm being so pathetic.'

'Because you're worried,' Sharon said simply. 'We all have certain expectations about childbirth and when things deviate from what we're expecting we feel cheated, but the truth is that plenty of people have less than perfect textbook births.'

'I know.' Tia sniffed again and gave a watery smile. 'I just want the baby to be OK.'

'Tia, nothing is going to happen to your baby with both Dan and Luca in charge,' Sharon said soothingly, gathering up Tia's belongings and handing them to her. 'Now then, can you manage these on your lap if I push you in the wheelchair?'

Tia nodded. 'Thanks, Shaz.'

Sharon pushed her up to the ward and helped settle her into a side room.

'I feel guilty, taking a side room,' Tia mumbled, and Sharon waved her hand dismissively.

'Nonsense. It's the least we can do for you and, anyway, for once we're not actually that busy at the moment. If we have to move you out, we will. In the meantime, the room is yours.'

Tia settled herself on the bed and gave a sigh. 'Am I allowed to move around?'

'Well, there's no way I'm bringing you a bedpan, if that's what you're asking,' Sharon said dryly. 'But, seriously, I think you should take advantage of the opportunity to get some rest. How's that pain now?'

'About the same,' Tia admitted, rubbing a hand across her swollen abdomen.

'OK. Well, I'm just going to sort out that dexamethasone and then we need to do those blood tests Luca requested.' Sharon walked towards the door and propped it open, smiling as one of the student midwives entered. 'Have you been shopping?'

'As instructed.' The girl passed two bags to Sharon who walked back into the room armed with magazines, books and flowers. 'Here we are—a few things to keep you occupied.'

Tia started to laugh as she poked through the bags. 'Shaz, I can't possibly eat all that chocolate! I'm the size of a house already.'

Sharon put her hands on her hips and surveyed Tia through narrowed eyes. 'Not a house. More a small cottage I should say, but it doesn't matter because the chocolate isn't for you. It's for us poor midwives who have to look after you.'

Tia shook her head, still smiling. 'And I suppose you're going to hide in here and read my magazines as well?'

Sharon clicked her fingers. 'Bother. You've rumbled my clever plan.'

'Thanks, Shaz.' Tia folded her legs underneath her and reached for one of the magazines. Maybe being in hospital wouldn't be so bad after all.

At least she felt safe.

CHAPTER NINE

SHARON sorted out the injection and the tests and then suggested that Tia take a nap.

When she awoke it was dark on the ward and Luca was sprawled in a chair by her bed, his eyes closed. Dark stubble was beginning to appear on his hard jaw.

'Luca.' She struggled to sit up, strands of sleek blonde hair falling over her eyes. 'How long have you been here?'

'About an hour and a half.' He suppressed a yawn and gave her a sleepy grin that did something strange to her insides. 'I've had a really good sleep. It seems that while no one seems to give a second thought to bleeping me at home, if I'm in my girlfriend's hospital room I'm given total peace and quiet. I'm thinking of leaving you here permanently.'

She smiled. 'I'm sorry I woke you.' Her voice was still scratchy with sleep and he reached out a lean hand and switched on the bedside lamp so that he could see her more clearly.

'How's that pain?'

Tia considered for a moment, rubbing her hand gently over her precious bump. 'Better,' she said with a nod. 'Definitely better. Maybe rest was all it took.'

'Let's hope so.'

Tia bit her lip, anxious for reassurance. 'Do you think the baby is all right, Luca?'

'The baby is fine,' he murmured, his voice deep in the semi-darkness. 'You are still feeling movements and I saw the trace that you had done before you went to sleep. There is no evidence of foetal distress. Go back to sleep now. The best thing that you can do for that baby is get some rest.'

Rest.

Tia snuggled back down under the covers and did as he'd suggested.

When Tia finally awoke the next morning she was feeling much better.

The pain had all but gone and the prospect of a day doing nothing but lying on the bed, watching television and reading the magazines that Sharon had brought her was suddenly very appealing.

There was no sign of Luca but presumably he'd had to leave before she'd woken up. She knew that he usually did a ward round first thing in the morning.

It was only as she lay doing nothing that she realized just how hard she'd been finding it to be on her feet all day at work.

One of the nurses brought her breakfast and she sat in bed and munched toast and drank tea.

'Lady Muck.' Sharon arrived a few minutes later, a broad grin on her pretty face. 'I'd be feeling quite jealous if i weren't for the fact that I'm about to stab you in the bottom with another injection of dex.'

'Oh, thanks.' Tia pulled a face. She'd forgotten that she was due to have another steroid injection. She knew that they gave steroids to women under thirty-four weeks because they helped to mature the baby's lungs in the event of a premature delivery.

She chatted to Sharon while she finished her toast and then wriggled down on the bed, screwing up her face as Sharon gave her the injection.

'I hope you don't expect me to thank you,' she grumbled pulling her nightie down and sitting back up. 'Horrible.'

'Yes, well, with any luck it will have been for nothing If you hang onto that baby, you won't need it.' Sharon sat down on the edge of the bed and checked Tia's pulse and blood pressure.

'Midwives should not sit on the bed,' Tia recited, and Sharon grinned.

'But I'm the boss. Are you going to report me?'

'Not for that. But if you carry on stealing chocolates when I'm asleep then I definitely am.' Tia shook her head, her expression one of complete disbelief as she watched Sharon eat four chocolates in quick succession, even though it was only breakfast-time. 'I've never known anyone eat as much as you. How do you stay so slim?'

'It's probably something to do with running round after people like you.' Sharon stood up and scribbled on the chart. 'Well, that's all fine. You're pretty healthy for someone who looks like a baby elephant.'

Tia laughed. 'I am huge, aren't I?' Then she stroked her bump anxiously. 'The scan didn't indicate I was any bigger than average but I feel like I've swallowed a balloon.'

'I suppose that's because you're basically a very small person,' Sharon observed, her eyes sweeping over Tia's arms and legs. 'Any size of baby would seem massive on you. Any more bleeding or pain, Tia?'

Tia shook her head and they chatted for a while longer, then Sharon went off to do her work and Tia snuggled down and promptly fell asleep again.

Tia woke up in time to eat her lunch and then slept right through until teatime when Luca strolled through the door.

Tia felt her heart miss a beat.

He was a spectacularly good-looking man.

She couldn't take her eyes off him as he sat down in the armchair by her bed and stretched long, powerfully muscled legs out in front of him.

'What a day.' He closed his eyes and let out a long breath. 'No one seemed to be able to manage a normal delivery.'

Safe in the knowledge that he wasn't watching her, Tia treated herself to a long look at him, her eyes sliding over his thick, dark lashes and resting on his roughened jawline.

He was enough to give a woman a heart attack.

His eyes opened and his expression changed as he intercepted her look.

'Tia?' His voice was gruff and he rose to his feet and settled himself on the edge of her bed, a strange light in his eyes. 'How are you feeling? Sharon told me that you've slept for most of the day. That's good.'

His nearness was making her whole body weak and before she could stop herself she reached out a hand and drew his head down to hers.

With a low groan his mouth closed over hers, his tongue seeking entrance as he kissed her slowly and thoroughly.

Her heart thumping, she felt one of his hands slide into her hair, holding her head immobile so that he could increase his access to her mouth.

Her body started to ache and burn as his tongue explored her intimately, his kisses growing deeper and more demanding. His free hand slid gently over her breast, cupping the fullness, teasing the peak with the rough pad of his thumb until she thought she'd go mad with frustration.

By the time he finally lifted his head she was shaking so badly that had she not already been lying on the bed her legs would certainly have given way.

'Cara.' His voice was thick with passion and he brushed his knuckles over her flushed cheeks with a rueful smile. 'I'm sorry. I should have shaved before I kissed you.'

'It doesn't matter.' Her eyes dropped to his dark jaw and desire curled deep inside her.

'Do you realise that is the first time in the whole of our relationship that you have touched me first?' His voice was soft and his eyes were strangely penetrating, as if he was trying to read her mind.

Tia dropped her eyes, thinking to herself that it was a good job that he couldn't read her mind or he'd be able to see just how much she loved him, and she didn't want that.

It would be more than her pride could bear to let him know just how deep her feelings were for him.

There was an exaggerated cough from the doorway and Sharon stood there, a wicked grin on her face.

'Sorry to disturb you two lovebirds. I'm supposed to be checking your blood pressure, Tia, but it's going to be sky high after that!'

Luca laughed and stood up slowly, as relaxed and self-possessed as ever.

'Absolutely. Better give her five minutes to get her breath back.'

Tia watched him curiously, her cheeks still flushed. He didn't seem to mind at all that Sharon had caught them kissing.

Still smiling, Sharon checked Tia's pulse and blood pressure and then listened to the foetal heart.

'You shouldn't be doing all this,' Tia said, watching her friend recording all the results. 'I ought to have a student midwife.'

Sharon looked horrified at the mere suggestion. 'I've already told you—we're not that busy today, so you can have star treatment.'

'Let's put her on the monitor for an hour,' Luca suggested, rubbing a hand over his face and suppressing a yawn. 'I might go and have a shower while you do that.'

He touched his rough jaw and looked at Tia with an apologetic smile.

'You go,' she said softly. 'I'll see you later.'

Luca left the room and Sharon sighed.

'That man is seriously gorgeous, Tia.'

'I know.'

Sharon's eyes narrowed. 'You do realise that he's crazily in love with you, don't you?'

Tia's eyes widened and she shook her head. 'Don't be ridiculous.'

'I'm not being ridiculous,' Sharon said, her tone dry.

'The man is crazy about you. For goodness' sake, Tia, why do you think he can't stay away?'

Tia shrugged. 'He's worried about the baby.'

Sharon arched an eyebrow. 'Oh, right. And wild, passionate kisses are the latest thing for averting pre-term labour, are they?' She gave a grin. 'I must have been reading the wrong research papers.'

Tia flushed. 'You've got it all wrong.'

'No.' Sharon's smile faded and she shook her head. 'It isn't me who's got it wrong, angel, it's you.'

'So if he's crazy about me, why hasn't he told me?' Tia asked, trying to sound indifferent.

Sharon gave a shrug. 'I don't know. I admit that's a mystery. But you haven't exactly been honest with him about your feelings either, have you? When did you last tell him that you love him?'

Tia shook her head. 'Not since that fiasco on the day of the wedding that wasn't.'

'Precisely.' Sharon breathed out heavily and shook her head. 'What a mess. The two of you need to have your heads knocked together.'

Tia bit her lip. 'Sharon…'

'All right, I'll drop it.' Sharon looped her stethoscope around her neck and moved towards the door. 'But take my advice. Any man who can kiss a woman like that is worth hanging onto.'

Tia watched her go with a faint smile. There was no doubt that Luca knew exactly how to kiss a woman senseless.

She touched her mouth with her fingers, remembering just how that kiss had felt.

Incredible.

But she still couldn't bring herself to tell him that she loved him. It would make her too vulnerable.

An hour later Sharon popped her head round the door to

ell her that Luca had been called down to Theatre and had
aid that Tia should have an early night.

Hiding her disappointment, Tia closed her book and
nuggled down in bed, deciding to take his advice. Sleep
ertainly seemed to be helping. She felt better than she had
or ages.

The baby was still very active and the pain had gone.

Maybe there really was nothing to worry about.

'ia awoke when the pain hit her.

With a muted gasp she struggled to sit upright, her hand
ressed to her abdomen as the severe cramping pain tore
hrough her insides.

Groaning softly, she bit back a sob and realised that the
oom was still empty. Luca obviously hadn't come back.
yes closed, she breathed gently, hoping that the contrac-
on would soon pass. Because that was undoubtedly what
was. She'd never had a baby before so she didn't have
rst-hand experience of labour pains, but the hand she had
laced on her abdomen told her everything she needed to
now.

She was definitely in labour.

Six weeks early.

Trying not to panic, she took shallow breaths and waited
or the pain to pass. Finally she was able to reach out and
ress the buzzer.

Polly, the night sister, was by her side in an instant.
'roblems?'

Tia nodded, her lower lip caught between her teeth. 'I'm
labour, Polly. Or at least I think I am.'

'Can I have a feel?' Polly sat down on the bed next to
er and placed a hand on Tia's bump.

Tia tensed as another pain hit and Polly glanced at her
atch, timing the contraction. After a few minutes she
ood up and bustled around the room.

'I'm going to put you on a monitor,' she told Tia, 'but

it does look as though you're in labour. I'll call Da
Sutherland.'

'Where's Luca?' Suddenly Tia desperately wanted hin
to be with her. It didn't matter whether he loved her or no
She trusted his judgement and she felt safe with him.

'He was in here having a kip and then he was calle
down to labour ward again,' Polly told her. 'One of th
registrars was having problems with someone and poppe
up to ask his opinion.'

And she hadn't even heard him leave. She must hav
slept like the dead. 'Will you call him for me?'

Polly nodded. 'Right away.'

Tia watched her leave the room and tried not to pani
The baby should be fine. She was just thirty-four week
pregnant, which was early, of course, but not as serious
early as it might have been. The baby might well hav
problems, but surely he shouldn't die?

Polly was back in the room a moment later with the CT
machine. The CTG—or cardiotocograph—gave a graph
record of the response of the foetal heart to uterine activit
as well as information about its rhythm and rate.

Tia shifted in the bed until she was more comfortab
and then Polly strapped an ultrasound transducer to her al
domen.

'Right…' Polly adjusted the strap and fiddled with th
machine. 'Let's see what this tells us…'

Tia relaxed slightly as she heard the reassuring gallopir
of the baby's heart.

Polly's eyes were fixed on the machine and she rested
hand on the top of Tia's abdomen to feel for any contra
tions.

Seconds later Tia felt the pain begin to build and gr
her. With a moan she shifted again, trying to find son
relief from the agony, but the pain was so intense she cou
barely breathe.

'Well, you're definitely having strong contractions

'olly muttered, watching the machine and then glancing at 'ia. 'I'll go and try Luca again.'

'I'm here.' His deep voice came from the doorway and e entered the room, his handsome face strained as he in-tantly assessed the situation. 'You are in labour, *cara*?'

The concern on his face and his gentle endearment made er heart turn over.

'I think so.' She nodded and gasped as another pain tore hrough her. 'Oh. Luca…'

He was beside her in an instant, sliding a lean, brown and over her abdomen, feeling the strength of her con-'action, murmuring encouragement to her as she tried to emember how she was supposed to breathe.

She sagged against the pillows as the contraction ended. Can we stop the labour? I don't want it to come early.'

Luca squeezed her hand and got to his feet in a fluid 10vement and looked at the trace on the CTG machine. We need to examine you.' He turned to Polly. 'Have you alled Dan?'

'Yes.' She nodded confirmation and Luca's mouth tight-ned.

'Well, call him again,' he growled, moving back to Tia, is tension obvious.

Polly vanished and reappeared a moment later with Dan, ·ho was the epitome of calm efficiency.

'You're determined to have this baby early aren't you?' e said lightly, smiling at Tia and taking the trace Luca anded him.

The next half-hour was a whirl of tests and discussions, nd all the time Tia struggled to cope with the contractions, ·hich were becoming more powerful by the minute.

Finally Luca raked a hand through his hair and sat down n the edge of the bed.

'We have all talked about it and we are agreed that we eed to get this baby out, Tia,' he said quietly, his dark yes holding hers. 'I know you don't want to have it early,

but we don't have any choice. Your labour is too advance
to stop it, and there is some evidence of mild foetal dis
tress.'

Tia's eyes widened anxiously. 'How mild?'

'Our baby is fine at the moment,' Luca reassured he
quickly, 'but we are all agreed that we should deliver hir
or her as soon as possible. How do you feel about havin
a section?'

Tia swallowed. This wasn't happening the way she'd ex
pected. Naïvely she'd expected a perfectly normal deliv
ery—the sort that she'd helped so many women with sinc
she'd qualified as a midwife. She'd never thought that she'
be in the 'complications' category.

Suddenly she felt hideously frightened and it must hav
shown because Luca quickly turned to his colleagues.

'Give us five minutes alone, please.'

They obeyed immediately and Luca moved closer to Ti
and took her hands in his.

'What is it that you're afraid of?'

She shook her head, unable to articulate her feelings.
don't know—everything. I'm afraid of the baby comin
early, I'm afraid of having surgery.' Her heart thudded fa
ter and she looked at him with scared eyes. 'I didn't war
it to be like this. I thought it would all be normal.'

His grip on her hands tightened. 'Not everyone is give
the perfect delivery,' he said softly, 'but what matters i
the end is that you are both fine. The rest of it we can de
with. Dan is one of the best surgeons I've ever seen an
I'll be there the whole time—'

'Can't you do it?'

His jaw tensed and for the first time in her pregnanc
she thought she detected signs of strain in his face. Mayb
he wasn't quite as relaxed as he liked to pretend.

'Tia, you know I wouldn't be the best person for this
His eyes locked with hers and he smoothed her hair awa

rom her face. 'I cannot operate on the woman I— on my irlfriend,' he amended quickly. 'Dan is the best person.'

'Can't I have a normal delivery?'

Luca let out a long breath. 'We could start that way and ee how it goes, but you're bleeding again and I'd rather ve were in control of the situation from the start. My in-tincts are that we should get the baby out now.'

And he had the best instincts of any doctor she had ever et.

'All right.' Tia pulled herself together and gave a nod. I just want the baby to be safe. Let's get on with it, then.'

'We'll give you an epidural,' Luca said, standing up and aaking for the door. 'I'll bleep the anaesthetist.'

The thought of having an epidural frightened her as well, ut she knew that it was much safer for the baby than a eneral anaesthetic. But what would it be like to be awake s the baby was delivered?

She tried to be rational. At least if she had an epidural en she'd be able to be a part of the birth.

And Luca would be there.

Fighting down the panic, Tia gave Luca a smile, but she new from the growing concern in Luca's eyes that he un-erstood exactly how she was feeling.

'We'll give you some gas and air until the anaesthetist rrives,' Polly said briskly, pulling the machine closer to ae bed. 'Do you want me to remind you how to use it?'

Tia gave a weak smile. They were all shown how to use in their training, of course, and she helped women use as and air on an almost daily basis, but it was quite a ifferent matter to be the patient!

'I tried it once when I was training,' she told Polly. 'It aade me feel dizzy.'

'Yes, well, dizzy might be a pleasant change from the ain,' Polly observed, her gaze sympathetic as Tia gave nother groan as a contraction gripped her. 'Let's give this

a try, and don't breathe too quickly. That's usually wh
people get dizzy, as you know.'

Polly handed her the mouthpiece and Tia breathe
steadily, screwing up her face as the pain intensified.

'Well done. Good girl.' Polly encouraged her gentl
through the contraction and Luca slid an arm round he
shoulders, hugging her against him as the contractio
ended.

'You need to start using the gas and air as soon as you
uterus starts to harden,' Polly reminded her, and Tia noc
ded, her face pale and drawn.

Luca stroked her hair and softly spoke to her in Italia

'What?' Tia looked at him, pain making her unchara
teristically grumpy. 'What did you say? I didn't understan
you.'

Something flickered in his dark eyes and he hesitated.
said that it will soon be over,' he muttered, and Dan sh
him a strange look.

'What? But I thought—' He broke off as he caugl
Luca's eye. 'Well, I mean…my Italian never was any goo
anyway.' He cleared his throat and turned his attention bac
to the notes just as Duncan Fraser, the anaesthetist, hurrie
into the room.

'I'm such a wimp,' she gasped, clutching Luca and pusl
ing away the gas and air. 'Why do women ever want na
ural births?'

She'd never known such agony.

'Labour is never the same for two people,' Polly r
minded her gently, rubbing her back to try and help rela
her. 'I've seen women deliver in hours and barely notic
and so have you. It isn't a competition, Tia. You just hav
to do what's right for you.'

Duncan made the necessary preparations and then move
closer to the bed. 'When this contraction has passed I nee
you to sit on the edge of the bed for me. We're going t

eed to work in between contractions, Tia, so if you feel nother one coming, warn me.'

Tia did as he instructed, gripping Luca's hand tightly.

'All right, Tia.' Duncan explained what he was doing in . calm voice and in no time at all the epidural was in place nd the awful pain was fading to nothing.

'Does that feel better?' Luca's eyes were clouded with oncern and she nodded.

'Much.'

'We're going to take you through to Theatre now, Tia.')an issued some instructions and Tia closed her eyes as hey wheeled her through the swing doors.

Why had this happened to her? Here she was, about to e operated on while she was awake. The thought terrified er!

Sensing her anxiety, Luca spoke quietly to Dan and then ettled himself on a stool by Tia's head and took her hand rmly in his.

'It's time we thought of some names,' he said, his eyes varm as he held hers. 'Something Italian, of course—Luigi, .eonardo, Gianfranco…'

Despite her nerves Tia smiled, grateful that he was trying) distract her. 'What if it's a girl?'

He gave a sexy grin. 'I hope it is. I'm better with vomen.'

And didn't she just know it!

Ignoring the flash of disquiet that his comment caused, 'ia concentrated on thinking of girls' names, only dimly ware that Dan had started operating. 'Daisy?'

'Daisy?' Luca gave her a horrified look. 'What sort of a ame is Daisy? Is that the best you can come up with?'

'I think it's pretty,' Tia muttered, her eyes rested on .uca's thick, dark lashes and the hard angle of his cheek-ones. 'Or how about Lily?'

'What is this preoccupation with flowers?' For a brief

second Luca's gaze flickered over the green sterile towel to his colleague who gave him a reassuring nod.

'I like Lily,' Tia said huskily, starting to relax now tha she realised she really couldn't feel anything.

'You are feeling all right?' Luca's voice was gruff and she gave a slow nod.

'Yes, surprisingly enough. I can just feel some pulling but it doesn't hurt.'

'I should think not!' Duncan looked horrified at the mer suggestion that any anaesthetic he administered could b less than perfect. 'How are you doing there, Dan? Any tim in the next ten hours is fine by me.'

Despite the banter, Tia knew that Dan was workin; quickly and only seconds later there was a slight commo tion and Luca straightened up, his features tense as Da lifted the baby out.

'Looks like you've got your flower, Tia,' Dan said cheer fully as he handed the baby to Luca. 'It's a little girl.'

'Oh!' Tia stared, wide-eyed, as Luca held the bawlin; bundle close to her. 'Oh, Luca…'

Tears slipped down her cheeks and she looked at th baby in amazement, thinking that she'd never seen anythin; so beautiful in her life.

'Can we call her Lily? Please?' Her voice was choke and for a moment Luca didn't speak, his dark eyes unusu ally bright as he held his tiny daughter in his hands.

'Lily sounds good to me,' he said finally, his voice de cidedly rough around the edges. 'Lily Zattoni.'

CHAPTER TEN

'LY...

Tia stared anxiously at her daughter. 'Is she OK? She ʜems tiny—'

'Not that tiny for a thirty-four weeker,' Julie, the paeᵣatrician, took the baby away for a quick examination and ᵤca prowled over to her side, watching every move she ᵢade.

'Are her lungs all right?'

His dark gaze was acute as he gazed down at his daughᵣr, waiting impatiently while the paediatrician examined ᵣr.

'Everything seems fine at the moment,' Julie assured ᵢm, wrapping the baby carefully in warm blankets. 'Obᵢously we'll need to watch her carefully and see how she ᵢpes.'

'I've found the problem,' Dan said as he delivered the ᵢacenta. 'A small section had started to peel away. It's a ᵢod job we operated or this could have caused us a major ᵣoblem later.'

Luca strode over to Dan's side and the two men spoke ᵢftly together as they looked at the placenta.

Finally Luca turned and returned to his seat by Tia's side, ᵢs eyes strained. 'You are feeling all right, *cara*?'

Tia nodded, exhausted but relieved that it was all over. ᵢow what happens?'

'You go into the recovery room and get to know Lily, ᵢd after a bit we'll take you to the ward,' Polly told her, ᵢishing off the swab count with Dan.

Tia lay there, gazing at her daughter, oblivious to the ᵢtion still going on around her.

Finally they finished and she was wheeled through to th recovery room.

'We need to give her something to eat,' Polly said, gatl ering the charts together. 'Are you going to breastfeed he Tia?'

Tia nodded. 'I want to.'

'OK, well, let's see if we can get her to latch on.' Pol positioned herself by the side of the trolley and togethe they tried to persuade Lily to feed. 'Your milk might n come in for a few days, but I don't need to tell you ho good for her the colostrum is.'

Despite both their efforts, they had no success.

'She's not doing it.' Tia's voice was choked and Luc gave a frown.

'Give her a chance, Tia,' he said gently. 'She's tiny, ca mia. It takes a while to get the hang of it and she is on just thirty-four weeks. Her suck reflex may not have d veloped fully yet.'

They carried on trying and then Polly tested the baby blood sugar. 'It's very low, Tia,' she said quietly. 'We r ally do need to get something into her. Can I give her bottle for now?'

Tia nodded reluctantly, disappointed that she hadn managed to breastfeed her daughter straight away but u derstanding that the important thing was that the baby ha a feed of some kind because she was so tiny.

But Lily wouldn't take the bottle either and there w something else that was disturbing Luca.

'She's grunting,' he muttered, glancing across at Pol who nodded agreement.

Tia's heart fluttered in her chest. She knew that gruntir was often the first sign of respiratory distress.

'But I thought her lungs were all right.' She turned Luca, visibly upset, and he gave her shoulder a squeeze.

'She doesn't seem to be as well as we first thought,' l admitted, his voice rough with tension. 'She obvious ısn't developed her suck reflex yet and she's going to ːed some help with her breathing. She needs to go to ›pecial Care for the time being, Tia.' He strode across to .e phone and spoke to the paediatricians.

Tia looked at Polly with horror. 'But I don't want her to ‹ to Special Care. I want her to stay here with me.'

Polly's eyes were sympathetic. 'I know that, Tia, but she ːeds some help. As soon as they've settled her you can › and visit her. We'll push you in the wheelchair.'

'Will you stay with her?' Tia turned to Luca, upset that ıe couldn't keep Lily with her.

'Of course.' Luca bent down and kissed her forehead.)on't worry.'

He scooped their daughter up gently and laid her care-lly on his shoulder. 'I'll take her up myself, Polly. You ay with Tia.'

Polly frowned. 'I ought to ask them to bring down an cubator.'

'I would rather get her up there fast.' Without further ›nversation, Luca left the room and Tia watched them, tally unaware that Polly was talking to her.

'Tia?' Polly finished checking her friend's pulse and ›ood pressure and frowned down at her. 'I asked if you ære in any pain.'

Pain?

'No.' And anyway she didn't care about pain. She just anted her daughter to be OK.

By the time Luca reappeared Tia had been moved to the ard and settled in a bed.

After a conversation with Sharon, who was now back on ıty, she'd persuaded the staff to remove her drip and her ıtheter.

'I want to be mobile as soon as possible,' she said stub->rnly.

Dan popped up to see her and checked on the wound ıd her uterus and asked about her back.

'It aches a bit,' Tia admitted, 'but I know that's perfect normal so you don't need to reassure me.'

Dan grinned. 'Having a well-informed patient is a mixe blessing. How's Lily?'

Tia tried to hide her anxiety but failed dismally. 'I don know. Luca's been up there for ages…'

At that moment Luca walked quietly into the room, o viously expecting her to be asleep.

'Is she all right?' Tia winced as she struggled to sit u right and Luca frowned.

'You are in pain?'

'No,' Tia lied. 'How is Lily? What have they done? she ventilated?'

Luca sat down next to the bed and dealt with the que tions one at a time. 'Overall, she's doing all right,' he sa carefully, and Tia's breathing quickened.

'But she's got plenty wrong with her, hasn't she? I ca tell that you're hiding something from me.' Her eyes fille 'I want you to tell me the truth, Luca.'

'I'm not hiding anything.' He took her hand and ga her a tired smile. 'She's just very small and 34 weeks is bit borderline, as you know. Some 34-weekers are perfect capable of managing on their own without help and the do fine. Others need help.'

'How much help? Is she being ventilated?'

Tia knew from her own experience as a midwife th plenty of babies born prematurely needed ventilating to a sist their breathing. Was this what had happened to litt Lily?

Luca took a deep breath. 'You know she was grunti and you know as well as I do that that can be a sign respiratory distress. She's also got a degree of intercost recession and mild cyanosis. They're giving her CPAP.'

Tia stared at him, aware that with CPAP—continuo positive airways pressure—the baby was able to breat independently but a continuous distending pressure was e

rted on the airway to prevent the tiny air sacs in the lungs
ollapsing at the end of each respiration.

'Are they measuring her oxygen saturation?'

Luca nodded. 'It's variable, but they assure me that we
an expect that with a 34-weeker. They're giving her ox-
gen and they've passed a nasogastric tube so that they can
ed her. Later on, if you have the energy, you could try
nd express some milk for her and they can put that down
ae tube. We don't want to waste all those precious anti-
odies and we need to start stimulating your milk supply
she isn't going to feed immediately.'

Tia nodded immediately. 'Shall I do that now?'

'No.' He gave a gentle smile and gently squeezed her
and. 'You need some rest. How are you feeling? I want
a honest answer.'

'I'm fine. I just want to get out of bed and go and see
er.' Tia looked longingly at the wheelchair. 'Will you take
ae?'

'Now?' Luca glanced at Dan who shrugged.

'I don't see why not. She's not going to get any rest
hile she's worrying like this. Take her up there if she feels
a to it.'

'All right.' Luca nodded slowly. 'But you need to have
ame more pain relief first.'

'Are you kidding?' Tia managed a wry smile as she got
ady to transfer herself into the wheelchair. 'After labour
ains, this is a piece of cake.'

Luca didn't smile. 'You know the rule, Tia. You have
ain relief before the pain comes back and then it's easier
control it. You don't wait until you're in agony.'

Tia looked at him curiously. 'Why are you so worried
out me being in pain? I'm fine, Luca, honestly.'

Luca let out a sharp breath. 'It was hell seeing you in so
uch pain when you were in labour,' he confessed quietly,
id then surprised her by scooping her up easily into his

arms and plopping her in the wheelchair as if she weighe
nothing. 'I am very relieved that it is all over.'

She stared up at him, surprised by the strength of h
reaction. She hadn't realised until now just how worrie
he'd obviously been. 'Will she be all right, Luca?'

'Tia, the girl has the entire paediatric department ho
ering over her,' he said dryly. 'Like you, I wish she wa
tucked up in here with us, but I'm not worried about he
Not at all.'

Tia started to relax for the first time in days. If Luc
wasn't worried maybe there was no need for her to worr
either.

She expressed some colostrum in the little room o
Special Care and would have spent all day with Lily ha
Luca not forced her back downstairs to her room for
sleep.

'You will not help her if you collapse,' he pointed o
roughly as he helped her back onto the bed.

Tia nodded and stifled a yawn, suddenly feeling mo
weary than she ever had in her life. She'd had a maj
operation, of course, so it was hardly surprising, and th
strain of seeing their tiny daughter lying in an incubat
connected to what seemed like hundreds of tubes was b
ginning to wear her down.

Luca looked as immaculate as ever but she could s
from the fine lines around his dark eyes that he, too, wa
feeling the pressure.

She was all too aware that, despite his own person
worries, he'd concentrated all his attention on supporti
her and overseeing the treatment their daughter was recei
ing. She loved him so much that it was a physical ache
her heart. Maybe it was time to tell him, she thought
sleep clouded her brain. Maybe it didn't matter that
didn't love her in the same way.

Tia slept on and off throughout the rest of the day, awa
that Luca was dividing his time between her room and th

pecial care baby unit where their daughter was being cared
or.

Sharon helped her express more colostrum and then
pushed her upstairs in the wheelchair so that she could feed
to Lily down the tube.

'Weird sort of breastfeeding, I know, sweetheart,' Tia
murmured as she fiddled with the syringe and watched her
tiny daughter smack her lips. 'Hurry up and learn to suck
and then we can stop all this messing around.'

'We'll still put her to the breast regularly,' Sharon said,
'but don't forget that she's only tiny and she'll get tired
easily.'

Tia looked at the baby wistfully. 'Do you think she'll
ever breastfeed properly?'

'Oh, yes.' Sharon was adamant. 'If you really want to,
I'm sure you'll manage it.'

Eventually Tia allowed herself to be wheeled back down
to the ward for some more rest.

The next day was frantic with activity and both Dan and
Duncan visited her to check that she was doing well physically. Despite the pain nagging in her wound, she was
determined to be as mobile as possible to limit the possibility of clots forming in her legs.

Lily's condition seemed to fluctuate although no one
seemed to be concerned that her problems were anything
other than something to be expected in a baby of her gestation.

'When will I be able to take her home?' Tia asked the
pediatric registrar and Julie gave a noncommittal shrug.

'You know better than anyone that I can't really answer
that. The official answer at this stage is that she could be
in until she should have been born—in other words, another
six weeks—but I hope it won't be as long as that.'

Tia sagged with disappointment.

Six weeks?

Six weeks until they could take Lily home and start t
be a family?

She spent most of the day with Lily, and Luca joine
her periodically, dividing his time between his new famil
and his busy job.

'I've spoken to Dan and he's agreed that I can take tw
weeks off when Lily comes home,' he told her in a husk
voice as they both leaned over the incubator.

Tia smiled up at him. Two weeks together? 'That's far
tastic. How did you manage to persuade him to let you d
that?'

'Threats mostly,' Luca admitted with a grin that melte
her insides.

'I can't wait to go home,' she said softly, and his eye
locked onto hers.

'Me, too.' He hesitated and his smile faded. 'There :
something I need to talk to you about. Something I shoul
have said to you a long time ago.'

Tia felt as though she'd been showered with cold wate

Was he going to talk about Luisa? Now, after all th
time?

Now that the baby was here, was he going to decide tha
their relationship was over?

Surely not. He adored Lily as much as she did.

But maybe he just wanted to be with Lily and not wit
her...

Hiding her panic, she concentrated her attention on th
baby and barely noticed when Luca excused himself to a
swer his bleeper.

She barely saw him for the rest of the day and when sh
finally went to bed her mind was still tormented by worr
and she couldn't settle.

Finally giving up on sleep, she glanced at the clock b
her bed and saw that it was still only two o'clock in th
morning.

Facing the fact that she wasn't going to get to sleep whe

e was this worried about Luca, she decided to pay an
promptu visit to Lily. Tucking her feet into her slippers,
e told the midwife in charge where she was going and
alked gingerly to the lift.

She was managing to get around very well, although her
ound still nagged painfully at times.

The lift moved silently upwards and the doors opened
th a clatter that was magnified by the strange silence of
e night.

The lights in the SCBU had been dimmed and Tia
opped to wash her hands and then walked onto the unit.

She stopped dead, surprised to see that Luca was there,
s broad-shouldered figure bending over their daughter's
t.

And by his side was a tall, elegant, dark-haired woman
nom she recognised in an instant. It was the same woman
e'd seen talking to his mother on the day of the wedding.
Luisa.

Even as she watched in mute horror, he slipped an arm
ound the woman's shoulders and bent to drop a tender
ss on her forehead.

Dear God, no!

With a whimper of denial, Tia turned and shuffled from
e room as fast as she could, determined to get back to
e sanctuary of the ward before she collapsed.

Because collapse she would. She was only too painfully
are of that.

How could she have been such a fool?

She'd known all along that he had a secret, that he'd
en involved with Luisa, but the truth was that she'd fallen
deeply in love with the man that she'd allowed herself
trust him.

But now that the baby had been safely born, he clearly
nted to be with the woman he loved.

And that woman was Luisa.

She was lying on the bed, tears pouring down her fac
when the door opened and Luca walked in.

He gave a sharp exclamation when he saw that she w
crying and was by her side in an instant.

'What's the matter?' His Italian accent was sudden
very pronounced. 'Are you in pain? Or is it hormones?'

Hormones?

Why was it that men were so quick to assume that wh
a woman was in tears it was caused by hormones?

He put out a hand to touch her but she flinched aw
from him and he frowned, clearly puzzled.

'*Cara.*'

'Don't call me that!' Her eyes filled again as she glar
up at him. 'Our whole relationship is a total farce, Luca

He stilled, his expression shocked. 'Tia, you don't—'

'I am such a stupid fool,' she muttered, interrupting hi
without thought, rubbing the tears away from her chee
with the palm of her hand. 'For a brief, totally delud
time, I really thought it could work between us.'

He frowned. 'Tia—'

'I was waiting for you to tell me, Luca.' She stared
him accusingly and reached for a tissue from the box
her bed. 'I wanted to see whether you were the same s
of man as my father.'

He was very still. 'Your father?'

'I told you that he had affairs,' Tia said hoarsely, 'bu
never told you how my mother found out, did I? She f
down some stairs backstage and was unconscious in ho
pital for a week. My father really thought she was goi
to die so do you know what he did?' Her eyes were brig
with tears of outrage as she looked at him. 'He chose th
moment to confess everything. My mother was lying u
conscious and he told her everything. All about the oth
women he'd been seeing—that their whole relationship h
been a sham. He thought that she couldn't hear him, b
she could.'

Luca's expression was grim. 'Tia, you don't—'

'She trusted him, you see,' Tia went on, her heart beating so fast she thought it would burst. 'And to find out that he had this secret life was just too much for her. When I heard your mother talking to Luisa the day of our wedding, it was like history repeating itself.'

There was a long silence and when he spoke his voice was soft. 'You heard my mother and Luisa talking?'

'That's right.' Tia nodded miserably, the words etched in her memory. 'Your mother said that it was a very sad day. That you were marrying the wrong woman for the wrong reasons and that you should have been marrying Luisa.' The tears started to trickle down her cheeks again and this time she did nothing to stop them. 'And then Luisa said that you'd told her that you would always love her. Which was all news to me, of course. Bad news. I was crazy about you, Luca. I really thought you were Mr Right.'

Luca's breathing was rapid and his face was dark with anger. 'Wait there,' he growled, turning on his heel and leaving the room, to return only minutes later, dragging Luisa by the arm.

He pushed her none too gently into the room and spoke to her rapidly in Italian, his expression grim.

Luisa listened and then glanced nervously at Tia. 'This is all my fault. Luca wants me to explain.'

'Don't bother,' Tia mumbled, reaching for another tissue and blowing her nose hard. 'I really don't want to hear it. I should have ended it the day of the wedding when I found out that that the pair of you were involved.'

Luisa's face blanched. 'That was why you refused to marry him? Because you thought that I, that we—?' She broke off and said something in Italian to Luca who shrugged, his eyes as hard as granite.

Strange, Tia thought dully as she tucked the scrunched tissue up her sleeve. For a man in love, he didn't look too happy.

'Tia…' Luisa's voice was suddenly shaking with nerve and she looked pleadingly at Luca who was totally unsym pathetic. The Italian girl took a deep breath. 'I think… seems as though you may have misunderstood—'

Luca growled something and she flinched slightly.

'I mean…' She cleared her throat and tried again. ' was— I'm not involved with Luca. I never have been. N in the way you imagined. But I wanted to be. I had a hug crush on him.'

She hung her head and Tia stared at her, uncomprehend ing. *A crush?*

'But I heard you and his mother talking. She said tha he should be marrying you. You said that he'd promised t love you for ever.'

Luisa nodded. 'It's true that Luca's mother alway wanted him to marry me, but it wasn't a realistic wish an it wasn't Luca's wish.' She bit her lip. 'The truth is tha Luca was kind to me, always, and I—I wished it would b something more.'

'But it never was,' Luca said, speaking in English fo the first time since he'd strode into the room, draggin Luisa with him. 'Luisa was a childhood friend of my si ter's. My mother, who doesn't have enough to occupy h mind, weaved all sorts of plans for bringing us togethe But they didn't work.'

Hope started to flicker in the back of Tia's mind. 'The didn't?'

'No.' Luca looked at Luisa and gave her a crooked smil the sort that a brother might have given to a sister. 'Whe ever Luisa and I went out, it was always with the famil We were never involved in a romantic sense.'

Tia swallowed. 'But you told her that you'd always lo her.'

Luca frowned. 'I may have told her that, but—'

'But he didn't mean it in a romantic sense.' Luisa spok in a pathetically small voice. 'When I found out he wa arrying you I went to see him at the hospital and—well, e was kind to me but very blunt. He told me again that e would never want a relationship with me. I was dread-lly upset and he did tell me that he'd always love me, ut of course he just meant as a friend. Deep down I knew ere was no hope, but I had a terrible crush on him. I was till kidding myself that he loved me when I spoke to his other the day of your wedding. I was so crazy about him made me do stupid things—do you understand?'

Tia thought she probably did understand. She knew just ow powerful an effect Luca could have on women.

'So you're saying…' Her voice cracked and she looked t Luca questioningly. 'You're saying that what I heard the ay of the wedding was nonsense?'

'Complete nonsense.' Luca's eyes gleamed. 'Something would have confirmed had you bothered to ask me. Next me you overhear something, it might be wise to discuss with me, *cara mia*. It might save us all a great deal of nguish.'

Tia glanced back at Luisa. 'So why have you come here ow?'

Luisa blushed. 'I've met someone,' she confessed, 'and e are on holiday in England. I wanted to bring him to eet Luca and apologise for my behaviour. I threw myself t him and behaved very badly.'

Tia flopped back against her pillows and stared at Luca, e colour rising in her cheeks as she met his eyes.

'Luisa, I believe your boyfriend is waiting downstairs.' uca barely gave her a glance but she took the hint im-ediately.

'Yes, I've got to go.' She hurried towards the door and ast a final apologetic look at Tia before leaving the room.

Tia stared down at the bedcovers, not knowing what to ay. She felt the bed dip and Luca's solid thigh appeared a her line of vision.

'Luca, I'm sorry,' she whispered, hardly daring to look

at him. 'I ruined the wedding and...I really thought yo
were in love.'

'I was in love,' he said quietly, reaching for her hand
and taking them in his. 'With you. From the first momer
I saw you in Venice.'

She lifted her eyes to his and shook her head slightly
'No.'

'Yes,' he said firmly.

There was a long silence. A silence that seemed to stretc
for ever.

Finally Tia shifted. 'But—'

'It seems to me that we still aren't talking enough, *cara*.
he murmured, his voice rough as he stroked her cheek wit
the back of his hand. 'So I'm going to talk now. It's tru
that Luisa had a crush on me and maybe I should have tol
you, but to be honest it didn't seem important. I was i
love with you and spending all my time trying to find way
to make you love me back. I thought that when I told m
family I was getting married the problem of Luisa woul
be solved.'

Tia stared at him. 'But I thought you were marrying m
because I was pregnant.'

He shook his head slowly. 'No. I was marrying you be
cause I was in love with you. Madly in love with you.'

'But when I told you that I was pregnant, you were ho
rified.'

He sighed and ran a hand through his hair. 'I know tha
it seemed that way, but it wasn't true. I was very pleasec
but also very afraid.'

'Afraid?' She was thoroughly confused and he gave
sigh.

'Yes, afraid. You see, I knew how wary you were c
men,' he said quietly. 'I knew that you were very confuse
about your feelings for me. I could see that what happene
between us physically confused and overwhelmed you, an

I was trying to give you space and time to adjust. And then we found out that you were pregnant.'

'I thought you didn't want me any more. You spent more and more time at the hospital.'

'That's true.' His voice was suddenly gruff and he walked slowly back to the bed and settled himself next to her. 'And the reason I spent all that time at the hospital was because I was desperate to finish writing up my research work so that I could be released early and take a job in England. I wanted to take you home, Tia. I thought things might be easier between us if you were in your own country.'

Her eyes met his, her heart thumping uncomfortably in her chest. What was he saying?

'I loved you from the first moment I saw you. But before you had time to get used to the idea you were pregnant, and I was so angry with myself for that. You were so wary of marriage, I should have given you time to adjust to the idea, instead of which I moved so fast you barely had time to think. And then you panicked. You were suddenly terrified of what you'd done, totally overwhelmed by the enormity of it. And I knew that I'd made a mistake to rush you.'

Tia nodded warily. 'How did you know that?'

'I could read your body language,' he said softly. 'Our sex life was as miraculous as ever but the rest of the time you were restless and unsettled. I was cursing myself for not being more restrained that first night together. I should have taken it slowly but at the time all I could think about was making you mine. I knew from the first moment I saw you that you were the only woman I wanted to spend my life with.'

Tia could hardly believe what she was hearing. *The only woman he wanted to spend his life with?*

'Really?'

'Really,' he said softly, a strange light in his dark eyes.

'And I thought that you felt the same way, which was why I had no conscience about rushing you into marrying me. On the day of the wedding, when I discovered that you'd gone…' He closed his eyes briefly. 'Well, let's just say that it was the worst day of my life.'

Tia was stunned. 'But you never told me that. You never told me that you loved me.'

'Because I didn't want to put more pressure on you,' he said. 'And I suppose because I'd never actually said those words to any woman and I found it difficult to say them.'

'I didn't know,' Tia said. 'I thought that you didn't love me.'

He closed his eyes and shook his head. 'Tia, everyone knows I'm crazy about you, except you. Sharon, Duncan, even Dan because I'd forgotten that he spoke reasonable Italian when I told you exactly how I felt in Theatre the other night.'

Tia stared at him in wonder. 'You told me that you loved me?'

He gave a crooked smile. 'And a few other soppy things that Dan obviously understood very clearly—I must remember to ask him where he acquired his knowledge of Italian.' He touched her cheek with gentle fingers. 'What a pair of fools we have been. When I discovered that you had left, I almost lost my sanity. I assumed that the baby had been the final straw and you had left in a panic.'

'But when you turned up in England, you still didn't tell me you loved me,' Tia pointed out. 'You said that we owed it to the baby to make our relationship work—'

'You seemed so determined to give up on what we had,' he said quietly. 'I used the baby to buy myself more time. Time to convince you that what we had was unique.'

Tia felt suddenly shy. 'And then you agreed to all my terms and conditions.'

'Of course.' He gave a wry smile. 'I would have agreed to anything to keep you by my side.'

She gave a little smile. 'You even stopped complaining
bout me working.'

He nodded slowly, his expression suddenly serious. 'I
nderstand now why you feel such a strong need to work.
t is understandable after such an awful childhood. You
eed to feel secure. But, Tia, you can trust me. I don't mind
 you want to work but I need you to know that I will
lways be here to look after you.'

'I know that. I love you, Luca,' she whispered softly. 'I
lways have.'

He gave a groan and scooped her into his arms, kissing
er gently on the mouth.

'Will you forgive me for rushing you? For doing every-
ning back to front?' He murmured the words against her
nouth, his hands sliding gently over her shoulders. 'I se-
uced you that first night without giving you time to get to
now me. But I always knew you were the only woman
or me.'

Tia pulled away from him, her eyes teasing. 'And what
bout all these other women that drool over you? What are
e going to do about them?'

Luca's eyes gleamed. 'I'm not interested, *cara*, you
nould know that by now. There is only one other woman
ho will ever claim my attention.'

Tia stiffened and then she saw the light dancing in his
icked dark eyes and she smiled.

'Lily.'

'Lily.' He repeated their daughter's name softly. 'Al-
eady she is turning my heart and my life upside down,
xactly like her mother.'

The look in his eyes melted Tia's insides. 'I love you,
uca.'

He murmured in Italian and bent his head to kiss her.
And I love you, too, *cara mia*. For ever.'

EPILOGUE

'IF YOU break the zip on this dress I'll kill you.' Sharon
stood back and admired her handiwork, her expression softening as she looked at her friend. 'You look beautiful an
you're a lucky girl, do you know that?'

'Yes.' Tia walked across the room to the Moses baske
where Lily lay fast asleep.

She *was* incredibly lucky.

'And this hotel is fabulous,' Sharon observed, glancin
out of the window towards the large ornamental lake. 'I'
say this for him, Luca certainly isn't stingy. All righ
We're due downstairs. The guests are waiting, and this tim
we're not giving them a fright.'

Tia smiled and bent to pick up the basket. 'She can sta
at the back of the room with you until we've finished.'

But Lily had other ideas.

The minute Tia picked up the basket she started to how
and Tia gave a groan of disbelief.

'No! Not now, Lily. You can't be hungry yet.'

'Just get downstairs,' Sharon said quickly. 'I'll keep he
happy until you're ready.'

Tia looked at her daughter and her heart twisted. Sh
was so tiny and helpless and she'd only been out of hospita
for three weeks.

'I can't.' She shook her head firmly. 'Not if she neec
feeding. I'll feed her and then I'll get married.'

Sharon looked frantically at the clock. 'Tia, you can't d
this again! Luca will have a nervous breakdown.'

'Except that this time I'm leaving nothing to chance
Luca's deep drawl came from the doorway and he walke

ver to Tia, his expression faintly mocking. 'Leaving me
/aiting at the altar again, *cara mia*?'

'Luca!' Sharon's voice was a horrified squeak. 'You're
ot meant to see the bride before you marry her.'

Luca smiled. 'I don't care what she's wearing as long as
he turns up.'

Tia looked at him anxiously. 'Lily's hungry.'

'Then feed her,' Luca said softly, removing his jacket
nd tossing it carelessly onto the bed. 'Otherwise you will
/orry and I don't want you to worry. I want this to be a
ay you remember.'

Ignoring Sharon's anxious mutterings about the time, Tia
llowed Luca to unzip her dress and settled herself in the
hair to feed the baby.

'I don't believe this.' Sharon's expression was comical
s she looked at them. 'You know that they're all going to
ink that you've done it again.'

Tia looked at Luca but he simply shrugged.

'We don't care what people think,' he reminded her
ghtly. 'They will wait, *cara mia*. Sharon, if it bothers you
 much, go down and tell them that we are feeding Lily
nd will join them in a moment.'

Sharon looked from one to the other and gave a sigh.
Maybe I'll do that.'

She left the room, closing the door quietly behind her.

Luca stroked Tia's cheek with a gentle finger. 'I thought
ou had changed your mind again,' he admitted gruffly,
nd Tia shook her head, her eyes soft with love.

'Never. But Lily started to cry.'

He gave a chuckle. 'I told you that you would be a good
other.'

'I love her, Luca,' Tia said in a choked voice, handing
im the baby as she rearranged her dress and got unsteadily
 her feet.

'I know you do.' He transferred the baby to his shoulder

and bent to kiss Tia gently on the mouth. 'And she is lucky girl to have you as a mother.'

Tia gave him a shy smile. 'I still can't believe we'r going to be a proper family.'

'Well, we are.' Luca held his daughter snugly with on arm and retrieved his jacket with the other. 'Are you read to marry me?'

Tia nodded slowly. Oh, yes, she was ready. She wa more than ready.

He smiled and held out his free hand. 'So do you thin we should get a move on before we give our guests a hear attack for a second time?'

Tia slipped her hand into his and her eyes twinkled int his. 'I do…'

* * *

Don't miss Sarah Morgan's latest novel,
Sale or Return Bride. *It's available in October 2005 in Mills & Boon® Modern Romance™ wherever Mills & Boon books are sold!*

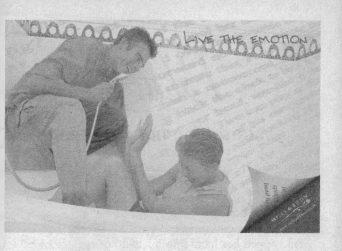

Modern
romance™

...international affairs
– seduction and
passion guaranteed

Modern
romance™

...pulse-raising
romance – heart-
racing medical drama

Tender
romance™
...sparkling, emotional,
feel-good romance

Blaze
...scorching hot
sexy reads

Historical
romance™

...rich, vivid and
passionate

28 new titles every month.

MB5 RS V2

GEN/14/RS3 V2

Blaze™

...scorching hot sexy reads

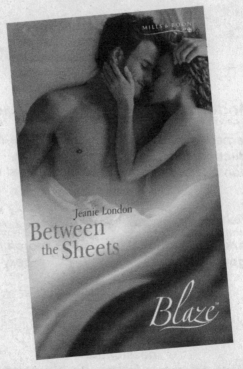

4 brand-new titles each month

Available on subscription every month from the Reader Service™

Historical
romance™

…rich, vivid and passionate

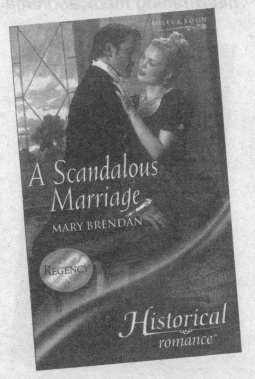

4 brand-new titles each month

*Available on subscription every month from
the Reader Service™*

GEN/04/RS3 V2

MedicaL
romance™

...pulse-raising romance –
heart-racing medical drama

6 brand-new titles each month

*Available on subscription every month from
the Reader Service™*

GEN/03/RS3 V2

Tender
romance™

...sparkling, emotional, feel-good romance

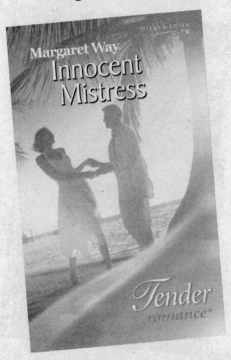

6 brand-new titles each month

Available on subscription every month from the Reader Service™

GEN/02/RS3 V2

Modern
romance™

...international affairs – seduction and passion guaranteed

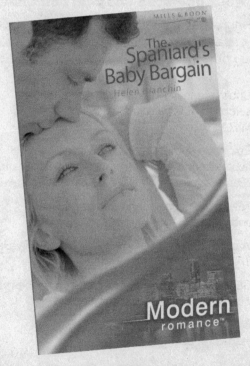

8 brand-new titles each month

Available on subscription every month from the Reader Service™

GEN/01/RS3 V

books authors online reads magazine membership

Visit millsandboon.co.uk and discover your one-stop shop for romance!

Find out everything you want to know about romance novels in one place. Read about and buy our novels online anytime you want.

✳ Choose and buy books from an extensive selection of Mills & Boon®, Silhouette® and MIRA® titles.

✳ Enjoy top authors and *New York Times* bestselling authors – from Penny Jordan and Diana Palmer to Meg O'Brien and Alex Kava!

✳ Take advantage of our amazing **FREE** book offers.

✳ In our Authors' area find titles currently available from all your favourite authors.

✳ Get hooked on one of our fabulous online reads, with new chapters updated weekly.

✳ Check out the fascinating articles in our magazine section.

Visit us online at
www.millsandboon.co.uk

…you'll want to come back again and again!!

WEB/RS V2